QUEEN
OF
AMERICA

Also by Luis Alberto Urrea

FICTION

Into the Beautiful North
The Hummingbird's Daughter
In Search of Snow
Six Kinds of Sky
Mr. Mendoza's Paintbrush (graphic novel; artwork
    by Christopher Cardinale)

NONFICTION

The Devil's Highway: A True Story
*Across the Wire: Life and Hard Times on the
    Mexican Border*
*By the Lake of Sleeping Children: The Secret Life of
    the Mexican Border*
Nobody's Son
Wandering Time

POETRY

The Fever of Being
Ghost Sickness
Vatos

QUEEN
OF
AMERICA

A Novel

LUIS ALBERTO URREA

Little, Brown and Company
NEW YORK   BOSTON   LONDON

For Cinderella, who saw this through beside me

Copyright © 2011 by Luis Alberto Urrea

Little, Brown and Company
Hachette Book Group
237 Park Avenue, New York, NY 10017
www.hachettebookgroup.com

First Edition: November 2011

Little, Brown and Company is a division of Hachette Book Group, Inc.
The Little, Brown name and logo are trademarks of Hachette Book Group, Inc.

The publisher is not responsible for websites (or their content)
that are not owned by the publisher.

Library of Congress Cataloging-in-Publication Data
Urrea, Luis Alberto.
    Queen of America : a novel / Luis Alberto Urrea. — 1st ed.
      p. cm.
    ISBN 978-0-316-15486-4 (HC) — ISBN 978-0-316-18764-0 (int'l ed.)
    1. Women healers — Fiction.   2. Mexicans — United States — Fiction.
  3. United States — History — 1865–1921 — Fiction.   I. Title.
    PS3571.R74Q44 2011
    813'.54 — dc22

                                                                    2011023065

                    10   9   8   7   6   5   4   3   2   1

                                RRD-C

                Printed in the United States of America

QUEEN
OF
AMERICA

Living with a saint is more grueling than being one.
—ROBERT NEVILLE

Prologue

AT FIRST, SHE FOUND IT DRY. Soon, and forever after, she would find it vast, dreadfully open, more sky than prairie, more prairie than mountain, more mountain than city. The whole would outstrip her ability to see, and she knew her days would end before she had seen one half of the continent and its rivers, its forests, its shores. Dry at first, then running, raining, flooding, wet. Then dry again. But now, in these days, for the first time in her life, she knew she was about to face the endless sea. The Saint of Cabora had discovered America.

To the sea. Among strangers. The rest of her life would be played out, she feared, among strangers. Like these well-meaning Americanos who, here in the summer of 1900, had taken over her existence.

She crouched against the wall of her train car, feral with shame and grief, skinny, silent, unwilling to eat or turn her face inward from the window that rattled and banged against her forehead for hundreds of hungry miles. She hid her bruises from everyone. She had been bruised before. They had tried to break her before. She was not broken. This was the worst part of her life. But she would find her way through it. She hid her thoughts.

Mr. Rosencrans had begun to think of her as a caged fox. Her other companions watched her surreptitiously, secretly afraid that she had gone insane. Mr. Rosencrans's son Jamie dared to sit beside her and take her hand. She did not speak to him, nor did she turn her face to him, but she allowed her fingers to be tugged, her fingernails to be polished by the pads of his thumbs. When she drew up her knees and placed her feet on the cracked leather seat, pulling herself into a tighter ball, he left her in peace.

She remembered the star-frost dawn when Huila first took her to

3

discover God. She'd watched the old woman talk to plants and thought her half crazy. She remembered the day Tomás realized she was his daughter, the way the emotions rippled across his face like wind on water, and the still moment when he mysteriously accepted her, like a man greeting his fate, for surely she was precisely that. She remembered her small chapel at the ranch at Cabora, its peaceful curved white walls of painted adobe. She remembered Cruz Chávez, the Pope of Mexico, so serious, so deadly with his big rifle and his scowl, so hilarious when she teased him. How unarmed he was when facing her. And his death far from her, how she imagined her letters to him burning and their ashes falling on his cold face like moths. War consumed her memories. Flames. Howls of rage and terror.

She tugged her old yellow rebozo over her head so that no one could see her face. She was nothing but eyes and she stared north from that right-side window, watching the tireless convolutions of the Arizona desert in their appalling sprawl and horrid writhing. Jagged peaks ripped at the overwhelming sky. Saguaro skeletons and dread black fossils of ruined ocotillo and creosote bushes battered by the white violence of the sun. Shadows spilled like dried blood at the base of shattered rocks. Volcanism. Above, vultures circled arroyos, waiting for dead rattlesnakes to ripen. Nowhere water, nowhere sheltering trees. Cattle were dying slowly from eating cactus and poisoned vines, their ribs already showing through their dusty sides like the rattling wooden bones of those dead cactus giants fallen, stripped of flesh by the sun, and leaving spindles of wood that looked like cages on the colorless hardpan.

The boy brought her a sweet roll and a cup of coffee from his father's hot bottle. She nodded and took the bread into the cowl of her rebozo. She smelled like roses, and her sweat was tart like marigolds. She smelled like a garden that could not be found outside the window.

They paused in Tucson. She craned around and stared at the city scattered to the south of the station. To the north, that great Frog Mountain where Mr. Dinges planned to one day find snow and bears.

She saw her companions staring at her, and she turned her face away from them again. It was a relief when they pulled out, and all the memories of baseball and the Van Order boys and the Arizona nightingales and the swan boats in the pond and the Yaquis embracing her father and Guapo El Chulo in far lamented Tubac fell back, and the town and the mountain and the San Xavier mission were never to be seen again.

It was a few hours to the next stop. Yuma. All she could think of was the dreadful prison—she had heard of the howling despair of the wretches buried in its baking cells cooked alive by the sun. Hours of cowboy ghosts, angry Indian wraiths, endlessly wandering the blank land, unhinged by sudden death, hungry and unable to eat, thirsting but unable to find water. She pressed her eyes shut and put her fingers in her ears.

In her mind, she was flying, flying like she had once dreamed she could fly, when she would take her friends through the cold clouds to far cities and the distant sea. She would put her feet in its insistent waters now. Perhaps she would simply walk into the waves and swim away, forever.

The Saint opened her eyes and watched the land unfurling, flopping, rising and falling like a flag or a sheet drying on a clothesline being tossed by the wind. In her mind she was out there, not in the dark squeaking car, and she was in the air, speeding, her hair unfurling behind her for a mile, her arms wide in an embrace of the wind, flying like she had once seen Huila do in her dream upon the llanos many years ago, Huila, drifting in the air as she came back from her journeys, coming down the breeze as if gingerly stepping down a stairway to the empty earth below. Teresita dove and swooped like a hawk over the cactus, over the boulders and hills and crags. The train rocked, its wheels endlessly clacketed on the rails, a vast sewing machine stitching America together, and its lulling rhythm was the closest she got to sleep on that journey. Her flying, the closest she now got to dreams, but she was learning fast: In America, you needed different dreams. And she did not yet know their language.

Book I

ANGEL OF THE BORDERLANDS

Part I

IN THE LAND OF DEVIL-MONKEYS

Dr. Braburn: Many people consider you a saint, due to your many healings. Do you consider yourself a saint?

Teresita: True, I have cured some, but I have never known how, and because of this I have never considered myself a saint. I have always been ashamed of that title.

—El Fronterizo

Nogales, Arizona
June 25, 1892

One

TWO RIDERS CAME FROM the darksome sea, black against the morning light, and they tore into the first Mexican village. They demanded, as they would demand in towns north, the same information: "Have you seen the Saint of Cabora?"

And at every dust-choked ville, in each forlorn rancho with nothing but skeletons mouthing the dry water tanks, in every charred Indian settlement, they were pointed north. That was all the People knew— she was there, far away, north. Gone. The People had come to fear unknown men seeking news of the Saint. Unknown men with great rifles and grim faces. Unknown men with questions. Such men had killed hundreds of the People and brought in hordes of slavers and soldiers to imprison others and drag them to their doom.

Always from horseback, sometimes from behind weapons pulled and cocked, shouted, rude, louder than the People cared to be spoken to: "You! Do you know where we can find the Saint of Cabora?"

No, it was better to shake their heads and point north. Nobody knew anything.

"We do not know her," they said. "They say she is in el norte."

Even those who felt abandoned by her, forgotten, dared not complain to these men. What if it was a trick? Some devilish strategy?

A voice in the dark outside yelling, "Long live who?" Think a long time before answering.

"Try looking in el otro lado," they said, turning away.

The other side; yes, of course. The United States.

The riders didn't know much—they were incurious men, for all their interrogations—but they did know their masters feared her return. And these two feared their masters. The great men in the great halls that the black riders would never see would burn the entire land to eradicate her. There was no failure available to the riders.

"She has not come through here?"

The People shook their heads in village after village; they returned to their meager labors.

"Who?" they asked back. "We never heard of her." Their lips fluttering with minuscule flags of burned white skin. At most they would look down and mumble, "That's an Indian thing." They scratched in dead soil, under white sun, with woven straw satchels of hard corn and clay jugs of muddy water and they did not look up to the riders, did not show their eyes. Something bad was crossing their land. They hunkered down, like their ancestors before them, and silently wished their saint good luck.

When there was a town big enough for beds and tequila, the riders watered and fed their horses, ate cooked meat with frijoles and tortillas, drank. People in the small eateries backed out the door. Women in the dingy hotels turned to the piano players and hoped the riders did not seek their flesh. These two enjoyed the fear they caused. Twin .44 revolvers, long big-bore rifles, great belduque knives like half swords. And that smell. They only smiled at each other. Sometimes they paid. And before light came, they left.

※

It was hard riding. Hot. They had no time to dawdle or bathe, no time for women. Most nights they slept under a delirium of stars, under slowly spinning heavens black and hard as ice and shattered along the horizon by bare peaks devoid of trees. One was stung by a scorpion; he pinched it and slowly pulled its tail off. They were sons of rocks and spines.

They shot rabbits from their horses and speared the little corpses on saguaro ribs and ate standing in the smoke of the fire. The smoke drove the lice from their chaps.

They pointed and nodded and grunted like the most ancient of wanderers who'd passed through here before there were horses. Talking dried out the mouth and the throat. There was nothing to say.

They stopped a lone ore wagon somewhere in the Pinacate desert and asked again: "Have you heard of the Saint of Cabora?"

"Yes."

"Where is she?"

"She went north."

"Have you seen her?"

"I have not seen her."

"Are you sure?"

The wagon driver hiding a small shotgun under his serape, and the riders, knowing it, fingering their pistols.

"Will you kill her?" the mule skinner asked.

They said nothing.

"Better her than me," he said, and shook the mules awake with a jerk of the ropes, and the heavy dark wagon groaned like a dreamer into the terrible light.

"She lives close to the border," he called back. "In the Pimería. Look for trees."

⁂

They exited Sonora through a defile in the rocks east of Nogales. The taller of the two was constantly watching the peaks to his right, aware of the Apaches hiding there—not afraid, but sick to his stomach when he imagined them coming like wasps out of some arroyo, and him mounted on his horse with Apache scalps and ears thronged across the back of his saddle. He would be roasted alive if they caught him. Still, it did not occur to him to remove the totems from the witness of the sun.

Around his neck, his companion wore a simple talisman on a black thong: one human finger bone.

They turned east and rose into foothills that seemed lent to this landscape from an entirely different world. Pine trees and oaks. Small streams winding down. Jaybirds and deer. They would have killed a deer for real food, but they were too close, they could feel it. The riders could not afford a shot now, even though the deer made their mouths water and their guts yowl within them. No, they would not signal their targets that retribution was upon them with an undisciplined rifle shot. They sucked pebbles so that spit flowed down their throats to fool their bellies. They had heard there was a great bosque of cool trees by water. The Girl Saint and her damned father would be cowering there.

Later, after their targets were dead and the scalps salted and packed away in burlap and sawdust, there would be venison. Meat steaming from the fire. Dripping fat like tears.

⁂

The cabin was so different from anything in Mexico. They could have been blindfolded for the whole journey and then been unblinded and they would have seen immediately they were in gringo territory. Perfectly squared walls. Neat fences. Hewn wood. White smoke unspooled out of the chimney and gave the air a scent of cedar, even where the riders hid above, in a strange small crown of granite. As if American tidiness could keep the devil at bay.

They were far from the cabin, but they could still hit it easily. They counted three horses. There were a few goats there too. The tall one held a spyglass to his eye. It wasn't good, but it was good enough. Ah, there she was—skinny, wasn't she. In a long pioneer dress. He scoffed. Stupid American clothes. He spit. She was casting some kind of water pan out among her chickens—milky water scattered the birds. She went inside. He adjusted his gaze to the window. There! There he was. Her father. The Sky Scratcher, the Indians called him.

Perhaps, thought the tall one, the devil is attracted to pretty little houses.

"He don't look that tall to me," the short man said.

"He's sitting down, pendejo," his companion replied.

He grunted, spit, squinted.

The Sky Scratcher was just a shadow through the cheap glass of the window. The rider shook his head. He could not believe they had glass windows. He had never had glass windows.

Just for that, they deserved what they got.

"They don't look special to me," the short one said.

"Cabrones," the tall one replied. "Bring me the rifle."

⁂

In his grove of cottonwoods and mesquites, Tomás Urrea lay in the ghastly heat of his little house. His head pulsed slowly with the crunching beat of his heart. Hungover again. Sick to his belly. Tired.

You know you are old when you awaken exhausted, he thought.

Tired of so many things. Tired of struggle. Tired of the pilgrims who still sought them out, hoping for a touch from his daughter. Oh, the Saint! They would follow her to her grave. And worse—his friend Aguirre had warned him that Mexico would regret letting her live. There would be men pursuing her.

The United States. Bad things were not supposed to happen here. He rubbed his eyes. He was tired of the United States. He did not want to admit the deeper truth: he was tired of his daughter.

He sat up slowly and stared into the murk. It was always dark in here.

"Teresita?" he called.

Why was he shouting? They only had the two rooms and a small kitchen off to the side. He could have whispered and been heard. But she was gone. Nineteen-year-old girls had a way of vanishing when they wanted to. Gone again—gone every day in the trees or out on the desert, cutting and collecting weeds. He shook his head. Talking to crows or something. Healing lepers.

He leaned over and spit on the floor. Why not. It was only dirt.

A shadow fell across the doorway. He felt around for his guns. Where were his pistolas? Not for the first time, he thought: How can I let her go wandering when I expect attacks from these goddamned religious fanatics? Back at their old hacienda, at Cabora, Teresita would have been watched over day and night. In his mind, he heard her voice. It had that tinge of disapproval that all young daughters seemed to develop and use when speaking to their fathers. That slight disappointment. *Perhaps,* her imagined voice said, *you were drunk when I went out and didn't notice I left.*

The outsider knocked on the doorframe.

Tomás stood and steadied himself on the table and then dragged his gunbelt out from a corner where he'd flung it on top of his wadded black coat. He went to the door, squinting—the damned sunlight hurt like a punch in the eye. He leaned on the frame and looked out. A pilgrim. But what a pilgrim stood there. Filthy, but they were often filthy. Skin dark as nutshells. But his eyes were pale grapes wobbling in his skull, bugged and sunburned. He had a reek about him of brown teeth.

"Where is the Saint?" this creature demanded.

"Otro come-mierda," Tomás muttered.

The man quivered.

"I do not eat shit," he said.

"You smell like it."

"I will see the Saint."

"You will not."

"Make way." He reached behind himself.

"What have you got there?" Tomás demanded.

He had a machete tucked in his rope belt. He started to draw it. Tomás snatched one of his pistolas out of the holster and hammered the pilgrim in the head with it and dropped him limp to the ground.

"Like a wet coat," Tomás said. He drew back the hammer and sighted down the blue-black barrel. He let the hammer down softly. Cocked again. The pilgrim moved in the dirt like an upended centipede. "I want to," Tomás confessed. "I really do." He let the hammer back down.

Several of the pilgrim's comrades hid in the shadows across the small clearing.

"You," Tomás ordered. "Collect this trash and be gone. And if I see any of you again, I will shoot you all."

They came forward with their heads bowed.

"Do you believe me?"

They nodded.

"Say it."

All they said was: "Sí, señor."

The short one retrieved a massive old Hawken rifle from a suede scabbard and delivered it to the tall one. He affixed a small bipod to the end of the octagonal barrel and flipped up the tall rear sights. The rifle smelled of oil. It was cool in the warmth of the sun. He rested his cheek upon the silky stock; it was carved with roses and hummingbirds. He drew a bead on the doorway, dark and empty. Then he swung to the window, to the blur of the man sitting within. Probably at a table. Reading a book. The gunman sneered.

He drew back the hammer—it resisted the pull just slightly; the liquid clicks of the gun's mechanisms as it prepared to shoot were soothing to him, like music. It was a five-hundred-yard shot, but downhill and no wind to speak of. He settled himself against the rocks, felt his ribs press into the earth, and he set the rifle tight to his shoulder and slipped his finger onto the trigger. Breathe. In. Out. Ignore the girl, appearing in the doorway now like a ghost in his peripheral vision. He could shoot the father and swing on her before she heard the shot. Papa would be dead in a cloud of red mist before the sound of the crack turned her head.

He fired; the window burst; the man's shadow exploded. Damn, the kick was brutal against his shoulder. He'd have a bruise. The girl spun to see what the shattering was. He took her with a shot drilled into the center of her back; she flew, disappearing like some magical act in a cabaret, into the deep dark of the cabin.

The riders got down to the cabin, to chickens still panicking and the tied horses sidestepping and tossing their heads. It was funny how strong the smell of blood was. The whole yard smelled of meat and old coins.

The short one threw a kick at a hustling chicken and said, "Supper."

His companion grinned.

They stepped into the cabin. It stank. So much blood in such a small space. They were both dead. The wall behind the table was sprayed with a starburst of deep red. More than dead. Those finger-length bullets tended to scatter the flesh. But their heads were intact.

"Drag them out," the tall one said. He grabbed Papa by the feet. The other took hold of the girl's wrist and pulled her out by one arm.

They yanked their belduques and bent to the scalping, avoiding the dark blood that still leaked from the tatters.

Her hair was red in the sunlight, her neck sugared with freckles.

The rider turned her head on her limp neck and looked at her face.

"Ah, cabrón," he said.

"¿Qué?" his friend said.

"This ain't her," the first one said.

"What?"

They looked at Papá, then kicked him.

"It's the wrong family?"

"Hmm."

They lit small cigars and stood there, stupid and hungry.

"I guess we keep looking."

"I guess."

"Burn the house?"

"Why not."

"But first..."

"First, we eat some chicken."

And they did.

Two

A DAY LATER AND miles beyond.

"The Saint of Cabora can no longer speak to the dead," Don Tomás Urrea said to the newspaper reporter.

Tomás turned away from the Arizona desert and regarded his interlocutor. The two men were sitting in the shade of the mesquite and paloverde trees of the rented bosque. Not far from them, the Santa Cruz River made its hot and languid journey away from Tucson, and on its banks a few cottonwoods had managed to grow—old grandfather trees, scarred by lightning and heat and drought. Don Tomás could hear them rustling in the desiccating breeze. His daughter the fabled Saint of Cabora regularly pointed out that the leaves of cottonwoods looked like hearts as big as hands, and they waved at you in the slightest wind. Beyond the trees, all was stones and rattlesnakes. He smiled ruefully. If they were in Mexico, he could show this reporter a bosque! Back there, he would have called it a huerta, and the mango trees would be dropping fat juicy fruit at his feet. But this was not the time for reveries, he told himself.

The reporter seemed to be waiting patiently as Tomás ordered his thoughts. Of course, the gringo note-taker could not possibly know of the endless parade of rattling ideas, memories, worries, regrets, schemes that tromped through his skull. Who could? Sometimes, if Tomás drank enough, he could postpone the haunting, he could trip the ghosts and make them stumble.

Tomás tried to focus, but all he could imagine were scenes of his lost life, turning to dust in Sonora. His ranch, gone. His woman, bereft and lonely. His wife too. And his children.

He wondered if his horses missed him. He wondered if his top hand,

Segundo, had whipped the tattered workers of the ranch into shape and earned him some profits. He wondered how a man made his fortune in the United States. Hell, how did a man even eat?

"Bosque," he said.

"Pardon me?" replied the reporter. They were speaking Spanish, but Tomás was convinced he had mastered English, and he intended to show this fool a thing or two.

"That is the name of this place: the Bosque Ranch."

"I see."

But he did not see. To be a ranch, a place needed cattle, horses, crops. Tomás and Teresita sleepwalked, stunned by their escape from death in Mexico. In unspoken mourning over the lost families and lovers, friends and memories cast out upon the sand by the violence of Indian wars, by the assaults of the government on their home. All Tomás had left was his great self. What else was there?

His daughter had her God and her herbs and her holiness.

She had ruined him.

He had been used to great bouts of superhuman activity. His days were filled with horses and vaqueros and cattle and laughter. Strong drink. Women. Always women! His days had been full of noise! And now, Arizona.

It was silent. He had never heard such pervasive silence. Except for the birds, which did not allow him to sleep in the mornings. The Apaches told him there were more birds in Arizona than in all the rest of the world, and he believed them. But you could not ride birds.

I will never go home.

※

In the bright house in Tubac, the Saint of Cabora cried out in pain.

"Be still, Teresita," her hostess said.

"It hurts!"

"Being a woman hurts," the lady replied.

Teresita closed her eyes. It was as if she were a small girl again, and her old teacher were speaking to her. Huila. Old Huila! Gone now to the place of flowers.

The women were preparing for a funeral, but, as is often the case, these survivors who attended to the details after a death felt a small giddiness just to be alive. Yes, a relative's death diminished them, but such passings also reminded them they were alive, more alive on some funeral days than on other days. Teresita thought: Life continues, even in this desert — weddings, births, illness, death — it is our story, always. No one dared laugh loudly when a quip lightened the room, but they avidly sipped their teas and their coffees and ate small pastries and perched on the edges of their chairs and stared at the Saint of Cabora as she spoke. Their eyes bright.

"Your father," one of the women said, "is quite charming."

"And handsome!" another enthused.

Teresita squirmed in her seat.

"We have fallen on difficult times," she said. "He is, though, still possessed of great charm."

"Is it true," her hostess asked, "that he nearly died to save you?"

Teresita felt shame. Her burden of guilt was heavy. Now, when she and her father scratched at each other in their endless skirmishes, she felt doubly guilty. Everything was confusing to her.

"He was heroic," she finally said. "In our tribulations."

The women passed looks around the room — it was all so thrilling.

"So tell us more," her hostess requested.

"¡Ay! Well, the soldiers came for me. They insisted I had inspired war. Revolt. Oh! That hurt."

"Sorry."

The women clucked.

"I did not inspire war, I never preached war. I was trying to tell the People of God's love... of God's justice."

The women looked at one another, nodded.

"I was to be executed. It was clear. I was sent to prison with my father. There...we suffered. Terrible things." She jumped in her chair. "But now I must suffer this torture instead!"

"Quiet now. Don't be a ninny," her hostess said.

Through the window, Teresita could see the twin cottonwoods at the Tubac river crossing. Teresita had stopped at the ruins of Santa Gertrudis Church for a quiet morning prayer. She enjoyed the sorrowful dilapidations, and the old fort still standing outside of town.

"I am not a ninny!"

She sat in the front room of Guillermo Lowe's house being attended to by his wife and some of the town ladies. The funeral was for Guillermo's father, William, down at the Cienega Ranch in neighboring Tumacacori.

"We were unexpectedly placed on a train," she continued. "And we were expelled forever from Mexico."

She squirmed.

"Sit still," Anna Berruel told her.

"I am."

"No, you are not."

"*¡Ay!*"

"It doesn't hurt, Teresita."

"But it does!"

Anna waved her tweezers in Teresita's face.

"You have one eyebrow! A lady does not have one eyebrow!" The gathered women nodded and murmured. "Do you wish to be a lady or not?"

"If you wish to find a beau..." one of the women said, her voice trailing off.

"I do not want a boyfriend," Teresita claimed.

"Yes, you do," said Anna.

After a moment, Teresita said, "Yes, I do."

They all laughed.

"One brow, why, it's...wanton," Anna scolded.

¡Por Dios!

Teresita could not believe that after all she had been through, people were still trying to make her into a "lady."

"Go ahead," she said. "Pluck."

⁕

Shade did not cut the heat.

The reporter had once interviewed Wyatt Earp, and this Mexican's mustache reminded him of the great lawman's. Though Tomás was tall enough and sufficiently craggy, and though he was momentarily famous, such a crop on the Mexican's lip seemed a real fumadiddle to the kid. These greasers and their pretensions. He smiled and focused on his satchel, fetching out a set of pencils and a leather notebook.

Don Tomás lifted a glass of dark wine from the wooden table. The reporter's full glass remained untouched. One of the table's legs was short and was propped up by a flat stone. The men sat on two rickety chairs. Don Tomás rested his boots on a third. He sniffed the wine right before he sipped it. All pleasure, he believed, could and should be doubled.

"So," he said.

He placed the glass carefully on the purple ring it had left on the gray wood.

"You have come to hear the story of what has happened since we were escorted out of Mexico."

The reporter opened his notebook so it lay flat on the table. He raised his pencil. His green bowler hat profoundly offended Don Tomás. Tomás could not understand why Americanos didn't doff their hats when addressing a caballero in serious matters.

"I would very much appreciate whatever of your story you might wish to impart, Mr. Urrea," the reporter said. "You are, what, some kind of Spaniard? A conquistador?"

"My family is Basque, originally. But we have deep historical roots in the Visigoth invaders of Iberia—"

"Yes, yes. Very interesting. You were imprisoned by the Mexican government, correct? Would it be improper to term you an enemy of the state?"

Don Tomás tipped his head politely.

"As you wish," he intoned.

"Criminal charges, correct?"

Silence.

"Might you be called a traitor, then?"

Slight cough.

If he had only seen Tomás riding his legendary stallions through Cabora, he would have known that Tomás's mildness was a harbinger of dreadful things, a sign that would have sent the vaqueros and ranch hands running. Tomás sipped his wine.

"I would like to hear about the Saint of Cabora. Your daughter."

In English, Tomás announced: "I know who is my daughter."

"Well?"

"Well what?"

"The"—he consulted his notes—"the 'most dangerous girl in Mexico.' That was according to Porfirio Díaz, the president of Mex—"

"Oye, cabrón," Tomás snapped, then switched back to English, which he thought was fluid and masterful. "Do you not think I know who is Porfirio Díaz?"

"Who Porfirio Díaz is," the younger man corrected. "Your English." The reporter smiled condescendingly. "A slight remediation, señor, for future reference."

Don Tomás turned his face to the young man with a small, skeletal smile.

"How kind," he breathed.

He was being ripped to pieces by the world, and nobody even noticed.

"So. As regards Señorita Urrea," the reporter continued in his schoolboy Spanish. The reporter pronounced it "seen-your-*reete*r." "Her mother is absent?"

"We do not speak of these things," Tomás muttered.

"She absconded, however."

Tomás adjusted his vest and his belt buckle and looked away. One shoulder shrugged.

"Is it true, what we hear about this healing business?"

"True?" said Tomás, considering it. "Define *true*."

"Is the Saint healing people, or do they only think they are being healed?"

"Ah," Tomás said. "Reality." He shrugged one shoulder again. Squeezed out a tiny reluctant laugh. He lifted his hands slightly. "I ask myself this every day."

"Do you have an opinion?"

"Yes," said Tomás, bored with this line of questioning. "I have several opinions. I manage to have an opinion almost every day."

The reporter crinkled his nose as if a bad smell had wafted in from the river.

"Opinions, then, about her being dangerous? If you will indulge me."

"We are in Arizona now," Tomás noted mildly. "Here, she is not so dangerous. Perhaps it is I who am the dangerous one."

The reporter chuckled.

Don Tomás lifted his glass.

"I said a funny?" he asked, reverting to English to show the kid he could.

These newspapers—all they wanted to write about was the Saint. The rural papers offered articles of faith, while the urban papers offered mockery. These incessant stories only fueled the madness. Even here, in this desert, eighty people a day could show up at any time demanding…miracles. Healings. Resurrections and blessings. Indians wanted to raid cities in her name. And the family's enemies, no doubt they were taking notice of this stream of mythmaking. The Great Depression of '93 was not helping either; the more desperate the pilgrims became, the more they scrambled after wonders. Trouble, trouble, trouble.

He slammed the glass on the table; the reporter jumped.

"The question is, do you intend to continue your outlaw ways here in the United States?"

"Ah, is this the question?"

A wasp buzzed around the table. It closed on the rim of Tomás's glass. It hovered and landed and tasted the wine.

Enough.

"I prefer bees," Don Tomás said.

"Excuse me?"

"Bees."

"Bees?"

"You are aware of bees?"

"Bees, señor?"

"Bees!" Tomás said. "Who do you think introduced domesticated bees to Sonora? I did! Who gave honey to Sonora? Me!"

The reporter said, "Yes, but we are in Arizona now. As you said."

He grinned at the patrón: *Touché!*

Tomás dropped his feet from their chair. The silver rowels of his spurs tinkled and rang like small church bells. He rose. He blotted out the sun.

"You see," Tomás said. "I prefer bees to wasps. Bees are more polite than wasps. And one thing I will not abide is rudeness."

He drew his .44 revolver from its holster.

"I cross-draw my pistola, left to right," he noted. "Like your own Wild Bill *Jee-coq.*"

He cocked it.

"Bees have the decency to die once they sting you. Wasps, you wave them away, you swat them, you flee from them, but they just keep on coming after you."

He fired once, exploding the glass and the wasp.

The notebook and pencil flew into the sky; the green hat levitated; the reporter dove to the ground and scrambled in the dirt. His chair landed three feet behind him. He had come all the way from Deming, New Mexico, and thus he began his return. On hands and knees.

"You bother me," Tomás announced. "You and your little hat."

He shot the hat. It scurried across the ground like a very agitated turtle. So did the reporter.

※

Teresita enjoyed the company of the good families of Tubac. Her father did not. He bristled at their kindness. He said all they had to offer him was charity. He refused to enter their homes because a man like himself did not beg for meals or ingratiate himself to neighbors for a complimentary glass of whiskey.

He was the patrón!

She could not, could not in any way, imagine a life trapped in their little vale, in their little country house, with no one for company. No friends. No conversation. Just their own remorse and anger. She was furious daily, and sometimes she trembled with anger and could not pray, for her quiet moments when she was alone with God were afire in her head with flame and ruckus and fighting.

She was angry, and she did not in any way believe that she deserved to feel that anger. But her old teacher would have told her that feelings are not right, and they are not wrong, feelings only are, and these were hers.

She was angry at her father for being drunk, for behaving like a spoiled child, for refusing to believe in her beloved God. Angry at Mexico. Angry at death.

Angry every time she looked in a mirror. Oh! She could hit herself in the face.

In the mirror, Teresita often saw an enemy.

The ladies in the front room of Guillermo Lowe's house fussed over her and patted her hair and applied creams to her brow. They poured small glasses of lemonade. They crunched thin cookies that blew ghosts of powdered sugar into the air as they breathed.

They took her to the upstairs guest room and they helped her change from her dusty black dress to her freshly laundered version of the same. One of them had a small veil for her. Funerals and weddings, she knew quite well, were what brought the ranchers together. And the women of the village of Tubac were going to make the most of their day.

※

Tomás reholstered his pistola and grabbed the bottle by the neck and strode to the doorway of his low slump-block adobe. The day seemed immeasurably improved. The caustic scents of the Sonoran desert seemed to clear his sinuses. They blended pleasantly with his gun smoke. He breathed deep, he took a swig, he dipped his head to enter the low opening.

He said, "Fate—I refute you!"

He considered this a peasant's hut. At Cabora, workers lived in huts like this. Ah, yes—irony. He was the hidalgo of nothing.

Inside, it was black and smoky and, if this were possible, even more stifling than outside. The great Saint of Cabora had filled the place with crosses and malodorous bundles of herbs and weeds. Alarming Indian carvings glowered at him from the shadowy corners. Flies immediately inspected his delicious nostrils.

Dolores, the chubby house girl, was inside, sprinkling water on the dirt floor. She had cooked him a breakfast pot of arroz con pollo that was already turning sour in the heat. The feathers of the unfortunate chicken stirred in the shadows outside the door. Great desert ants were trying to drag them away.

"Has that skinny bastard gone yet?" he asked.

"¡Ay, señor!" Dolores cried in theatrical shock.

She knew to pantomime horror over his outrageous behavior. It was one of the only things that brought him pleasure. Dolores was a student of men. She knew they needed their legends about themselves more than they needed family, drink, or love. Even with his trousers down, a man would pause if you stroked his myths about himself.

She was terrified of guns, and the Sky Scratcher was given to shooting things lately. He would occasionally unleash bloodcurdling shrieks of sheer boredom, and then, she knew, he would be likely to squeeze the trigger. There were four bullet holes in the roof already. She was getting used to his outbursts.

He watched her out of the corner of his eye.

She sidled up to him, sweeping the floor without raising her eyes, but also brushing his thigh with her epic buttocks, a carefully orchestrated accident.

¡Ah, cabrón! he thought, his loins percolating immediately. This again!

He may have considered hanging himself several times over the past six months, but he still knew a thing or two about the ladies, and as long as there were ladies in this desert, he would live to see another day.

"Come see," he said.

They peered out the window together.

The reporter was scurrying through a wall of tall weeds and shoulder-high desert grasses; mourning doves and quail exploded from cover, marking his passage.

Tomás laughed.

Dolores turned away to sprinkle water and lemon juice on the floor; she glanced over her shoulder. She knew he was half drunk. He was asleep every day by five o'clock. He was a ruin, but he had more centavos than she did, and she meant to get as many of them away from him as possible before he ran out completely. Nothing personal.

"You are so bad," she scolded.

"By God," he muttered and threw open another shutter to illuminate her better.

"Americanos are not as rude as you!" She poked out her tongue.

He reached for her. She shied away. "Come here, you!" he said.

"Where is the Saint, señor?" she asked.

"The Saint!" he roared. "What is she, my mother?" He stomped around in a circle, bumping his head on a ristra of chiles. "The Saint is out saving the world!" He smiled falsely. "Come," he said. "Show me your bottom."

"Oh my," she replied.

"As a favor. Biscuits for a starving man."

"I have to work to pay my debts," she demurred.

"I have coin!"

"Look, then," she said.

With studied shyness, she turned her back and began to raise her skirt.

He swallowed more wine and breathed out slowly.

Her bloomers came into view, a gift from Tomás himself, given to her last Christmas. He felt almost saintly when he saw them. He thought Teresita was not the only good person living in this house. Saint Tomás of las Nalgas.

Dolores squirmed as she moved one side of the off-white cotton down her right hip. Startling, delicious brown skin revealed itself, curving to shadow.

"See that?" she teased.

"Yes."

"Another?"

"Oh yes."

She rolled the white cotton off her rump and allowed her fundament to wobble.

"Yes!" Don Tomás Urrea said. "That's better."

"Give us a kiss," she breathed.

He fell to his knees.

Three

ELSEWHERE.

Celebrants of the Santa de Cabora rose in strange outbursts of glory in several towns south of the Arizona line. Before she had been ushered out of Mexico, she had physically walked among them, and her presence had largely held their madness in check. But now, with her gone, all they had left was her legend. And a legend is a relentless and cruel thing, a hungry master not satisfied until fed by great madness. They were children abandoned by their mother, and their joy carried rage within it; their exultations led to fire and smashing glass. Her calls for peace seemed to coalesce in the night, accumulate mass like icicles, and then be found on tables in the morning glowing dull yellow, made brass, but for some, transformed into bullets for rifles and battered pistolas with grips made of wrapped hemp rope and hand-carved cottonwood root.

In a Sonoran town near the coast, the Teresistas had gone mad with love. They'd begun by praying in their small Catholic church, crying out for Teresita to return. Someone had a bottle of her bathwater, still smelling of roses, and when it splashed among them, holier now than holy water, they flung themselves into the aisles, they cried out in Hebrew and the forgotten tongues of angels. Pictures of Teresita appeared from under blouses and from mochilas as if they were a visitation from Heaven, as if she herself were in the pictures somehow, or could hear their cries, or could feel their tender grasping, and they kissed her, rubbed her on their hearts, fought over her as they flung her likeness among themselves. And when the priest tried to stop this sacrilege, they fell upon him with love and they beat and kicked and pummeled him and left him prostrate before the altar as they burst from the doors and infected the passing citizens with Joy. It was all love. They set fire to the cantina in love, and they beat the drunkards with sticks. The drunkards joined them in Joy, blood streaming down their faces. It was all to be healed, if they only celebrated her holy name! The dead would return! The dictator would be overthrown! The crops would be watered and the animals would come back and all the Yaquis who had been dragged off in the slave ships and the death trains to the terrible haciendas of the south would return in glory!

Two American ranch hands, on a deserved vacation from punching cows in Yuma's brutal sunfire, had made camp near the sea. B. Andrew Laird and an unnamed companion had fished and hunted and drunk tequila far from the woes of work. Now they saw the glow of the burning and the smoke, and they heard the great laughter and singing coming their way as the pilgrims marched out of their town and into the wilderness, flinging themselves into the grace of Teresita, who might have ascended to Heaven, they did not know.

"What in hell is that there?" asked B. Andrew as the Joy came toward them.

They never got their boots on. The crowd flowed over them like ants. It was a great mass of chanting and yelling and joyous violence as they kicked and punched the Americanos. Held aloft were nude men, helpless in the grip of the holy ones. And B. Andrew felt himself lifted and stripped—they ripped his britches off him as they passed him over their heads. Then they tugged at his shirt.

"Andy, we gone be unshucked in a minute, as naked as them two greasers over there." The unnamed buckaroo was down to long johns and socks.

"¡Viva la Santa de Cabora!" the Teresistas were chanting. "¡Viva la Santa de Cabora!"

"If we don't try something now," B. Andrew called to his friend, "we is cooked."

"Andy! These bean-eaters is gone kill us," his amigo noted.

So B. Andrew took up the call—what else could he do?—and joined the Joy and shouted, "Long live the Santa de Cabora!"

The crowd faltered.

"¿Viva Teresita?" it asked.

"¡Viva! ¡Viva Teresita!" he hollered.

His friend took up the cry: "¡Viva la Santa de Caboolah!" he shrieked.

Suddenly, they were deposited on the ground, stripped naked, embraced, and slapped on their backs as they covered their parts with shaking hands and tried to smile at the Joy lest it turn again and kill them in the name of love.

"¡Amigos!" the Joy crowed. "Benditos sean."

And the Joy hurried away, waving ax handles and rifles and whirling rosaries like small lassos. Laird and his compatriot ran in the opposite direction and managed to catch an apron-faced mare they shared bareback all the way to San Luis, where, sunburned bright red and peeling, they were arrested by the Mexican sheriff for riding naked in the center of town.

⁘

Horses. Ironclad wheels. The loud cry of a brake lever outdoors.

Don Lauro Aguirre, the best friend of Don Tomás, entered the room. He pulled off his hat and opened his arms, but his imagined abrazo faded immediately from his mind.

Tomás stood with his trousers pooled around his ankles; Dolores had her skirts thrown over her head.

"Oh my," Aguirre said. "Excuse me."

He hurried outside, wiped his brow with a bandana, and huffed a single laugh into the cotton.

Ay, Tomás, will you never change?

He waited, knowing his old friend would only rush so much.

⁘

Don Tomás strode purposefully out of his house in greeting. His white shirt was half untucked and hanging over his belt. His black vest lay open across his belly. He embraced Don Lauro and slapped him on the back. He held Lauro at arm's length and cried, "Let me look upon you!" Aguirre was deeply embarrassed to note that Tomás had tears in his eyes.

Lauro had been there at every turning in the fate of Tomás and his family. It had been Aguirre, curse him, who had taught Teresita to read. He was the family intellectual. And now he was a great newspaperman in El Paso, Texas.

"You have come a long way."

"I brought you a sheet of jujubes," Don Lauro announced, retrieving the wax-paper rectangle from his small pile of valises. Tomás snatched the sheet of brightly colored candy from him and gnawed off a piece as if it were jerky.

Wagons had once brought hundreds of pounds of delights to his rancho, and Aguirre had been there for that. Now a sheet of jujubes was the most exciting thing in his day. He stopped eating and dropped the candy on the table. It tasted stale.

He put his hands in his pockets and studied his boots.

"And Teresita?" Aguirre asked.

"Away."

Dolores came forth, deeply flushed.

"The help!" Tomás said, reviving himself, gesturing. "Have you met the help, Aguirre?"

"Miss," said Don Lauro, flushing bright red as he tipped his hat.

"Señor," she said with a slight rolling curtsy. "The sweeping is done, Don Tomás," she called.

"Ah!" He spun around. "Excellent! Thank you. And take the rest of the day off!"

"Gracias, señor," she said, bustling away toward Tubac.

He turned back to Don Lauro, waving her off absentmindedly.

"I miss my old staff at the rancho," he said.

"But you are making the most of it."

"One does what one can."

Tomás noticed the reporter's abandoned glass of wine on the table. He caught it up and gestured with it. "Welcome to my estate! What's mine is yours!" He barked out one bitter laugh and gulped the wine. Skittered the glass across the wood. He gestured at the nothing around him.

Looking up, he noticed the wagon that had brought Lauro. A swarthy bastard sat upon the high box, dangling the reins for a team of mules. The sides of the wagon were great wooden shutters, gaudy with red and gold paint, tied to rusted iron hooks in the wooden frame. Its hinged roof was tall—taller than the driver. The wooden flaps said: MUSICAL MISCELLANY.

"What is this?" Tomás demanded. "Are you traveling in a rolling whorehouse?"

Aguirre studied the new wrinkles on his friend's face. Unkempt hair. Poor Tomás.

"It is a traveling pianist and his driver," Aguirre said.

"¡Qué!" cried Tomás. This might be a lively day after all. His spirits were already lifting. "And the driver. Why do I recognize him?"

"Why," Don Lauro replied, "that is Swayfeta."

"I am Swayfeta!" the driver called. "Guide, contractor, mule skinner! El Paso!"

Having delivered his résumé, he sat back and grinned.

The wine was making Tomás feel a bit wobbly. He squinted.

"¿Quién chingados es Swayfeta?" he asked.

"We met him in Cabora. On that fine day when Lieutenant Enriquez and his men were guarding the wagon train. Do you remember?"

"The Arab!"

The Arab tipped his cowboy hat to the two Mexican gentlemen.

"As salaam aleikum," he said.

"Andale pues," replied Tomás.

His attention had drifted to the shadows where an Apache friendly sat backward with his legs crossed on his white-faced horse, observing them with a slight smirk on his face.

"By God," he cried. "You lurking savage."

Lauro jumped — he had not noticed the native.

"Sky Scratcher, I brought your bug juice," the man said. He nodded to Aguirre. "I am Venado Azul."

"Delighted," Don Lauro heard himself intone as he caught himself in a small bow. "Lauro Aguirre, at your disposal."

"What did you find for me?" Tomás demanded.

"Not easy, man like me, buying bug juice!" Venado Azul scolded.

He spun himself around the right way and nudged his horse in a loose half circle, then plodded forward. He reached back to his saddlebags and produced two bottles; the fluid in one was brown as toilet water. "I have a whiskey. It will kill you, I think," he said. "And I have a good burgundy. Three bottles." He shook the corked bottle; the wine was black.

Tomás snapped his fingers.

"Burgundy," he said.

Blue Deer handed it over, one to Tomás and two to Don Lauro. Tomás dug in his pocket for some money. He couldn't find any. "I had some gold a minute ago," he muttered, forgetting that Dolores had the coins in her apron pocket now. Don Lauro ended up paying for the wine.

"Lovely doing business with you," Tomás said grandly.

Blue Deer wiped the Mexican's fingerprints off the coins with a red cloth and put them in his pocket. He dropped the wicked brown bottle back in his bags. He'd find a mule skinner in the mountains who would pay the going rate for it.

"I shouldn't sell liquor to Mexicans," he noted as he prodded his horse to head out. "You can't hold your liquor."

"I'll show you who can't hold liquor!" Tomás erupted, but he was too focused on removing the cork from the bottle to take action. "I'll... shoot you off that...apron-faced...nag!" The cork popped. "Andale." He sighed.

"You should try tulapai. Apache beer." Venado Azul nodded sagely. "You see some visions then."

"Adios," Aguirre said to Venado Azul.

Venado Azul tipped his hat to them and turned his horse away due east. He knew better than to veer north and face cavalry idiots in the arroyos. He was going to ride straight up the mountains and vanish into the Cochise Stronghold.

He stopped and looked back.

"How is the Saint?" he asked.

Tomás replied, "Saintly."

"I saw that story."

Tomás shrugged. "Pick up any newspaper," he said.

"There are pilgrims coming," Blue Deer warned. "Singing."

Tomás nodded. "The world has gone mad," he said.

"Do you know what is mad?" the rider said. "In Tucson I saw white men in a field. Some of them were throwing white rocks at others. And the others tried to hit the rocks with sticks. Then everybody ran around in a circle." He shook his head. "I don't think you muchachos will last too long, acting like that."

"Then you can take back everything we stole from you," Tomás said.

"Oh," Venado Azul replied, "don't worry. That day is coming."

He kicked his horse and was gone.

"He startled me," said Lauro.

"I thought you were stouter than that," Tomás muttered. He was starting to slur his words. That simply wouldn't do. He pulled himself erect. "I—" He intended to announce something, but his mind drifted.

"Yes, yes," Don Lauro chimed in, hoping to cover for his friend's woeful condition. "You fear no man. You fear no god. You ride the chubasco and saddle the volcano."

Tomás smiled. He stared at the ground. He sighed.

Aguirre took his arm and led him toward the table.

"My days..." Tomás sighed. "I am a ghost, Aguirre. I am already dead...." He sat down and put his hand over his eyes.

Embarrassed, Aguirre offered a conversational stratagem: "This rock throwing and stick swinging the Indian claims to have witnessed."

Tomás slumped in his seat.

"They call it baseball," Don Lauro continued. "It is a sport. Not a rock, but a ball. Not a stick, but a bat."

"I know what it is, cabrón," said Tomás. "You think I don't read newspapers? Do you think I only speak to Indians?"

Tomás sat there in the same chair he had been seated in earlier. He poured Aguirre a snootful in the dirty glass and tipped the bottle to his lips. He took a long pull.

Me vale madre, he told himself, which is how he stirred himself, finally, fatalistically, daily: I don't give a damn.

"Tell me about this piano," he said, waving the bottle toward the wagon.

⁂

For the first time in many weeks, something entertaining.

Tomás was excited. Why, he remembered the days at his uncle Miguel's home when gambling wagons rolled up to the great doors, and revelers came from all the ranchos. Tomás and Aguirre unhitched the eaves of the wagon and manhandled them up, where they were tied off and remained open like great bat wings. Inside, the pianist had been asleep in a cot tucked behind the upright piano on the bed of the wagon. Mirrors and gilt paint added a festive tone to the arrangement. He rose and shook out his red velvet coat and finger-combed his hair before donning his gray beaver-felt top hat.

"That hat," noted Tomás, "is as tall as a man from Michoacán."

The pianist was named Wolfgang Emiliano Froelich. He had hired Swayfeta to wrangle his magic wagon from El Paso in the hopes of procuring a saloon engagement for the winter. Tomás noted the piano had a pair of bullet holes in its side.

"Gentlemen," announced Wolfgang, "permit me to entrance you with the most popular songs of the day. Tunes enjoyed by royalty and fine households alike in such faraway wonderlands as New York, London, Paris, Washington—"

"And Parangarícutirimícuaro!" Tomás yelled. It was his favorite word, the name of a town back in Michoacán. He had almost forgotten it. He was finally having a good time.

"Play, please," Aguirre said.

Wolfgang eyed the bottle of burgundy. He licked his lips a few times to convey his unquenched thirst, but Tomás was not responding. Wolfgang sighed. He sat on his piano bench and arrayed sheet music on its small stand above the keyboard.

"We begin with the musical sensation of last year, 1892's grand composition 'Daisy Bell.' By the songwriter Harry Dacre. Known popularly as 'Bicycle Built for Two'!"

He pounded it out, to the delight of the Sky Scratcher. He demanded it be played again. When he discovered the song had lyrics about a fine young woman perched upon the seat of a bicycle built for two, he organized Swayfeta and Aguirre into a men's choir and bellowed the lines with immense gusto. Aguirre was more than happy to sing; he had, once again, come to his compadre's rescue.

⁂

They were fully engaged in the newest musical sensation, Mrs. Hill's "Happy Birthday to You," when the procession heading down to the Lowe funeral in Tumacacori passed on the trade road beside the bosque. Three carriages in black mourning bunting rolled slowly past the gulley, and the raucous bellows of laughter and shouting reached the occupants clearly. The piano was quite loud in the midafternoon stillness, and it gave the entire desert a festive saloon feeling. This was, of course, mortifying to Teresita. She pulled her black veil over her face and turned away from the fine people who sat on the seats around her. They tried to remain expressionless, but really. Don Tomás! At a time like this! He was simply too much!

Teresita hung her head. Wished for the wagons to hurry so her father's debaucheries could no longer be heard. Her string veil was too thin to keep out his voice or hide her shame. Even the crows seemed embarrassed.

The funeral-goers pretended they didn't hear Tomás bellow: "Hoppy bort-days to joo!"

They all jumped, however, when he shot his pistola into the air.

The wagons moved on by at their slow pace, and one of the mourners patted Teresita on the arm.

"I suppose," she said kindly, "that your father will be indisposed and won't be attending the funeral."

No one else said anything.

❋

By midnight, the killers' horses moved among shattered tiles of flat slate by feel. Their horseshoes made small screams against the black rock, casting forth sparks that danced away to die immediately among the cool gravel and bones. Nothing could be seen of the riders. They were as deep in night dark as if the high dome above them had melted and poured over their heads. The iron shrieks, the clops of the hooves, the gasps of breaths moving in, moving out across a blind horizon.

Four

WHEN TERESITA RETURNED IN the night, she found the scattered ruins of her father's little party. Wolfgang was asleep again behind his piano, and Swayfeta slept on the ground beside a small campfire. He was wrapped in a horse blanket, and the mules, freed from their traces, sniffed him and seemed to think uncharitable thoughts about him. He muttered, "Get away from me, you knob heads." He rolled over.

She could hear Don Tomás snoring inside the house.

There was Don Lauro! He was slumped over the outdoor table, his few cases piled around his seat, and an oil lamp sputtering beside his head. He rested his cheek upon his crossed arms, and open upon the wood, a French poetry book: *Les trophées,* by the Cuban José-María de Heredia. Moths fluttered around Aguirre's head. He would be mosquito bitten in the morning, and his neck would feel as though it were broken from his ridiculous posture. That and the wine headache would be epic. She looked around her. Empty bottles lay on the ground.

She leaned down and kissed him on the cheek.

"Too bad for you," she whispered.

Three pilgrims hunkered in the shadows beyond the wobbling light of the fire.

"Yes?" she said.

They came forward.

Suppurating wounds. The stench of bad meat coming from their injuries. Adoration in their eyes. She wanted to sleep. She smiled at them. They prayed. She laid her hands upon them, then moved them away from the wounds and said her words and the pilgrims gasped and cried out softly and the wind kicked the treetops and the bats could almost be heard above them making their silent screams and kissing sounds and the moon was a thin curl of orange cotton floating in a pool of oil and the wounds burned and tickled and the pilgrims fell to their knees and kissed her hands and she said, "Rise—don't do that," and refused to accept their meager payments and patted them and embraced them and sent them away with bundles of herbs, saying, "It is late—go to sleep!" They left laughing and waving, and she knew she could not enter her house until they were far gone, because her own presence, her backlit waving, was their benediction, and they would look for her until the dark and the trees and the curve in the road stole her from their sight. She knew that when her work was done, her work was not done.

Entering the stuffy house, she saw that her father had not made it to his bed but lay on his back in the middle of the floor with his arms cast wide. His pistol was in one hand, and an empty bottle was in the other. Over him, before she shut the door behind her, she sketched the sign of the cross. Then she went into her room and closed that door.

Finally. Quiet. Alone.

※

Dawn.

Three vultures flew in languid circuits from the Bosque Ranch to Nogales and across the invisible line far south to Alamos, Sonora. They picked over the skeletal remains of a calf in the old Cabora pastures, and they rose high enough to see the River of Spiders threading its way down the great Sierra, where so many had died in Teresita's name. The thin smoke of the burning of Tomóchic had long since dissipated, but the ash clouds formed dust devils still, the remains of warriors and rebels who died with their somber leader, Cruz Chávez, in that forgotten war. Cruz, the self-appointed Pope of Mexico, Teresita's friend. Gone now, to cinders. Those vultures saw it all, saw the small flecks of color that were Yaqui warrior bands moving against the mounted Rurales and cavalry on the bloodred plains and the black smear of the Pinacate desert, volcanic shadows on the land, dead rivers like scars on the back of a slave. They veered on the wind, their black glistening wings barely moving, their great feathers spread like dark fingers reaching for the souls that still fluttered in the hot winds, looping, spilling down the sky from the tides of slaughter. Cabora, Alamos, Nogales, Temosachic, Bavispe, Huatabampo, El Júpare, Tumacacori, Tubac. They went south and they went west, and they went east, and they went north, searching endlessly for the dead. And they found the dead everywhere.

Coyotes scrambled through the dawn with human flesh in their jaws where soldiers or bandits or Apaches or Rurales or rebels or cavalrymen had torn rancherías apart, scattering the walls in splinters, shooting the pigs and dropping the families in the gravel akimbo, untucked, half naked to the unforgiving sun god of their ancestors. Horse thieves ran from Arizona and New Mexico with remudas of stolen pintos pursued by orange wedges of roiling dust as they fled, American lawmen riding hard after them. Ambuscade and capture, assault and matanza. The Americans moved against the Apaches, the Apaches moved against the Mexicans, the Mexicans moved against the Yaquis. Rattling like leg bones all across the land, lone dry stalks of corn shimmied and worried in the breeze, their kernels pilfered by crows, their flaxen tassels detaching and sailing away to fall among pack rats and field mice, joining the stray cotton threads of the dead to make underground nests for writhing pale masses of blind infants.

And messiahs bred and sprouted in the hills. Each flood of arterial blood watered a new crop of visionaries. Dancers stomped in circles until blood seeped from their feet calling the old gods to return, calling on Jesus Himself to raise His fist and smite the invaders. And the Hail Marys whispered in fear in wagon trains and adobe huts as the desert warriors seemed to fall out of the sky like hornets went unanswered. These desert gods required a new form of prayer. They did not respect the faith of those about to die.

All across Sonora, into Chihuahua and back to Sinaloa, the followers of the Saint of Cabora stirred. How many starfish scars of bullets on how many backs moved among these crowds? They were followers of Teresita, turning her name into the name of a movement: Teresistas.

No longer followers of presidents, no longer Yaquis or Mayos or mestizos, not even cristianos anymore. They were pilgrims from some other world. Pilgrims from the place where Cruz Chávez lived forever with his deadly long gun. Pilgrims from the very heart of Teresita herself—even those who had never seen or heard her knew she would smell like roses once they fell against her bosom and breathed her in. They believed her picture would stop bullets. And they believed that were they to be killed, her tender gaze could lift them from the grave.

You could not touch God, but you could touch her.

The vultures moved like black angels, watching. Miners came out of the mountains in slow avalanches of donkeys loaded with ore; Chinese railroad laborers bent to the rails or scurried across the border to Texas;

Mormons sought Lamanites in the desert; and there was no telling which nation was which. And when their circuits were complete, the great birds drifted north again and circled the Bosque Ranch, hoping the great death would reach Arizona.

❋

Lauro Aguirre, bent over his drunken table and snoring, was caught in a muzzy fever dream. He stumbled into the Pillar of Boaz and knocked it over, greatly embarrassing himself as the gathered Freemasons guffawed. Then, to his shame and arousal, he realized he had forgotten to don his trousers and he stood before the assembled congregants naked from the waist down, except, in his dream, the men had become Methodist churchwomen on a Sunday morning who had not yet noticed his nakedness. Oh, the agonizing tingle in his loins! Yet…yet…his aching neck. His sore shoulder. And something touched him. Was this too the dream? A hot little…something…patting his cheek. He grumbled. He twitched. He blew fetid air from his lips, trying to drive it away. Yet it tapped him, then grabbed his lip and tugged.

Aguirre opened one eye and beheld a demon. Its insane face bore a mask of dark fur, and its red eyes goggled at him. It hung out its tongue. It giggled horribly in his face and grabbed his cheeks with two hot little hands. Aguirre shrieked and fell over backward. The beast flew from the table, waving a long ringed tail in its wake.

"The devil!" Aguirre gasped from his position on the ground. "A monkey!"

"Good morning, Don Lauro," said Teresita from the door.

"A devil-monkey!"

"No, no. That is only a chulo."

"A chulo! A chulo! What is a chulo?"

"That," she said. "A coatimundi."

"Don't tell me this beast speaks Latin!" Aguirre cried.

From inside the cabin, Tomás shouted: "A raccoon, Aguirre!"

"That," announced Aguirre the scholar, "is no raccoon!"

The creature sauntered around in a circle, its tail straight up in the air forming restless small curls above its back. It strode over to Teresita and leaned against her leg. It sneered at Aguirre and sneezed.

"My God," Aguirre muttered.

"I named him Guapo," she said. She laughed at her little joke: *guapo* and *chulo* were both versions of "handsome." She said, "Guapo El Chulo."

Aguirre laid his head back in the dirt.

"Oh," he noted. "My head."

Teresita said, "Shall I make you some coffee?"

But Aguirre had drifted back to sleep.

※

Tomás felt forgotten, and Teresita hoped to be forgotten. But Tomás was wrong, and Teresita did not get her wish.

They slept. Tomás groaned through his nights dreaming of his lost love Gabriela Cantúa. The woman of thundercloud hair. Cinnamon thighs. He raised a knee and smiled in his sleep. That skin, that skin! That cream and bronze skin anointed with honey and blessed by his tongue! He would not be distracted by Dolores if Gabriela were beside him. He would not even be distracted by his own wife, Loreto. There was no limit to which love would not go! Honey...on her breasts. Both knees up now, Tomás chuckled. Deep red wine in her fragrant navel...

Teresita suffered through her nights, twisted in the hot rough sheets. Dreaming of all her sins and failures. Dreaming of Cruz Chávez and the warriors of Tomóchic dying in flames and bullets, ripped apart with her name on their lips. Oh! She jerked awake with a soft cry several times a night, thinking she saw their ghosts lurking in the corners of her room. All she could do was sip tepid water and wait for dawn to come, praying, hoping God would see fit to lift His blessing from her and allow her...silence. Allow her love and a small garden and daughters of her own. "Remember me, dear Lord," she prayed. "Remember to forget me."

She was always up before Tomás.

She looked down on her father now and kicked the sole of his boot.

"Levántate, Pápi," she cooed.

Then she kicked him again, hard.

"Get up!"

❉

Don Lauro rose, one side of his face pocked with welts as if smallpox had somehow swarmed out of the green river and destroyed him. His neck was frozen at a terrible angle by the pain, and his mouth felt like a pig wallow. He peeled himself from the earth.

Tomás came staggering from the house with a tin coffeepot burping out little billows of steam like a small train. The hair on one side of his head stood straight up, and his paper collar had popped loose and was sticking out.

"I have Arbuckle's!" he exulted.

"Ah, Arbuckle's," sighed Aguirre.

It was everybody's favorite coffee—it was mostly the only coffee they could get. They both gave the name a Mexican spin. They called it "Arr-*boo*-kless."

Aguirre carefully sipped his coffee while Tomás took a great swallow to prove to the universe that he was macho enough to scoff at the pain of his scalded throat.

They sat at the little gray table and stared at each other.

"You should have warned me," Tomás said.

"About?"

"About los pinches Estados Unidos!" Tomás replied.

"What of it?"

Aguirre's head was throbbing sickly. He thought he could hear his brain crunching like boots on gravel. He was silently praying, promising God not to sin again if He would only remove this ghastly sensation from his skull. He could ask Teresita for a healing, but Tomás would never let him live it down.

Tomás produced a thin flask from his black trousers and waggled his eyebrows as he doctored the coffees.

"This is America, correct?" he demanded.

"Mf," said Aguirre, holding his hands over his eyes.

"Where are the Americans? Eh? Good God, man! Where are the pinches gringos!" He was roaring, Aguirre thought. He wanted his dear friend to shut his bellowing mouth. "I am *forced* out of *Mexico* as a *threat* to *Mexicans* and they send me to *America*." The words were bursting in Aguirre's poor head. "And *what*, Aguirre, my dear *son* of a *whore*, do I find in *America*? I find nothing but *Mexicans!* Mexicans, Germans, and this damnable *Arab!*"

"As salaam aleikum," Swayfeta croaked from his bedroll.

"Andale pues," said Tomás.

Aguirre sipped his coffee. The rum steaming in the cup entered his nostrils and seemed to melt a bit of the cotton in his forehead. He sipped again.

Teresita came out of the house in her stifling black dress.

"I wish we had bananas," she said.

Tomás looked meaningfully at Aguirre.

"Of such small tragedies are our lives composed," he said. Or he thought he said. He tipped a little more motivation from the flask into his cup.

"Daughter," he called. "Have some Arr-*boo*-kless!"

Suddenly, Guapo El Chulo hung his head over the edge of the house and shouted: "Keet-keet-keet-keet!"

Aguirre leapt to his feet, but Tomás simply drew his pistola and fired over Guapo's head. Guapo retreated at great speed.

"Filthy beast," he announced.

"Father!" Teresita scolded and stormed back in the house. She did her best to slam the door. It squalled and shuddered and stopped a few inches from the frame.

"Is there any wine left?" Tomás asked Aguirre.

Teresita slammed pans behind them.

"See what I must put up with?" Tomás said.

Five

IT WAS ALREADY EIGHT in the morning. The entire day was wasting away. Teresita sat inside, writing on a pad by the orange light pouring in through the shutters. She had to go out into the desert and collect plants. She shook her head. There was simply too much to attend to. Her father—well, he was useless. She spent most of her energies tending to him. Perhaps Aguirre would help her father. She stood and leaned out the window to spy on them at their table.

"I refuse," Tomás was announcing, "to acknowledge your perfidious implications!"

"Seriously, though," Aguirre said. "You seem...heavy."

"Heavy!"

"Not heavy, perhaps...¡pero lúgubre!"

"I'll be damned!"

"Burgundy, for example. Es muy sentimental. As I say, a lugubrious drink. Especially for this heat. I recommend an amber liquor. Perhaps even a clear or slightly off-yellow liquor."

Maybe not.

She withdrew her head and sat back down.

She licked the end of her pencil and bent to her pad. She needed several herbs and leaves. What her teacher Huila would have called "little sisters." Teresita smiled. *Yerba santa,* she wrote. She was not sure she could find it here in this desert, but she would look. Beside its name she wrote *consumptive's weed*. Everywhere she looked, the poor seemed to be coughing up their lungs. You could never have too much lung medicine.

Huisache, the catclaw. She smirked. For hangovers. But she wasn't going to tell those two—let them suffer a bit.

Desert willow, more medicine for the lungs and the coughing.

Cardo santo, the prickly poppy. She might have to climb a hill for that. For sunburns and warts, yes, but she preferred it as a tea for the urinary discomforts women often suffered. She had heard that men were cured of their softness problems with their little branches when they drank it, but men did not often mention these difficulties to her.

She looked around the room. What else? It would never hurt to stock up on sunflower and silver sage. But of course.

She scribbled again.

Matácora, the leather stem, the sangre de Cristo. How could she forget? What an indelicate root to be named after Christ's holy blood! Though Huila would have seen the humor in it—after all, if one was cursed with hard dry stools caught in the culo, then the sangre de Cristo would seem holy indeed when it cleared the blockage right out. "Oh, Huila!" Teresita said, speaking to her dead mentor as if she were in the room. And who could tell? Perhaps she was.

She tied on Huila's old apron and she put a knife in the right pocket. She needed it to cut samples. Huila would have also used it to puncture any evildoers she met along the way, but Teresita refused to harm any man. If a bad man came, he would have to kill her. She was not going to shed human blood in anger. Huila would have scolded her for this willful pacifism. Huila believed to her marrow that some men deserved to bleed.

Teresita did not smoke, so she had no use for Huila's old pipe and redheaded kitchen matches, yet she kept them in the left pocket anyway.

She stepped out the door.

Tomás was pounding the table and rising from his chair. They had apparently moved on to philosophy:

"Don't condescend to me with Kant!" he roared.

Unperturbed, Aguirre lifted an infuriating finger and said, "Delving further..."

Teresita walked away. Squabbling magpies. She whistled. Guapo trotted out of hiding and cast a suspicious over-the-shoulder look at the men. She closed her ears to their shouting and tried to listen for the distant shimmering of wind in the saguaros.

It was hard to find God with so much ruckus. She was not bothered by the squalor. Her holiest days, after all, had been in the mud and stench of the peon colony of Tomás's great ranches. Huila had often told her that people sought God on mountaintops, but mountaintops were too small for anybody to stand on. If you really wanted to find God, you would have to stand in the mud like everybody else. All this noise. How could anyone hear anything?

⁕

The assassins did not know where to find the Bosque Ranch, but they coerced vague directions from informants along the way. It could be anywhere between Nogales and Tucson, but they'd been told to find the ruins of a cathedral in the desert, and within five miles, they would find this bosque. Good enough. They had found men with less information than that plenty of times. Just the names of a prostitute and a town were often enough for them to find a target and take him. Those were the best because the men could not fight or flee with their pants down.

They had only to eliminate the enemies of the state. They had no opinion. They had eliminated many enemies. They didn't even shrug when an assignment came, because it was only a problem to be solved, and never a moral reflection. How do we ambush these Yaquis or Apaches or bandits or liberals, and where do we put them when they're dead? Death was a practical thing, no more mysterious to them than a bucket or a hammer.

If they found women, they calculated only if there was enough time to enjoy them before they killed them. If there were children, they had only to determine what would be most expeditious—to kill the children first, or the parents. Children were easier—one shot each annihilated them. It was just their scampering that made things complicated. They could run like scalded dogs, those little ones.

As for the moral toll, it was on the heads of those in Chihuahua City, on the heads of those in Mexico City. These two had never even been in a city. Those who did live there, those fine thinkers and gentlemen, they were the ones who dictated. They paid other men to kill their chickens and their enemies. They remained clean. The assassins merely followed their orders. Neither was a churchgoing man, but they both left the burden of guilt to God and their masters.

The motherland was more important than the individual lives of peasants and traitors. And the children? Wasn't it a gringo general who'd said about Indian babies "Nits make lice"?

They were comfortable—they were traveling the land of Indian wars and slaughter. America was full of killers. No one here would care.

All was calculation and discipline. Not heat, not hunger, not rain, not cold stopped them. They were as relentless and dark on the landscape as ants. No stops in hotels or towns now. No towns. They chewed jerky and drank dirty water from their bottles. They rode on.

Far behind them, the old man stood in his stirrups.

He was parked atop a red ridge sparkling with agates and infused with fossils. He did not require a telescope. He could see them perfectly well. He cradled a massive Sharps Big Fifty rifle across his lap as he sat comfortably on his wicked black stallion. The Sharps rifle weighed over sixteen pounds, and it smelled pleasantly of oil. Its slugs were as big as thumbs. If he calculated for windage and arc, he could drop the assassins before they even heard the sounds of the shots that killed them. What would they have thought if they'd known their very own set of calculations was now being levied against them?

"Sons of whores," he muttered.

He nudged his horse forward and followed them across the desert, along the abandoned border.

Thinking about a big cup of coffee.

·❋·

Late in the day, when Teresita returned to the house, she found her father strumming her guitar and regaling Don Lauro with ballads and corridos. They were apparently friends again. She had painted small blue flowers on the guitar, and her childhood scrawl spelled out her name on the neck. Her father's recovery seemed complete.

Tomás stopped strumming and observed to Aguirre, "She spends her days away from home and wanders back at sunset."

"Have you spent the whole day here?" she asked mildly.

"All the damned day," her father boasted.

"Válgame Dios," she said, the reproach that had passed down through generations of women brightly shining at the core of the phrase.

He ignored it.

"Teresita!" he cried, as if he'd just seen her.

"Yes, dear Father?"

He waggled his eyebrows at her, incapable of controlling his flirting even though she was his daughter. She was distrustful of the whole scene. A command performance for her beloved Don Lauro.

"We have decided upon a treat for you!" her father proclaimed.

"Oh?"

"A small surprise." Aguirre smiled, tipping his head in a courtly gesture. "To brighten your day."

"Yes?"

She could smell herself. Her sweat still smelled like roses. She had smelled like roses since those troubling days in Cabora when the powers had come upon her. Others found it lulling and lovely. To her, it was just sweat, and it embarrassed her. What nineteen-year-old woman wants to reek of sweat, even if it smells like flowers? All she could think about was a dip in the green river with a bar of lye soap.

Tomás declared: "I have contracted for a wagon! For tomorrow!"

"A wagon, Father?"

"Absolutely!" he cried.

"A treat, you see," said Aguirre.

"To Tucson, Teresita!" Tomás could barely contain himself.

"Really?" She smiled.

"We shall see baseball!" he exclaimed, waving her guitar in the air.

Tucson! The city! She was immediately excited.

"Might I buy a new dress?" she asked.

Tomás squinted at her.

"Frankly," he said, assenting, "that old black nun's habit of yours needs to be replaced."

Aguirre stood, bowed to her, and intoned, "Vive le haute couture!"

Teresita rushed inside, gathered fresh underthings and soap and a tatty towel and her hairbrush, and ran to the river, where she pushed through the wall of reeds Tomás had woven together for her so she could bathe in privacy, though Guapo and his chulos gathered across the way and stared at her, amazed that she would wallow in the water like that.

Six

THEY'D GOTTEN UP BEFORE the sun. A ride could be had from Tubac to Tucson for fifteen cents per passenger on the wagon of Mr. Alphonso Dinges, and Tomás had added a dime per head for Mr. Dinges to swing down to their little rancho and collect them. Before loading, they all stood around the outside table sipping boiling Arbuckle's and eating Mexican sweet rolls. Slender Mr. Dinges and Tomás took great pains to keep the crumbs out of their mustaches. Don Lauro dribbled coffee onto his goatee and stained its few white bristles a yellow-brown. Teresita could not believe Don Lauro already had white hairs on his chin and, she noted with a small smile, poking from his nostrils. ¡Ay, Dios! She enjoyed her coffee with honey and the last of the slightly curdled cream from their blue pot.

Mr. Dinges understood Spanish—though he called it Mexican—perfectly well. But he preferred to answer in his own American.

"Dinges!" Tomás exulted.

"Aye."

"To the city!" he cried.

"A' righty," Mr. Dinges said, nodding. "Jes' lemme slurp this'n down right here." It sounded like he'd said "rat cheer." Mr. Dinges gulped his coffee and gasped in delight and then hurried inside to put the cup in the wash bucket.

Tomás and Aguirre glanced at each other, dropped their dirty cups on the table, and grinned: these gringos and their ways! Such mess could be left for Teresita or Dolores to take care of when they got home.

The group strolled to the wagon, kicking up a haze of dust in the flat morning heat; all sounds fell to earth like feathers—even the calls of the birds had lost their sharp accents. Tomás buckled on his double-pistol gunbelt as they walked. His gold watch chain bounced against his abdomen as he strode through the day, his white sleeves burning brightly against the dark cut of his vest. He tipped his smart black American cowboy hat down over his eyebrows and fancied himself a pistolero, like the legendary Bunbury of the roving gang the Iberians, of radical Sonora. The watch in his pocket used to play music when he opened its cover, but that mechanism had died since he'd left Mexico.

Each of the travelers carried a small carpetbag with a fresh change of clothes. Tomás carried his coat over one arm; Aguirre, as always, wore his—that Aguirre, he wasn't one for shirtsleeves. Teresita wished she owned a parasol.

Mr. Dinges took Teresita's arm and helped her up into the former prairie schooner now stripped of its bows and canvas and decked out with three narrow rows of benches open to the air behind the helms-man's perch.

"Up ye go, Miss Saintie," he muttered.

"Gracias," she said.

He clambered up to his high bench, leaving the gentlemen to help themselves up. His sombrero was vast and droopy; it kept the sun from his face and from the back of his neck, and should it rain, its shape would gutter water away from his eyes and keep it from running down the neck of his shirt. Three quarters jingled in his pocket. His wagon was big and bright and only had three arrow holes from its original travails on the Camino del Diablo. Mr. Dinges was happy. It was a good day.

The juggernaut was pulled by four swayback mares who had seen long years in front of plows and who now were resigned to pointless trudges back and forth across the desert. But Mr. Dinges spared the whip and put honey on their oats, and besides, Tucson was rife with aromatic horses and donkeys, and they enjoyed that. There were mules to threaten and ponies to snicker at. It was a living.

Mr. Dinges shook the reins and said, "Hup-ho, ladies. Hup!" The metalwork jingled like Christmas, and the horses took their eternal plodding steps and the wagon jerked once and creaked to life and started its long rolling into the sun. "Hup, now, hyah."

Teresita unfurled Huila's yellow rebozo and covered her head. Her old teacher would have pointed out the importance of showing humil-ity to the Creator. But Teresita mostly wanted to keep the terrible sun from burning her brow.

"Mr. Dinges!" Tomás crowed. "Are you not a great historian?"

Mr. Dinges chuckled.

"Aye, seeñor. Aha."

"Tell Mr. Aguirre here, a great newspaperman from the grand city of El Paso—"

"El Paso! Mm-hmm. Do tell."

"—tell Mr. Aguirre what the Mexicans call Americanos in these parts."

"Oh my!" Mr. Dinges said. "My goodness. In front of the Saint?"

"Be bold, Señor Dinges!" Tomás hollered. "She is a big girl!"

She laid a hand on his back.

"Is fine," she promised, practicing her English.

"Aha! Ahum. Aye, they do. The Mexicans roundabout call the gringos los Goddamns."

Tomás roared with laughter. He slapped Aguirre's shoulder.

Aguirre asked, "And why is that?"

"Well, I suppose we say 'Goddamn it' all the goddamned time."

"Brilliant!" Tomás cried. "I love America!"

Teresita covered her mouth with the edge of the rebozo and laughed until her eyes watered.

※

They had been rolling now for an hour.

"You could travel for a year," Tomás said with despair, "and never get anywhere."

Dinges was bent to the sun as if he were carrying it on his back.

"Whose land, Dinges?" Tomás called.

"Papago."

"The mighty Papago," Tomás intoned. "Scourges of the Camino del Diablo! Warriors of the desert! Eaters of Mexicans! Isn't that right, Mr. Dinges."

"Yep, well, I wouldn't know nothin' about that."

Aguirre looked about fretfully.

"Eaters?" he mumbled.

"Oh yes!" Tomás narrated: "Fifty years ago, the Papago were involved in war with the Mexicans. And the gold prospectors. They said they ate pilgrims. Scared them, eh, Dinges?" Mr. Dinges hunched his shoulders to deflect Tomás's voice like so many pebbles. "The Camino was a bad road, eh, Dinges?"

"Bad enough."

"Bad enough!" Tomás repeated. "Indeed!"

Teresita ignored him.

"Dinges!"

"Aye?"

"How old is this big saguaro cactus?"

"Oh, he be three hunnert goddamn year, I'd reckon."

"And how much water do you suppose it holds?"

"Well now, ahum, I'd say that there holds about three hunnert gallon."

"Do all saguaros do things in threes, Dinges?"

"I haven't thought about that one."

Tomás pulled his flask and tipped it up for a small jolt.

He lay back in his seat and watched buzzards circle high above him like great catfish swimming in a pond.

☀

Mr. Dinges pulled the wagon up to the adobe gate of San Xavier del Bac Cathedral in the heart of the desert. The old Spanish mission gleamed white as a beacon beside a small dark hill in the shape of a cone.

"The Dove of the Desert," Mr. Dinges announced. "Next stop, Tucson."

He didn't give them time to inspect the church. He took on a dark-skinned trader with a woven sling full of merchandise who was bound for Tucson. The man paid Mr. Dinges five cents and settled down on the last bench.

"Hola," Tomás said.

The man pulled an orange-painted wooden flute from his sash and began playing a meandering indigenous tune.

Mr. Dinges pointed out the arched doorway to Teresita. "See that there carving up on the archway? That be a mouse to one side and a cat t'other. Ye ever see nothing like that on no church afore?"

"¿Perdón?"

He translated it into Spanish for her.

"They say that when the cat gets across that arch and ets the mouse, then ye know the world's endin'."

Teresita found that delightful. She was going to comment, but some of the sand people recognized her. They waved. Somebody called out, "¡Viva la Santa!" She raised her hand to them. She gave them the gift of her direct gaze and her smile as the wagon groaned away from the old white adobe church and rattled into the northwest.

Tucson, ahead, a dark bundle of sticks and a maze of whitewashed boxes and a few plumes of smoke rising at an angle. Southwest of it, the tormented and mysterious Yaqui mountains, and to its north the vast wall of the red and saffron Frog Mountain, the complex of peaks and canyons that sealed Tucson off from the rest of the world.

And up into the scattered tiny rancherías and tumbledown adobes of the south end of the old city. Dogs and chickens and some running children. But the general trend was toward boojum trees and scarred-up saguaros. They could smell cooking smoke.

Tomás pointed.

"Mexicans!" he cried.

Don Lauro felt vastly superior to this town.

"El Paso," he sniffed, "is by far the grander settlement."

"I'm a-gone hive off the highway," Mr. Dinges announced. "We take the ol' main drag into town from here." The wagon creaked left, its wheels knocking down and up through a small brown rivulet running along a trench that vanished into the O'odham territories. They rolled down Calle Meyer, a dirt track bounded on either side by low adobes.

Teresita could barely contain herself. So many people! Horses and carriages, a bright yellow paper kite, music from a Mexican brass band coming from a stand-alone cantina in the shimmering heat waves of the hardpan. She could see the elaborate San Agustín Cathedral far ahead and three or four two-story buildings. A real city at last.

Tomás noted the appearance of the Arab's piano-wagon in the distance, making sad rounds in search of a welcoming cantina.

"Whoa!" hollered Mr. Dinges, dragging back on the reins. He kicked the brake lever forward with his right foot. The wagon squealed and a thin bit of smoke rose from the axle. The mares stopped and stomped their feet in place before slouching immediately into their naps. "Hop out, now," he said. "I be here for ye to-morrow at three. It be another twenty-five cent each to get home."

They struggled down—again, Mr. Dinges offered his arm to Teresita and ignored the gents. The Indian trader in back hopped off and trotted down the street.

"Most enjoyable," Don Lauro said to Mr. Dinges, tipping his hat politely.

"Yep."

Mr. Dinges hove back aboard and irritated his mares by awakening them and turning them toward Tubac. The Urrea party watched them clop away, angrily nipping at each other in their traces.

"Those horses," noted Tomás, "are saying, 'Goddamn it.'"

He laughed and Aguirre snorted.

"It's a joke."

Teresita took up her small bag and stepped to the curb.

"Yes," she said.

Her father rolled his eyes.

"A sidewalk," she said. "Wood."

"Shall we find lodging first," asked Aguirre, "or food?"

"I see a saloon," said Tomás. "Didn't you recommend amber fluids?"

They wandered down the wooden walkway, Tomás's boot heels clomping loudly as he went along.

Three Americanos burst out of the saloon's swinging doors and hurried toward them. Aguirre and Teresita instinctively got out of their way, but Tomás held his ground. Tomás Urrea stood aside for no man. He believed anyone hurrying in his direction was about to deliver news or praise or both. He grinned and began to raise one hand in greeting. The leader of the three, a burly bastard with a great kerchief around his neck, threw up his hands and then double punched Tomás in the chest, bellowing, "Get out of my goddamned way, greaser!" Tomás flew backward off the raised walkway and crashed on his ass in the dirt street. He was too astonished to draw his pistolas and shoot these rude fellows. He simply sat and gawked as they receded.

Teresita rushed to his side and reached down to help him up.

"What did they call me?" he asked as they stumbled out of the sun and hid in the shadows of the overhang of the saloon.

Seven

THEY FOUND A ROOMING HOUSE on Calle Alegría that took Mexicans, and they set out their belongings in their three rooms; though the heat was intense, the mattresses on the beds were fat and comfortable. Teresita loved the white lace curtains in her window, though her view was of the back end of a blacksmith's shop, and she could hear clangs and curses and the relentless *whoosh* of the bellows. She did not care — she had her own washbowl and pitcher, her own towels.

They took a few minutes to recover from the sidewalk assault, and when everyone felt that enough time had passed for Tomás to regain his equilibrium, they set forth to find a bistro for a midday meal. A stroll down Alegría brought them to Calle Real, where they took a left and headed toward the Elysian Grove Barrio.

The walk did Tomás a world of good. He pointed out interesting details as if he'd been raised in Tucson. Gesturing to a picturesque string of donkeys jostling for shade under a cottonwood, he said, "Ah, the poor burro! Consider his fate. Born to bear burdens for lazy bastards all his days. Then he dies, unsung and unmourned." He took a lugubrious turn and proclaimed, "A fate many of us must share."

Ignoring this outburst, Aguirre quipped: "The cowboys call donkeys Arizona nightingales."

As if in response, one of the burros let rip an obstreperous hee-haw.

They burst out laughing.

Feeling lighter after the donkey's serenade, Tomás led them to a small eatery that exuded comforting aromas of garlic and hot lard. Aguirre nobly preempted any worrisome scene by announcing, "It is my treat, and I will not abide any argument!" The Urrea family bowed their heads and accepted. They took a corner table, and Tomás ordered beer for himself and Don Lauro, while Teresita asked for lemonade. They glanced at the menu, which was chalked on a square of slate mounted on the wall.

When the waiter came back to take their order, Tomás said, "I'd like sopitas!"

"Sopitas?" the man said.

"Right. Sopitas!"

"What's that?"

Aguirre held up a finger.

"Tomás," he said. "I believe in the United States they call them chilaquiles."

"Chilaquiles, then, my good man!"

The waiter looked at him.

"Eh?" he said.

"Christ, man!" Tomás cried. "Torn-up tortillas fried in a pan with salsa and an egg! For God's sake!"

"Oh," the waiter said mildly. "You mean migas."

Tomás let out a choked cry.

"We don't serve migas. How about scrambled eggs."

Tomás laid his head on the table.

"I have died." He moaned. "I have died and awakened in Hell."

Aguirre thought it prudent to keep quiet. He sipped his beer. The waiter turned to Teresita. She beamed.

"I'll have sopitas," she said.

⁂

"That was funny," Tomás told her as they walked into the south end of the city. "That pendejo didn't know what to say." He laughed. "'I'll have sopitas'!"

She bowed her head and smiled.

They were on their way to Carrillo's Water Gardens. Rumor had it that a lake was to be found there, and they might rent a little paddle-boat to float in festive circuits accompanied by ducks and swans. There were rose gardens too, though Teresita had no desire to smell roses.

Tomás noticed a small group on the other side of the street keeping pace with them and watching their progress.

"¿Y éstos, qué?" he said.

"Yaquis," Teresita said.

Aguirre was very interested in this situation, since his revolutionary theories dictated that a sure way to topple the Díaz regime in Mexico was to enlist the combative Indians in a general uprising. From the safety of his offices in El Paso, he had launched a steady stream of broadsides into Mexico recommending this very thing. Many of them included a portrait of Teresita herself, her hair unbraided and cascading in a startling waterfall around her shoulders. He had pilfered the image from an album at Cabora. In white letters across the bottom, it said: TERESITA URREA, THE SAINT OF CABORA, THE SOUL OF TOMÓCHIC. Though hundreds of these relics had flown off his printing presses and onto the walls of huts and jacales all over the borderlands, Teresita had not yet seen one. He had remembered to forget to show her.

"Must you attend to them?" Tomás sighed, gesturing toward the indigenous contingent.

"I must," she said.

"Yes. Well. Abracadabra."

He lit a thin cheroot as she walked across the street.

He and Aguirre watched Teresita speak to the Yaquis, who gestured and bobbed their heads. Not a festive-looking people, Aguirre thought.

Serious, even somber. They were pointing at Tomás, who had busied himself with blowing smoke rings and looking through them at Frog Mountain. Exquisitely bored.

Teresita came back across the street.

"Father?" she said.

"Hmm?" He was imagining the delightful downy line of nearly invisible hair running south from the bottom lip of his distant love Gabriela's delicious belly button. The way her skin formed little goose bumps as he blew on that downy line...

"They do not want to speak to me," Teresita said.

"Oh?"

"They asked to speak to you."

He took the dark cigarro out of his mouth and stared at her.

"What did I do?" he asked.

"They said they want to meet the Sky Scratcher. The man who saved Yaquis from starvation and murder in Sonora."

He was almost stunned.

He smiled.

He tossed his smoke aside, brushed back his hair, straightened his vest.

"I suppose," he said, "it would be rude to keep them waiting." He stepped off the curb. "My People!" he cried, raising his arms.

Don Lauro Aguirre took Teresita's elbow in his hand and said, "Behold, the legend."

The Yaquis closed around Tomás and took him in their arms.

※

Greatly refreshed by his public acclaim, Tomás set a martial pace to the pond. He delighted in the ducks and bought bits of biscuit from a young Mexican girl; he joined Teresita in tossing these crumbs among squabbly waterfowl while Don Lauro negotiated for a small paddleboat. They boarded and took a ridiculous cruise in oblong circuits. The water was thick and green, and white feathers floated upon it like tiny galleons. They were so happy in their boat that they realized they had completely forgotten the baseball game they had planned to witness that afternoon. They immediately made plans to see the next game the next day and continued to paddle about. "Can we afford another night?" Teresita asked. Her father simply put his finger to his lips and regarded the ducks.

This was, perhaps, what saved their lives.

As they were frolicking in the Carrillo Garden, and then shopping for fruit and sweet rolls in the original Elysian Grove market—where they were astounded to find a black bear chained to a stump in the quarter-acre backyard—the riders from Mexico were standing among the ruins of the Spanish church in the desert near their home.

It was eerie, though eeriness was an effect lost on the killers. The walls were broken, tumbled in on themselves. Pigeons flapped in the spears of sunlight. The place stank of skunks and mold. Its white-washed bits of wall were smeared with great gouts of black from an old fire. They could see the rusted holes where the spikes had once held the grand cross above the altar. Rust ran down the wall like blood. The men pissed in the rubble.

Soon, they were entering the bosque in far Tubac. The two men crept forward on their trained horses. Horses that had hunted men long enough to know how to be silent among them until the chase was finished. The assassins didn't even have to hold the reins. These horses were as dependable as hunting dogs.

They separated and came in from opposite sides, pistols drawn, long belduque knives in their left hands, carbines half pulled from their saddle scabbards. It was too close for the Hawken—it rested behind the tall one's saddle, wrapped in a Navajo blanket and tied down with deer-hide thongs.

They scanned the silent little tumbledown farmstead; they couldn't help but snicker. How the mighty had fallen. There were only a few chickens to represent the great Urrea cattle herds of the past.

The tall assassin stepped his horse from the shadows to the north and signaled his companion that all was clear. They would set up an ambush and slaughter Urrea and the Saint when they returned. Perhaps there was something worth stealing in the little house. Perhaps they could enjoy the Saint before she died. The second gunman, in fact, was about to say to his compatriot: *I have never lain with a saint before.* He half turned and rose in his stirrups and said, "Hey," to his companion.

Simultaneously there was a meaty *thunk* and a cloud of dust that exploded from the rider's chest. In that same instant, he was airborne, somersaulting across the open space, and only when he hit the ground did the report of the big Sharps rifle catch up to the hit and boom in echoes from a distance. The first assassin had only the merest moment to realize that his partner was dead and that he himself was doomed when the immense punch struck him through the shoulder and threw him ten feet from his horse. He did not live long enough to hear the thunder of the shot that killed him.

The horses were too well trained to run. But they were confused. They skittered a bit, danced in place with crazy cue-ball eyes. When they settled, they nosed the dead men. They didn't like the smell of blood, though they were used to it. They did like the smell of the grasses and weeds that grew in the clearing, and they turned their backs on the assassins, promptly forgetting the dead as they began to fill their bellies with dandelions.

After a while, the old man rode in slowly. He had slipped the Big Fifty into its sheepskin scabbard, and he rested a .44 revolver on his saddle horn. He was thinking about how the buckaroos called saddle horns biscuits, and he wished he had a damned biscuit right then. The Urreas were gone. He smiled. He spit at the dead men.

"Chingados los dos," he muttered.

His hip ached a little as he dismounted. But by God his eyes were still good—he had tracked these two halfway across the world. And now look at them. They were going to be a real problem when the family got home, but so be it.

He looked around until he found a pick and some shovels in Tomás's toolshed. The old man had been born in a house that looked very much like the shed. Oh well. If you were born a crow you couldn't expect to live like an eagle.

He grabbed the ankle of the nearest corpse and dragged it away, deep into the trees of the bosque.

⁂

Fred Ronstadt's band, the Club Filarmónico, was playing on the shore of the pond.

Torches were lit by nearly invisible workers. Tomás and Teresita danced a jarabe to the melodious skronking of the brass and violins. Don Lauro busied himself taking notes on the flora and fauna — tiny bats like black moths circled the green water as the sun set; the far crags of Frog Mountain burned vermilion and orange in the sun glow. Fine ladies in white dresses spun parasols over their shoulders and tipped their heads to caballeros in striped trousers and long coats. It was so civilized. And above the edges of the pond, the darker men and women of the town wandered along, glancing down at the "gente decente" disporting themselves.

When the music ended, the three friends walked back toward their rooming house, but Teresita stopped in a few shops and emerged from one in a pale dress with frills around the neck. She was blushing at the extravagance, but Tomás sang her praises.

They dined near the cathedral, then joined the strollers on the main street for a slow promenade. The town was flickering with guttering lights. Carriages and wagons rumbled by. Laughter seeped from the cantinas, and Teresita volunteered to go to bed so her father could slake his endless thirst. He kissed her cheek and dashed down the sidewalk, thinking already of tequila and lime.

"Tomorrow," he called. "Baseball!"

Don Lauro tipped his hat to Teresita and left her at the door.

"Keep him out of trouble," she said.

"That is what I have always done," he replied.

Eight

EARLY THE NEXT DAY, too early in Tomás's opinion, a helpful Yaqui man in the street directed the Urrea clan to the field in Marana where the Yori madmen were playing their ball-and-stick tournament. Teresita was delighted to hear the mother tongue again and chatted amiably with him for a few moments before Tomás made his impatience known. "Lios emak weye," she blessed the man as they parted. He stared after her and smiled.

Tomás hired a carriage to take them to the field — Teresita in her new white dress. He gave the driver an extra dime to find Mr. Dinges and let him know they would be returning to Tubac the next day instead of that afternoon. Aguirre had wrangled a straw hamper from the rooming-house maven, and he had loaded it with bolillo rolls and cheese, boiled eggs, a few apples, water, and some red wine. Tomás was smoking furiously, and Teresita could tell he was hungover yet again and trying to choke his headache and queasy stomach with smoke. But the day was fresh, and she wasn't going to let his behavior spoil it.

Butterflies settled at the edges of noxious puddles in the dirt street and fluttered their wings in praise.

"There is evidence of God for you," preached Tomás. "He gives you donkey piss and you mistake it for fresh water."

He smiled at them both, feeling he had scored the first point of the day.

Don Lauro was deeply offended by this, but he feared Tomás's ridicule, so he stayed silent.

"Perhaps the butterflies understand what we don't," Teresita mildly replied. "Everything God puts before us is a blessing — we are simply too blind or foolish to understand it."

"You would know," he said, just to have something to say.

"Yes," she replied. "I would."

Aguirre said, "Look at the mountains!" quite brightly.

Another moment saved.

※

Tomás approached the dirt diamond with a great smile on his face. The Americanos on the teams were all wearing ridiculous little pin-striped pants that reached halfway down their legs. One team's had blue piping; the other, red. This absolutely delighted him. "Long johns!" he enthused.

The players trotted about importantly, and they did deep knee bends and stretches. A few reprobate cowboys loitered about the far left field aboard their tough little ponies. Tomás could tell, even from a distance, that they were laughing. A vaquero was the same in any language! More pleasant than the cowboys, however, were the ladies sitting on blankets under the few paloverde trees or under vast sunshades, their handles sunk in the dirt. He sucked in his gut and stood a bit taller and smiled down upon them.

Aguirre offered Teresita his arm, and they strolled like an uncle and a young niece to the shade of a mesquite tree that actually had a rough patch of grass beneath it. Off to the west, Picacho Peak stood amusingly, looking like a slouch hat knocked cockeyed. But only Teresita thought things like mountains were funny. One had to understand their language.

Aguirre spread out a blanket beside the hamper, and Teresita lowered herself and commenced to fanning her face with a lacy hankie.

"Beastly hot!" noted Don Lauro.

"I believe I will take a sip of water," she said.

The boys in their summery uniforms shone like little candles. She watched them trot and throw the balls to each other. Their hair bounced in the sun. Their strong legs were quite attractive. Men with dark beanie caps hollered at the boys and seemed to chase them around like a small herd of goats. All very amusing.

Tomás was wandering around, nodding amiably at all the picnicking women on their quilts.

"Baseball!" he was saying. "Baseball!" It was apparently his favorite new American word. It came out "*beizy*-boll."

Suddenly, a small collection of duffers hobbled out of the little clubhouse and entered the baseball diamond. All players stopped their hustling and doffed their caps. The old-timers tottered to the mound and commenced a martial racket on drums and fife.

"What is this?" Tomás demanded.

A handsome Mexican woman seated on a small folding chair near him said, "These are heroes of the American war." Her hat was adorned with cunning little silk flowers that made her head seem to be a garden of great tenderness.

"Which one?" he quipped, smiling at his own wit. "They have so many!"

"The one between the states," she replied, fanning herself lightly with a newspaper. "The big war."

Aguirre excused himself from Teresita and hurried forth. Uncorking a draft of erudition, he stepped up to his friend and the woman. "Of course," he offered, "we all know our celebrated Cinco de Mayo commemorates the defeat of Napoleon the Third's invading troops in heroic Mexico. However, most aficionados of history miss the fact that Napoleon was marching north to lend support to the American rebels! Indeed, the Confederacy might have prevailed over the Union if Napoleon's army had arrived in time. But we all know that they did not." Beside himself now, he muttered, "¡Viva México!"

They looked at him. Tomás had an utterly blank smile on his face that stated, in no uncertain terms, *Shut up!* Tomás turned to the fine lady and said, "He remains a patriot."

She reached up.

"Hand, please."

"But of course!" Tomás effused.

He took her soft hand and helped lift her and held on a half beat longer than necessary. Just to let her know he could make her forget the doldrums of this charred spot. That he could see into her soul. She withdrew her hand from his grip and adjusted her horticultural hat.

"Gracias," she said.

What a peach! What music in her voice! Tomás glanced over at Aguirre and winked.

"Remove your hats," she said.

They did.

"He is Don Lauro Aguirre," Tomás offered. "Formerly an engineer, but of late a very famous newspaper man and publisher in El Paso, Texas!"

Aguirre bowed and said, "Delighted. At your service."

"Sir." She smiled, tipping her head. "I am Juana Van Order, from Solomonville."

Tomás dared to kiss her hand. Ah! The delightful knuckles smelled faintly of orange peel. Once again, she retrieved her hand from his grasp.

"I am," he proclaimed, "Don Tomás Urrea. Currently, ahem, residing in Tubac. But most recently of Cabora, near Alamos, Sonora."

Tomás Urrea: back in top form!

"Cabora!" she replied. "Are you familiar with the Saint?"

"Familiar!" Aguirre cried. "He is her father!"

She gasped.

"And there is the Saint herself!"

They spun around and beheld Teresita putting her hand upon the head of a raggedy urchin with bare feet. She carried a small clutch bag, and she reached in and drew a few coins out and handed them to the boy. She smiled and waved.

"My, my!" rhapsodized Juana Van Order.

"Yes," Tomás boasted, "my dear daughter, buying shoes for poor children."

"I should like to meet her."

"Ah."

"My boys and my husband would like to meet her as well."

"Ah!"

He stood in the same spot and didn't seem about to budge.

"My younger son is a great aficionado of hers."

"Fancy that!"

"He has a picture of her, can you believe it?"

"Such miracles!"

"Some huckster is selling them, I suppose."

Aguirre adjusted his collar and smiled faintly.

"Why, I never," said Tomás.

He grasped his hands behind his back, hat hanging down upon his rump and bobbing, and rocked up on the balls of his feet. They stood there in silence, regarding the fife-and-drum ensemble tootling through a few more martial pieces meant to rouse the crowd. Scattered applause met each pause between songs.

"¿Le gusta el baseball?" Juana asked Tomás.

"Like it? I love it! It is the sport of kings!" he bellowed.

Two further duffers staggered out to the mound now, one carrying a Union flag and the other bearing the Confederate Stars and Bars. An announcer sallied forth with a huge white megaphone at his mouth, hollering:

"Join me in honoring the heroes of the War Between the States!"

The cowboys whistled a few times. The people around the field groaned to their feet and clapped. Several doffed their hats. Tomás put his back on. The music resumed. Tomás scoffed at the fife player squeaking away like a baby chicken.

"That little flute looks like a rolled taquito," he quipped.

The fine lady smiled.

Emboldened, he added, "That flute player—I don't know how he was a hero. He seems a little feminine, if I dare say so."

He chuckled until she said, "That is my husband. Mr. Van Order." She smiled up at him. "He played the fife in many battles. He was shot twice and lost his leg at Chickamauga."

"By God!" Tomás cried. "He has a peg leg?"

She opened her parasol and used it to subtly separate herself from him.

⁕

Before the game began, Mr. Van Order limped toward them. Tomás grabbed Mrs. Van Order's empty chair and rushed to him. "Sit!" he cried, seizing Mr. Van Order's elbow and forcing him into the seat.

"¿Habla español?" he asked.

"Po'," Mr. Van Order replied in Italian, inadvertently answering Tomás's question completely.

"Ah!" Tomás said. Then, in his best English yet, he announced: "Is hero! Your leg! Berry brave, berry strong. ¡Y la flauta!" He mimicked the fife.

Mr. Van Order looked to his wife for guidance in this situation, thinking that the tall Mexican was disporting himself like a wild man.

"My dear," the fair Juana called. "This is Señor Urrea, the father of the Saint of Cabora!"

Various handshakes and pats on the back followed, accompanied by questioning glances cast at Teresita, who seemed perfectly happy at a distance, watching all the handsome young men in their outfits galloping and trotting around the diamond, clapping their hands, hooting "Ho!" and "Hey!" and catching the whizzing balls.

"Mr. Urrea," said Mr. Van Order. "Perhaps your daughter can grow me a new leg."

Tomás looked down at him gravely.

"This is silly," he lamented.

Mr. Van Order busied himself with a warm bottle of beer. Tomás and Aguirre were delighted to help him uncork an extra pair of flagons. The three men engaged themselves with the first inning of the game. The first batter took his stance, bent slightly forward with his bat raised over his shoulder. In his extraordinary English, Tomás confided to Mr. Van Order: "Is look like he crap pretty soon!"

Juana drifted back to Teresita. Soon, the men were vaguely aware of the females laughing behind them, and they suspected the women were laughing at them, but the exciting *crack* of the bat hitting the ball kept them focused on the game. They all, in their own ways, loved the beizy-boll.

※

The Solomonville visitors were ahead by one run when they took a break.

"Best two out of three, you know!" Mr. Van Order explained.

Aghast, Tomás inquired, "How long is this series?"

"Today's about it. We played two games yesterday."

Thank Christ!

"What a shame," Tomás mourned. "To cut short."

"At least we're winning," Mr. Van Order replied.

They availed themselves of more lager.

Mrs. Van Order turned to Teresita and laid her hand on the Saint's arm.

"My son," Juana said, in Spanish, "will not believe you are here."

"Which one is he?" Teresita asked, looking at all the pretty boys in the sun.

Juana smiled. She knew romantic excitement when she saw it. Why, for all her fame and holiness, Teresita was just a nineteen-year-old Mexican girl. Juana knew all about being a Mexican girl. She knew what Teresita was feeling at that moment. Watching all those big boys with all that shining blond hair. Why, when Mr. Van Order had appeared before her with his medals on his lovely blue uniform coat, she had felt a flutter that had run from her belly to her knees. No one felt love more profoundly than a Mexican girl.

"I have two boys," she said. "John is the tall, darker one out there. A great batter, if I do say so. He thinks he's growing a mustache."

They laughed.

"Harry is my baby. He's the light-haired boy near first base. Do you see him? He's your great admirer."

Teresita stared and smiled faintly. Behind them, people had started drifting to the field. Small groups gathered, watching. Harry was a youth with pale skin burning pink in the sun.

"Yes," she said. "I see him."

"How amusing it would be," whispered Juana Van Order, "if my Harry should become the beau of the Saint of Cabora!" She was not so much *forward* as she was *familiar*. That wonderful instant bantering that happened among the women when the men were not near.

"Ay, señora," Teresita cried, hiding her face with her hankie. "¡Por favor!"

They giggled.

But Teresita stopped giggling when young Harry trotted toward them, his hair gleaming in the sun, his cheeks round, bright from exertion. He had dirt on his knees and apparently on his bottom, for he batted at it with his cap, and puffs of dust flew out behind him as he jogged. Why, he looked just like an angel. She imagined a cherubic boy like that might be a good fit for a servant of God such as herself. And she liked his muscles.

"Father!" cried Harry. "Did you see that last play?"

Mr. Van Order struggled up.

"Indeed I did, Harry boy! A remarkable save!"

Harry had snagged a low line drive down the right foul line one-handed as he sailed sideways through the air, then crashed to the unforgiving soil with the ball held aloft for all to see.

Harry laughed and took a stoppered bottle filled with water from his father and guzzled it; the water fell from the corners of his mouth, and his Adam's apple bobbed. He toed the soil. His legs were long and restless.

From her seat, Teresita thought he was as lovely as a young horse.

"Son," said Mr. Van Order, "I would like to introduce you to my new friend Señor Tomás Urrea."

Harry stunned Tomás by turning to him and greeting him in perfect Spanish. "Buenas tardes, Don Tomás. Yo soy Harry Van Order, a sus ordenes." He offered his hand for a firm handshake.

"Mi amigo Don Lauro Aguirre," Tomás said.

Harry turned to Aguirre and bowed slightly.

"Es un placer, señor," he intoned.

Such manners! Well-bred! Aguirre beamed at the lad.

"Son," said Mr. Van Order. "I believe I have a surprise for you."

"Oh?"

"Sonny boy, take a wild guess who is Tomás's child."

"I could not."

"Try."

Harry laughed, shrugged.

"A hero of yours."

"Billy the Kid?" Harry said.

The men laughed politely.

"A girl," his father prompted.

"A g—?" Harry stared at Tomás. Harry liked girls.

"Don Tomás," Mr. Van Order explained, "owned a rancho in Mexico."

"Cabora," Tomás offered—he couldn't help himself. A good drama really helped the hours pass.

"Oh my Lord," said Harry.

The men smiled. Tomás slapped Harry's arm. Mr. Van Order took him by his shoulder and turned him around.

"The Saint," he said.

Teresita waved.

"Holy..." breathed Harry Van Order, "...smoke."

Harry's older brother, John, sauntered over to them with a towel around his neck. He was taller than Harry, dark-skinned, though that could have been from either his mother or the sun. He pushed his brother, and they roughhoused for a moment. Mr. Van Order chuckled. "Oh, these boys!" he said.

Teresita regarded him from her puddle of shade. Oh, this one. This one was strictly on the devil's payroll.

Tomás noted to Aguirre: "This muchacho has his mother's looks."

"Why, my dear Urrea," Aguirre replied. "He looks just like you!"

When John heard that Teresita was sitting nearby, he spun and stared. She made him blink. He had not been much interested in this saintly folderol Harry had been going on about, but she was as fresh as a damned daisy. He smiled at her. She smiled back.

"Harry's idol," he said.

He immediately appalled his brother; he strolled over to her and announced, "My little brother is in love with you. After the game, you need to eat with us so I can watch him squirm."

Harry was so mortified that he ran back onto the field, cheeks burning.

"You might find out which one of us is the better man," he said. He winked and grinned. "At least," he said, "the taller man." Teresita looked up at John, dark against the sky, and thought he was rude. Horribly handsome.

"Be kind to your baby brother," Juana said.

John kissed his mother on the cheek.

"Mama's boys are the best," she said.

"Me?" he cried.

"Both of you."

He trotted away, punching his father on the shoulder as he passed. He held out his right hand, and a baseball appeared there as if by magic. He pivoted as he ran and threw the ball to deep left and shouted, "Catch it, you lummox!" He forged on into the burning sun.

Mr. Van Order dragged his chair back to his wife and Teresita, where he sat and patted Juana's hand as the final innings of the ball game played out in dust and whistles, laughter and mild applause.

Behind them, the slowly swelling mob had unfurled a banner.

VIVA LA SANTA DE CABORA.

Harry Van Order, at first base, bottom of the ninth, watched them unfold the painted sheet, and he missed the ground ball that his brother scooped up and threw to him. The runner thundered past him as he fumbled for the ball, which had taken on a life of its own and was hopping around his feet like a drunken toad. The enemy scored three runs off his error. Solomonville lost the game.

Enraged, John ran over and slugged him in the shoulder, and they wrestled furiously in the dirt. The coaches of both teams dragged them, spitting and cursing, apart. John kicked at Harry. Harry threw a handful of gravel at John. Teresita watched them as they were hauled behind the clubhouse, where the dust of their ongoing battle drifted to view in periodic billows.

Mr. Van Order shook his head.

"Boys," he lamented.

Teresita was thinking she could beat John Van Order in a fight.

Nine

BACK AT CABORA, BEFORE the troubles destroyed everything, Teresita had tussled with the vaqueros like a scrappy boy. The Sonoran sun, in her memory, was buttery yellow and somehow less brittle than the Arizona cauldron of fire that turned the center of the sky dead white at noon. She was skinny under its light, and her shadow was blue as it puddled around her feet. Arizona made her feel angular, a rattling scarecrow made of bones and regrets.

In Sonora, and before that in Sinaloa, she had been thin but made of flesh. She could outride the other children on the ranch, and some of the vaqueros thought she could outride them too. She could definitely outplay them on guitar. They included her in their wrestling matches, and she could exert some tremendous power to make herself too heavy to budge. She would taunt them. "Come on, big men. Knock me down!" And they would line up to heave a shoulder into her. They, who were twice her size. They would batter themselves against her small frame and be unable to move her.

Teresita often laughed out loud when she thought of those days.

Very little, now, made her laugh.

Her teacher had tried to show her that it was all a question of balance, that without balance, there could be no control. And she had exercised control ever since—her thoughts, prayers, actions, behavior were all under endless scrutiny. If not by God, then by her father, and if not by her father, then by the People. They had once been her neighbors and friends, and then they became her followers. She felt a small chill of horror. Followers! It was terrible to have followers. But it was more terrible that part of her liked it.

Of course, she could not control her fanatics, only herself. Balance, again. When she had followers, she was watched over by the government and the newspapers. People copied her words in notebooks. She caught herself wondering what she had said and worrying all night if this time her careless utterances would lead to someone's death or some outbreak of madness she could not have foreseen. Sometimes you just want to speak without measuring your words! Sometimes you want to laugh and sing! Sometimes you just want to ride your horse!

No wonder she relished her sad small memories of Cabora. Blessed obscurity. Nobody was watching her. Certainly not her mother...She closed her eyes. Balance, she told herself. Control. Thoughts of her mother. Those were unwelcome invaders, for they filled her with sorrow and shadows. Teresita did not like to cry. She did not like to demonstrate that weakness to the world. Besides, she told herself, if she cried in public, some maniac would rush up and catch her tears in a bottle to sell later.

Oh, Mother.

Mother, gone and never returned, wandering somewhere in Mexico, perhaps to this day. Mother, a small shadow of memory, not real enough to have a face in Teresita's mind, for she had left before Teresita could even speak. Driven by poverty, fear, and shame into the life of the wandering immigrant, the trudging nameless dark ones who were seen on the outskirts of every town. Still, in her dreams, when Teresita flew far over mountains and slipped down the winds to dip her toes in the ocean she had never seen with her eyes, she saw her mother. Small Cayetana Chávez. Hair done in elaborate waves, pale color painted on her Indian cheeks. Red glistening lacquer on her lips. Her mother, dancing in the wobbling glow of paper lanterns hung over plazuelas in Mazatlán. Teresita had hovered above her mother like a hummingbird; Cayetana's dresses were red, like flowers, and they spun out around her knees as she twirled with workmen and cowboys, lawyers and butchers, all the men taller than she, and still beneath her. None of them worthy of her laughter or her touch. Mother.

Teresita could cry out, she could whisper, but never, in any dream, did Cayetana hear her daughter's voice.

And when she moved on to another town, Teresita would fly through clouds and rain, under ice-cold stars and under the orange Mexican moon, to find her.

She pulled her hair back and tied it with a ribbon as Aguirre's rented carriage banged toward Tucson after the game.

⁕

Well. Enough of that. It was far more amusing to remember her donkey Panfilo. It was delightful to relive the first real meals she enjoyed when Tomás saved her from her poverty and allowed her to enter his world of finery, crinolines, and shoes. Ah! Squash blossoms fried in egg and filled with white cheese! Fideo soup with chicken, lemon juice, and banana slices! Turkeys stuffed with dried mangoes, apricots, pineapple, and raisins! Platters of tiny fish sun dried and crisp, tart with lime juice and dribbled with bloodred Tabasqueño sauce! Such food. She'd thought no one had ever seen food like this in the history of the world. Before Tomás, a poached iguana and half a bolillo roll was a feast to her.

"No wonder I was a skinny child," she muttered.

"What was that, my dear?" asked Aguirre.

She shook her head.

"It was nothing," she said.

She pulled Huila's rebozo over her head and hid her eyes.

If she could only control her thoughts, she believed, she might be able to control her life.

She put her hand on her father's knee. Startled, Tomás turned to her and smiled. He patted her hand.

"It will be all right," he said. "You will see."

How could he tell what she was thinking? It seemed to be a father's small magic.

Teresita laid her head on his shoulder. She sighed. He put his arm around her and noted, not for the first time, how slight she really was. How small her shoulders, how bony she felt.

"I promise," he lied. "Our troubles are behind us."

※

Supper with the Van Orders started in a slightly uncomfortable haze. The Urrea company was shown to a long table spread with a fine white cloth in the biggest hotel in town. Tomás made a great show of slipping money to various obsequious servers. Teresita had not sat at a table like this since before she had been harried from her home by soldiers and taken off to the prison. Through the windows of the dining room, she could see vague shadows of faces on the street, peering in at her. The brothers had apparently already recovered from their dustup.

Approaching the table, the party divided. Teresita and Juana sat side by side at one end of the table, and Harry wrestled his way into the seat directly across from Teresita. He was red-cheeked and confident, absurdly pleased with himself to be facing her. His mother clearly found this precious and softly nudged Teresita in the ribs, and the two of them snickered, baffling and alarming Harry. At that moment, Tomás and Van Order took the far end, and John and Aguirre formed a buffer zone between elder males and tolerant females. Harry was adrift, a free agent. Teresita was not used to being sequestered. Her usual place was directly across from her father, where she could argue the events of the day and the books they had read.

Tomás announced, "Apparently, the women have formed a union."

Harry startled Teresita by pulling a folded picture of her from under his off-white cotton shirt. Upon seeing it, Don Lauro Aguirre cleared his throat and touched his lips with his napkin. Tomás paused in the middle of a bon mot to note, "Some cad has made a religious relic of my daughter!" Aguirre coughed. Mr. Van Order patted him on the back.

"Here, here!" he said. "You're not choking, are you?"

Harry studied the picture as if it were a construction blueprint, as if he had secured a commission to inspect the real article and ensure that it matched the plan. For her part, the Saint did not enjoy being reviewed in this manner. Yet when Harry's eyes turned away from her to the far end of the table, she grew impatient and anxious for his gaze to return.

The first course was served, white tureens of the Mexican soup known as cosido. The beef had been boiled gray, but the broth was clear, and onion, potato, and small red flecks of herbs floated in schools around the shoal of meat. In each bowl, a segment of corn on the cob joined the meat.

"Waiter," Tomás announced grandly, "some red vino with the soup!"

"Certainly," the waiter said.

The Van Orders were impressed.

Teresita sipped her water and spooned broth into her mouth. Tomás was breaking the bank now. She shook her head. She avoided the meat. She watched Harry watch the older men, his college. Juanita sparkled beside her. The men slurped like beasts as they attacked the overcooked beef.

Upheld by the heroic translations of Aguirre and John, with the occasional interjection from Juana and the generally unwelcome yet tolerated intrusions from Harry, the men engaged in a multilingual conversation that no reporter could have accurately recorded. Aguirre mentally registered an observation: For men of ideas, language is no barrier! He would include it later in one of his notorious broadsides.

"See here, Tom!" Mr. Van Order said. "This Díaz—a tyrant! You're in America now, my friend. There is no going back."

"No," Tomás agreed.

"Make the best of it, boyo!"

"Indeed."

"You must become an American citizen if you hope to make anything of yourself in this country." Mr. Van Order gulped wine and put down his glass decisively, point well made!

"Yes, yes," said Tomás. "I have already applied for citizenship, my dear Van Order. Both with excitement and a twinge of regret. I am now, however, in the—¿cómo se dice?"

"Probationary period," Aguirre offered.

Tomás pointed at him. "In that. Three years." He held up three fingers Mexican style—including his thumb. Juanita chuckled and held up three fingers American style—no thumb, only fingers. Tomás stared at her hand.

"It is a beginning," Aguirre murmured.

Tomás changed fingers.

"Well! After three years, we will see, won't we, if it is for the better or the worse when I become an Americano."

Tomás and Juanita drank a mock toast to each other.

"It is very delicate," Tomás confided. The men all leaned in. Juanita finished her soup. Harry turned back to Teresita and studied her. It was about time, she thought, as she acted irritated with him for looking at her like some sort of puppy. "You see," Tomás said, "the political situation dictates a certain . . . delicacy."

"Delicacy," Aguirre concurred.

"My landholdings in Mexico. I am responsible for family."

"Families," Aguirre interjected.

Tomás cast a censorious eye at him.

"I must make my moves quietly, lest the government take my lands, my ranchos. All is in peril, amigos. We must be discreet."

They all nodded wisely.

The waiters made the soup bowls vanish.

The second course descended. Tomás announced, "More red wine with the meat!"

He turned to Aguirre.

"Who is lugubrious now, cabrón?" he said.

※

John, like Harry, watched the adults with avid curiosity: the libertine Tomás, that prig Aguirre, and his dear old papa were bright red in the face and animated with vino and manly twaddle. Romantics, all of them, romancing one another. Predictable too: war stories and fables of horseback exploits. Horses! John hated the goddamned animals and would have liked to see them all boiled in stews. Nor did he share the gents' seeming fascination with wide-open plains and rugged savage mountains and the predations of the intriguing red man. God! A world of repetition and dull replication. John Van Order imagined himself in a city, never to smell horse crap again.

He glanced at Teresita. He liked her eyebrows. She looked permanently startled.

Down the table, his mother and the Saint were in their own cloud. John had been stunned to learn that when his mother was younger, she had been known as la Yaqui. How was this possible? Like many sons, John could not believe there was anything mysterious, unfathomable, or interesting about his mother. It was God's commandment that parents were dull. And here, suddenly, his dowdy mother — dear though she be, the queen of popovers and pies — was positively...giddy.

"Mother," he said. "Have you been drinking?"

He was appalled when Teresita and Juana burst out laughing at his expense.

"Teresita," Juanita said. "What is the word for 'serpent'?"

"*Bacote.* In Mayo."

"I remember! What is the word for 'bird'?"

"*Huirivi.*"

"I remember! What is the word for 'lice'?"

"*Náinari.*"

They laughed out loud.

John said, "Mother!" There was nothing funny about lice! Not, at any rate, to decent ladies.

They snorted. John tossed his napkin on the table. Harry's head swiveled back and forth, an idiotic half smile on his lips along with lamb grease.

"What are you looking at, fool?" said John.

"I do not know, brother," Harry replied. "I can't figure out what it is yet."

It was all coming back to Juanita Van Order.

"Mother. Really. People are starting to look."

"Jita se guaria?" she said to John in Yaqui.

"Eh?" he replied.

"She said 'What do you want?'" Teresita translated. The women laughed. She turned to Juanita and said, "Es yecca-ara."

They laughed again.

"What?" John demanded.

His mother said, "She says you have a big nose."

Offended, he scooted his seat closer to his father and turned his back on the babbling woman who had apparently been reduced to savagery by this so-called Saint.

"Witch," he muttered.

Teresita whispered to Juanita, "Omteme."

Juana shrugged. "He is often mad, isn't he, Harry?" Harry blushed when Teresita looked at him. "Harry." His mother smiled. "My little bunny." Of course, she said *tabu,* so he didn't know what she'd said.

Harry had sat there holding his picture of Teresita the whole time. Now he refolded the picture and tucked it inside his shirt, next to his heart. He secretly extended his legs under the table and tapped Teresita's foot with his own. She jumped. He looked away, but kept smiling. She scooted her feet back an inch. He reached out and tapped her again. Oh! She looked at him. He glanced at her and ducked his head but smiled so hard he looked like his cheeks would pop like balloons. He was blushing! But he tapped her foot again. She covered her mouth with her napkin and snorted. This was...she didn't know what it was. She thought she should be outraged, yet she found it hilarious. Carefully, she put out her foot and tapped the top of his. He dropped his fork.

John turned back to them, his ears still red with anger. He raised a faux toast to Teresita.

"You ain't much to look at," he noted, "but brother here can't seem to get enough of you!"

"John!" his mother scolded.

Teresita kept her eyes down, things clear. John Van Order wanted to be her beau. Well, well. Harry tapped her toes.

Ten

TERESITA WISHED SHE HAD a pocket watch like her father; this meal seemed like it had been going on for twenty hours. Her bottom hurt. She was tired. She could smell herself. She didn't know if it was lovely or appalling. The People said it was evidence of God's grace. But it always made her self-conscious.

Harry leaned toward her.

He said, "You healed Fulgencio Ortiz."

"Excuse me?"

"You healed old Fulgencio. From San José! That's how I heard of you."

"Oh…" Now she was blushing. "I meet so many people." It was dreadful talking about it.

"He was crippled," Harry offered. "You made his leg straight."

There was no way to address this kind of comment. Nothing one said was sufficient. Nothing sounded right.

"Praise God," she finally mumbled, so self-conscious.

"But how'd you do it?" Harry asked.

"I did not," she replied, shifting in her uncomfortable seat. "God did it through me."

John guffawed, and she did not know if he was laughing at her or at one of her father's japes. He never looked her way.

"It is a blessing," she said.

Suddenly, John turned to them and said, "She's one of them yerb women." He grinned at her. "Working those Mexican yerbas."

"Mind your own business," Juanita scolded.

Harry hadn't been drinking the wine, but he looked poleaxed by the whole event and hung his face around to stare at John. Then he swung his dog eyes back at Teresita.

"The Ortiz family lives near us," Harry said. "San José ain't far."

"Yes," said Juanita. "Their whole town reveres you."

Teresita sipped water so she wouldn't have to speak.

"You should move to Solomonville," Harry encouraged. "Be near us!"

Juanita grinned at her son.

"You are so forward, bunny."

Sadly for Harry, Tomás heard that one and turned to them for a moment and cried, "Does your mother really call you *bunny*, young man?" Howls of derision from the male end of the table.

Harry laid his foot against Teresita's and fumed.

When dessert came, a bread pudding dotted with raisins and drooling a bit of sugared rum, Harry pulled a face.

"This dessert is a tad stale," he said.

"While you," Teresita replied, "tend to be a bit fresh."

She lightly kicked his ankle.

☀

After dinner, as the two families parted, Harry blushed vivid red when Teresita kissed him lightly on the cheek. Abrazos all around, hearty promises to keep in touch and to drop in at Solomonville soon for a visit.

When it came time for John to bid Teresita farewell, he surprised her by offering a very decent bow from the waist. He took her hand in his and kissed her middle knuckle, looking up at her from under his eyebrows.

"Don't forget me," he said.

"I might," she replied.

"I won't let you," he said and tipped an imaginary hat before vanishing in the gloom.

When she finally rested her head on her pillow in the rooming house, Teresita felt almost dizzy. It must have been the sun. It must have been the rich food and the late hour. She told herself it was not, not, the Van Order boys. She felt light taps on her toes, though, more than once as she drifted off.

☀

After a night of bad sleep, she was not thrilled to be remounting the creaky step to Mr. Dinges's tiresome wagon. Tomás and Aguirre were rumpled, seemed morose. Hungover again, she reckoned. Mr. Dinges knew enough to let them all be. He busied himself by chatting with a German shopkeep riding home to Tubac. The two men seemed to have an endless supply of goodwill toward bacon and both spent many minutes expounding on every miraculous facet and permutation of bacon: Bacon and eggs! Bacon in thick slabs in saddlebags! Bacon grease on your face to cut sunburn! The smell of bacon! Bacon wrapped around fried chunks of rattlesnake! Bacon grease in a biscuit! Salted bacon lasting forever on the trail! It was making Teresita queasy.

Behind her, Tomás snored softly.

Aguirre just stared at the landscape, looking a hundred years old.

⁂

Mr. Dinges left them, tired and sunburned, on the road between Tubac and the Bosque Ranch. They dragged their bags along the path in the afternoon sun. Horned toads lay in the cactus shadows like mottled dropped pads of the nopales. They were the same colors as the gravel they rested on, and both men missed them entirely. Teresita watched a nervous javelina shake his head at them from the western edge of the wilderness, his little tusks making idle threats. The men missed this too. Crows scolded and insulted them happily as they jumped from one raggedy treetop to the next. No sign of Guapo anywhere.

"I would keep walking south," Tomás announced. "Right back to Mexico!"

"Except," Don Lauro replied, "they would kill you."

"There is that," Tomás conceded.

They skidded down the gravel slope of the road, into the mesquite shadows. They walked down the skinny trail to their sad house, and Tomás stopped abruptly. Teresita ran into his back. Aguirre, lagging behind now, didn't notice. Tomás pulled his pistola and put his finger to his lips. There, before the house, stood three horses. Two of their heads drooped in the classic pose of the siesta, but a fine black stallion perked up and swiveled his ears toward them, quite alert.

Tomás stepped forward and sprang into the light of his clearing with the gun extended before him. He could smell fresh coffee. Smoke was rising from his chimney. He sniffed. By God! Some son of a bitch was frying his eggs inside his house!

"Show yourself!" he bellowed.

The invader stepped out of the gloom. He was guzzling coffee from one cup and held another cup in his opposite hand, ready to guzzle that one too. He squinted at Tomás and spit once.

"Hello, boss," he said.

Teresita cried out and ran past her father.

"Segundo!" she yelled and knocked the coffee mugs from his hands. He chuckled. He lifted her off the ground.

"I'll be damned!" Tomás said as he beheld his old foreman. "You are the last man I expected to see today."

Then he began to smile.

Then he began to laugh.

"I told you!" he shouted. "I told you things were fine! I told you things were going to get better!"

He rushed to Segundo and gave him a pummeling abrazo.

"I brought you some horses," Segundo lied. "And this big rifle."

Eleven

TERESITA WAS IN THE kitchen half of the cabin, but she did not mind. She was working on some rice in the largest frying pan, melting lard and dicing red onions. Waiting for the onions to become as clear as small windows before dropping in the yellow rice and frying it. She would fry the rice until it, too, became clear. Then she would add water and spices and boil the water off in several rounds of cooking, until the rice was swollen and tender. She would add diced tomatoes, green tomatoes, and tomato sauce, holding off on the diced chiles and cilantro until the very end of the cycle. Salt, garlic.

As soon as Dolores reported for work, she would send her back out to buy two chickens that they could dismember and boil in a broth of consommé, onions, celery, sage, lime, and red peppers. Teresita poured sweat as the smoke unfurled around her. She had tied a red rag around her head and fancied she looked like Manuelito, her Chiricahua Apache teacher, with his fierce warrior's bandana. For just a moment, she wondered if he thought of her. Her volumes of hair were pulled back in a long mare's tail. Manuelito would have braided his, she thought.

Beside the rice, the dented coffeepot blurped and bubbled merrily. Steam filled the smoky room. She tipped water from the clay jarrito into the rice pan; it hissed. The billow hit her face. She wiped her brow with her arm. She smiled. Segundo was here. She was happy, and happiness made food taste better. Cooking with happiness for your loved ones was like laying hands on the sick. It was a great medicine. Teresita often wondered how men did not realize this about women — that their wives and daughters, their sisters and mothers, in this most basic form of service, were spell casters. If women found out how powerful they were in their slightest exertions, in their pain and joy, in their love, she would be out of business. Lord! Let it be soon!

She peeked out the window. Three of her loved ones were gathered at Tomás's little ceremonial table. They were all smoking black cigars. They were spitting, slamming their hands on the wood. Guapo El Chulo ran by and feinted an attack at Segundo's backside before diving into the weeds at the far end of the clearing. Their top hand didn't know how close Guapo's claws had come to his buttocks.

Teresita cut an onion and wept. Onions could cure impotency. Oh my. She sighed. She smiled. Just what those men did not need.

Outside: laughter.

Curses.

Shouts.

※

"You have brought me great joy, Segundo," Tomás said.

"Good to see you too, boss," said Segundo, taking a last puff of his cigarillo.

"And what else have you brought me?" Tomás asked.

Segundo sauntered over to his horse and pulled a heavy oilskin package from his saddlebag. He walked back to the table, looked into the distance, paused. Tomás, clearly agitated, wanted to leap from his seat. As if teasing a hound with a chunk of sweet bread, Segundo feigned tossing the bundle on the table but didn't. Tomás jumped a little. Segundo smiled, dropped the packet with a loud thud.

"I brought this," Segundo said rather mildly.

Tomás peeled back the top flap of the package and let out a cry. Money. Bundled stacks of colorful pesos.

"¡Ah, cabrón!" Tomás shouted.

Segundo sat back down and patted his belly.

"I've been managing the ranchos pretty damned well," he said.

Tomás leapt up, grabbed him, and kissed his brow.

"Not that well," Segundo noted.

When Dolores appeared in the clearing, she was immediately smitten with Segundo. He in turn promptly twisted his gnarled and sunbeaten visage into a leer, ghastly and exuding profound affection. "I did not know," he announced, "that Easter lilies could grow so gentle and lovely in this terrible desert." She almost fainted and rushed into the cabin with Teresita.

"Steady," warned Tomás.

Aguirre snuffled and chortled into his goatee.

When Dolores exited the house to get the chickens, Segundo leapt to his feet and said, "I thought I heard the wings of angels beating musically from Heaven above, but it was merely the gentle patter of your delightful little feet!" She cried out and jogged away.

"Seriously," said Tomás.

"I will ask Teresita to introduce me to that fine woman," declared Segundo. "But first, I must learn her name." Were they wrong, or did that grizzled old coyote trot over to the house like a teenage boy?

"That is the most unseemly thing I have ever witnessed," said Tomás.

"You have been bested, my dear Urrea," gloated Aguirre. "A better bull has entered your pasture."

"Bulls?" cried Tomás. "What is this about bulls!"

Segundo came back out with a big mug of Arr-*boo*-kless.

"Dolores is mine," he said. "All right with you boys?"

Tomás leaned over and spit.

Aguirre patted Segundo's arm and smiled.

"I believe you will require a little of that money back," he said.

Segundo thought about it.

"Boss," he said. "Give me a loan."

⁂

Even Dolores sat down to eat. Every time she smiled, Segundo made a face in her direction that conveyed the depth of his agony. She was, he made clear in his silence, the most desirable and witty woman in Arizona—perhaps in the entire country. She was startled by this and didn't know why she hadn't noticed it sooner. When she passed Segundo the salsa pitcher, he gasped as her fingers touched his. He put his apparently wounded digits to his mouth. "Such sweet injuries." He sighed. "Your touch tastes of strawberries."

"Jesus Christ!" Tomás protested.

The remains of supper were abandoned on the table, and a second and third. Guapo El Chulo raided the dirty plates and feasted on chicken and tortillas and pickled carrots and gobs of cold rice colored gaily with vegetables. The campfire was lit and the guitar made the rounds. Teresita sang corridos to great applause. Segundo spooned with Dolores, and Tomás was astounded and deeply hurt to see her making a cat's cradle for him with white yarn and reducing ferocious Segundo to a small schoolboy giggling and mewling hideously at her ridiculous stratagems. Don Lauro Aguirre could not have been happier as he leaned back in his seat and sipped a delightful cognac that Segundo had requisitioned from Doña Loreto Urrea's grand house in Alamos, La Capilla.

Tomás wandered away to water the creosote bushes. He went a discreet distance from the gathering to relieve himself, and it was there, looking upon the trunk of a mesquite, that he saw blood. Odd. He looked around. A thin spray on the rocks. He buttoned up and went to the side of his house, following the trajectory of elongated drops. Blood on the adobe brick. By God! He inspected the horses. One had blood on its saddle.

He snuck to Segundo's horse and sniffed the long Sharps. Its barrel still smelled of gunpowder. Well, well. He lit a cheroot. He knew right away what had happened.

He strode up to Segundo, who was happily mauling Dolores.

"How soon?" he said. He glanced at the horses.

Segundo looked up at him.

No one else at the party knew what they were saying, but these two understood each other perfectly well.

"Soon, I figure."

"How many?"

Segundo shrugged.

"As many," he said, "as it takes."

Tomás stood with his hands on his hips.

Segundo said, "Boss."

"Yes?"

"They will never stop."

The fire continued to crackle and throw sparks.

✳

Tomás had been scared, and ashamed that his emotions were so baldly obvious, but before Segundo made the inevitable gentleman's gesture of "accompanying Dolores home," Tomás had asked him: "What of my Gabriela? Has she sent word to me?"

Segundo had gone to the saddlebags again and produced a paper bundle.

"This," he said.

"No letter?"

"None."

Segundo and the cook made their way into the night.

Tomás left Aguirre and Teresita to their own interests. Aguirre had taken out a volume of verse by the poet Martí, and he droned on in sonorous interpretations of the Cuban's tropical largesse. Teresita closed her eyes and rocked as if listening to the greatest symphony.

Tomás took his bundle into the house. With trembling fingers he tore the paper. The whole thing was soft, pliant. Cloth. He tattered the paper and her nightgown fell out, redolent of her, sweet with her perfume, spicy with her scent. It was the softest thing he had touched since he'd been exiled from Mexico. He smelled it. Smelled her. Buried his face in his Gabriela's scent. Alone, in his smoky hut, Don Tomás Urrea wept.

※

Farewells. Good-bye notes. Surly payment of pointless bills. Handshakes and final cups of tea with platters of crullers. Dolores took Guapo El Chulo home with her. The rituals of parting had been attended to, and there was nothing for it now but to go.

The wagoneer Swayfeta had made his way down from Tucson, happy to be returning to El Paso. Stripped of its piano and its bat wings, the wagon was tawdry in the morning light, gray and splintery. The family's few goods were piled in back. A comfortable chair took up the middle, and Teresita sat there with her books. Aguirre, Segundo, and Tomás manned the three horses; Tomás was delighted to be bristling with the weapons of the dead assassins, his new belduque knife gleaming at his hip. Teresita thought that if they'd given her a horse, she could have outridden all of them. Maybe those bad Van Order boys would find her a pony. She settled back comfortably and opened Anna Berruel's parasol. She wondered if Harry intended to keep tapping on her foot.

Off to the side, Dolores wept copious tears.

"Farewell," Segundo said tragically. "My delicious little bun of breakfast pastry."

"Damn it, man," muttered Tomás.

He twisted in his saddle, looked around. This was familiar. Leaving again.

"Swayfeta!" he bellowed.

"As salaam aleikum," the Arab replied.

"Andale pues," said Tomás, and spurred his horse away from the bosque.

⁑

And now it was a trio, three riders leaving Culiacán and galloping north, toward Guaymas and beyond. They rode two pinto ponies and a gelding palomino. Each carried a Winchester repeating rifle in a leather scabbard, and they bristled all about with smaller weapons. Their packs were loaded with jerky. They came on like a black wind, scattering wild dogs and crows. They never slowed when they roared through villages. And the People turned their backs to them, bent to their tiny corn milpas, or hid in their houses. The thunder of the horses' hooves announced them before they could be seen, and the sound receded, stormlike, into the distance as they passed. Drumming, drumming, drumming on to the heartless border night.

Part II

THINGS FAR AWAY AND DEAR

The saintess can hardly be called beautiful... but then she is "interesting" even if she's thinner'n a bed slat, and wears a philosophical air, has bright lustrous eyes, and in more ways than one sugests [sic] the Boston girl, the habitué of the Concord school of philosophy. And when she substitutes a black silk dress and Seville lace for that yellow, blue [and] black polka-dotted gown, she looks quite recherché. Teresa no habla el Ingles worth a cent, and the Herald *reporter had to talk with her in Yaqui, which she speaks fluently. She can't even say "howdy" in Iowa English.*

—El Paso Daily Herald, 1896

Twelve

SAN JOSE WAS WORSE for them than Tubac. But it was peaceful. Though the nights could be cold, the people were warm. The land was wild, and the Van Orders were a manageable ride away. Solomonville amused Tomás because it was as worn out as far Ocoroni, Sinaloa, where he had once dreamed of a great life while eating mango slices red with chile powder and crunchy with sea salt. The people of Solomonville did not have mangoes, but they were people who remembered mangoes, so he had something to talk about with them. For Teresita, it was like being caught in amber; Ocoroni had been, until Tucson, the most established city she had ever seen. But then they arrived in San José... well. At least there weren't many distractions.

Their new home, rented with the money Segundo had brought them, tucked up against great boulders and blackened barrancas, was baking hot and drafty when there was a draft, which was seldom. It was an off-plumb two-room wooden thing, weathered into a condition more splintered and discolored than Swayfeta's old wagon. Snakes followed pack rats into the main room, which served as kitchen, sitting room, and Tomás's bedroom. He often retired at night to find lozenges of rodent scat tossed across his cot like handfuls of seed. He slept with Gabriela's nightgown wrapped around his pillow. In the mornings, he was leery of putting his feet down after having brushed a sidewinder's dry scales with his toes and narrowly escaped a strike. But the snake was chilly and lazy and was probably not really interested in killing him, just in getting him off its back.

Teresita had troubling dreams in that house. She dreamed of a warrior from Tomóchic, dead now for three years beside his pope, Cruz

99

Chávez; the dear José, or Saint Joseph, as he called himself after she cured him of a goiter that hung off his neck purple as an eggplant. José. She barely even knew the man. Why should she dream of him? But she did, several times. José came to her rattling door with his hat in his hands; his white hair was brown now, and his bent back was straight. He was somber. And in every dream, he asked Teresita if he might move into her house with her, find shelter, for he had been wandering all night.

She couldn't eat breakfast on those days. She wished her old teacher were with her now to explain these dreams, but if Huila had been there, she would likely have told Teresita things she did not want to hear. And after three dream visits, she did not answer José and left him outside, and she saw him scowling at her from a wagon that rattled away into the darkness, and though she waved at him and called out, he did not respond. But his face was not angry. All she felt from him was sorrow.

She busied herself with small chores, shaking the spectral gloom of the dream out of her mind. She hung her clothes off nails hammered into the walls of her trapezoidal bedroom. It was dark, and she was constantly on the lookout for black widows, who seemed to find her one milky window irresistible. Every few days, the recessed window well had a ragged black-widow web in one corner, and Teresita had to capture the spider in a glass jar and transport her, bouncing like a deadly black grape, to a far rock outcropping.

Scorpions too. One day, as she availed herself of the dreadful outhouse, a scorpion dashed out from the wood and plunged into the bloomers pooled around her feet. No amount of careful foot lifting would reveal the beast, and Teresita failed to see the humor in her insane bare-bottomed explosive dance out the door with her underwear flapping around on one ankle. After rattlesnakes and black widows and scorpions, the befuddled tarantulas that tap-danced slowly into their house seemed as mild as puppies.

It was in their first week in San José that Don Lauro Aguirre's cryptic letters began to arrive for her. The regional mail carrier clopped up the arroyo on his melancholic burro and blew a shrill two-note call on his tin whistle. Teresita rushed out and was thrilled to see her name on an envelope. From Texas! She paid the man a few centavos and stroked the donkey's handsome forelock and took the stiff envelope inside and commenced to construct herself a pot of tea. She set out a cup on a small towel on the table in front of her father's empty bed. She lit two tallow candles that cast wobbling yellow light in the room. She poured the tea — flowers and lemon — and dipped a golden coil of honey into the cup and sat excitedly with Huila's knife in hand. As she slit the back of the envelope, she said, "¡Ay, Don Lauro!" as if they were in one of their old chats. Anything could be in the letter. It was so exciting.

Within the envelope lay a folded card of off-white vellum, heavy and rich. She felt it, slipped her fingers along the fibrous edges of the card, before opening it. But she stared blankly at the message within. Then, baffled, she turned it over and checked to see if she had missed something. There was nothing else, no greeting, no signature. Simply one word, written with a quill, neatly, with no great flourishes:

Ferocity.

She hid the card under her bed and was bothered by its message day and night. Ferocity? Whose ferocity? Sometimes she muttered "What?" out loud. It was the rudest note she had ever received. Perhaps he had been drunk. Or had gone mad. Perhaps he had meant to quote some beloved French poet and had simply forgotten after jotting the first word. Sometimes she took the note out and looked at it again, as if it would reveal some hidden meaning to her.

Ferocity.

She grew tired of the one-word diatribe and consigned Don Lauro to the trash heap with a shrug.

Until the mailman's two-note fanfare sounded again, one week later.

She paid again, stroked the donkey again, made tea again. She smiled. It was a game. Surely. Don Lauro was engaging her in a piquant folly. She poured her tea. Perhaps he had realized his bizarre error and had rectified it with a more complete letter.

The message this week:
Justice.
She threw the card into the fire.

One week later:
Destiny.
She didn't bother with tea the fourth week.
Liberation.

Then:
Retribution.
She took up her pencil and bent to the table and carefully wrote a small reply that she handed to the irksome mail carrier the following week after he had given her yet another card. If he had an opinion, his face did not show it. He must have thought Teresita had a fervent love affair brewing with some distant Texan, but he did not mention the scandal to anyone.

Aguirre:
Revolution.

᠅

Teresita:
Bunkum.

᠅

Satisfied, she swiped one of Tomás's new horses and barebacked into the hills so fast he couldn't have caught her even if he'd set out right after her. She hammered the hills with the assassin's horse, leaping carelessly over small ravines where rattlesnakes awakened from their slumbers and furiously threatened shadows that had passed over their heads in their dreams. She laughed and shouted as loud as possible—she was far away from anyone, far from anywhere where anybody could hear anything. She yipped and yowled until coyotes in the bushes were moved to melancholy enthusiasms and answered her as she flew beyond them. Her braids came undone. Her hair opened around her shoulders like great black wings. Her face burned in the sun.

It had been so long since she'd ridden that her thighs burned and her legs shook when she dismounted. But nobody would know that her knees were wobbling under her skirts. She walked through her chores that week thinking of freedom.

The next week, there came no card. In a way, she missed the mail. Still, she smiled as she went about her business in peace. Six travelers from Las Cruces had to be fed and given shelter as she attended to the painfully infected birth canal of an expectant mother. A buckaroo with a barbwire slice through his left eye was dragged in unwilling and cussing by his compañeros. Two little boys from the village brought their sick goat. An old woman from Salome could not stop bleeding. Teresita cleared her thoughts with the needs of the pilgrims.

Until the following Wednesday, when the old donkey of doom sadly meandered to her door again.

Aguirre:
Lead them.

A raven insulted her from a dead tree. She heard, but did not see, hummingbirds whirring in the still air. Dragonflies rattled like toy kites. Teresita put the card back in its cream envelope and tucked it into her blouse. Three peasants were on their way; one of them struggled with a rough wooden crutch. She stood tall, threw her head back so her chest was open, open to the sky, open to the sun, her heart shining and hot inside her, her feet rooted in the earth, pulling sustenance from the deep shadows beneath her, and she raised her hand to the pilgrims.

"Come to me," she said.

Thirteen

TOMAS AND SEGUNDO BUSIED themselves with expeditions, sometimes staying away overnight as they prowled the crags on the far eastern, New Mexico side of their great landscape, sometimes driving their horses up into the mountains to their immediate north. On these days, Juanita Van Order came to stay with Teresita. Her boys camped outside the house, well past the fences. They were bemused by their mother's insistence that they not show themselves. They were hurt, though neither would admit it beyond making trusty and blustery statements about the vagaries of women. Harry, who had never been with a woman, was all hearts and valentines—he pined and sighed until John wanted to kick him in the rump. What a girl. Whereas John, who had been with four women, only one of them a sportin' gal from Safford, burned. No pink blossoms or bluebirds; it was all smoke and heat. He stared toward Teresita's vale and felt despair—felt the endless openness of this charred land closing over him and suffocating him. He had taken to stealing his father's rum and sipping it until the pain within dulled to coals.

Harry had a little boy's trust in life. And he was partial to the ladies, young and old. John wasn't all that moved by them. He suspected they were all working some angle—who wouldn't, to get out of the desert? They observed the hubbub at Teresita's door.

"I think she's plumb holy," Harry argued.

"Dang, son," drawled John. "You ever think she might be crazy?"

"Don't you say it."

"I went and said it already."

Harry threw the punch; John nabbed him around the neck and threw him down like a steer for branding; they wrestled in the dust.

The women enjoyed their days without men. They examined plants, shared recipes and folktales, laughed and relished phrases like *Caita tigua* and *Nech che biu graia*. "Sing to me." "You are shameless." Days without Spanish. Occasionally, they took fresh popovers or pies out to the sulking boys.

Harry blushed and fumbled. John gave Teresita the old wolf eye, looking up from under his brows — it had worked on the hooker. But Teresita seemed immune to it. In fact, she saw reason to sidle up to Harry and nudge him with an elbow. John saw this. And he affected a stoic and monumental presence, ignoring her and scoffing at her baking baskets. It added some interest to the days, but life was pretty much a vastness of boredom.

The only thing that truly livened things thereabouts was the languid, sad campaign of wanderers and pilgrims seeking her hands on their burns and their scars. They brought her chickens or bruised fruits or eggs in payment for her ministrations. She asked her helpers — girls from the jacales and small rancherías nearby — to use these supplies to feed the weakest and smallest of the patients.

There was no extra food anywhere in the valley. The cows were dark and bony and looked as though in place of milk they would give drafts of dust. Dirt farmers grew potent green chiles, and beans straggled up trellises, but only enough for the farmers' families. Where local people could siphon water out of the Gila, they grew corn and tomatoes. But there was no cheese to be had. No fruit, though Juanita brought Teresita cans of peaches. The well was hot and smelly, a home of mosquitoes and odd water bugs that walked on the cloudy surface of the water in hectic assemblies.

"We have no meat," a pilgrim said to her.

Teresita looked around her. She pointed to the bounteous stands of wild beavertail cactus.

"Then fry nopales," she said.

Teresita's house thus became the place in the valley for fried eggs and diced cactus. No tortillas. No dessert.

It was either, she knew, do work or sit. "If you were born to be a hammer," Teresita told herself, "do not curse the nails." Still, on some days, she was the nail, and they were the hammers.

"What do other girls do, Juanita?"

"Chores. Cooking. School. Romance. Dances."

⁂

Scorpions in the toilet were worrisome enough, but the pilgrims outside the outhouse door were worse. They would listen there unless Tomás chased them away. They would whisper to her or knock as she sat on the stained plank within. They waited outside with their sad cow eyes and did not allow Teresita to eat her meager breakfasts. On many days, she stepped out to them with a crust of roll in her mouth. If there were children—well, so much for that. She would feed her sweet rolls to them. Tomás yelled at her: "You literally give them the food from your mouth!" He heard himself say, every day: "What is the matter with you?" For once, Tomás was happy he had lost everything in Mexico because this time the pilgrims couldn't destroy his crops or his herds. Just his bread box, just his paltry larder. He noticed his nopal cactus hedges were disappearing. He started calling the pilgrims locusts.

He found his daughter completely lost to reason, and he must have been a fool to allow it. But he could not imagine how to stop it. Perhaps, he thought, if they went to the highest point of the highest mountain, and if he chained her to some stone, and Segundo and he shot these beggars until all of them were forests of bone far below...

The faithful wondered why Teresita and Tomás did not attend their church services. But how could they? For Tomás's part, church was now and forever out of the question. God? Tomás would like to slap God in the face.

John Van Order asked her one Sunday as she was setting out to pick tiny flowers from the weeds, "Aren't you going to church?"

"I am the church," she said.

He thought on that one for a while. He wasn't sure he understood it, but he was partially convinced that he didn't like it. It was easier for John if he didn't talk to her much.

Harry, though, tried to speak to her as often as possible. Once, before running away with embarrassment streaming from his head like purple smoke, Harry, giggling, had brazenly called her sweetheart. She expected more from a young man than that.

She walked out into the sun and forgot about all of the people around her.

Coyotes, skunks, centipedes (masiaca).

Gila monsters, jackrabbits, roadrunners, snakes (bacot).

Chollas, locoweed, lizards, crows, vultures, jaguars, blackwater (chuculibampo).

And the humble, hungry, restless horde of wounded, coughing, bleeding, pregnant, impotent, blind, crazy, malodorous, beautiful, sad-eyed people.

※

Aguirre:
Evolution.

※

John, who was often recruited by his mother to guard the gates of Cabora Norte (Tomás's little jest), had never seen anything like this slow lava flow of hopeless cases. He was astounded to see bare feet in the hideously punishing gravel of the hot desert canyons. He was anxious whenever Indians approached—Indians from tribes he had never seen before, from tribes he had only read about in frightening penny dreadfuls, novels of slaughter and bloodshed where these dangerous savages visited unspeakable horrors on lone white women in besieged shanties upon nighted plains. Comanches. Pimas. Strange tribes from Mexico.

Who were these Tarahumara runners who thudded in from the distance and stayed for only the briefest moment at Teresita's door before running away again? They were like ghosts.

He thought they would eat her if they could. They would nurse on her like shoats until she was dry as the dirt. He would save her, he told himself. He would take her to Chicago or New York.

Still, there were fewer Mexican pilgrims every day and more American Mexicans. He didn't even know what to call them. There was no handy term for them. He didn't mind the fine gringos in their expensive rigs, their carriages and their cabriolets. He didn't mind their picnics and their frilly idiotic parasols. It was largely a festive day at the zoological society for them. He had never seen a zoo, but he had read of them. Besides, the rich ones often brought bottles of wine or beer, and he could cadge a drink or a half-emptied bottle off them. He didn't even mind the Mexican shopkeeps and pretentious businessmen like Aguirre. They struck him as false too. Just like the happy Americans.

But these peons! These brown poor! It made him ashamed to be half Mexican when he saw these shambling paupers with their rotten teeth and their skewed eyeballs. Begging for water or a piece of bread. Greasers, all of them. It wasn't the first time he'd cringed over the Mexican poor; Americans laughed at them and called them lazy, criminals. Stupid, they were stupid. They *had* to be stupid. He sometimes roughed them up with the butt of his rifle just to get them away from him, back out the crooked gate and off to the hell they had come from.

Harry thought it was all quite exciting. John half expected his brother to throw himself at her feet like the pilgrims and seek some "miracle." It was, John thought with clenched teeth, all too much.

He preferred busy days to slow days. The thinner the crowds, the deeper the boredom. If he could charge each of these half-wits a nickel, he would be a rich man. Any day away from the industry of Sainthood was the best.

She seldom even looked at him.

·⋇

Don Tomás petitioned the United States government repeatedly for naturalized status. He was denied twice; with Mr. Van Order's help, he lodged his complaint, only to learn that it was Teresita the U.S. didn't want, not him. Teresita threatened not just Mexico's security but this country's as well. The government wanted assurances given under penalty of imprisonment and expulsion that she would spend her probationary period within one hundred miles of the border, not agitating Indians. All the U.S. needed was a new round of ghost dances and uprisings.

Don Lauro, settled and thriving in El Paso, suspected the worst. He suspected that the Díaz regime had pressured Washington to keep her in range of their assassins. Aguirre knew that Mexico was far from finished with its saint.

Tomás wasted no time and immediately reapplied in both their names.

Fourteen

From:
Don Lauro Aguirre
Prensa El Independiente
El Paso, Tejas

To:
Don Tomás Urrea
San José, Arizona
c/o Solomonville General Delivery

My Beloved Companion, You Degenerate Wretch, Tomás:

Things are excellent in El Paso! Even a dissolute drunkard like yourself could be happy here. It remains urgent that you cast off the dreary sackcloth of your Arizona encampment and join us immediately here on the banks of the surging Río Bravo. Or, as they call it here, the Río Grande. Honestly, not so grande in my opinion.

Still, one could spit into the motherland from the American side. Imagine the glory of watching from El Paso one day soon as the glorious revolution across the wild river frees the motherland! The dictator topples and the populace rises to its blessed destiny! Liberté! Égalité! Et cetera!

It is clear to me, my dear Urrea, that the hordes of pilgrims who assail you will not abate soon; frankly, this is all to the revolutionary good! They are the warriors of tomorrow, marching to a free Mexican morning.

However, it is also clear to me now that your dear daughter—our Teresita!—will require a more civilized society to secure her safety. The Americans are in league with the tyrant, of this I am assured! Danger lurks in every defile, in each canyon! Here, we have paved streets and some few electrical lights. We are a modern city with all the amenities. We are largely Mexican here, and we are disposed to revere and protect the Saint. In El Paso, we have struck a balance— fragile as it might be—between the empires.

One could do business in two nations at once—one could make a double fortune.

I urge you to consider this move soon. I can begin to procure you a reasonable home in the foothills that gently flow from the Franklin peaks. Below you, the river and Ciudad Juárez. Yes, the dictator could send more assassins north. But imagine, if you will, my dear amigo, the difference between a modern city-in-full and an outpost in the savage territories. We have a full contingent of gendarmes. Sol-

diers. It would seem to me that security is assured in El Paso. How simpler to find sanctuary in a city!

Consider my offer!

Come!

Loyally,

Your Servant, and a Better Man by Far,

Lauro Aguirre

⁂

From:

Don Tomás "El Santo de Cabora" Urrea

San José, Arizona

c/o Solomonville General Delivery

To:

Don Lauro "Robespierre" Aguirre

El Independiente

El Paso, Tejas

Pinche Aguirre,

Cómo chingas.

How it darkens my day whenever another letter from you arrives, you pretentious bastard.

I do find pleasure in your pages later, though, when I retreat to my outhouse and require some fancier paper for my delectable bottom. My bottom, you should note, resembles two luscious scoops of flan blushing with caramel, a feature I will gladly share with your wife, should you ever find a woman who can stand you. Until that blessed day when Our Beloved Savior bestows a wife upon you, I will comfort myself with servicing your mother.

Aguirre! I am bored to tears in sweet San José. Canst thou tell?

Tubac was as cosmopolitan as Paris compared to this. The dreadful lines of cow-faced seekers have thinned, but they will never stop. Yes, I am aware of the dangers here! Yes! I have hired those dullards the Van Order boys to guard the…ahem…ranch in my absence. If I stay here, I go mad. I sneak away and shoot rabbits with Segundo.

Teresita resembles a holy scarecrow. I can't stand the heavenward gaze. So Segundo and I haul our asses up the mountains and cuss and drink like men.

We have our own river, you know. You're not the only one with a damned river. The mighty and noble (not quite true on either count) Gila. I would like to ride down it on a raft toward Yuma and sneak back into Sonora. Let them put me up against the wall and shoot me! To be home again. To be home.

Did you know, my old friend, that Coronado and his Spaniards climbed these very peaks? I follow his path up, up, farther every time, our horses drinking from the shallow river that falls from far Morenci and Clifton. All about, there is lumber! Why, no one in these high valleys has organized a good cow operation, and it hasn't crossed their minds that there is a fortune to be made in pine trees. Lumber! Simply there. Free for the taking.

Lauro cabrón—a man could start anew up there where the air is clear.

I continue to petition our noble hosts' government for sanctuary. Anything you can do to expedite this process will be deeply appreciated. I may never wrangle citizenship for Teresita…but you and I both know she lives in some other world anyway. If I can make her safe, I will feel vindicated.

I miss you, cabrón. I miss… oh hell, I could make lists for one hundred pages of what it is I miss. Good tequila? Sí. A big bloody steak? ¡Claro que sí! I would be thrilled to simply see a street. *A woman who is not the wife of some one-legged war hero or a leper crawling to Teresita on tattered knees with seventeen rosaries around her neck. No, more than a woman. Ten women. A hundred women.*

I would run past them all for one small glimpse of my Gabriela. Poor goddamned me.

Yours,
(Can You Believe These Pendejos Call Me)

Tommy

PS: I am intrigued by your suggestions of life in El Paso....

⁂

To:
Gabriela Cantúa
Rancho Cabora, Sur de Alamos
Sonora

From:
Teresita
In Exile

Ay, Gaby—

Is this all there is for me?

If you were only here. I cannot tell you my sorrows, for you would weep and I would be guilty of breaking your heart. We are alone here, and lonely. There are funny boys here—one mean and sulky, one silly as a little girl. I wish either one of them would be a man and demand my hand and ride me away from here! I have seen in their magazines such magical places! Places of the kind I dreamed of when I was a girl. Have you seen San Francisco? It is far from here, but it seems lovelier than any city I have seen before. It is by the sea, dear Gaby. The sea! Can you believe I have never seen the sea? Can you believe I have never seen a real city? A city! I have seen cities only on those long-ago nights when we all held hands and flew in our dreams. Or were they dreams? I cannot remember now.

What is the matter with these cowboys? I am waiting for one of them to take me to San Francisco! There are no men in the United States. Just boys.

We have been in Arizona two years now, and it feels like ten. I have a friend here named Juanita. Do not be jealous! She is older, not quite like Huila. Perhaps like a mother. She has taught me to sew and to bake. I never knew how hard it was to make a pie of apples. I had never heard of a quilt and am surprised that a blanket made of old shirts and dresses is at once so difficult to make and so dear to the Americanos. You would be surprised, though, how sacred it feels to lie beneath the stories that each panel seems to whisper. One day, I will make you a quilt. First, I have to get some more clothes. I wear my dresses until they tatter. I don't mind. No, really. Stop laughing. (Besides, I was never as fashionable as you.)

Poor old Don Lauro seems to have gone insane. I think he has been sipping laudanum or absinthe. (I am so bad!) He keeps sending me notes. But they are all stupid. One-word messages that make no sense. I don't know—Kill! Something like that. Guns!

Frijoles!

Coffeepot!

Father pines for you. He is often difficult, I will admit it. He is too proud to mention you. But he must surely pass away without you near him. As must I . . . Oh, write to me and tell me everything there is to tell. Spare me no detail. What did you eat today? Did you have coffee? Are there any new horses?

(Women here are plucking their eyebrows—it's the newest thing. You should try it.)

Sabotage!

Power!

Father has even abandoned bees.

If only you could be with us now…
Teresita

PS: Remember to say your prayers; God is our only true hope.
PPS: El inglés es imposible.
PPPS: Hats! Murder! Pudding!

Fifteen

TO HIS BROTHER'S PROFOUND amusement, on Saturday nights Harry Van Order snuck onto the property and left flowers outside Teresita's door. He stole white roses from his mother's dearly-fought-for patch of earth where her dishwater tempted a garden from the grit. He thought white roses were divine. So did the javelinas that came out of the desert after he crept away and ate them before dawn. They loved him.

※

Here came the Apaches. They walked their horses in from the great playas out to the south and east—vast wobbling hallucinogenic tan sand flats, quivering in sun, heat shimmers silver as water out there where nothing dared grow. They seemed to drip upward, those languid riders, elongating in the heat waves, the mirages of their bodies breaking to quicksilver beads and lifting into the trembling air so their hats seemed to drift toward the sun and blink out. The land itself looked like flesh, and it joined the vision of the bodies of the warriors dissolving, as if all flesh were being pulled away to Heaven.

From their small rise, Tomás and Segundo watched them come. Who else could it be but Apaches? They had come down from the formidable mountain wall of the Cochise Stronghold. Tomás knew the very defile they had come through, the secretive angled canyon that veered away from the desert into a narrow cut that opened to unexpected creeks and cottonwoods before offering precipitous trails into the warriors' high retreat.

All the men of the region except Tomás feared the Apaches. Indians liked the Sky Scratcher. He bore the mantle of their affections with ease. It didn't occur to him that they respected his defense of his daughter more than they respected him. Though they all knew he had saved the Yaquis from starving once. News like that never ceased its roving from mountain to mountain. Still, one never knew.

Segundo kept his rifle handy. These little bastards made his scalp crawl. He knew the stories—who didn't? How they tied men to wagon wheels and set the wagons afire, laughing and commenting as the men burned and screamed as if they were some kind of critics watching a play. Segundo understood actions like that. But he didn't intend to be the subject of such attentions. He was too old for that kind of foolishness.

The riders walked the horses calmly in their direction, raising no dust. The animals were small, mean. Knotty bundles of sinew and muscle. The riders wore red shirts and yellowed tanned-hide leggings, and the one in front wore a Mexican sombrero. There were three of them, and they were leading two horses piled with bundles.

"Segundo," said Tomás. "What do you see?"

Segundo, known as Buzzard Eye due to his supernatural vision, took the cigarillo out of his mouth and spit some tobacco.

"Boss," he drawled. "Three Apaches. Looks like three other cabrones, all dead, hanging on them two horses in back."

"Mexicans?" asked Tomás.

"How can you tell?" asked Segundo.

"Short hair?"

Segundo squinted.

"Looks like no hair at all."

Scalped.

"Mexicans," said Tomás.

Since the beginning of the War of the Apaches, the tribe had no love in its heart for Mexicans. The Mexicans were worse than the Americans, and the Americans were very bad. Villages had been wiped out in the Mexican raids, whole family lines spilled in the dust and lost forever. The Apaches had relieved their sorrow all down the Mexican coast. They had sacked Mazatlán and set it to the torch.

The riders halted within hailing distance.

The leader raised his sombrero.

Tomás laughed.

It was Venado Azul.

Tomás waved him on.

Venado Azul tapped his horse's flank with the Mexican hat and came on. He was grinning. He worked the big hat back onto his head and raised a hand.

"Sky Scratcher!" he called. "You still drinking too much liquor?"

"Every chance I get!"

Venado shook his head.

"Better than milk, I guess," Venado said. "You people keep nursing like baby goats."

"Where did you get that hat?" Tomás called. Segundo slid the rifle from its scabbard and laid it across his lap.

Venado Azul shrugged. "I had to take it off one of these boys so I could lift his hair." He jerked his head back toward the bodies. They seemed to be wearing shiny black cloaks, but these were merely flies, jostling upon the softening men. Their heads were all bright red. As the horses walked, the dead men's spurs pinged and chimed a small, festive melody.

"Who are these unfortunate Christians?" Tomás asked.

Venado was looking at Segundo.

"I am Blue Deer," he said.

"I don't give a damn!" Segundo cried, Sharps now raised.

"These boys," Venado said to Tomás, ignoring Segundo's outburst. "Assassins. Heading for the Saint. We caught 'em." He smiled.

His companions untied the thongs holding the bodies to the horses and kicked them off. The bodies hit the ground like sacks of beans. Clouds of dust and irritated flies swirled around them. Tomás had seen dead men before, and the way they flopped always made him queasy. He hoped Teresita was right, that there was some sort of heaven. Even a hell. Anything was better than the indignity of being dead. He spit when the smell got to him. Dead men were as appalling as dead cows or dogs. No angels in sight.

Venado took a leather pouch from his shirt pocket.

"I think this was their bounty."

He jingled the pouch.

"Keep it," said Tomás. "For your people."

Venado tossed the pouch to his companions, who wheeled and rode fast toward the mountains.

"They don't like that rifle," he noted.

"Goddamned right!" blurted Segundo.

Tomás rubbed his eyes. Even he had to admit this frontier business was exhausting. Guns. Scalps. Riders. Perhaps Aguirre was right about El Paso and sophisticated society. He imagined, for a moment, an exotic tall glass of sarsaparilla.

"How do you know," he asked, "about these poor bastards' intentions?"

Venado was looking around. He pulled a toothpick out of the hatband and stuck it in his mouth. He had a mild expression of serenity on his face.

"We... talked," he said.

"Jesus," said Segundo.

Venado saluted them with one finger, tapping the immense brim of the hat.

"Give our love to the Saint," he said.

Segundo snorted.

"Love," Segundo said.

Venado regarded him. He pointed at the dead men, dark upon the soil. They were absorbing all the sun in the land.

"Sometimes," he said, "love is very, very hard."

He lowered his head so his face vanished in shadow.

"My advice? Do not tell her why she lives another day. This"—he waved his hand lazily—"it ain't to her taste."

He kicked his war pony and accelerated into the sun.

"Holy Christ." Segundo sighed.

Tomás slid off his mount.

"Love is hard?" he said. "Love is hard? I'll tell you what's hard. Dragging these dead sons of bitches into the arroyo. That's what's hard. Get off that horse, you lazy son of a bitch, and lend a hand."

Segundo took his time getting down.

"You're the boss," he said.

They bent to their work, holding their breath, thinking of things far away and dear.

Teresita was on her knees inside the smoky hut of Magdalena of the Goats. That was the only name she knew for this place—when the pains came and the water gushed, the girls had come running and crying, "Magdalena of the Goats is having her child now!" Teresita had gathered her things quickly. Huila's sharp little knife. Matches. Yerba buena, yerba mansa, cotton root, three small clay jars of aromatic pastes. She threw her rebozo over her head and stalked through the heat behind the frantic children. In these moments, she felt as if her teacher walked beside her, whispering the ancient secrets in her ear. She walked quietly, feeling every step in the earth, telling herself to be calm, for if she was not calm, the little mother would be panicked and jittery. She remembered her lessons: Bringing a child into the world was like taming a skittish horse. It was in the voice, the eyes, the calmness of the partera. For if the midwife was not ready, who was?

The first thing was to test the air in the room. It did not smell sweet, but nothing in this valley smelled sweet. She had to sniff through a curtain of spoiled-beans-in-the-pan smell, of smoke and of sweated clothing in a dark pile by the bed. It was the scents behind that told the tale: the tang of fresh woman-sweat, the stark redolence of fear and pain, the coppery wet smells of the passage opening and the fluids moving. Blood. Musk. But no rot, thank God. No odor of death in the room.

Teresita had the girl up on her hands and knees, great belly hanging toward the earth.

"You may cry," she said calmly. "You may weep and cry out. We were all brought here in pain. But we were all called to come make this a better world. It hurts because it is worthy of pain. Each birth brings the promise of great justice. It is a great wonder. I am here now to help you." She reached under the girl's body and placed her hands upon the distended belly. She held it up. She laid her head against the girl's straining back. "Breathe," she said. "Feel me. I will take your pain. Feel me."

And Magdalena of the Goats cried out. Spreading from Teresita's hands came heat. Tingling delicious warm tendrils. A flow, a tide of soaking heat.

"Suffer no more," Teresita whispered. "I am here."

The girl squatted and in a swoon of time that could have been a minute or forever, her body trusted the infant into Teresita's hands.

The girls helped the mother down. Teresita wiped the child with a clean cloth, sucked the mucus out of his nose with her mouth. She spit the plug into the corner. He screamed his outrage to the universe, his little face red and furious. He urinated in a great arc that went over Teresita's shoulder. She eased the afterbirth onto the mat on the floor and quickly sliced the cord with Huila's knife. Boiled threads tied off the end of the cord.

"You have come here," she said, "to love. Love strong, live well, endure."

She anointed the baby with herbs to keep the mosquitoes away and placed him on Magdalena's chest. He attached to her with a frantic suction that seemed to want to pull her all the way inside his tiny body. Everyone laughed.

Teresita pressed a moist white towel to the opening between Magdalena's legs. It blushed pink, then deep red. She applied a poultice there to keep the blood clean and the tissues healthy. She took Huila's matches and lit sage in a small saucer and smudged the mother and the child and the room itself. The girls sang to the mother and her son. Teresita cleaned the mat. Then she sat back on her haunches and smiled. She was soaked in sweat.

"Let's have coffee," she told the girls. "I wish we had bananas."

The girls had never seen bananas.

When they brought her a mug, she asked for sugar. There was no milk, even goat milk, for Magdalena had not been able to work her flock.

"Tomorrow," she promised. "I will milk the goats."

"Quiet now," Teresita said. "You will tend to your son." She snapped her fingers. "You, girls," she said. "Milk this mother's goats!" They rushed outside.

She sipped her coffee and regarded Magdalena and her boy. In her pocket, Aguirre's latest missive said: *Today.*

For once, his message made sense to her.

Teresita said, "Amen."

Sixteen

GREATLY OFFENDED BY TERESITA'S apparent rejection of his flowers, Harry Van Order in turn greatly offended Teresita by not coming back to her home. She did not enjoy admitting it to her father, but she was not only offended but also deadly bored. Harry vanished, and John seemed to drift farther and farther from her house until he looked like a black ant on the ridgeline to her south, standing guard in wretched silence. How had she lost them both? What had she done?

"Everything I touch turns to mud," she said into the air.

She studied each letter from Don Lauro, and she fretted over each telegram from the U.S. government in the ongoing struggle over their immigration status. The Americans were still insisting she stay within a hundred miles of the border in case she needed to be deported. When the day came that Don Tomás was cleared and given full resident status, she surprised him by asking, "Is El Paso near the border?"

"El Paso is the border."

"Then I want to go to El Paso."

"Just like that?"

"Just like that."

"For good?"

"For good."

"Why?"

She blew air out of her mouth. She raised her hands and revealed their hut, the incandescent black rocks all around, the dead sky. She tipped her head sideways and squinted at him as if she were concerned about his evident lack of cognitive reason.

"I am dying here," she said.

"Daughter," he said. "I died a long time ago and woke up in Hell."

Then he grinned like a little boy. She was astonished — and angry — to realize that Tomás had simply been awaiting her permission to go. Cruz Chávez, rest his eternal soul, would not have sought permission. Were there no men left anywhere? Tomás was supposed to be her father. Why did she have to mother him?

In her mind, she heard Huila's voice as if it were coming through a hole in a wall of years, faint, muffled: *You are old enough to stop thinking like a girl. You are old enough to stop worrying about your father. If you were born to be a mother, stop being an infant.*

Teresita held her fists to her temples.

She wondered if God would be angry with her if she threw all the plates against the wall.

John Van Order moseyed along on his way out to the road.

"You look a mite cranky," he noted.

"Oh, be quiet," she said.

He offered her some advice: "Kick a pilgrim."

She listened to him laughing as he went around the bend and through the broken gate.

※

And came the awaited day.

They boarded the train in the screaming heat of June at a desert platform with a rickety water tower and drooping telegraph lines etching graceful black curving segments across the horizon. Segundo left before they boarded, riding for Cabora. There was no way he was going to step onto a train. He had it on good authority that once a vehicle exceeded forty miles an hour, all the oxygen would be sucked out of the riders' lungs and they would suffocate. Everybody back in Sonora knew this. Besides, once the train reached its impossible acceleration, if the riders were not dead yet, the force of gravity would destroy them should they rise from their seats. He imagined bodies flying backward in the train cars and smashing in hideous tangles of broken bones and tattered limbs at the end of each one as the train kept moving but gravity held these poor victims in place until the wall rushed forward and destroyed them. To hell with that! He laughed at Tomás as he rode away. Good luck, pendejo! he thought. Too bad about Teresita, though. None of Segundo's friends had ever traveled more than a hundred miles in their lives, and there were certainly none who had ridden trains. He was not fooled by the age of science.

Mr. and Mrs. Van Order had brought Teresita and her father down from the property in their carriage. A small wagon trundled along behind them bearing the aged trunks with their things. Juanita had packed Teresita a small case with a few of her own extra dresses; they had to hide this in the wagon lest Tomás find out Teresita had accepted charity. Better — he would have proclaimed — to rob a bank.

Teresita wore her best white Tucson dress. Tomás looked smart in his vest. They mounted the steps of the train at eleven in the morning; Teresita pretended she did not notice the Van Order boys. Harry had tears in his eyes as he watched her board. John, sitting atop one of the horses Segundo had liberated from the bounty hunters, kicked Harry in the shoulder.

"Why don't you wave a hankie?" he taunted.

He turned his horse and walked it away from the station. He simply chose not to watch the scene and affected a deep fascination for the sallow flats to the west. Just like that? he thought. It ends on a whim, and they get to go to a city while I stay here? He wanted to come undone all over the scene, shoot some cactus, kick and howl. "Well, shit," he told the horse.

Teresita nodded to the ragtag pilgrims and followers who scuffled around the station, unable to understand what was happening. They believed that Teresita was going on vacation to Texas, a far land that they would never see. Such were the wonders of the Saint of Cabora! "She does what she pleases," someone said. Others nodded. "She travels the world like a dove." Mothers told their children the Saint could fly to Texas if she wanted to. But she was going by train to keep the land from going wild—imagine the Indians seeing her flying in the air! There would be uprisings all along the border!

Fathers hung their thumbs in their belts and scuffed the dirt and opined that the Saint was going to procure mysterious potions and cures. Don Tomás, it was rumored, was buying arms for them so they could ride into Mexico to liberate it. Teresita would bless the bullets with mysterious Yaqui herbs so the bullets would not only find the bad men even in the dark but also return to the shooters to be shot at enemies again and again. God bless the Saint of Cabora! Thanks to her, one man with one bullet could win any war.

If they had understood that she was abandoning them, they might have set fire to the train on the spot.

Kisses, hugs. Juanita was a little startled at how easy it seemed for Teresita to leave her. Juanita was weeping, but Teresita was all business. Curt, even. Gone as if she had never been there at all. She didn't wave.

They could not know how many friends Teresita had lost. How many places. How much love. How many faces had haunted her and passed into the unclear past like dust, like cook-fire smoke. Although her ghosts no longer spoke to her, they were more real to her than the world she daily walked across.

Tomás, however, made great gestures of farewell. Abrazos and back-slaps. Great bowings and bellowings. Long, sad gazes into Juanita's eyes, which somehow delighted her husband—such yearning looks affirmed for Mr. Van Order that any man on earth would give his own left leg to have such a fine woman but only he, the Mighty War Hero, had managed to snag her. However, Tomás's eyebrows warned everyone in the station, should the slightest opportunity arise, he would fall on her like a rainstorm and sweep her away with his wicked, wicked love. He bent, kissed her hand for the last time, and breathed in her luscious knuckle scent of garlic, horse sweat, and lilac.

Juanita and her husband stood up on their carriage and waved, but Teresita never even looked out the window.

*

The train lurched once and hove to, then settled into its side-to-side waddle down the rails, clicking pleasantly.

"Different from the last train ride," Tomás noted.

"At least no one is pointing guns at us," she said.

She rubbed her eyes.

"I am excited, I must admit," her father announced. He slapped his knee as if a burst of enthusiasm would confirm their delightful future. He nudged her in the ribs and guffawed. "Here we go!" he said.

She was too tired to be excited. She stared out the window at the tiresome landscape. Desert. Where were the trees?

"What is El Paso like?" she asked.

He pulled his flask from his pocket, unscrewed it, took a gulp, smiled, sucked air, and took a second swig. "Rico," he said. He replaced it in his pocket, withdrew a black cigarillo, bit off the end, produced a redheaded lucifer from his vest pocket, struck it on his boot, and lit up. He shook out the match and tossed it over his shoulder. He blew a puff into the air and said, "Desert."

She slumped.

"More desert?" she said.

"What's wrong with deserts?"

She gestured out the window: yellow and tan. Rocks. Dead spindles that might have once been plants.

"I thought all you mystics," he observed, "went to the desert."

"All I have ever seen is deserts. I am tired of deserts."

They contemplated the various shades of dun as the world rotated past their window.

"It's not fair."

He gritted his teeth. Fairness? She wanted to discuss fairness? Ah, the young, with their endless shovel-loads of horseshit.

"Why can't we move to a city? Why can't we live by the sea? John Van Order told me about New York City! Why can't we live there?"

Tomás laughed a small puff of smoke. John Van Order! What did that dirt-clod waddy know about New York?

"Don't be an idiot," he said. "El Paso is a city."

Stung, she turned away and felt her face burn.

"Look!" Tomás cried, as if he'd seen a great stone temple. "A cow!"

His effort was not appreciated.

She moved to another seat and stared to the south. At least the mountains that way were blue. At least the far Mexican sky had amassed vast black cliffs of rain clouds.

Deserts and mystics, she thought. Yes, Jesus went to the desert, Elijah and Moses. But this desert was already ruined. Beside the rails, a dirt road scrawled itself along, and destroyed wagons lay beside it like skeletons. Burned and tumbled adobe huts marred the land. Trash blew into the creosote bushes.

"Men have destroyed it," she mourned.

He put his hands on his face and scrubbed it, as if he could tear out his own eyes. The nasty black cheroot between his fingers dropped ashes on his hair. Women! A daughter was as impossible as a wife! What did they want! Ridiculous creatures! He should have had only sons! Jesus Christ—a saint no less!

She turned as if reading his mind and glared at him.

"Is that how we look at our father, young lady?" he heard himself say. It was damned absurd, and he knew it.

She rolled her eyes.

"Charming," he said. "Why don't you spit on the floor while you're at it."

"I didn't say a word."

"Oh, you didn't need to say anything, Teresita. Your face is quite eloquent." He turned to the window. He muttered in immense self-pity: "Generation of father haters!"

Her mouth dropped open in silent protest.

He infuriated her! It was all so unfair! She never asked for anything. Why bother? He was so cheap, so drunk, so self-indulgent, asking would be of no use anyway. No friends. No boyfriends. No school. No anything.

She stomped her foot.

"I'm tired of being told what to do," she announced.

"Oh really," he said mildly. "What a pity. Perhaps you should move away and start your own life. Until then? Oh! I suppose I have to continue protecting you and caring for you! So terribly sorry."

She actually made a growling sound.

"Did you just growl?" he squeaked.

"I—absolutely—did—not—growl!"

"My God! Just like an animal!"

"Why can't I decide where we go for once?" she cried.

"You?"

"Yes. Me."

He laughed.

"You did decide. You said, I want to go to El Paso. Now, damn it to hell, we are going to El Paso. Who denied you the, the, the *right* to declare where you wanted to *go?*"

"I had no choice!" she shouted.

A small family at the far end of the car turned and stared.

"¿Qué?" she snapped.

"Nuff'n," said the father, and they turned away.

Tomás maintained his coldest smile.

"No choice?" he said.

"Women have no choice in this world," she muttered.

"You're joking."

She stared at him.

"You're a girl," he said. "You're not even a woman yet. And I am the father here."

"But—"

"But nothing." He dropped his cigarillo on the floor and ground it under his heel. "As long as I am your father, and as long as you live under my roof, eat my food, spend my money, I say what we do. Once you marry and live off some other man, it is not my concern any longer. Do what you please." He sat back and crossed his arms. "No man can control you anyway."

"God controls me," she boasted.

"Yes. Your big husband in the sky."

But he wasn't done. He got to his feet unsteadily as the train rocked. He was not flung against the back wall. He leaned toward her and hung his finger in her face.

"I gave up everything for you! Everything! I asked nothing in return. Nothing! The very least you could do is respect my authority!"

He stormed out of the car and slammed the door. She could see him on the platform between cars. He was leaning on the rail with his head down, engaging in poetic postures like some angry little boy.

"Grow up," she muttered and stared at the emptiness around her.

-*-

They slept fitfully. Their backs hurt and their bottoms ached as if they'd been kicked. They were hungry. The vastness of the desolate land fluttered outside the windows like wind rippling a flag. Tomás jerked awake and sat watching his daughter. She snored. He was thrilled to know something new about her. He lit up another smoke, and he tasted it and put it out. His flask was empty. He closed his eyes and thought about the future. He thought about all the things he might do to make himself again an honored, respected gentleman.

They pulled into El Paso a long time later in clouds of steam. Aguirre had assembled a great welcome for them. Teresistas held up banners. A brass band tootled insanely. Sombreros flew in the air. Politicians with sashes and straw hats stood around importantly. Scores of tiny Mexican and American flags waved. Women in fine dresses held the hands of children in cute little charro suits. Police fretted at the edges of the assembly. Aguirre stood among a throng of spies, secret operatives, Mexican revolutionary theoreticians, Freemasons, and one priest. Teresita and Tomás were astonished to observe their first Negro faces. Uproar and excitement. The crowd screamed. The brass blew a fanfare.

"Oh no," said Tomás. "Not again."

They did not know that this same crowd had assembled the day before and waited for hours, only to greet an empty train. And here they were again. Most of them. Shouting.

Seventeen

THE TWO YAQUI WARRIORS had been watching from the hills. They had seen the Great Joy consume the towns south of Nogales. The Teresistas had poured out to pillage and burn, crying out their love as windows shattered. They had not been far away when the crowds overtook the hapless American cowboys and nearly beat them to death, leaving them naked and kissed in the desert sun. They had consulted the old men, the Dreaming Men, who had gone far in the night and seen the Saint in her journeys, had seen the souls of the fallen making their way across the dark plains. They had seen the visions of the war to come, and they wanted to start it now. They wanted to burn the land. They wanted to unleash the fury of God. They dreamed of the far prisons in Quintana Roo and Yucatán exploding, throwing Yaqui and Mayo slaves out into the jungles like lava from a volcano. They wanted to dream their warriors and brothers and mothers and sisters home. They silently called out to them to kill everyone they could find as they fought north, to clean the pestilence from the land and return to the holy light of the Río Mayo and the Río Yaqui valleys. *Home.* Was there any sweeter word? *Home.* They wanted all souls home. They dreamed for days. They saw Federales and Rurales falling, their sand-colored uniforms blooming in red gardens of blood.

And these two men had been blessed by the Dreaming Men and sent to Nogales and were unseen by the Mexicans and the mestizos. Just two more desert Indians. Two more tall men with bluntly chopped obsidian hair and off-white clothes, their feet black in their huaraches, their faces grim and carved like hawks as they walked the Sonoran alleys. Mexican soldiers eyed them, but they never faltered, never looked aside as they walked. Their language passed back and forth between them like a murmur of wind in the ocotillos. They watched the border crossing, and the American guards. They sniffed the American air that came across the line with American smoke, the smells of American beef and American bread. They watched the fat bright American citizens parading not twenty feet from the shambling silent Mexicans. And they made their way up the sharp hills to the south of Nogales, where the barrios bristled in the arroyos, and the wild dogs scattered after rabbits, and the Indians spied on the guard posts on both sides of the border. The warriors walked high and sat low and watched. They watched the sun set, and they watched the sun rise. They watched the buildings across the line. Nogales, Sonora, was a mirror that reflected Nogales, Arizona. They had pictures of Teresita under their shirts. They waited there. It would be a good day. They prayed. They did not joke or laugh. Soon, they knew, the rifles would come.

Eighteen

IT WAS NO COOLER in El Paso.

Their wooden house at the corner of Overland and Campbell was stifling. But they didn't care. It was neat and pastel-colored. White shutters bracketed the windows. "It's a dollhouse!" Teresita exclaimed as she ran from small room to smaller room. Tomás was astounded to find perforated, soft toilet paper in the water closet. He enjoyed using the peasant's vernacular for this magical room, calling it the excuse-me (el escusado). He shook the fluffy papers in Aguirre's face and laughed. "What is this?"

Aguirre beamed as if he himself had invented the silky bum tissues and boasted, "Paper for the toilette, mon ami. Why, we have had this paper since 1877!"

It was too good to be true.

"By God!" Tomás breathed, and he celebrated the welcome invention with a toast from his flask. The United States had it all. Pampered nalgas.

"This is the greatest country on earth," he said.

Aguirre dipped his head, representing the humble nation.

Even Teresita sidled up to the paper and gave it a little pat. Civilization. She went to her blue room and shut the door. She threw herself on her bed and stretched and smiled. She kicked off her shoes and sent them flying to the corner. She hiked her skirt and kicked her feet in the air. A breeze lifted her sheer curtains and they moved like moth wings, like blessing hands passing over her in prayer. The curtains had come from Montgomery Ward's catalogue and had cost $1.27, but they could have come from Heaven. She laughed at herself. Really. Did she have to find holiness in everything? Was the toilet paper made of angel feathers? She snorted. She bounced. The bed squealed. She pulled the pins from her hair. She kept her skirt up so the breeze could cool her legs. Her bare toes digging in the coverlet felt so good she wanted to get up and jump on the bed. So she did.

Teresita and Tomás had been lucky to get there; just the year before, the massive rail strikes in the United States had stopped thousands of trains all over the country. One never knew if the rail system would suddenly choke and die again. They considered themselves doubly lucky to have arrived in a safe haven — craziness was afoot in the world. People said it was the End Times come upon the world at last. Christ Himself would return before the dreaded 1900 began, and He would be wielding His terrible sword of judgment. Groups in the hinterland were preparing bundles to take with them when He called the saints to Heaven and the dead from their graves. They would lie in fields and await their godly levitation to glory, then drag home mosquito-bitten and thirsty to hope for demolition some other day.

Far from God, Chicago had been consumed by great riots, and the cities felt as though they would ignite along labor, poverty, and racial lines. At least, this was what Aguirre's companions reported. For all its gunfighters and border brigands, El Paso was a peaceful enough destination from which the Urreas hoped to watch both the United States and Mexico evolve, to use Aguirre's newest word.

The future was coming on fast. There was no escaping it. In Germany, the mad Dr. Diesel had invented an engine that, it was said, would drive all tomorrow's commerce and personal transportation, thus replacing the horse, even perhaps the steam trains. Newspapers were alive with this sort of thing almost every day, inventions, conglomerations, fantasia. Tomás could not wait to goggle at the front page over his eggs each morning. Out of loyalty, he read Aguirre's tiresome rag—all revolution and bizarre tales of saints and miracles and, well, a bit too much about Teresita in his opinion. But at least it was in Spanish.

He tested his English against the *Times* and the *Herald,* and when a letter or small item critical of "the Saintess" appeared, he hid it from Teresita. Like the morning he saw in the *Herald*: "Santa Teresa has such power over the ignorant Mexican peasantry that she could, if disposed, stir up the worst kind of revolution." Better to simply tear that page out and wrap the coffee grounds in it.

If the gringos had seen the politicians and professors and businessmen and the furtive spies Aguirre brought around, they would have gone berserk. But as long as they thought she was inciting only peasants, he and his daughter were all right. And yet the rail lines that converged on El Paso, lines from New Mexico, California, Mexico, brought the faithful and curious from unimaginable places. He had been astounded to meet a doctor from New York who had taken his vacation to observe the healings. How much more amazed was he when a family from Scotland made its way up their street with an offering of buttery sweet biscuits.

He buried the coffee grounds in the bin under orange peels and stale tortillas. Teresita didn't need to see such newsprint, even though she didn't seem to care what anyone thought about her anymore.

"I am beyond all that," she told him. "It is all an illusion."

"Illusion," he repeated.

"I maintain my serenity."

"Ah," he said. "Yes. Now you are the Buddha."

He thought this was funny; she ignored it.

Tomás's uncle the great Don Miguel saw to it that proceeds from the ranchos were shipped to Tomás, and these happy packets of money arrived regularly. They wanted for nothing. Oil lamps, iron pans, fresh blankets, a maid, a gardener, assistants to attend to Teresita's nonexistent ledgers and paperwork. A tally, they had decided, needed to be made. Even of Tomás's nonexistent businesses. They ate good steak—or he did; she made do with fruit and eggs and bread and tamarind juice.

"You don't know what you're missing," he gloated as he slurped a powerful bowl of menudo turned red with hot sauce.

She looked into the bowl and said, "It looks like leeches floating in a bowl of eyeballs and blood. It smells like the inside of a dead horse."

She tenderly patted his shoulder and left the room.

He fought down rising bile and ate the rest of it just to show her how good it was.

These were their days at the beginning in El Paso.

※

They lived not far from the central section of the city. Mejicanos lived below the centro, near the river. The rich bastards lived up in the foothills in nice brick houses, and the fattest of the high-climbing Mexican pols squatted there among trees and parks above it all. They consorted with lawyers *and* judges and drank and danced except in election years, when they descended to the barrios and squinted compassionately and clicked their tongues over the plight of the gente. *The People.* Tomás almost banged his head when he heard *the People* spoken again—he would never escape the moiling upheaval of the masses. Frankly, he wanted to be up in the hills with the big brick houses and the alcoholic sellout Mexican hostesses with their swollen rumps and gringo-lawyer husbands. Yes. Big houses. Tipsy little dumplings sitting on his lap.

His own house was tidy and bright. Its windows sported white curtains all around. The porch was small but held two chairs and a square table. Cats visited regularly, and the mockingbird that stood vigil in their small lime tree bombed them furiously. Behind the building, the jagged Franklin Mountains jutted into the sky. The ghost of a long-dead Spanish monk was said to wander up there with his burro; travelers had witnessed this ghastly wraith beside the road to New Mexico. Lost gold mines in the Franklins waited for rediscovery, loaded with millions of pounds of Spanish ore and Catholic jewels. Tomás thought it would be a good idea to waylay this ghostly monk and escort him to the cave, for he was clearly keeping the treasure to himself. He planned to ride up there and liberate the fortune as soon as Segundo arrived. All that good money was wasted on Catholics, he thought, and how much worse to let a dead Catholic keep it.

Coffee with Mexican eggs on flat corn tortillas in the mornings.

"See here," Tomás announced, shaking his paper at her. "They have discovered a mysterious rayo X that will allow doctors to peer into the human body."

"Medicine men can do that already," she countered.

"There seems to have been an automobile race," he reported. "The vehicles drove from Chicago to some other city. They traveled at a speed of five point six miles an hour. An American won. Two thousand dollars."

"Americans always win."

"How can you say always?" he demanded. "It's the first pinche auto-car race in history!"

"Americans always will win," she said. "They invented the auto race so they could win it."

"Ha!"

"They invented the border so they could invent Mexico and beat us in every race."

"By God," he said.

He rattled his paper.

"Your poisonous attitude," he sniffed, "can hardly be seen as saintly, I must note."

"I never said I was a saint," she replied. She looked at a buttery piece of toast and tossed it back in its plate. Sniffed the coffee and found it wanting. She bit into a slice of melon. "I am a prophet."

"Oh God, no," he said. "What you are is nineteen years old."

She wandered back to her room to read.

He shook his head. He guffawed. He pulled his flask from his pocket.

❋

Aguirre had delivered the newest sensation, H. G. Wells's *The Time Machine,* to them. Teresita, enjoying the services of a reader-translator hired by Aguirre, shuddered at the dreadful depictions of the Morlocks. She believed in things like Morlocks and took to locking her windows at night. ¡Lúgubre! Far more grim, however, was Hardy's newest, *Jude the Obscure.* "Obscure, indeed!" Tomás muttered.

There was immense excitement in the Urrea house when Tomás got his hands on a Kodak pocket camera. Teresita often snapped pictures of her clients as they gathered on the porch. There was nowhere in town to process the film, however, so she never saw the prints.

And more. The strains of America's most popular new song at an open-air concert they'd gone to down at San Jacinto Plaza on a Sunday evening. It was called "And the Band Played On." (Tomás was delighted by the romance of its opening lines, and later he often crooned them at inopportune moments in his exemplary English: " 'Casey would valz with a strawverry blonde.'" He liked that idea.) After the concert, he had walked with new friends to the burly Río Grande and stared sadly at Juárez. Then, to finish off the evening, he had cajoled them into taking him to Chinatown so he could watch the fugitive Chinese immigrants in opium dens. He was very interested in opium, though he did not dare to smoke it in front of his esteemed associates. But he sniffed the air and then thought, perhaps, he felt a bit more serene.

But far more astounding to the Urreas than the developments of 1896 or the complexities of life in El Paso were the small miracles of their own home. Water, for example. Water ran through pipes and filled bathtubs. Water sluiced out their toilet. Teresita could spill water in the side yard and coax gardens from the soil. Sunflowers, silver sage, poppies, geraniums, coneflowers, cosmos.

She ate nasturtium leaves in her salads — they tasted like pepper. It was a ragtag garden, though — she was averse to pulling weeds. She had an inordinate fondness for dandelions. Wicked thistles pleased her, for they attracted butterflies. For Teresita, the garden existed both on the ground and in the air.

When she had a moment to rest, it was her greatest pleasure to sit at the table on her porch with the bad cats from the neighborhood at her feet, the mockingbird yelling threats and obscenities from the tree, and the buzzing universe of color, bees, butterflies, and hummingbirds, beside her house. The occasional dragonfly rattled up from the river and hovered around the porch, seeming to study her face. She did not read. She did not pray. She simply sat. She never said a word. All she did was smile.

She was certain that bigger cities were out there, waiting.

❈

Teresita had seen an advertisement in Don Lauro's newspaper for an herb emporium down on Stanton Street. She was thrilled that one could simply enter a shop and gather leaves. This seemed too marvelous to imagine. No hiking into the wastelands? No knife or shotgun?

This was the modern world at its best. Damiana? Hinojo? Rafa de víbora? Right there in jars on the shelves to be had for a few centavos and a pleasant word.

Don Lauro often stopped by the Urreas' small house to observe the milling crowds. It sometimes threatened to become a rabble. One over-crowded day, he recited a favorite poem to calm them. Most of the people on the street had not heard poems and seemed to think the great man was preaching scripture to them. His mellifluous voice rang out and caused them to bow their heads.

The single-file line jostled down Campbell Street and went around the corner onto Overland. Still, for all its civility, the mob of the needy disturbed the Urreas' neighbors, and when they weren't glaring from their closed windows, they were placing flowerpots and benches across their gateways to keep any beggars from their yards.

Righteous revolt, Aguirre wrote in his notebook.

Teresita had taken to sitting at her table on the porch surrounded by candles and fresh flowers and water and coiling plumes of incense. She greeted the seekers quietly—too quietly for Aguirre to catch a word of the consultations. It was fascinating the way they knelt at her feet, held her hands, even laid their heads upon her knees. They often wept, but just as often they laughed with her. Although he could not hear their words, her laughter rang out clearly. It was a strong, loud laugh, all belly. Sometimes, whatever the pilgrim said made her laugh so hard, she wiped tears from her eyes and shook her head.

He couldn't say he saw a great change in the cured sufferers. They hobbled down the steps in the same way they had struggled up. Bent backs remained bent. He never saw the lame and halt rise and dance. He didn't see the blind cast away their white canes and run free. Yet they came away smiling, and some of them blessed those waiting behind, as if the newly cured had absorbed some sort of sacred charge.

On one occasion he glanced up—Teresita was waving him closer.

He edged through the crowd and looked up at her.

"Ferocity!" she mocked, then laughed at him.

He looked around.

"Fanaticism?" he asked.

She took a sip of water.

"Faith," she replied.

He tipped his head: point, Teresita.

"Uncle Lauro," she said. "I would like to visit the Farmacia Río Grande on Stanton Street. Por favor."

He bowed slightly.

"Absolutely."

"Will you take me?"

"I will."

"Tomorrow, then."

He started to reply but saw he had been dismissed. She had already turned to her next client, a fellow with an eye as blue-white in the middle as a clot of curdled milk. She took the man's chin in her hand and turned his face to one side and looked into the dead eye. Aguirre noticed the man was trembling like a newborn colt.

He put his notebook away. Teresita was magnificent on her porch, fully in her powers. He whistled as he walked off. Everything was coming together. He, too, believed in the hand of God. He knew where it was pointing. It was pointing at him.

Nineteen

TOMAS WAS ALREADY OFF doing business when Don Lauro Aguirre pulled up before the house at eight the next morning. Tomás had become a progressively stranger creature to Teresita, some visitor from a benighted world. He drifted to sleep in his chair as he read at night, jerking awake with a loud "Huh!" and making believe he was agreeing with something she hadn't said. Lately, he had begun picking his teeth with pieces of thick paper. Outside, he honked and spit as if the world had earned the product of his sinuses. Had he always been so unsavory? She could not remember. And now he had developed a perverse love of great, malodorous wheels of cheese. He brought these giant rounds home in twine nets, coated in red wax and smelling like stinky feet. He seemed to think that nasty cheese was a high point of human endeavor. He blew his curdled breath in her face. She wondered if all fathers were so blissfully unaware of how embarrassing they were. At least Don Lauro made some effort to earn and keep her respect.

When Aguirre pulled up to the house, the light was still slanting onto the street, yellow and orange and slightly blue in the far corners. Breezes freshened by the river swirled dust and butterflies along the stone curb-side. Aguirre's cabriolet was polished — its black work shone like obsidian, and its gilded trim was electric with sunlight. A few believers stood around on the street corner, watching her house with hope on their faces. There weren't yet the milling crowds, though trash had accumulated in the roadside plants. The believers shuffled toward him. Aguirre saw in them the greed he'd observed at raffles and church bazaars. He shrugged off his impression and stepped up and knocked. A house girl opened the door to him and ushered him into the tiny parlor.

"What is your name?" he asked.

"Mississippi, mister."

"Ah." He wrote it in his notebook. This was history.

"How old are you?"

"Fourteen."

"I see. And where are you from?"

"Tennessee."

"Good. Good."

Mississippi had come from Tennessee, but Aguirre missed this delight. He had written *Miss Hissippy*. Odd name — perhaps Russian. But he approved of a young lady who demanded respect and called herself "Miss." He put away his notebook.

Teresita came out in Juanita Van Order's yellow polka-dot dress. She was as bright as the sunflowers outside the window. Well, with the dots, she was perhaps more like a stand of black-eyed Susans. She nodded to him and took his arm and was happy to be guided to the carriage and lifted to her seat with all the chivalry Don Lauro could muster. He climbed up beside her and settled his hat on his head. It was one of those turtlelike bowlers that so offended Don Tomás.

"This day," he pronounced with a flourish of hands, "is *foudroyant!*"

She eyed him, silent.

"Dazzling."

Aguirre clicked his mouth at the horse and they rolled.

❄

Everyone in the pharmacy was thrilled to meet the Saint. They had read about her in the papers, though none of them had seen her in person. She was fascinated by a black Mexican woman working behind the counter. She had not heard of such a thing.

"Where are you from?" she asked.

"El Golfo."

"I love your skin," she said. "May I touch it?"

The woman offered her cheek, and Teresita stroked it.

"It doesn't come off," the woman said.

They laughed.

Teresita had no money. Aguirre had to smile. Going to a store was apparently beyond her life experience. He pulled wadded dollars from the pouch he carried under his jacket.

He did not understand the value of things that thrilled her. A noxious black twig that looked like it was ready for a trash fire made her cry out in joy. She laid curling long leaves into a sheet of newspaper and rolled them up carefully while nodding wisely at him as if he knew what magic potion they would brew. She sniffed at a clay bowl of dirt.

"What is this?" she asked.

"Graveyard dirt, miss."

"Graveyard dirt?"

"Yes, miss. Taken from a murderer's grave."

"Ay, Dios," she murmured. "Do you use it to heal?" she asked.

"You use it to kill."

"I see."

She dusted off her hands and moved on. Aguirre glanced into the bowl and averted his eyes. It occurred to him that he was dipping into forces beyond his understanding.

The day's purchases came to five dollars and seventy-five cents. They placed the bundles of herbs in the back of the wagon, and Don Lauro turned the carriage toward downtown. "Have you ever eaten ice cream?" he asked.

She shook her head.

They clopped over the cobbles and through the dirt of the bright streets. Teresita had never seen so many people so well dressed. The buildings all about were huge, casting shadows that were alive with pigeons. They rose two and three stories, and some of them were fronted with brick or white stone. It was like passing through a great marble range of mountains. Festive American and Texan flags formed colored waves in the air above the cliff faces. Hotels. Banks. Stores. She saw that El Pasoans bought many kinds of clothing, many cuts of meat, many sizes of boot, many brands of gun.

Aguirre nudged her and pointed out a tall fellow striding along distractedly. He wore his hair a bit curly at the collar, and his mustache was wider and blacker than her father's.

"That's the sheriff of Las Cruces," Aguirre said.

"He looks mean."

"He's Pat Garrett," he explained.

"Oh?"

"He killed Billy the Kid!"

"Oh!"

She craned around and stared at the lawman. He glanced at her. She waved. He raised a finger and stepped into a saloon.

Teresita let out cries of delight when the mule cars rumbled along on their tracks, happy trolleys pulled by nodding philosophical mules. And bicycles reduced her to wild laughter. Great high-wheeled rattling machines with capped boys perched on their seats, charging in and out of the shadows of fat cottonwoods along the streets and acequias.

They took in the bustle of workers at Bassett's lumberyard, and they stared at the young Negro children in front of St. Clement's Episcopal Church, which looked like it had been built with planks from Bassett's. Aguirre pointed out the Ames building. "Home of the *El Paso Times*," he sniffed. "The enemy." He shook his fist at the building, and they both laughed. "They used to sell boots there," he said. "I daresay the establishment was better used in that service."

Down to the corner of Texas and Mesa. The Segundo Barrio was near, as was the river. Don Lauro helped Teresita down and walked her to the Elite Confectionery on the corner. The floor was made of echoing tile, and the white counter within was curved and long. It was cool inside. Teresita loved the smell of cakes and sugar. Don Lauro ordered two toasted cheese sandwiches with bottles of Houck and Dieter strawberry sodas. He confided, "The brave Mexican freedom fighters across the river drink Houck and Dieter. We drink in solidarity with the revolt."

She lifted her bottle to him in a toast.

"Ferocity," she said.

"Er, yes."

"Justice."

"Indeed."

"Evolution."

"I—?"

"To death!" she cried.

"Oh, now..."

She tinked her bottle against his and drank deeply.

The sandwiches glistened with delicious grease, and yellow cheese drooled from the soggy bread. This cheese did not smell like her father's cheese. Teresita licked the rubbery goo off her fingers. She had a rime of grease around her mouth, which Aguirre, feeling avuncular, dabbed away with his napkin.

Pushing away his plate, he said, "Now, the ice cream."

"I can't!"

"You must."

"I'm full."

"It melts and fills in the gaps. It will fit. We must have dessert."

"I'll get fat."

"Fat and very, very happy."

He raised a finger and requested the specialty of the house. This was a concoction known as the Elite Baseball. This made them both smile as they thought back on that afternoon that already seemed one hundred years gone — the Van Order boys in their silly uniforms and their thrilling antelope speed in the field of play.

"A revolt is coming," Don Lauro murmured.

"No."

"Revolution, Teresita."

"I will have none of it."

"You could lead them!"

"I could not."

"If you were to ride at the head of a column of bold warriors, what city would not fall?"

"If I were to lead an army, cities would fall down, all right. They would fall down from laughter."

"Teresita!"

"Not today, thank you."

"Revolution is God's work."

"Healing is God's work," she demurred. "Childbirth. Making honey. Not shooting people."

He drummed his fingers.

"Perhaps revolution is how a culture heals itself."

Teresita said, "Oh, look. The ice cream is coming." Then, without glancing at Don Lauro, she said, "This *saint* business—it is invented by newspapers to sell beans and saddles."

He blew air out of his puckered lips as if he'd burned his tongue on hot food.

When the bowl of chocolate and vanilla ice cream—in round baseball-sized scoops—topped with cascades of chocolate sauce and nuts landed before her, all Teresita would say was "Oh my." She silenced Aguirre by attacking the bowl savagely. She never looked up at him. He was appalled to hear her grunt in delight.

She licked the bowl clean.

※

"Ice cream is the greatest food ever invented," she said, sighing.

Her stomach gurgled as they rolled across downtown, but she didn't care.

The editorial offices of *El Independiente* smelled of ink, cigars, and hair pomade. A fellow in a starched shirt with a paper collar was bent to a horrid clacking machine, banging away at a set of recalcitrant keys that, once struck, sent metal arms pounding into sheets of paper. The whole thing was most appalling, and it slid a roller back and forth with irritating pings of bells.

Don Lauro showed her to a seat at his desk.

"My empire," he said, opening his arms as if to hug the room.

"It's very interesting," she offered.

"I want you to work here with me," he said, sitting down at his desk.

"Excuse me?"

"Here, Teresita. I want you to help me edit this newspaper."

She sat back in her seat. He expected her to gasp, or cry out, or refuse his offer out of hand. But she did not. She smiled. She rubbed her stomach.

"Edit?" she said.

"Yes! We can write together!"

The man at the type machine turned and glowered at them and made a small noise in his throat and went back to hacking.

Thinking he was really smart, Aguirre said, "This is true healing, Teresita. Healing of the mind!"

She snorted.

"I have written articles before," she said. "It was interesting. But hardly sacred."

"How wrong you are." He startled her by slamming forward in his seat. "No, no, no. No!" He rose, he paced. "We tell the truth here. We reveal the history of the moment. We uncover the liars and depose the wicked. We give voices to the voiceless. I would venture that this work is sacred indeed!" His finger was raised to the ceiling.

"¡Sí, hombre!" the typist exclaimed, then went back to work.

"Ah," she said. "Revolution again. Perhaps you should collect stamps, or butterflies."

"It is not a hobby! It is a calling!" Aguirre thundered.

She riffled through some pages on his desk.

"What miracles would we celebrate now," Aguirre insisted, "if no one had bothered to write the scriptures?"

She looked up at him.

Oh yes, he thought, that was good.

"So," Teresita said, "the Bible was God's newspaper."

"Well! I, er...Perhaps."

"These scriptures," she said, staring at the pages. "Bottles of elixirs to cure drunkenness. Oh, wait. Here is a story about a gentleman caught stealing ladies' clothing from a line near the river. Ah! An advertisement for a six-gun. Quite sacred."

She crossed her arms and looked around the room.

"And," Don Lauro said, using his final stratagem, "you will earn money, so you can repay your father for his incredible sacrifices on your behalf."

She hung her head. She was angry—she recognized an underhanded ploy. But it was a good ploy. She felt guilty every day. Tomás made sure of that.

"I will not violate my principles," she said.

"No."

"You can't change my words."

"Never."

"I will have freedom to say what needs to be said."

"I swear to it."

"I will not advocate violence."

"Well! No..."

"We will hire women."

"I...Right."

He put out his hand. She looked at it. Should she agree? What of her pilgrims? She knew what Don Lauro would say: *You will address the needs of many more pilgrims through the newspaper than you could see in a score of days.* She could help Don Lauro bring justice to the very People she had sprung from, the People she might never see again. Justice. Evolution. Her head spun a little.

"Besides," he said. "You're bored. Newspapers are great fun."

She smiled up at him.

Reluctantly, she put her hand in his. They shook.

"Don't expect much," she said.

He waved that off with a "Pah" and broke out a box of cigars. He snipped the ends off two of them and handed her one. Its end immediately became soggy in her mouth. It was a small swamp that was dropping tendrils of tobacco on her tongue. She spit them out. Put the fetid end of the cigar back in her mouth, tried not to swallow the brown spit that flooded her tongue. Men, she thought, must be crazy. He struck a match and lit her stogie, then put flame to his. She pulled a humorous face. She didn't mean for it to be humorous. "Puff it," he said, sitting down. He was having a wonderful time. Teresita was game. She could outride him for sure. She could beat him in a wrestling match, she was pretty certain. She knew she could play guitar better than he could. She sucked once.

She spit the cigar onto the floor.

"Gack!" she cried.

She coughed, spit, bent over coughing with her tongue hanging out.

He leapt up and pounded her back.

"That is the worst thing I ever tasted!" She gagged.

He smiled.

"You'll get used to it," he said.

Smoke hovered over her in a shroud.

Twenty

IT WAS NOT LOST on Tomás that he was unemployed while his daughter now had two jobs—Saint and girl reporter. He had not heard of any girls reporting for newspapers. It felt indecent to him, yet it was less irritating than her pieties. Of course, neither career yet paid Teresita any money whatsoever. Things in America were upside down.

At night, she was exhausted and sullen after her endless ministrations and occasional outbursts of fanatical rhetoric delivered to the bovine faces of the mob, those low folks the locals called rascuaches. He laughed. *Rascuache!* What a word. It even sounded dirty and flea-bitten. He immediately composed a lyric:

> *There was a young man in huaraches*
> *Who seemed to be very rascuache*
> *He came up to my knee, he was covered in fleas*
> *And his britches were covered in patches.*

"By God!" he raved. "It is art!"

He hurried to mail a copy of his poem to Gabriela in far, far Mexico.

A next concoction: The scribbler Aguirre with his damnable notebooks descended on their dining room at night and drove Teresita into fits of nervous jitters with his enthusiasm for the horrible truth about the massacre of Tomóchic and her followers there. Tomás was against this project—a book no less. But Aguirre assured him in surreptitious hissing conferences on the back porch that this publication would transform their standing in society and would, indubitably, bring them great fortunes. Tomás didn't point out that a book about an obscure indigenous slaughter printed by a small Mexican newspaper in El Paso on yellow newsprint and in Spanish was not destined to overwhelm the American populace. Why bother?

Aguirre set a pot of coffee and a quiver of pens upon his desk and tipped his head to her.

"I just wanted a normal life," she dictated. "I wanted to be pretty and attend dances with my friends. Who did not desire romance, pretty dresses, and a peaceful home full of babies?" She tapped on the table with her fingernail to make sure he paid attention. "I was just a girl when holiness was dropped on my head. I did not ask for it. I was chosen."

Aguirre wrote none of this—he drafted the first lines of his incendiary introduction instead.

Teresita gamely set her jaw and narrated whole scenes to Aguirre, who scratched away in his ledgers like a madman. She even, to her detriment, read Aguirre letters from Cruz Chávez. These letters often made her weep, and she writhed afterward in terrible dreams. She yelped in her sleep and cried out. Yet she believed the story had to be told. She owed it to her fallen friends. She owed it to the People.

Tomás, lurking in the back room and listening to these writing sessions, did not know that rebel maniac—the Pope of Mexico!—had written so many letters to his daughter. Unsavory. Goddamn, as his American friends liked to say. He smoked. He fretted. He wished he could get his hands on Juanita Van Order. He crept out the back door and walked the silent streets of El Paso, wondering where he'd seen those opium dens.

It was Don Lauro's idea to call their project ¡*Redención!*

Tomás, making a weak effort to bring sanity back to the house, said one day, "What redemption? Everybody was killed."

But nobody listened to him.

※

Came the day when the young reporter was given her first assignment. One had to accommodate the Saint's schedule, Aguirre was well aware. She had to learn, however, that some stories were simply too important to history, to the entire furthering of the human race, to be stopped by rascuaches, peasants, Indians, and beggars. "I will come for you at six o'clock on Monday morning," he warned. "Be ready. Be fed. Wear appropriate clothes." By this, he meant no polka-dot party dresses. She was deeply offended—as if the Saint of Cabora did not know how to dress.

That morning, hoping to shock Don Lauro, she appeared on her porch in a pair of Tomás's trousers. Aguirre almost fell out of his carriage. Not from outrage but from a great sense of looming history. Why, the warriors of dear Chihuahua, those daring raiders who crept the desert wastes and set ambuscades for the dreaded Rurales, practiced their own form of women's suffrage: their women carried rifles and strapped crossed gunbelts across their chests and wore men's trousers! Aguirre cursed himself for not bringing a photographer to capture Teresita's revolutionary resolve. He rose in his seat and raised his arms. *Solidarity. Fraternity. Liberation.* These all burned in his head. Puzzled, Teresita watched a faint billow of ruby-red and gold light seem to spiral off his scalp and evaporate in the air above him. She had not seen soul colors very well since she was a child. She shook her head. Perhaps it was a trick of the light. She didn't have time to think about it—Aguirre was laughing and prancing around the cabriolet to take her arm. In a minute's time, they were trotting through the drowsy streets, watching the sun cascade down the delightful facades of the buildings all around them as small dogs scattered and the crazy little birds of Texas squabbled. She'd barely settled in her seat.

America was just too fast.

☀

A new photograph of Teresita was circulating on that day. It showed her standing behind a chair with angels and cherubs surrounding her. Aguirre had secretly printed several hundred of them, and now the Teresistas in Sonora distributed them among their warriors, for the fight was approaching and they would need her protection. In El Paso, Mexico's greatest spy, Victor Ochoa, had one such photo. Ochoa, Aguirre's mentor, had vowed to keep its provenance secret from the Saint. He was a man of intrigue. He could keep his mouth shut. Had he not faced certain death penetrating the bastions of power in Mexico City to report to his comrades? Had he not carried dangerous billets-doux between the nations tucked in his boots? Had he not prospered in Los Yunaites Estates as a businessman and thus opened the doors of gringo power as handily as he had plumbed the Mexican government's depths? He had!

He drew himself to his full height so his gathered followers could regard him in the morning light.

Ochoa stood in the desert northwest of El Paso in sight of the New Mexico border. He wore jodhpurs tucked into tightly laced knee boots. His tan shirt was visible under an open brown wool army jacket. The cross-chest strap for his handgun gave him a smart, military mien. On his head, a stiff brown U.S. campaign hat, with its flat brim and dimpled crown. His goggles lay on his upper chest, held around his neck by a loose leather strap. He slapped his gloves into the palm of his left hand.

"¿Dónde está pinche Aguirre?" he demanded.

This moment, June of 1896, would be remembered, Ochoa knew; history would be made. And it was imperative that he make that history now, in time for Independence Day, so the Americanos would look upon Mexicans as the great race that they were. The twentieth century would be the era of the Mejicano. And *here,* now, if Aguirre ever arrived, he would grab the reins of that coming century and ride it forward in the name of his bronze race, his sons of the Fifth Sun, his beloved children of Quetzalcoatl. Yes, they would see today that a Mexican could fly. The first man in the air! Let Jules Verne chew on that.

His ornithocopter stood a short distance away, overseen by three assistants. It chuffed softly, its boiler building up a head of steam in its central stack. Ochoa had affixed the angel-crowded picture of Teresita before his pilot's seat, located behind the steam tank. Yes, it would be a triumph for them all—Aguirre knew his peasants. Ochoa would soar into space in the name of Mexicans, but also in the name of the Saint of Cabora. Thus the uprising would begin. And Ochoa would bomb the enemy from above, dropping bottles of kerosene from his agile craft as the oppressors scattered in fear below him.

He slapped his hand some more and waited.

※

"The trouble, my dear," Aguirre postulated as they bounced away from the city, "is that we Mexicans are baroque to our bones, while the Americanos are modern. But today, Mexicans leap ahead! Today, Mexicans shed the baroque and rush to the forefront of modernity."

Teresita had no idea what he was talking about, but she nodded politely.

Ochoa, he told her, was a patriot. A leader. A guide to the expatriate warriors of El Paso, and a mentor to *El Independiente.* Ochoa had had his hand in the Urreas' immigration struggle. The great man, master of espionage, thirty-third-degree Mason, Rosicrucian, was also a student of da Vinci. And he had furthered da Vinci's ancient plans for a flying machine by relying on Aguirre's legendary engineering skills. Indeed,

Aguirre humbly let it be known, the flying machine could not have been created without his talents. She cooed—men liked that. Aguirre said, "One does what one can, Teresita!"

For three years, they had plotted and sketched out the epochal ornithocopter. It had not been cheap! Oh no—the parts had to be machined by hand. Few men—perhaps none except them—could create a contraption that would leap and scoot through the air like a dragonfly. It was a great honor to her that Ochoa wanted her to cover the event for the newspaper.

"You represent our traditional ways, and he represents our future."

"I see," she said. "Out with the old, in with the new."

He sputtered, but she smiled and looked at the sere mountains.

When they arrived at Ochoa's launching site, she beheld the great man in his military garb. Behind him, the machine stood, looking ugly as a pig. It was a small wagon frame with four auto-car tires in place of wooden wheels. She jotted notes. The boiler heated the small silver tower, out of which rose a rotating pole with a great white canvas umbrella atop it. A McClellan saddle with stirrups faced the silver steam tank, and levers jutted out from each side. Several cameras were trained on the contraption, and Ochoa maintained a mysterious silence as he gestured meaningfully but did not speak.

Teresita stepped forward.

"Señor Ochoa," she said.

"¡Ay!" he cried. "¡La Santa de Cabora!" People applauded mildly. As if Ochoa hadn't been expecting her.

"Would you care to comment on this interesting craft?" she asked.

"It is a secret," he confided.

"But the newspaper is here. The cameras," she said.

"Yes, of course. After it flies, there can be no secret! Only before!"

She wrote this down.

She saw the picture of herself mounted on the craft.

"What is this?" she demanded.

"It is a picture of you," he said.

"I can see that," she replied. "It's hideous."

"No!" he said.

"Awful. I look like a corpse with paper angels hanging from wires."

He studied the picture for a moment. He was busy. This business was irritating. Men's doings were always being delayed by women's shenanigans, he decided.

"It is sacred," he intoned.

"It's ridiculous."

"B—"

"Do you see any angels around me?" she demanded.

"Well, no."

"Angels," Aguirre pontificated, "can only be seen with the eyes of the heart."

They both glared at him. He withdrew to a safe distance. She turned back to Ochoa. He was looking around for help now.

"I must be going," he announced.

Ochoa mounted the saddle and put his goggles over his eyes. He removed his campaign hat and placed it on Teresita's head. He gestured for her to back away. "Shade yourself," he advised. He picked up a leather helmet and squeezed his head into it. Everyone clapped more robustly. He waved her back with his fingertips. She hurried to Don Lauro's side.

"Extraordinary," he breathed. Then directed her to note this utterance in her notebook.

Ochoa peered at three gauges on the tank. He turned a black valve, and a great puff of steam chuffed out and dissipated in the air. The machine shuddered. They all clapped again. He turned a red knob. The machine began to whine. They cheered. They whistled. Ochoa took hold of the lever on the left and drew it back. The pole rotated and pumped. The white umbrella spun, slowly at first, then faster and faster. The pumping made the umbrella rise and fall as it spun. It made loud unfurling and snapping sounds like the sail of a boat in a stiff wind. Clouds of dust began to swirl around man and machine as if they were in the midst of a dust devil. The contraption jittered and began to hop in place. It tapped from tire to tire as if it were excited and wanted to run and jump in a lake.

"Behold," Aguirre shouted, "the future of the Mexican race!"

Ochoa slammed the other lever home and he launched into the air.

The copter rose two feet and slammed back to the ground.

"¡Ah, cabrón!" Señor Ochoa could be heard to utter.

The machine leapt again. Three feet. Slam. Leap: six feet. Slam.

"¡Chingado!" he cried.

Buckaroos hollered, "Ride that sombitch!"

Horrible gasps and screams of steam spurted out. The clanging of the machinery was deafening. The machine tipped away from them and scattered the photographers, who ran, shouting, trying to save their cameras as the machine frog-hopped at an alarming angle.

"¡Jesús!" Ochoa yelled.

Teresita's picture tore loose from the engine casing and looped through the air as he retreated at an increasing rate.

The machine would not rise into the sky. It would only jump, and it farted and wailed and threw bolts as Ochoa rode it up a small hill. They saw him on its crest, bouncing horribly with his legs akimbo, before the machine leapt off the far side in a horrid eruption of steam, dirt, and rocks.

They heard one last cry from the world's greatest spy before the crash: "Oh, Ga-daaammett!"

Aguirre hung his head.

"The future," he mourned, "shall be deferred."

He pointed at Teresita's notebook.

"Quote me," he said before hurrying off to see if Ochoa was alive.

Twenty-One

THEY WERE SCREAMING WITH laughter. Tomás was on his back on the floor. "He flew off a hill?" He gasped.

She was wiping tears from her eyes.

"He bucked over the hill! It looked like a giant iron toad!"

"No!" He gasped again. "Stop!"

"He cursed every time he hit the ground," she said.

He rolled over and got to his knees.

"I beg you by all that is holy, stop. You're making me wet my pants."

She hopped once. "¡Ah, cabrón!" she cried. She hopped again. "¡Ay, Mamá!" She hopped. "¡Ay, caramba!"

Tomás crawled out of the room.

"I must now escape to the excuse-me."

"Go," she said, raising a holy hand in blessing.

She sat at the dinner table and poked at a bowl of sliced melons. Her shoulders still shook when she pictured the scene. She scratched her head with both hands, shook out her hair.

Tomás came back in the room. He was no longer smiling. He looked, in fact, like a sad child. His shirt was untucked and his hair was mussed.

"What is it, Father?" she asked.

"There is no water," he replied.

"¿Qué?"

"They have turned off our water."

He had a paper in his hand. He had lifted it from the small table near the door. He held it out.

"Who did?" she demanded.

He shrugged.

"El Paso. The neighbors. There was a letter."

"When did that come?"

"Last week."

"And you did nothing?"

"I didn't think they were serious."

She stood. She took the paper from him and stared at it.

"But why?" she said.

He hung his head.

"We bring a bad element to the street," he said. "Your... followers. Disreputable. Something. The decent people, they want us to move."

She sat.

He sat.

They stared at each other.

"But you didn't do anything," she scolded, like a mother whose son has not done his homework.

He dug his thumbnail into the table's wood.

"I guess not," he muttered. "I can't do everything."

She sighed.

"Don't even start," he said.

"I wasn't starting anything."

"Yes, you were."

"I was not!"

"You were criticizing."

"I wasn't the one who ignored the letter!" she said.

"See?"

He crossed his arms and looked away.

"Thank you very much for your support," he said.

She ate a slice of melon to collect herself.

The beams of the house creaked and cracked above them.

He cleared his throat.

"What do we do now?" she asked before he could say anything.

He shrugged one shoulder.

"We move," he said.

He blew air through his lips.

"Again."

Thinking: Are you happy now?

Thinking: Damn you.

They took great care to not look at each other for a long, silent time.

"Good night," he said.

His door closed silently and his bedsprings creaked.

Teresita went from lamp to lamp then, blowing out the flames.

⁂

Don Lauro Aguirre and a bandaged Victor Ochoa hauled the Urreas' belongings away in a rented flatbed wagon as the neighbors glared and clucked and scowled at them from their porches. Tomás and Teresita rode in Aguirre's cabriolet down the street behind them. Teresita steered, for Tomás was hugging a wheel of Parmesan to his chest as if it were a baby, shielding it from evil. People waved as they passed, but to Teresita it seemed that they were jeering. Her face burned.

They hauled up to the front porch of a rooming house on Oregon Street at the edge of the barrio. The Negro hotel was down the road, and handsome women stood there with their children eyeing the great arrival. On the far corner, a cantina favored by bandits and rebels stood in a cloud of cigar smoke and ruckus. Tomás was scowling furiously, but he cheered up when he saw the cantina. "I see my cathedral," he quipped. But Teresita was happy to see that, indeed, a church stood on the corner opposite the cantina. "And I see mine," she replied. Both accepted that they had scored cheap points.

There is our life, she thought. Expressed in stone.

"Where do we live now?" Tomás called.

Aguirre pointed.

"Top floor. Northwest corner."

Tomás looked up, craned around. Three Mexican and two black kids waited to help them move their things upstairs. Tomás looked back up the hill.

"We used to live up there," he said to the kids.

"What happened?" one asked.

"I killed the neighbors," he said.

The boys' eyes widened.

Across the street from the rooming house stood an empty lot. It was about an acre in size. Drunks lounged comfortably in the dirt. But he noticed people were moving into the space. He thought he saw some of them carrying canvas—a tent.

Oh, he knew what that meant. There were no surprises left for the Sky Scratcher. There would be more tents. There would be bonfires and barbecues. There would be flags and tooty-tooty bands. Evangelists and revivals, endless preaching for Teresita and against her, and those damnable hymns. Indians and vaqueros. Fulsome children with watery angelic eyes. Assassins. Gunmen. Mexicans. Spies. People stood in the street and pointed at them. Jumbles of drunks and revelers tumbled in and out of the cantina, and shouts and drunken greetings rolled up the street at them. Teresita waved.

"Don't encourage them!" Tomás snarled.

It would all start again. Oh, hell. All of it.

But now Teresita had a high window from which to look down and bless her fanatics.

Tomás comforted himself with the thought of shooting the pilgrims from his bedroom.

From the cantina, two dangerous characters sauntered into the street. They were followed out by a slender woman with spiky hair. They all stared. They strolled toward Teresita and Tomás. One had long black hair and leather pants, a billowy poetic white shirt.

"Who is this dandy pendejo?" Tomás wanted to know.

The other bad boy wore his hair only to his shoulders, but this was still shocking to Tomás. He laid his cheese aside and fingered his pistola. The two bad men wore pistolas too, slung low on their hips. Skinny bastards, Tomás thought. No hats.

Aguirre fell back and gasped. "It is the Iberians!"

Tomás gripped his pistola harder. The dreaded Iberians! Crept into the United States from Chihuahua, no doubt looking for banks to rob. The gunmen stood in the road and stared at the Saint. Tomás knew he could draw and fire in a second if he had to. Still, he secretly loved bandidos and lamented the fact that he had never run off as a lad and joined the gang of the topless female scourge of Mexico, La Carambada.

Tomás gestured with his chin.

"¿Y tú, qué?" he challenged.

The one in the leather pants said, "Soy Bunbury, de los Iberos. Este es Valdivia."

Aguirre already had his notebook out, but Bunbury pointed at him.

"No interviews," he said.

Although Teresita resented the photographs of her that adorned so many walls, if she had been given a photograph of Bunbury of the Iberians, it would be hanging in her bedroom.

He looked up at her under his eyebrows, like a wolf. John Van Order looked at her that same way.

"¿Qué hubo, mi santita?"

My little saint! She squirmed.

Tomás thought it was insolent.

"Aquí nomás," she replied. "Echando relajo."

What? What? Tomás's head swiveled between them, incredulity on his face. She said she was just hanging out? Enjoying the relaxation? What? Talking like a drunk to these cabrones? Saints didn't say these things.

"¿Y ésta?" she asked, nodding to the woman.

"Es Rakel La Pocha. My historian," Bunbury said.

The two killers smiled and posed handsomely: cheekbones, pouts. Rakel spit.

Teresita said, "You must be very famous to have your own historian with you."

The wicked Bunbury looked around and grinned.

"You are more famous than I," he said.

"Mine is a different audience."

He stared up at her.

"I don't think so," he replied. "Who is more of an outlaw than a saint?"

"Benditos sean," Teresita said, raising her hand.

Tomás goggled. Blessed? Blessed be? Was she kidding? These evil sons of bitches, blessed?

The bad men dipped their heads a smidgen.

"Oh, please," said Tomás.

"Gracias, Santita Guapita," Bunbury said. He pronounced it "Grathias."

All right; Tomás was going to shoot them. They were calling his daughter cute right in front of him.

He started to speak, but Valdivia lit up a smoke and offered him one. He stalled and considered. A notorious pistolero was offering him a smoke? By God! He took it and said, "Grathias." Everybody was Iberian.

Valdivia wore a guitar on a strap across his back, and it hung head-down like a rifle.

"One day," Bunbury said, "we will write a song about you."

"I would love to hear it," she replied.

"Shh," suggested Tomás.

Ochoa and Aguirre stood with their mouths open.

Bunbury shook his head sadly and smiled up at her.

"When we are in Hell, Santita, and you are in the Kingdom of Heaven, remember us. Come near the gates. We will serenade you."

He winked. He dug out coins from his tight pockets and tossed them to the boys gathered around him. He hung his hands off his silver concha belt.

They turned and strolled back to their bar for another round of drinks. Bunbury had a bottom that Teresita did not want to look at. The gunmen moseyed as if daring anyone in El Paso to shoot them. Rakel La Pocha had knives tucked in the back of her belt.

"I was ready to blast those knot heads," Ochoa said.

Tomás sat back down and put his head in his hands. He'd thought there was going to be a rousing gunfight right there on the corner of Oregon. But Valdivia had fine tobacco, he'd give the Iberians that much.

"Oh God," he said. "It will never end."

Teresita hopped down, all grins.

"Those fellows," she noted, "weren't so bad."

"They wanted to kill us all," Tomás said.

"Father," she scolded, "they wanted to see me. Everyone wants to see me. Didn't you know?"

She joined the kids as they started to unload the boxes from the wagons. Tomás kicked back and tipped his hat to keep the sun from his eyes. He muttered, "But you like everybody." He closed his eyes. Better to be asleep than to be the way he was. Which was small—small and dry in the vastness of the yellow desert sun.

※

There was no room for most of their things, so Tomás rented a storage shed around the corner. The stench of Tomás's cheese immediately attracted mice, which began tunneling through their belongings. They dug comfortable tunnels in the Parmesan and ate themselves to sleep.

Teresita set about tidying up the apartment. The building was made of brick, and it soaked up the heat and turned into an oven. They kept the windows open, but the incessant noise of the street assaulted them at night. Mexicans raised a ruckus late into the night, they heard. The cantina seemed to be a center for cross-border fraternity: Americanos shot off pistolas outside and broke bottles. The Negro hotel was quiet by eight o'clock, but the downtown doves in their red skirts and loose tops who snuck between it and the next-door building screeched and hooted with their drunken buckaroos until dawn. Carriages, wagons, galloping horses.

Tomás was appalled when the church bells went off first thing in the morning. He leapt from bed and yelled "Shut up! Shut up! Shut up!" out the window. In the Segundo Barrio, even God was a troublemaker.

And, as he had predicted, the camp across the street began to grow. That one tent went up, its striped top attracting wanderers, and as soon as that outpost was settled, a second tent appeared. Between and behind them soon opened taco stands and charqui smokers making strips of black jerked beef. Donkeys loitered in the shade of the building as their owners made themselves small plots in the dirt from which to stare up at Teresita's window. The borrachos of the barrio had never seen anything so entertaining, and they sat upon the small porches of the downstairs apartments passing their ten-cent bottles of red vino, commenting as raucously as crows.

He caught her, late one night, peering out the window at the humping, bumping mass in the field.

"Are you all right?" he said.

She just stared.

"Are you sleepwalking?"

When she spoke, it was almost a whisper.

"They are faceless," she said. "There are so many. I cannot see them any longer. I cannot remember any of them."

She reeked of roses.

He steered her to bed.

※

If he could only charge a few centavos to each of these pilgrims, Tomás thought, he could buy a new Cabora in a year. But Teresita was adamant. Aguirre, however, was making a small fortune selling Teresita's photographs—his agents skirted the edges of the crowd with stacks of the sacred relics, selling them for a dollar. It was absolute robbery. Tomás dug around in their trunks and found a picture Teresita had signed and meant to mail to poor stupid Cruz Chávez. He stole it and bargained with Aguirre. He got a good price for it. Teresita's autograph drove the fanatics wild.

July.

When they heard explosions and gunshots and screaming coming from the sky, they leapt from their beds. Dreadful fires flared through their curtains. The sky must have been burning—red, green, blue. Tomás drew his pistola and plastered himself to the wall, holding Teresita back with one hand as he peeked through the curtains.

"Ah, cabrón," he said.

He drew back the curtain for her to see. Skyrockets flew from the rascuache camp and from the hills behind. Glittering sky bombs rained down from the Franklin Mountains on the city below. Teresita laughed and clapped her hands. They leaned there on the window ledge and watched their first Fourth of July.

Twenty-Two

REVOLUTION.

The great Nogales raid began before first light on August 12, 1896. Forty warriors climbed into the hills in Sonora and huddled, rifles across their knees. Benigno Arvisu, Victor Ochoa's local operative, fed small twigs into their little fire. His compatriot Manuel González was the leader of the group. Manuel had survived the terrible cannonade and burning of Tomóchic. He had been to Cabora and seen Teresita at work. Now they looked out upon both Mexico and the United States. There was a garrison below them full of soldiers, but the warriors trusted that the barbwire fences between the nations would keep the Americanos on their own side. If the Americanos rode into the battle, Manuel, Benigno, and all of their men would surely die.

Oh, but they reminded themselves, each in his own way, that they were blessed by the Saint. Them. They bore her holy image inside their tunics and shirts. Her holy face would stop all bullets—this, Ochoa and Arvisu and González had promised.

"Tell us about the Saint," a voice requested. "You saw her at Caborca." They had already mistaken the name of the ranch for the name of the town in the west.

"She was like a figure made of light," González told them. "She made us all laugh. She blessed Cruz and his fighters."

They nodded and murmured and smoked and stared into the fire.

"She smelled like flowers."

"You got that close?"

"I did. She laid her hand on me. I smelled her with my own nose."

Benigno nudged him.

"You couldn't have smelled her with anybody else's nose," he said. They snickered. They elbowed each other.

"Can I touch you?"

"You can."

The warrior touched the hem of González's serape.

"Bendita," he said.

They touched their angel pictures now.

Manuel carried pages of the *¡Redención!* articles folded in a cotton pouch that dangled from his neck. He tucked it away against his heart.

Those articles! Teresita had busied herself in her writings with messages about fate, destiny, and God's bounty. These pieces clearly galled Don Lauro, and he had steered her to more political bits—pensées on the fate of the Mexican dictatorship, for example. "How do you feel about the deaths of so many of your innocent tribesmen?" he'd offer over coffee and pig cookies.

"It tears out my heart. I am consumed with horror. I pray for justice to come, of course."

The next day, a headline: "The Girl Saint Cries for Revenge!" Subhead: "Justice Will Come in the Form of God's Wrath, She Avers." Aguirre had taken her sentiments and transformed them into ferocious proclamations.

"Teresita will protect us," Manuel said. "Teresita will watch over us."

"They say she can fly," one warrior said. "Is it true?"

"Yes." Manuel González pointed to the sky. It was flat black, a painted ceiling. Stars were smeared across the vault of the sky like flour. "She can see us all."

"She's asleep," Benigno said.

"In her dreams! She sees!" Manuel hissed.

Ah; the warriors nodded. They were Yaquis and Mayos and two mestizos. They knew about the Dreaming.

"She is always with us," Manuel promised. "Always. Always. She will bless our bullets to fly true. Her holy face will stop the enemy's rounds from killing us."

"Yes, we know."

"Claro que sí."

"Amen."

"Yes."

This was good. They felt happy. They would attack the border. They would incite a new shooting war in Mexico, and the killers of the People, the dictators and the soldiers, would fall. They smoked more mapuche cigarettes wrapped in corn sheaves.

"May God guide us," Manuel said.

"Let us," added Benigno, rising and dusting off his pants, "kill them all."

⚜

The forty men dropped out of the Sonoran hills and silently moved along the line. They could walk right up the main street from the American border shack. The only American border guard was a young cavalry rider in a small booth. He was lit by an oil lamp, and he was mostly asleep, and when he looked up and saw an Indian peering at him, he said "What?" before the stock of a rifle slammed into the bridge of his nose and dropped him, snorting blood and snot, to the sand. The warriors were gone before he even moaned.

They fanned out in the dark, heading south like a flood after a night rain—each of them with a directive, each with an ambush point to man in the slumbering town. Ochoa had trained Benigno well, and they had fought many battles back when the Yaqui wars were hot on the land, when they thought the revolution was about to ignite. Well, things seemed to find their own time. Men could not dictate the will of God.

Dawn was coming, but they were already in place. Six riflemen crouched in the little park. Ten men took up their positions across from the barracks of the guards and the soldiers. Men lurked behind corners at the mercantile, the post office, the little Hotel Nogales. Manuel González cut the telegraph lines and shimmied back down the pole and picked splinters out of his thighs as he crouched behind a barrel across from the customhouse.

Ochoa had told them, "Disrupt trade first. Business is their religion! Kill their profits, and you kill them."

As soon as roosters started crowing across the border in Arizona, he rose and shouted.

"¡Viva la Santa de Cabora!"

They jumped to their feet all around him and took up the shout.

And they fired.

※

Soldiers poured out of the barracks to a rain of bullets. Two Federales died immediately. Church bells rang. The fire station's bell on the American side clanged along with them. The Mexican sheriff jumped from his bed in the hotel and tumbled downstairs in his long johns, racking rounds into his Winchester. The thunder of massed guns overwhelmed the day. Dust. Running. Screams.

American cavalrymen leapt from their beds and were on their horses in minutes. They charged up and down the line, unsure of what to do. They waved handguns, tried to point their rifles into the melee. They were the only defense against invasion.

Dogs fled. Horses panicked and charged, whinnying and kicking. Barrels, windows, bottles in the saloon, jars and flowerpots on porches exploded. Dirt, shards flying everywhere. Men falling. Hollering. Cats scrambling. Chickens, in a hysterical burst, left feathers swirling in the street.

A speeding wagon was peppered with shots and overturned, throwing its pilot in a hideous rolling tumble across the cobbles.

Manuel González danced like a drunkard at a party as fifteen rounds from three directions slammed into his chest and belly. Benigno watched him dance and die from behind a water trough at the mercantile. Manuel shook, his shoulders shrugged rhythmically, and he lifted and moved backward through the air, his rifle loose in one hand and his red bandana the same flashing color as his blood gouting in jets all around as he spun, spun, one foot on the ground, one raised, his hand in the blizzard of rounds going to his heart, to his pictures of Teresita, the look on his face one of bewilderment as he soared. Teresita could not fly. He was flying. And the bullets tattered her to rip through his heart.

"¡Cabrones!" Benigno shouted, and stood up into the whirlwind.

※

It might have been due to the bells or the shouting of the federal troops on the Mexican side or the endless roar of gunfire, but the cavalrymen in Arizona could not contain themselves and jumped their horses over the gates and low barbwire fences and invaded Mexico. The young lieutenant at the head of the column shouted, "Boys, they're coming our way!" which made no sense, since it was the Americans heading toward the Mexicans. But nobody noticed in the din of rifles and bells and screaming horses.

Benigno and his boys shot their way into the customhouse and barricaded the doors and then shot at everything that moved. Bullets blew bright holes in the walls, as if a hundred eyes of angels had opened in the dark and cast beams of light into the gloom. But if their gaze fell on you, you would bleed and die.

Teresita's face did not stop a single round that day.

⁂

Hours later, the dead raiders were set out on the street. During the battle, they'd seemed twenty feet tall. Now, emptied of life, they looked small and pathetic. They weren't even gruesome. As citizens came down the sidewalks and stared, leading their children by the hands, there were few rivers of blood or piles of viscera. These warriors looked asleep. One who had been shot through the jaw had a comical rag tied around his face and looked as if he were waiting for a barber to pull an aching tooth. People pointed at him and laughed. The dead men's heads were propped against the wall of the customhouse. The angle would have hurt if they'd been alive.

Manuel González, their leader, lay a bit apart, set out perpendicularly to them, across their feet, with his ankles crossed. People walking by kicked him. He seemed to nod when they kicked him, sometimes turned his head as if checking to see who was bothering him. His blood had ruined Aguirre's newspaper inside his shirt. He was half staring into the sky. Dust turned his black eyes gray.

Twenty-Three

THAT SAME MORNING, REBELS attacked customhouses across the sweep of northern Mexico. They attacked Ojinaga, and they all died. They raided Juárez—in El Paso, Aguirre and Ochoa had assembled on the roof of the ice cream parlor to watch—and were destroyed by the garrison of Mexican federal troops stationed there. The expatriate revolutionaries smoked cigars on the roof and mourned. They could hear every shot, and the cries of the fallen drifted across the river with the clouds of dust and the bracing smell of gunpowder. Ochoa gestured toward the south and stated, "All this because your saint will not fight like a man." Aguirre knew this was unfair, but he also knew this was a good line, and he made it—in gentler, more reverential tones—the subject of editorials and broadsides. For a time, Tomás banned him from their boardinghouse, declaring him a traitor, but only until the next boot dropped. Díaz in Mexico declared the revolt a plot by Teresita herself, laying the blame for the violence on her, thundering that she be extradited immediately to face her belated fate in the motherland. The Mexican ambassador to the United States made his case in Washington for the festering indigenous danger of Teresita and her agitators—she had brought terror across the border and threatened to unleash new waves of scalpings and uprisings among the savages in the great southwestern territories if she wasn't exiled in reverse! Really, he pointed out, the great Abraham Lincoln himself had once hung a score of recalcitrant Indians when the security of the country called for it. Teresita had, the ambassador insisted, earned her place beside her Yaqui rabble, dangling from a tree.

It took all of Ochoa's vast network of influence, debts, favors, and operatives to stay the hand of the U.S. government. When Aguirre and Tomás were speaking again, Tomás—who now had gray hairs in his sideburns and mustache—jeered at Aguirre. "Nice work, you son of a whore! You had a one-day revolution!" His laughter was cruel.

※

When she stepped out to see how the morning would look, Teresita found a letter from the archangel Gabriel on her front stoop.

At first, she thought it was an editorial response to one of her articles for Don Lauro or, worse, another insult after he had suggested she was the reason for the revolution's failure. How could she both inspire the revolt and destroy the revolt? Herbs and spirits were so much simpler than this.

If she were more like her father, she would work up a good long curse. She never knew what new irritation or panic would hit on any morning. She certainly didn't expect a letter from Heaven.

Gabriel had lovely penmanship. His words lifted into curlicues, inspired no doubt by the trajectory of his wings as he flew. *Those who do not follow me,* he wrote, *shall be slain by my sword. I am a general in the army of the Lord. Believers shall forever march under the shadow of my wings. It is mankind's choice—glory or death.*

He signed it *The Angel Gabriel.* It didn't say *Sincerely.* There was no PS.

Attached to the heavy cream paper was one large, white feather.

It wasn't the strangest thing that had ever happened to her.

She awoke before dawn and washed herself and made ready her clothes. As she did each morning, she prayed, she honored her ancestors, she prepared a clear glass of water to put on the altar with her sacred objects and her cross. There was no way, in Segundo Barrio, for her to walk out to the fields of Itom Achai and greet the sun. What fields? And how would she maneuver through the crowd? No way to find power spots under trees to consult with coyote or semalulukut or the sly libélula—old dragonfly, her friend. What trees? But God could come to her room as she had once gone to His. Oh, death. She had been dead—it was hard to believe now that she was alive again and it meant being so hot and tired and bored.

Tomás had asked her what death was like, and she'd said, "Cooler than Texas."

Indeed, Heaven was breezy. God's hair, locks full of stars and waterfalls, had blown slowly around Him, she recalled. But she could not remember His face. Still, she'd know Him again when she saw Him.

Getting up from bed was so hard. Her body ached because she could not sleep well feeling the tidal swell of all those souls outside her windows dreaming about her. Huila used to say, "The hills are ancient, but they still are covered in flowers." She smiled. She was feeling the age, but the beauty was fading.

How easy, she remembered, it was to die. Why did we fight it when it came? It was like lying in a feather bed, after the pain and fear had passed.

As she washed herself with her soaps and tepid water, staring in the mirror as she bent to the basin, she could see the small wrinkles beside her eyes and mouth. Her eyebrows were growing back together. No wrinkles in Heaven, she thought. Lots of deer, though.

She hadn't seen Gabriel in God's valley. She had seen old Yaquis there, walking in the small hills where the sunflowers grew. She was curious about what moved him to write to her now. And if he could write her letters, would her dear Cruz Chávez or Huila ever write? How she would love a letter from Huila! Her eyes welled with tears. She splashed water on her face. No time for that. People were waiting. But she wondered, as she went back down the stairs, why Gabriel was in such a bad mood.

Once the reporters started to arrive, she found out.

※

Lately, she knew, they had been saying she was a mesmerist, that she somehow put her followers in a trance. Before, she would have laughed at them. She would have been fierce about it. But now... She had been away from her home, her land, her teachers for so long. She didn't think she was putting anyone in a trance. She was almost sure she was passing the power of God through her body. Don Lauro told her that her power was political, not holy. Of course he would. She sniffed her arm. She still smelled like roses, but she could barely smell it anymore. That was what holiness was like. Holiness coming down on her every day, she was ashamed to admit, was a crashing bore. It started out bright gold, vivid red, delicious purple. Over time, though, with no respite, it faded to gray.

It was harder in the rooming house. There was nowhere to go, nowhere to meet the seekers, nowhere to escape them. A wine-sotted borrachito on the ground floor had one of the empty-lot-facing doors up three stone steps from the street. He let Teresita sit in his dark room and wandered the streets drinking red wine and bumming smokes while she did her work. The old paisano's room smelled vaguely of dirty clothes and urine. She burned her incense and candles and hoped for the occasional breeze to stir the stink. No wonder the Bible promised golden mansions and great feasts in Heaven. This was a life of dust and ordure.

Her first clients were elderly Chinese, hiding in the city's shadows from the anti-Chinese expeditionary forces that rode into barrios and rounded up the illegal "celestials" who had come north from Mexico to work the rail lines and slaughterhouses. The old ones were awake before the Mexicans, and they smiled at her or stood stoically, sometimes unable to tell her what ailed them but pointing at body parts. They talked to her about chi, which made Tomás smirk when he overheard it, because in Spanish *chi* meant "urine." Sometimes, the old ones would take her hands in theirs, dry and soft and hot as little birds, and they would position them near spots on their bodies, nodding, whispering in their language that she somehow understood. One Dr. Chai sometimes spoke poems to her as he tried to show her where the cardinal spots for healing could be found.

After the Chinese came the banged-up buckaroos and the dented cantina boys and the feverish doves from the alleys. Teresita took them all. She knew whom Jesus knew. She helped whom Jesus helped.

And then the citizens of El Paso. And the citizens of Ciudad Juárez. And the travelers from New Mexico and Colorado, and then California and Missouri. They came from Chicago and New York. How she longed to see New York! And they came from Scotland and Ireland. They came from Mexico City and Havana. She greeted them all equally, the fine businessman, the prostitute, the Indian guerrilla, and the nun. It was her calling to accept them and offer them God's gift. Day after day. Sometimes they just wanted to see her and touch her hand. Sometimes they cried out when she raised her hands, and swooned at her feet. Sometimes they knew they were dying and merely wanted a kind send-off and an assurance or two. Nothing startled her. There was no malady, stench, wound that shocked her. She preferred the cures she could offer with herbs. Herbs relied on her expertise, her training. They could be measured. She knew what tea eased pain in the womb; she knew what ointment drew pus from a cut; she knew what leaves chased worms from the gut. Beyond the herbs was all faith. Yet, like the smell of roses, faith sometimes waned. Sometimes it also turned gray.

"Who am I but a woman?" she asked a deaf old man from Bavispe.

He smiled at her. He bent in a deep bow. He kissed her hand.

Tomás watched as he always watched, with one hand near his pistola. "All beggars," he said. "You have a ministry of whores and orphans and beggars."

"These are the blessed poor whom Jesus loved," she replied.

"You're not Him."

At night, she knelt on the painful wooden floor and prayed. Tomás was down on the stoop, unwilling to be exposed to any more sanctity. It felt like typhus, some holy miasma in the air that choked him. Malaria.

"Father!" she cried to her Lord. "It is not what I thought it would be. I don't know where to turn. Where is my refuge? Or am I greedy to ask?" Tears rolled down her face. "I am so tired, Lord. I am afraid. Those around me have used me. Those who follow me do evil. Those who are against me seek to silence me. Please, Father. A sign. Won't You offer one small miracle for Your poorest daughter?"

She heard crickets, but that's all she heard.

※

The Nogales raid exploded in the newspapers a few days after the dead were buried. Reporters came—more New Yorkers. The *New York Times*. The *Los Angeles Times*. Newsmen from Tombstone and Mexico and Fort Wayne, Indiana, jostled with her followers.

Military men stood guard around the rooming house. Pinkertons asked to speak to her on behalf of the United States government. The

People could not get to her. Soon, the room was full of scribes and detectives and officials. Ochoa didn't dare show his face.

Headlines threw her words on breakfast tables all over America. "Had No Part in Them! Asserts Girl Saint about Mexican Uprisings."

A rock came through a window.

Signs bobbed in the street.

VIVA SANTA TERESA.

U.S. FOR AMERICANS, MEXES OUT.

Tomás recognized one of the old Rurales who had come to Cabora years before and shot a pilgrim. He was dressed as a peasant and hobbled piteously among the thwarted followers outside the phalanx of reporters. The man had suspiciously bright white bandages wrapped around his arm and leg. When he pushed his way into the room, he locked eyes with Tomás, and the Sky Scratcher cross-drew his .44 and lodged it in the Rural's left nostril.

"Calma, guey," he breathed. "Easy now, my son."

He reached into the assassin's shirt and withdrew a saltbox derringer. Its four fat barrels made it a squat, ugly piglet of a gun. Tomás held it up in his left hand and shook it in the assassin's face.

"And this?" he asked.

"You got me," the Mexican admitted. "Are you going to kill me now?"

"Why shouldn't I kill you?"

"The Saint wouldn't approve of it."

"You were going to kill the Saint!"

"I had my orders."

"Asshole," Tomás said.

He drew back the hammer of his .44. Those in the room gasped. The assassin's eyes bugged. Teresita cried, "No!"

Tomás spun the man around and kicked him in the backside, sending him tumbling into the street. He scrambled to his feet and dashed away, pursued by fanatics. Tomás pocketed the derringer and holstered the pistola and squared his shoulders. He was heroic—he caught his reflection in the wall mirror and scowled furiously and handsomely at himself. Adjusted his vest.

"Teresita," he announced into the overcrowded room, "we need to talk, and we need to talk now, and we need to talk alone."

The gathered scribes shuffled out and even Teresita had to admit that things were becoming impossible.

"I tried your city," he said. "I don't like it. I'm sorry. Cities are for idiots, weaklings, and eggheads. Cities are full of smoke, piss, trash, and cabrones."

She said nothing.

"I urge you, with the strongest possible sense of responsibility as your father—I am still, you must admit, your father—that you consider, at last, I mean, *Christ, consider* stopping this madness for *one short season.* Please! We retreat. We do not concede defeat, nor do we—oh, hell— renounce *Jesus Christ.* No! Of course we don't! Don't be silly! My dear girl, do I look like I'm joking? I am not. God"—he held a hypocrite's hand over his heart and gazed skyward—"God calls us to duty, it's true. But He also calls us to rest. On the seventh day and all that."

She watched him.

"Rest, I tell you. I don't know about you, but I am goddamned tired. Fed up, in other words. Done. Bored. I shit on cities! So!"

He strode around as if hiking a hundred miles across the llano, bumping into things as he gestured wildly.

"I propose to you, *just as a brief respite,* mind you, a retreat. We go back. Yes, to Arizona. But wait! We go back, but we go into the high country. My God! Are you aware of the high country? No, of course you aren't. But it is cool there. They have pine trees and rivers."

"Cool?"

"Damned cool, Teresa! It even snows up there. Come. Let's go. Let's go recoup. Eh? Ha-ha, eh? I see you thinking. I see you smiling. Just think: We can ride horses where nobody knows us. No more assassins. It's safe, it's quiet."

He waggled his eyebrows.

"Oh, my dear. The clouds pass close enough to touch. And there are Indians."

"Indians?"

"Indians all over the mountains."

"Indians."

He sat on the old man's bed beside her chair and took her hand.

"We shall make a home there. I can start Cabora Norte there. I will build you a chapel. I will build you a clinic. Whatever you want. But please, please, I implore you, for this once, allow us to live in peace."

She closed her eyes. She trembled. She fretted her hands together.

"Is it truly possible," Tomás asked, "that God would have you, of all His servants, spend the rest of your life in danger and misery? Really? What kind of God is that?"

"Oh, Father," she whispered.

Finally, she wept.

Twenty-Four

BEFORE TERESITA AND TOMAS boarded the train to Solomonville, Aguirre and Ochoa pulled up to the station in Ochoa's flatbed. Their driver was a notorious agitator and street musician, the ponytailed ruffian Romo. He was an associate of the Iberians, and he could be seen and heard singing drinking songs on corners with Valdivia and Bunbury. Aguirre, Ochoa, and Romo secretly pulled back the edge of a tarp they'd laid down so the weeping fanatics could not see their load. Under the big greased sheet lay dusty rifles. Romo gestured with his hat: *Behold, the grand prize.*

"What is this?" Teresita demanded.

"Bless them," said Ochoa.

"You're insane."

"Bless them, I said."

"I will not."

"Your followers are being slaughtered in your name. Your ancestral lands are stolen and given away to the oppressor. You play the holy clown while your sons and daughters are destroyed. How dare you not protect them. Bless these guns, or you are killing these people."

Aguirre nodded sadly.

"Evolution," he reminded her.

She looked at Romo.

"What have you got to lose?" he said. "Hell, you already lost everything."

"Fine."

She raised her hand over the guns once. Cameras clicked. She threw her hand behind her and hurried into the train car. Aguirre felt a coldness in his right cheek, and that side of his face went slack and numb. He clutched it and felt the spit drool out of his mouth. The numbness faded away after three days, but he retained a certain fear of Teresita ever after.

※

Back across the desert. Back across New Mexico. Back through Spanish bayonets and creosotes, into the mad rocks and saguaros of the Sonoran desert.

Tomás was serene. He sat with his feet up on the seat before him, working on his teeth with a pick. He didn't smoke and he didn't drink.

"El Paso," he said to her. "Didn't care for it."

"I loved El Paso," she said. "I didn't like the complications."

Teresita spent most of the trip asleep. She could not believe how tired she was. It was almost as though once she'd admitted that she was weary, her body betrayed her. Even her mouth was tired. She did not want to speak to anyone, even God. She did not even want to use it to chew—she never wanted to eat again. She wished to be sent to a convent where the sisters took vows of silence. If they would only let her sleep for a year.

In her mind, the high country was almost as colorful as God's heavenly valley.

"Are there deer?" she asked Tomás.

"Of course. Trout too."

She nodded.

"What is this place called?"

"Clifton."

"Cleeptong," she repeated.

"Cliff Ton. The town of cliffs. Cliff-town."

"Cliffs?"

"Oh yes. Mines. Mines everywhere. You'll love it."

She fell asleep and saw Huila in her dream. The old healer was walking ahead of her, looking back over her shoulder. Teresita tried to catch her, but she could not run fast enough. "Come back!" she called, but Huila never slowed down. On her back, she carried a woven mochila, and the satchel held within it everything that Teresita had ever known or loved. Just before she disappeared over a small ridgeline, Huila turned around and stared at her. She waved once, then stepped over, out of sight.

※

To get to Clifton, they first had to return to Solomonville. They arrived as if erasing their original journey to Texas. The same train came back along the same track into the same rattling station. Nothing had changed at all. Even Mr. Van Order and Juana stood beside their same wagon, waving again.

Teresita dragged herself from her seat. Tomás bounded. He was almost flying. He shouted happy orders at everyone. He hustled her through the car, actually smacking her backside.

"¡Muévete!" he encouraged. "Move it, lazybones! ¡Andale!"

She was...appalled...but she laughed, against her will.

Tomás made an acrobatic leap from the train car's iron step and landed already in a slight bow before Juana.

He swept her hand to his lips and kissed the fragrant air a half inch from her flesh.

He spun on Mr. Van Order and smacked the dust out of the man's coat in a series of brutally fraternal abrazos.

Teresita was just stepping out, squinting in the sun, when Mr. Van Order gestured behind him.

Tomás turned and let out a bark of joy. Segundo! That old buzzard! Back from Mexico!

And then Tomás let out a cry the likes of which Teresita had never heard.

His hands rose to the sky.

He fell to his knees.

Gabriela Cantúa was standing behind Segundo, and she came forward and bent to Tomás and accepted his weeping face and pressed it to her bosom.

Part III

OF LOVE AND
THE PRECIPICE

Teresita's father chose Clifton, Arizona, because he had visited there while the family was at San José. He had liked the town for its natural beauty, reminiscent of Alamos, as well as for its bustling mining activities. He acquired a few acres of land with several small houses in the narrow valley in the lower part of town, just north of the San Francisco River. The location was sufficiently remote to discourage agents of the Mexican government and religious fanatics with designs on Teresita's life.

—WILLIAM CURRY HOLDEN, *Teresita*

Twenty-Five

SUCH BEAUTY, SUCH SILENCE, such clarity.

Children everywhere.

Segundo's wagons brought more than Gabriela—they carried an army of Tomás Urrea's offspring, along with a chest of gold Mexican pesos, comfortable beds, a sewing machine, a hundred rifles, twenty pounds of sun-jerked beef planks, cotton material in drooping bolsters— red, blue, white, checkered, black, yellow. Something called calico. Tomás made everyone laugh when he announced upon seeing it, "El calico me da cólico."

The boys nudged one another.

"That cloth's so ugly it makes the boss sick," they confided.

Segundo brought delicious dried tamarinds, bisnaga and camote candies, blocks of panocha, tin bins of fermenting maíz masa that might not make tortillas anymore but could make corn beer and Indian tejuino. Segundo brought tequila. He brought long stalks of sugarcane, great burlap sacks of pinto beans, bags of dried corn kernels, lime, a heavy stone-lidded pot of clover honey, chiles verdes, chiles Tabasqueños, chipotles and jalapeños, guayabas and mangoes. He had a sealed pot of the heinously pungent little objects known as nanchis. Neither Teresita nor the animals would touch a nanchi. He brought a potted avocado tree and a potted olive tree. And, on his second trip up from Alamos, he brought the Tubac house girl, Dolores.

"I would like to introduce you to my fiancée," he announced.

Teresita stifled a snort, but Tomás shook with a palpable fit of the horrors.

※

He was making a home for his beloved, the exquisite Gabriela Cantúa. Mother of his daughter Anita, as precocious at six as Teresita had been when she was a child. And Gabriela bearing him another already! And the children of his marriage, here for the wonders of America. American educations. American careers.

The months in this property below Clifton and Morenci had been kind. Fruitful. Tomás enjoyed sun, hard work, familia, money, and cascades of mother's milk showering his face in the holy debauchery of his bedroom. "It is my little fountain." Gabriela blushed as she erupted. "Gushing for you." His beloved tasted of sugar.

He strode about again in tight black trousers with silver-studded belts. Gabriela loved to cook, and even though they had an American woman who made their meals all week, Gaby took over on the weekends. Her cooking had given him a paunch, but he did not care about his paunch. He celebrated steaming pork carnitas falling into tender riots on his tortillas. He drooled like a dog when the chiles rellenos were searing on the flame, their caustic smoke announcing them to the world, their fat bellies gurgling with yellow cheese as they wore their egg-batter coats into the frying pan. He crunched a hundred fried tortillas awash in pico de gallo salsa and crushed avocado wedges with lime. He sucked goat cheese off the tips of his fingers; he sucked salt and chile powder off orange slices; he sucked marrow from deer bones; he sucked coffee out of his incredible whiskers. His whiskers threw small bolts of white across his lip now, and he also did not care about these. He slung his pistolas low, like the Iberians had in far El Paso. He used eyeglasses to read, las antiparras, but he didn't complain about this either. Perhaps, oh, if there were the slightest quibble, it would be that his tender, his holy, his wicked Gabriela had limited his access to liquor. Of course, he found his ways. A barn could hide much brandy. His one glass of delightful port wine with supper was often his twentieth drink of the day.

He was busy again! Fences. Cows. He hired and fired workers before there was any work to be done. He busied himself in exquisite misery with great ledgers where wavering lines of brown numbers danced as he held his head and delightedly cursed his fate. He had dung on his boots again—and a woman who did not allow him to track it in the house. He had money. If he could rope the money and brand it, he would.

He rode a savage little pony that Venado Azul had brought him from the desert playas of eastern Arizona. The pony was never tired and never scared, ignored lightning and thunder, stomped rattlesnakes to death, chewed through hitching posts, and stripped paint off the sides of buildings with his great yellow teeth. The animal mounted cows, donkeys, other horses. He ate books. The pony hated pigs but loved the barn cat, and they spent many hours in confabulations behind the stacked hay bales. Tomás named him Caballito Urrea, and the pony was not alone; all the animals had apparently been adopted by the family. The bull was El Toro Urrea. The sow was La Cochita Urrea. The green parrot was Periquito Urrea, and he was apparently an egomaniac, for he spent his days announcing "Periquito! Periquito!" to the world. Perhaps he thought they were all named Periquito too. The chickens, alas, did not earn family names, though Teresita and the horde of small Urrea children did grant them titles in secret ceremonies: Misteriosa, Feather Brain, El Drumsticks, Aunt Ca-Ca Maker, Mr. Ochoa.

Tomás busied himself with the colorful town up-mountain from them. Clifton's elite found him delightful, and they were insatiably curious about the Saint. Moved yet a bit baffled by her enthusiasm for miners and house girls and burrito makers in smoky little kitchens. Dr. Burtch, the great physician of the town, often sat on the porch and chatted with Teresita about things medical. She narrated various recipes for potions that he could experiment with in his clinic.

Tomás had barely mentioned in his various enthusiastic outbursts that very few fanatics came to their door, aside from the insistent Dr. Burtch. He had paused long enough to congratulate himself on his brilliance—who was going to drag all the way up these mountains?

Especially if they were dying! Ha. It must be sad to be them, he told himself. But he put it all out of his mind because there was work to be done. There were horses to ride, neighbors to cajole, trees to fell, a lumber mill to be designed. He telegraphed Aguirre and requested his assistance.

⁂

Caballito Urrea merely tolerated Tomás, but he seemed to enjoy Teresita. He had many opportunities to know her well—her boredom was complete. She had so little to do. Her father was far too busy to even notice her. And Gabriela, well—she was a mother, and a stepmother, and a wife. She was so adult, suddenly. Who did she think she was? She and Tomás muttered little endearments to each other that others couldn't hear, and they flounced around giggling like chulos. What kind of behavior was that?

But Tomás had been drunk with Gaby since he'd first seen her all those years ago in her father's rude little roadside eatery. Smitten by her hair and her saucy attitude and by something else ineffable, some feminine magic Teresita had studied but failed to comprehend. Whatever it was, it was enough to pry Tomás from his marriage to the formidable Loreto Urrea and engage him in this vast romance, this epic of delights. Teresita had never known what to think of her father making off with one of her girlhood friends. It was baffling. Irritating. But it was... Tomás.

Little Anita tried to follow Teresita around, but she was impatient with her sister. Anita thought Teresita could teach her things. But Teresita was not yet ready to be Huila. She loved the girl, but really. In the parlor, Anita made her demands known.

"Teach me. Take me with you."

"Go away," Teresita scolded. "You're bothering me."

"I want to learn."

"This is not for children."

"You were a child, Teresita."

"Yes, and look how I turned out! Now scat."

Tomás overheard this conversation and pulled Teresita aside after Anita had huffed upstairs.

"Not for her," he said.

"What is not for her?"

"This, this God business of yours."

He stood shaking his head with a sour look on his face.

"God?" she said.

"God!"

He looked like he was smelling something foul. "I don't want you spoiling this house with your fanatic God complex."

She reeled.

"Do you hate God so deeply?" she asked.

"I hate your obsessions. I want them to be absent from now on. No sainthood in my house."

"Father!" she cried. "It is my calling!"

"No. No. Not here, not now." He stormed out of the room, then stomped back and held a finger in her face. "Yes, you were the Queen of the Yaquis. What did it get you? Nothing!" He crossed his arms. So did she. "What will you be now? Queen of America?"

He had the audacity to laugh in her face and dismiss her rudely by walking away.

So Teresita had cause to lead the little Apache pony out of the corral and leap upon his back on many days. His skin would quiver when she mounted, as though her body were sending an electrical charge through his. The climb did not impress him. Crags and defiles were his steady diet—he swallowed miles tirelessly. He knew mountains.

All up in those high hills were Mexican copper miners and Indians. Over in the hamlet of May Queen, she visited the Garcia family. Their father, Don Bonifacio the Elder, had just broken his ankle at the Morenci copper pit, and without his efforts, the family could not afford to eat. Yes, the mountain was paradise. But even in paradise, the Mejicanos were often hungry.

She set his ankle and rubbed aromatic herbs upon it to lessen the swelling. Then she bound it tightly in long dark roots with soil still clinging to them, with crushed leaves soaked in alcohol packed directly on the flesh, and then wrapped the whole thing in white cloth. He would always walk with a cane, but he would walk.

She dropped by the Calvillo home, the Fernandez house, was delighted to meet Aguirres who had never heard of Don Lauro. The Dawsons had secretly helped Apache warriors escape the cavalry in the old days, and they cooked her beans with fried nopales. She drank tea and coffee and orange juice. She ate pan dulce and cookies and slices of sweet potato pie. Doña Calvillo took to calling her La Cookies. The neighbors in that Morenci block made it, as they made everything, into Spanish: La Cúquis.

She crept through valleys no one had homesteaded. She shivered deliciously on the banks of small creeks that fed into the San Francisco River. Secret tributaries where trout loafed in shadows beneath trees that had arrowheads in their heartwood. She perched on boulders in the clear streams and watched the trout drift backward with the current until they got near a drop-off, where the water — like languid soft- ened green glass — swelled and foamed white and plunged. And when the fish were almost to the point where they would be dashed backward down the falls, they would flick their tails lazily and shoot upstream to begin again. Teresita, drinking yerba buena tea from her flask, always laughed when the fish seemed to look at one another and ask, *How did you like that?*

One day, she discovered a New Mexican gold miner named Silver City Slats. "For my rib bones pokin' out! I was al'ays skinny!" He had poached a calf from Tomás's field. She didn't care. The stinky old man walked like a mule and had one milky eye.

"I can fix your eye," she offered.

"What's wrong with my eye?"

He delighted her by uncovering his simmering pot of son-of-a-bitch stew.

"This here's my own recipe."

It was made of tongue, brain, kidneys, marrow, and stomach lining. Cooked with vicious red chiles from Hatch. He'd cut some carrots, wild onions, and watercress into it. Added a few roots and a purple turnip. He served himself a great glob of stew on a tin plate and was astounded when Teresita turned down his invitation to grub with him.

"Find any gold?"

"I'm inches away."

"How long have you looked?"

"Twenny year."

She rode on.

No one knew where she was, so no one worried about where she went. She stood on the lip of the copper mine pit watching hunched men the color of earth struggle up and down the dirt ramps. On the far side of Morenci, she and Caballito Urrea found ancient stone circles and squares, the ruins of eldritch homes of a people who had, perhaps, seen Coronado himself and his gleaming conquistadores struggling into the mountains. They might have died at the Spaniards' hands. She found a half-shell temple that had a small altar cupped within it, and on the altar, a mummified rattlesnake. She knew it to be sacred, but if the good people of Clifton found it, they might see it differently.

It wasn't lost on her that some of the mountain católicos did not approve of her. They were calling her the Witch of Cabora rather than the Saint. *Witch, Saint*—neither meant much to her. Still, it shook her profoundly when she'd been buying some licorice in the Hygienic Market and a child had whispered, "¡Es la bruja!" and her mother had grabbed the child's hand and yanked her away from Teresita's side. Better to keep the village of the ancients a secret. If she was being selfish, so be it. It gave her a place to pray.

Caballito Urrea spent his time eating columbines and yellow wildflowers. The only ones who could bother them here were ground squirrels, which waddled up to sit beside Teresita and wait for her to distribute cherries or peanuts. Whistling little fussbudgets.

And the ghosts. But the ghosts kept to themselves and stayed out of sight.

Sometimes she slept in the sun with the Apache war pony standing over her, sniffing the air. She was very tired. She found that if she stared at a small nugget of cloud in the sky, she could make it unfold and spread out above her. The clouds opened their wings like hawks, hovered, drifted away. And, when she was absolutely sure no one would see her, she cried.

꙳

To avoid censure, Segundo called Dolores his wife, and they moved into a small clapboard house to the side of the church, close enough to the rail lines to hear the clanging and chuffing of the trains. Groaning ore trains came right through the center of Clifton, carrying their precious green rock down to the burning plains. Segundo liked the sounds of trains. They made him happy. He liked to sit at the picturesque little station and smoke and watch the locomotives come and go.

But nothing made him happier than Dolores. He called her mi chatita, for she did have a bit of a pug nose. He was convinced that all men desired her, and he turned nervous from keeping an eye on her whenever they walked to the store or went to church. As everyone else was praying, Segundo was casting an outraged eye all about him thinking, ¡Pinches cabrones! Thinking: I see you, you filthy little bastard! It made him tense. One of the Smith family noted to the padre after Mass: "He's a tetch snorty."

And Dolores, who had never felt love in her life, was blessed with utter amnesia. She had no memory of her former ways and suddenly believed herself to have always been an upright Catholic woman of the highest moral standing. For her own sanity, she stayed away from the tremendous doings at the Urrea ranchito. She preferred to believe that Tomás had never existed and was now being played by a handsome actor.

Teresita meant to ask Tomás how he felt about Segundo and Dolores, but she didn't get a chance. Breakfasts were boisterous affairs with wiggling children arrayed along each side of the table—some calling Gabriela Mámi and some calling her Doña and some calling her Gaby. It amused Teresita to call her Mother, and Gaby in turn was delighted to call her my child, and Gaby sat there glowing like the Madonna at her end of the table, Segundo as crusty as a bowl of chicharrónes enjoying his second morning meal at Tomás's left hand. Teresita often took her food in the kitchen with the cook, Mrs. Smith. She was a virtuoso of this new thing the Urreas had never seen before, los pancakes. They called them panquéquis. Mrs. Smith baffled everyone by calling them splatter-dabs.

Eggs, brown and still warm from Misteriosa and Aunt Ca-Ca Maker, fatback bacon slabs, fried beans, cheeses, onions, tortillas cooked in lard and lying like tawny magic carpets beneath the drooling eggs, diced nopal cactus, melons, oranges, coffee, and watery milk. A platter of pan dulce, all pale yellows and tans and pinks and sparkling with sugar. Teresita was stung that nobody seemed to notice she was standing at the chopping block eating her fruits and her cream clots and sweet rolls, but her father was suddenly out the door with comedic bellows and outrageous orders barked at scuffling men from Solomonville and Safford, the whole ruckus drowned out by hammering and shouting and cattle lowing and horse shrieks.

Then, lunch: fried steaks, gravied pork chops, and more beans, more tortillas, bowls of fideo soup, chicken legs—poor Mr. Ochoa was dismembered for the platter—fried tater wedges, great stacks of chiles and jícama in lime juice and leaves of lettuce under dribbles of oil and lemon and salt, cilantro, pickled hot pepper carrots, boiled eggs crunchy with salt and blushing pink from chile powder, deviled eggs (another Mrs. Smith secret project), tomato slices from the backdoor vine, yellow rice with bits of onion and festive red tatters of fried tomato, more coffee and milk and now tea and sarsaparilla in bottles and orange sodas and clay pots of steaming hot chocolate. Fish soup and fish albóndigas and catfish fried in cornmeal on Fridays, the barn cat finding ingenious ways to invade the house and lurk conspiratorially under the table on these evenings. Bowls of canned peaches ended these feasts, along with ginger and cinnamon cookies in the shapes of animals, chocolate squares and rum cakes and strange things called scones all studded with raisins that Tomás did not like one bit. Visitors often joined the tribe for these lunches—that ol' Dr. Burtch ate like a sparrow—and Teresita was of greater interest to strangers than to the family itself. Before she could engage her father in a satisfying debate about *Dracula* or the latest attempted raid by Teresistas on Ojinaga, it was time for the siesta.

The children, who were Americans and didn't appreciate the great Mexican traditions, scattered to their games and their sports and their chores while Tomás and Gabriela retired to their upstairs boudoir. Teresita found it wise to exit before the inevitable sounds of creaking and thumping headboards resonated through the parlor and caused the cook and the house girl to blush and frown and secretly laugh.

"Them Urreas," Mrs. Smith confided to Mr. Smith, "is rutters."

Suppers came late, Sinaloa style. After so much gluttony in daylight, the nine o'clock meal was light. Cooked pumpkin or squash, served cool. Puddings. Breads. Melon and strawberries in cream. Milk all around.

And to bed.

When school started, Teresita helped Gaby get everyone in order and watched them head off like a meandering line of sad goslings up the hill to Segundo's wagon. The old pistolero didn't seem to mind delivering children to school at all. Segundo didn't seem to mind anything anymore.

Everyone was extremely happy.

Except Teresita.

Twenty-Six

YOUNG AL FERNANDEZ WAS a skinny kid who skipped school to go to the station and watch trains. He lived in the house with big flowerpots on either side of the door farther up Segundo's street. He loved trains so much that the engineer of the passenger line gave him a striped trainman's cap. He wore it every day, and even when his father hid it from him, he'd find it and get out the back door so he could catch the afternoon ore hauler as it pulled like a giant rattling curtain across the drama that was slumbering Clifton. Al knew everybody, and he knew everything. He was a historian by nature. Lacking a jailhouse, the miners had dug a deep, narrow shaft and closed it off with bars, and that's where bad men and drunks were locked to wait for their trials. When it was empty, he sometimes snuck down there to hide from patrolling schoolmarms hunting him down.

Al sat near Segundo while the old man smoked and basked like an ancient lizard as he waited for the train to come. Al stretched out his legs in emulation of the pistolero and they silently took the sun together. After a time, Segundo wordlessly donated a bottle of strawberry soda to the kid. The closest they got to talking was Segundo's laughter when the truant officer came for Al and hauled him away.

※

Al led Teresita up the slopes to a hidden cave. They squeezed in and found a tarnished Spanish helmet inside. "Don't touch it," he said. "I think it's cursed."

Teresita felt curses flying all around them. She believed the earth was angry because of the mines. She felt the restless spirits of the dead wandering the hills. The anger of the conquistadores. It was frightening.

Her father would never go to Mass, but the rest of them did and sat there knowing perfectly well that they were all living in sin. Worse, her father was lying to the American government—he was trying to register Gaby as a U.S. citizen and claimed all the children in the house were theirs! That they had been married for years! Everyone knew perfectly well that he was married to Loreto in Mexico. But nobody seemed to care. "All the Mexicans do it," he said in one of their rare chats. "You always lie to the government." Yet they called *her* bad names behind her back? It wasn't hard to see devils in the air.

Through Segundo, Al met the Santa de Cabora. He was shy. You didn't just walk up to a witch and say hey. But he knew she was historic.

One day, Al showed her down the narrow prisoner shaft on the west side of town. It was empty for the moment, and she slipped down, feeling choked by the stone tunnel. At the bottom, it opened up into a small cell with a bench carved in the raw cliff rock. She could see up a long borehole to the barred round window at the top. An eye of blue sky looked down at her; in its center, a dark pupil formed by a hawk. The stones were unhappy; she could smell it.

Teresita had to bless this mountain range.

She had Al lead her on a climb up the two highest of the San Francisco peaks. Each climb took an entire day. Al was all too happy to miss school.

At the top of each peak, she placed a wooden cross she had fashioned from her father's fence slats and painted white. She placed the first cross so it faced east, and the second so it faced west, the happy town resting between them, blessed at sunrise and sunset. She prayed and murmured and wept at each cross while Al Fernandez sat on stones and watched her, eating rock candy and wondering if she was crazy or holy.

They came down the second peak in time for the evening train. Segundo was there with his wagon. Teresita saw Al off with a pat on the head and a handful of coins.

The boy doffed his engineer's hat once and nodded to Segundo, who merely lifted one corner of his mouth in response. They watched the kid trudge uphill to lie about another day at school. Teresita turned back and looked at Segundo.

Don Lauro stood beside the wagon, beaming.

"My child!" he cried.

She flung herself into his arms.

She had never been so happy to see anyone.

He patted her on the back.

"I am so happy you have come," she said.

"Are you crying, my child?"

"Only with joy, Uncle Lauro."

Segundo pursed his lips. He felt wise. Women were like that. He had learned this from his Chatita. These emotions they had. He nodded sagely at Aguirre.

"Teresa," Aguirre said, "I have a surprise for you."

She pulled back. She seemed as nervous as a sparrow to him. He gripped her arms and felt bones. Did nobody feed her up here?

"What is it?" she said.

"Me," said a voice behind her.

She turned around. A terrible fellow in a hideous red silk cowboy shirt festooned with gaudy roses and piping stood smirking at her. He wore absurd violet boots made from some sort of alligator skin. He wore a yellow cavalry bandana at his neck, and his pants had thin red stripes. He was a one-man parade. He held a toothpick in his mouth, and his hat was black with a white feather in its band. He smiled. Gold teeth under a pencil-thin black mustache.

"¿Qué pasa, flaca?" he drawled.

Flaca! How dare he call her skinny! She turned to Aguirre.

"That's Johnny Urrea," he said. "He joined me in El Paso."

"That's what I call myself," said the dandy.

"He wanted to come see you all."

"Is he a reporter?" Teresita asked.

"I'm right here," Johnny Urrea said. "You people. Still talking about cabrones like they wasn't even there. That ain't holy, is it."

"I'm sorry," she said, face flushing.

"I'm a card player," Johnny offered. "Pistolero. A powerful rancher too." He laughed.

She stared at him.

"Give me a hug," he said. "Just don't paralyze me this time with your little 'powers.'"

"Ay, Dios mío," she said. *"Buenaventura."*

"Who else?" he confessed. "Really, sister, are you stupid or what?"

She went to him and gave him a tentative hug.

He smelled like cologne.

"Our father," he noted, "is going to be impressed when he sees me."

She thought: I doubt it.

※

When she was small, still undiscovered by Tomás and still unwanted, Buenaventura had appeared on the rancho looking for his father. He was a terrible child, but he was her only protector when things were bad—and things were always bad. He had never gotten over his resentment when Tomás took her in but refused him any measure of love or acceptance. He secretly thought of himself as the Bastard Son. And he had used that rage to fuel himself. Frankly, Segundo was more of an influence on the boy than his own father, since Segundo was the only one who had ever taken him in.

Years later, his jealousy pushed him to mock his bastard sister at every turn. Unlike his great father, he did not love Indians. Her Indian ways appalled him and seemed affected and stupid. Little Miss Has Her Own Bedroom wearing her rebozo, talking Yaqui. Little Miss Father Buys Me New Shoes. While his mother coughed out her lungs alone, and he slept under bushes until Segundo took him in and fed him beef.

He loved her. He loved Tomás. Why did they not love him? What had he done? He had been a hero to her! If he hadn't saved her when she was lying beaten and snotty in a pigpen, if he hadn't carried her, smelling like pee and mud, through the night and to that damned witch's door, to that nasty Huila, then Teresita wouldn't even be the Saint. He had fought for the ranch. He had fought for his father. But there was never anything left for him.

Yes, he was illegitimate — Tomás's bastard son. But so was Teresita. Why had she been accepted when he had not? And when her mother's family had balked and mistreated her, Buenaventura was there. Who was there for him? Who had ever taken him in when he was hungry?

One day — a day he regretted, and not simply because it had cost him — he had vexed Teresita and humiliated her by screaming insults about her Indian blood. And she, even then feeling the surge of powers in her body, lost control and — when he thought of it, he winced. His shoulders hunched. Because he had nothing to compare it to. It was a bolt of pure anger. It was cold, and it was hot. It flew from her eyes, or her hands, or her gut, or her heart, or the awful Indian spirits he was convinced followed her in a warrior band. It pierced him and stole his speech and froze his mouth and paralyzed his limbs. Even now, years later, he walked with a limp. It had been harder to demand respect since that day. Then they were gone, and he was the boss. And this is how he became a dandy, Fast Johnny Urrea.

He still feared her.

*

It was an uncomfortable scene at the dinner table. Tomás had sent Gaby and the children away — he wasn't about to contaminate them with the foolery of this swaggering nitwit. Besides, when Gaby considered the various partners Tomás had left scattered behind him, she grew sullen and refused to make love to him. Her belly swelling with his next heir was driving him mad with desire. He could not keep his hands off her belly, her swelling bottom. Her breasts were still heavy and veiny from the last child. He had to shake his head and refocus on

Buenaventura, who happily poured himself another cup of coffee. Teresita came from the kitchen and placed a plate of pig cookies before him. Those pig-shaped gingerbread cookies were every child's favorite.

He sneered.

"I hate that shit," he said, then gobbled one and slurped his black coffee to wash it down.

Out on the porch, Aguirre and Segundo sat in rocking chairs, maintaining an uncomfortable truce.

"Jules Verne is erudite," Aguirre was saying. "But he is no match for the fevered nightmares to be found in Wells!"

"Goddamn," Segundo agreed falsely, blowing smoke.

Teresita grinned, laid a hand on her brother's arm.

He jumped.

Tomás eyed them both, raised his eyebrows at Teresita.

"So," he said.

"Yup," Fast Johnny said. "I'm through with Mexico. It's a dung pile."

Tomás twiddled his fingers.

"I'm on my way to California. You want to live, Pop? San Francisco's for you!"

Pop? thought Tomás. *Pop?*

"You," said Johnny, nudging Teresita, who gazed upon him with adoration that he could not see. "You need to shake the dirt off your feet, skinny. Come to San Francisco. I'm going to catch a ship to China."

"Oh!" she said.

"Absolutely not," said Tomás. "And what brings you here?"

"Business," said Johnny, smiling broadly. "I took care of the ranch."

"How so?"

"Sold it."

Tomás simply stared.

"You . . . sold . . . my ranch."

Johnny gulped some coffee, licked the crumbs of his cookie off his lips. "Sold it. You ain't coming back."

"It wasn't yours to sell."

"It was all mine to sell," Johnny corrected him. "I was your only heir."

"Heir!" Tomás roared.

Teresita shivered. Segundo clomped inside.

"Something wrong?" he said.

"Kill this little bastard!" Tomás cried.

Johnny grinned, shrugged, leaned over and spit on the floor.

"Hey," said Segundo.

"Hey," scolded Teresita.

"You can't kill me," Johnny said. "I am *your* little bastard." He laughed. He pointed his fingers like a pistol and shot Tomás. "Daddy!" he announced.

He threw an immense bundle of worn bills on the table.

"I took all the money from the sale of Cabora to Don Miguel, el patrón. He gave me my cut." He gestured to his clothes. "I'm spending it real well. And he asked me to drop off this cut to you, dear Father."

He slammed his hand on the table once and rose.

"I'll borrow a horse," he said. "I don't feel like we're going to have a family reunion. Besides, I hate the smell of animal dung. You should do something about that."

He flicked Teresita's hair as he went by.

"I just made you rich," he said. He leaned down. "Meet me in San Francisco."

He started to whistle as he stepped out the door and skipped down the steps.

Aguirre peeked in the room.

"Is it safe to come in?" he asked.

They all shouted, "No!"

Twenty-Seven

ANITA BORROWED A DONKEY from the paddock and followed Teresita and Caballito Urrea uphill. They veered off the road and cut along a deer path that switchbacked over raw slanted cliffs. Swallows tumbled out of cliff nests and cut the sky with their scissor tails. Vultures had wing tips that seemed to be reaching for the tops of pine trees like ten-inch fingers, and small angry birds harassed them until they flew out of sight. Crows were irritated at the riders coming through their territory and voiced insults and questions as they went from spire to spire, dead tree to ledge, looking down at the intruders and then looking at one another in apparent disbelief. An escapee yearling cow was feral and sly in the bushes, thinking itself invisible because its head was buried in greenery.

Teresita, far ahead, was in her white dress; she'd pulled up her skirts indecently, and her brown legs were bare to the sun. Anita did the same, though the donkey's spine felt like it was going to split her bottom in two as she bounced and jounced after her sister, and its fur, so soft at first, started to burn her thighs and sting the insides of her knees. This riding—overrated. But it was another gleaming day in the mountains. The air felt thin as paper, as if their faces might tear it and pass through into something beyond.

Teresita ignored the little scamp following her. She was wandering over the side hills and the abandoned camps scattered in gray planks beyond the winding rail lines that seemed to swirl down the mountains like vast carnival rides. Her horse, given free rein, moseyed ever upward. Teresita scrubbed the visions of Buenaventura out of her eyes, squeezed the memories of faces, names, whole years out of her head. Oh, to be free of them all—Cruz, Huila, Buenaventura, her terrible aunt and her flailing wooden spoon. She wondered where Harry Van Order had gone, he of the blushing-little-boy face and the hopeless cowlicks. And John, so mean, so tall, away to Chicago, chasing dollars and finery.

They drifted up and up until they were roaming the old slopes of Shannon Hill and its cemetery, the whole hill a home of the dead. There were houses not far from the old graveyard, but the graveyard was where Caballito Urrea took her. He was not interested in mestizos' homes and their smells. He was interested, like Teresita, in herbs and flowers. Horses understood healers: healers smelled like plants.

He shuffled along the old fence, and he sampled the weeds outside the boneyard. A happy dog galloped along between the graves, chasing a twirling scrap of paper that he caught in his fool mouth and released in the wind so he could chase it again. His barks were small as stones and fell dull on the ground. It was a gravel lot, curving with the slow curl of the world's horizon, silent save for two small boys tossing a béisbol at each other across the far dirt road. Their mother came out and shouted at them — Teresita heard the door smack tartly as they went in. She sat astride her horse and waited for her insistent little sister to catch up.

The graves were sad, yet the place felt friendly. Lonely, but not unwelcoming. The endless wind of the peaks whispering and sighing through corroded iron plaques and crooked stones. She squinted. A lone man stood out there among the farthest crosses, thin, tall, with long hair blowing around his head. For a startling moment, he looked like Cruz Chávez. But no. He was thinner. Fairer. Clean-shaven. Black vest and white shirt. He turned his head and looked at her, but she could not tell from this distance what expression was on his face.

Anita trotted up. The donkey was not happy about the climb. It huffed and stomped its foot and made disgruntled donkey noises.

"Hush," said Anita.

They dismounted.

"Ow. My butt."

"That's what you get," Teresita scolded her. "If you think I'm rubbing potions on your nalgas, you're crazy."

Anita giggled.

"Why did you follow me?" Teresita demanded.

"I want to learn."

"I am not your teacher."

"You're the Saint."

"I am not a saint."

"Well, I love you."

"Oh," said Teresita.

She put her hand on top of Anita's head.

"Are you not afraid?" she asked, gesturing toward the graves.

"No. Not with you here."

Teresita shook her head.

"Don't put your faith in me, child," she said. She began to walk. She crossed her arms as though to keep the wind from entering her chest. Anita could smell her. She loved that smell—sometimes, when her big sister was out, she snuck in her room and sniffed the roses from the pillows on her bed.

"I am as empty as these graves," Teresita said.

"Ay, Teresita."

Anita rushed to her and hugged her—her arms came around Teresita's hips.

"When I die," Teresita said, "you make sure I'm buried well."

"You won't die."

"Oh, I will. I won't be here long, Anita. Not very long."

The crazy dog joined them. He was trotting sideways, wagging furiously. He offered Anita the scrap of paper in his mouth, but when she reached for it, he tore away and jumped around with it.

"Idiot!" Anita yelled.

They laughed.

He crouched before them and dared them to take his paper.

Teresita shook her finger at him.

He twirled joyfully.

She shook her head. She was distracted. She had been staring across the bare ground at the Indian man. They could hear his voice. He was singing.

"What is he singing?" Anita said.

Teresita shook her head. Shrugged.

"Let's get closer," she said.

"Let's spy on him," said Anita.

Teresita took her hand and walked in his direction without walking directly toward him. She kept an eye on Caballito Urrea—escape was always a concern now. She needed to know she could leap aboard and gallop away, dust blowing in an attacker's face. She would not harm anyone intending to harm her, but she would kill anyone for hurting Anita.

They walked, studiously reading what stones they could see among the weathered planks and rusted iron markers.

His voice came in the dusty breeze as if it too were dusted.

Teresita froze in place and gripped Anita's hand more tightly. Her eyes grew wide. She stared at the ground.

"What is it?" Anita asked. "What, Teresita?"

"Maso bwikam," Teresita breathed.

"What?"

"Shh. Deer songs. Shh."

They listened.

Aa sewailo malichi yewelu sika
Yo chikti yo sea yeula sika
Sewailo malichi rewelu sika
Yo chikti yo sea huya aniwapo
Yeulu sikaaa...

A tear fell from Teresita's eye. Anita watched it roll to the edge of her big sister's chin, tremble, and fall.

The dog came over to them and sat at their feet.

"What is it, Tére?" she asked.

"It is the story of a deer, a fawn. Covered in flowers. Out in the wilderness of flowers, going from blossom to blossom."

Anita looked across at the singer. He was staring at them. She waved at him. He nodded.

Teresita had thought she would never hear the mother tongue again.

The singing stopped.

"Uh-oh," said Anita. "Here he comes."

"Look busy," Teresita said.

They turned away from him and tried to make it appear that the ground was deeply fascinating.

He walked forward, stopped a respectful distance from them. He crossed his arms behind his back and gazed at them.

"I work for your father," he said. "I am Guadalupe."

"I am Teresita."

He grinned.

"Yes. I know who you are. And this little one?"

"Anita," Anita said, raising her chin to him.

"My little sister," said Teresita.

He nodded.

They looked at each other.

"That dog," he said. "His name is Wo'i."

" 'Coyote,' " Teresita translated for her sister. "Is he yours?" she asked.

He shook his head.

"Then how do you know his name?"

"I just named him."

The dog looked up and wagged.

Anita liked it that the man and her big sister were chuckling.

"You," he said to Teresita. "You were in Sea Ania?" The flower-world.

"Perhaps. I was somewhere."

"Did you see God?"

"I did."

"What can you tell me of God?"

She smiled.

"God is not a white man."

They burst out laughing.

Guadalupe said, "Don't tell me God's a Mexican!"

"No, no. I don't think so."

Anita's head was swiveling between them.

"He might be Sioux."

"Ay, ay, ay," Guadalupe said. Then: "Was Sea Ania as they say?"

"It was."

He nodded.

"Deer?"

"Deer."

He smiled.

"Water?"

"Plenty of water. The grass was like a thick blanket."

He nodded.

"Gracias," he said and turned and walked away. He stopped, turned back, and called: "Your father keeps you from your destiny." He walked on. They watched him recede in the distance and vanish over the lip of the hill.

"He had no horse," noted Anita.

Teresita smiled.

"Maybe he flew."

They laughed.

As they walked, Wo'i followed them, ferociously guarding them from weeds and the horse and donkey.

Anita said, "What was that? That...Ania?"

"Sea Ania. The flower-world."

"Flower-world?"

"The other side."

Anita looked at her.

"The world in the east," Teresita said. "The world that mirrors our world. Has no one taught you anything, child?"

And she bent to a trembling little weed and started telling Anita stories about the plants and the deer and the movement of grace that flows like water across the sky and lands in our hands, and then she made the girl rub her hands together briskly and raise them to the weed to feel its billowing, silent singing. Their hands were their ancestors' hands, moving through the air and back, back, hovering like prayers through ten thousand years.

Twenty-Eight

TOMAS WAS NOT HAPPY about the dog. Wo'i sat on the porch at Teresita's feet grinning at the world, thumping his tail when horses, donkeys, the pig, the cats went by. However, when a buckaroo appeared, or a mill worker with a pine-tar-dripping plank, he'd set off in demented assaults, yowling and barking and trying to bite the man's heels. From his seat, Tomás tried to kick him, but Wo'i seemed to find this hilarious, and he scooted sideways and started his moronic dancing, begging for more kicks to dodge. "Are you responsible for this?" Tomás asked Teresita. She shrugged and ate her orange slices with a vague smile. His moods, he reflected, could still be amusing. He flicked his cigarillo stub at the dog and lit another. "Filthy beast," he said. Suddenly, Wo'i spied an unfortunate Dr. Burtch coming through the gate and sped off in a frenzy of rage and chased the doctor back out of the yard and up the road. Tomás burst out laughing.

"Perhaps," he noted, "the dog is not as bad as I thought."

He said to her, "What's wrong with these Americanos? They don't have any drive—nobody thought of ranching cattle here before. Milk, Teresita! Right now these poor cabrones have to bring milk up the mountain! I'll give them their own fresh milk."

"Perhaps you can bring them bees as well," she said.

He stroked his whiskers.

"Perhaps."

She was delighted to be chatting with her father as if nothing strange had ever happened. She knew the moment would be brief, and it was delicate. It was made of ashes. It could blow away in an instant. So she busied herself with her bowl of sliced oranges and relaxed as he boasted.

"Milk! And firewood! Can you believe they buy lumber and ship it here? And they have to scrounge about in the hills for firewood for the winter. Ha! I can give them wood, and I can make sure they don't cut down their trees to heat their asses when it's snowing." He shook his head, raised his hand, and smoked. "They needed me here to organize them, my dear."

Wo'i focused their attention when Guadalupe the deer-song singer appeared at their porch steps. He didn't remove his hat. He had his hands in his pockets. Tomás found this insolent in and of itself, but Wo'i simply wagged his tail and shuffled over to the untidy Indian and butted his head against Guadalupe's knee. Tomás stood up and glowered.

Guadalupe called to Teresita, "¿Qué hubo, Cúquis?"

Cookies? Cookies? Tomás felt for his pistola, but it was inside, hanging on a peg by the staircase.

"¡Lárgase de aquí!" Tomás scolded.

Teresita smiled at Guadalupe.

"¡Andale!" Tomás shouted. "I'll fire you the next time you speak to my daughter like that."

Guadalupe looked sideways at him and dipped his head.

"Whatever you say," he said.

"You're goddamned right, whatever I say, desgraciado!" Tomás was red in the face. He threw another kick at Wo'i. "And take this jackal with you!"

Guadalupe made kissing sounds at the dog and backed away. He winked at Teresita and walked, very slowly, down the slope. Wo'i followed, casting accusatory looks at them over his shoulder.

"Who—in the hell—was that," Tomás said, not really asking. He stomped inside, and she could hear him buckling on his gunbelt. He stormed around in there, shouting: "Coffee! Where is my newspaper! Did I or did I not just ask politely for some *coffee!*"

A mother with a shawl over her head came forward, bent at the waist. She struggled from the gate to the porch. Her body moved with painful, mechanical ticktocks, like the pendulum of an old clock. Her face was gray. Her brow was knotted. Teresita saw the shadows of clouds around her head. She was dying.

She called, "Santa Teresa. I have an issue of blood. I have great pain."

Teresita wiped her hands on a cloth and raised them to the woman.

Oh, day of sunlight unfurling in waves like golden curtains in the breeze, day of white tree trunks and golden leaves, day of the river ringing in small bells and singing in voices from the back of a church; butterflies blew up from the gardens like colored paper; the air was sharp, almost cold, and it carried the scents of cut wood, smoke, flowers and animal dung, snow far above them, and water. The distant, amusing tang of a skunk wafted down the valley. Wo'i was apparently chasing another poor cowboy across a field—his demented barking echoed off the barn and the mill until the shriek of the spinning blades cutting pine trunks drowned him out.

"Come to me," she said. "I will ease your hurt."

The woman winced up the steps. Teresita did not help her. She watched the struggle, judging it. The woman said, "I have brought you a gift." She extended a cloth wrapped around sweetgrass and sage. Teresita claimed it without a word. She took the woman's hand and helped her sit gingerly in the chair. Teresita could smell the blood under her skirt.

"Ay," the woman said.

"Shh."

They sat quietly for a moment.

Teresita rose and stood before her.

"I am here," she said. "You are with me. Here, now. This pain, this disease — they were with you yesterday. But you are with me today. And here, there is no room for your pain. We invite it to go home."

She put her hands on either side of this harried, plain woman's face.

"You are so pretty," she said.

She ran her thumbs down either side of her face, sliding the wrinkled and beaten skin until it lay smooth.

"Blessed among women," Teresita said.

She kissed the woman's forehead.

"Daughter of God."

The woman was baffled, even alarmed. She had never been praised. She had never been blessed in this fashion. She trembled.

"Do you believe me?"

"I will if you say so."

"I say so."

She squeezed the woman's face and gently shook her head, slowly, almost imperceptibly.

"You," Teresita said in a whisper, "are holy. You are worthy of this day."

Teresita stared in her eyes as if she were going to enter her head through them and live there. The woman didn't blink. Teresita smiled at her.

"Do not be afraid," she said.

"I . . . am not."

"Good."

"I believe."

"Good."

She knelt at the woman's feet. Her knees popped. She smiled.

"Did you hear that?"

The woman found herself laughing. She had not laughed in weeks because the pain was so great. And the shame. The cloths under her skirt were already full.

Teresita shook her head.

"The knees are the first to go," she said.

"The knees and the hips!"

"Oh, I know it. Being a woman...hmm." Teresita shook her head again. They were both laughing as if they were at a garden party.

"Have an orange slice," Teresita said.

She put her left hand out and pressed it against the woman's belly. With her right hand, she made signs over the woman's head. She never got to the orange slices. She gasped and closed her eyes. She opened them and stared above the valley.

She could see eagles far over the peaks, and they were circling slowly in the endless wind.

Heat moved up her torso.

The woman's knees slammed shut, then sprang open.

Teresita touched her head.

"Oh," the woman said, and she began to weep.

"God," Teresita said, "give this mother back her blood."

Teresita could feel the sickness inside the womb swarming up the insides of her arms like dull brown smoke. She felt weak. It slithered, the smoke becoming a snake. The sickness coiled inside her, and she would have to pray and cleanse herself to move it out into the mud where it belonged. She dropped her head and reached out into the woman's agony and took hold of the slippery knot of the heart of the illness. It wanted to escape, to hide elsewhere in its victim, but Teresita's authority was complete. Her hands were tingling, burning with life. Her will could not be denied. "Come now," she said. "Come now and leave this good woman in peace."

The woman cried out once. She sobbed.

"Pain?" asked Teresita.

"Relief."

The woman hung her head down until it rested on Teresita's shoulder. Teresita put her arms around the slender shoulders. The woman's breath was bitter, but Teresita knew it would sweeten day by day.

"I love you," the woman said.

Tomás watched from the doorway and then silently crept back into the house.

Twenty-Nine

FIFTY DONKEYS ARRIVED IN a grouchy pack train led by arrieros from New Mexico who did not spare the whip. They came up the mountains in a straggling atajo, the old-time mule trains Tomás had once seen in the Yaqui hills of Sonora. Everything reminded him of everything else; his mind fluttered and flew, seemingly out of his skull, as it took in the great world. The thought of money brought it right back, however, to perch and focus where it belonged.

The arrieros were a scruffy bunch, and they hobbled about on bandy legs as if barely capable of walking. Once they were off the backs of their yellow-eyed mules, they were like crabs. They asked for food, pay, and a place to sleep. They called the bunks in the worker's dormitory cootie cages. Nobody knew what they were talking about.

Tomás immediately deployed the donkeys with fifty men leading into the hills. Each donkey had its own aparejo packsaddle, ready to carry its load of wood. Teresita guided wood scavengers to the many valleys, canyons, and wilderness defiles where she had found hundreds of fallen trees and old trunks ready to be collected and trimmed for firewood. It was an army. Among these wood hunters rode Guadalupe, but Teresita ignored him. Her father had made it quite clear that fraternizing with the workers was forbidden. The humor in this situation was not lost on her.

The year 1899.

A long season of peace. Four years in one place—it was hard to imagine. Teresita told Anita, "I wish life would speed up." Wisely, Anita said, "I don't know if that would be a good idea." As Don Lauro Aguirre might have stated in one of his broadsides, *The fair sisters of the mountains were about to learn whether this desire was wise or not.*

Aguirre had shipped a phonographic machine to Tomás. It was a sensation. No one in Clifton had ever seen such a device. They gathered in the parlor and requested the tune—the only tune—to be played again and again. Assenting, Tomás inserted the red wax cylinder in the maw of the contraption and spun its handle, whereupon the trebly notes of "A Hot Time in the Old Town" assaulted their ears. Gabriela found it quite irritating, but Teresita was utterly fascinated by this new technology. Later that year, the newest popular song in America arrived by post: "On the Banks of the Wabash, Far Away."

"¿Qué es un Wabash?" Tomás wanted to know.

The fame of the phonograph was so wide that it lured the Van Orders up from the flats to listen. It was a pleasant visit, with Juana and Teresita dancing to the herky-jerky music as the men drank, smoked, guffawed, and boasted. There had been no word from wicked John for a year, but Harry, Teresita's beau, had found true love and hoped to marry an Irish girl. Teresita hid her distress.

The Urreas also acquired the latest scientific breakthroughs—cold cereal and aspirin. Gaby could not get enough of the flaked corn, and she ate bowls of it for breakfast and lunch, much to Tomás's disgust. "Vegetarian!" he accused. Aspirin was of great interest to Teresita, for it offered to do some of her heavy work by way of a small pill. She welcomed it, testing its simplicity with her own monthly stomach pains, and found it did work.

They received magazines: the hilarious humor compendium *Life;* Gaby's favorite, *Good Housekeeping;* Teresita and Anita's delight, *National Geographic;* and Tomás's sacred *McClure's.* The occasional Sears, Roebuck catalogue came, and Segundo enjoyed sneaking peeks at the drawings of women in their underwear.

Life was so good that nobody even noticed the Spanish-American War had come and gone the year before. "Spaniards? Cubans?" Tomás said. "Pah!"

They were not left alone. Visitors to the Anglo mine owners and businessmen of Morenci and Clifton were inclined to stop by the Urrea ranch to see the "Girl Saint" they had read about in the newspapers. Dr. Burtch brought them to dinner, and Anita and the other children were constantly dolled up in precious outfits and made to parade about in rosy-cheeked, silent performances for heavily scented, high-hat-wearing gringos. The Englishmen, mine managers mostly, were hilarious. They had a faint stiffness about them that repeatedly parted like a curtain to reveal a stinging wit. The Irish were more like Mexicans and quite comfortable to be around. New Yorkers fascinated Teresita most; their funny, honking accents, yes—but also their head-spinning sophistication, the way they simply owned the room when they entered. They lived in her dream city, city of mystery and culture, towers, and, she had heard, a park full of tigers and bears.

Everyone loved the scratchy music machine.

Teresita stepped out onto the porch to escape one such crowded music party. The night was heavy with crickets and night birds. Frogs in the shallows raised a wild hosanna. She fanned herself—who knew that fine Englishmen and rich bankers could be so hot and sweaty? Life was full of wonders.

She sat on the steps of the porch.

And he was there.

"Cúquis," he said.

"Lupe."

He was tall against the stars.

"I was waiting for you."

"I see. Waiting like a coyote to strike his prey."

He was startled by this.

"I don't see it that way," he said.

Guadalupe Rodriguez kept to himself. He worked harder than any three of the other men together. But he seldom spoke or joined in the workers' celebrations. He stayed away from town, and he avoided church. Nobody even knew where he came from—he'd just appeared one day, carrying an ax and heading into the woods. He kicked a squat former shrimper from New Orleans out of his bunk and moved in and took a tin plate at feeding time and scooped up three servings of beans. He had a Winchester '73 that was bright and well oiled, and he produced a very old Buntline Special revolver that was about as long as Wo'i's leg. "Touch these," he said to the other workers one night, "and you die."

"Right," one of the men said in the dark. "Good night to you too."

Later:

"Pendejo."

The men snickered in their cots, but they did not touch Lupe's weapons.

Segundo assumed Tomás had hired him. Tomás thought Lupe was one of Segundo's Neanderthal henchmen. He just got in line on payday and accepted his small pouch of coins and went back to the bunkhouse to sleep.

She felt a thrill when she saw him. It made her feel strong to ignore him. But she longed to hear that accent, those occasional words in the mother tongue.

"I want to be with you," he said.

"You are right there."

"No. With you."

"Who else are you with, Lupe?"

"You think you are funny."

"I know I am funny."

He crossed his arms, kicked at the dirt.

"How's the dog?" she asked.

"He ran away."

"Shame. He was the best part of you."

"You're teasing me."

"Am I?"

He blew air out in a near whistle.

"Your father hates me," he said, perhaps angling for sympathy.

"Yep."

This took him aback as well.

"If he catches you creeping around here," she said, "he will ventilate you."

He snorted.

"I am a bad man," he said.

"I believe that."

"I can't be chased away so easily," he boasted.

She rubbed her face with both hands. Boys, boys, boys. How many boasts would she have to endure before she died? She stood, brushed off the back of her skirt, squared herself, and faced his shadowy bulk.

"Lupe?" she said. "You will have to do better than that." She yawned. "Frankly, that bored me. Now go away. Your mommy is calling."

She went inside and slammed the door.

She was smiling as the next round of dancing began.

⁂

The next time she saw him was down along the San Francisco's banks; she'd been following the river away from Clifton. It cut and wandered in these mountains on its way. It was rocky, hot, then turned a corner and fell in among cottonwoods and slanting pines and turned cool. Flowers exploded on the edges of the shade—blue and yellow, visited by fluttering little paper confetti that revealed itself to be butterflies and red dragonflies and golden-eyed water flies with great delicate wings. Wasps with hard stone-yellow backs fussed busily among the wild anise and watercress plants, snipping and scooping balls of mud from the black shore. Teresita could see small golden glitters in the mud. Rich dust of ore tumbling unseen out of the peaks. She loved that the wasps' nests would be decorated with gold and copper, the finest walls in the entire region.

As she walked near reeds, small frogs launched themselves with chirps of alarm, her stroll seeming to set off a great green popcorn cook-off.

Out of sight of the rancho, she found a place between the roots of an old oak that formed a seat. She nestled in it and rested her spine against the trunk of the tree. She asked the oak what it thought of the day.

Tomás would have suggested she be committed to an asylum if he heard that, but she knew that one's back should often press against a great wise tree. She could feel its profound age and patience through the cotton of her blouse. Besides, it was comfortable. Bees worked the weeds all around her. Humming and muttering. The water's whisper. The birds. The sun. She closed her eyes.

Something woke her. Her eyes opened slowly. She smiled at the day. She stretched. Her bones creaked, and she yawned, wide as a cat.

She looked downstream, and here he came. She could see his hat above the reeds. His oddly bouncing gait, the force of his movement. His head was down, his hat covering his face. He didn't seem to know she was there. He was carrying something.

He stepped through the wall of reeds and stopped. He carried a fawn in his arms. It still bore white speckles on its tawny back. It was tiny in his great embrace. The fawn turned and looked at her.

Lupe grinned up at her.

"Saint," he said.

He came forth and knelt and gently put the fawn down before her on wobbly legs.

He stroked its neck. Teresita put out her hand — the fawn licked it.

"Malichi," Lupe said softly — little fawn. "Dogs got his mother."

She put her hand on its back. It nudged her with its nose.

"Here we are in the huya," he said. The wilderness. She looked at him. "Things happen. Sad things."

She was in love with the tiny deer.

"Can you save him?" Lupe asked.

"I'll try."

He nodded.

"I will carry him for you," he said and took the fawn back in his arms and rose taller than the trees. He put out one hand and took hers and helped her to stand.

By the time they passed through the rancho's fence, they were laughing.

Thirty

MALICHI FOLLOWED TERESITA around wagging his little tail. When Tomás saw them go by, he cried, "¡Epa! ¡Teresita! Did you use your powers to turn your dog into a deer?" He didn't even wait for a response. He didn't want to know the answer.

Segundo, who was becoming more useless the older and happier he got, sat in the rocker on the porch with a pot of coffee and a platter of sweet rolls.

"Boss don't like the deer," he noted mildly.

"No," she said.

Malichi stuck his head under her skirt and lifted it. Segundo regarded her knees. He smiled benevolently, offering his blessings upon the earth.

"I can slaughter him for you," he offered.

She swept Malichi into her arms and hurried away.

"I like venison," he muttered as he picked raisins out of his scone and stretched out his aching legs. Ah, the sun. He chewed and sighed and counted the hours until he could return to plump little Dolores.

※

1899/California

From: El gran chingón

Skinny, ¿qué pasa?

I seen everything in sant fransissco. Its more than our big father seen anywere. He think hes so smart and hes not.

I meet the chinos you love so much. They got
duck with heads on in windows you can eat all
crunchy with sour pepper soup. Pinchis chinos
and mexicanos own sann fransis.

They got fogs that cover up the city like las
cortinas from your fancy bedroom Skinny like I
never had until now. You got to see my big bed.
I bet my bed be as big now as your bed. Ha how
you like that

Our pendejo father never didn't believe in me
so what I am Johhny now. They love me here. It
is full of boats, sour bred, kites in the parks.
And many bad girls. You know what I likes. And
the girls liking me!

Get here before I sail away.

But don't bring him.

Buena V. Johnny

＊

Tomás stood on the porch and glowered.

Teresita led a parade of her siblings through the yard. She, Anita,
and the Cabora forces, followed by the Alamos children and that
damned deer, the pig, some ducks that had somehow decided Teresita
was their mother, a goat—where the hell did the goat come from?—
and the barn cat, with its crooked tail held stiffly aloft and forming
slow happy arcs over its spine. The children were banging pots and toy
drums. Teresita strummed her infernal guitar. They were all chanting
some nonsense, but he could make out "maso bwikam" amid the infan-
tile blather.

Gabriela clucked disapprovingly. "She should grow up," she muttered, and banged back inside.

Tomás spit and scratched the small of his back where the sweat that was brought forth from his gunbelt caused a rash. Behind him, Segundo snored softly.

Tomás noticed workers smiling at Teresita as she stomped along. They were mocking her, he was certain. If they were mocking her, then they were mocking him. Oh, for the days of real mastery in Cabora. A flogging or two would liven up the establishment! But Dr. Burtch and the pinches gringos of Clifton would not appreciate a whipping. No.

Tomás stole one of Segundo's sweet rolls and had at it. He patted his expanding gut. It pained him sometimes. And if he drank too much coffee, his heart fluttered in his chest. It sent a chill into him when it banged. He would not say it *frightened* him. He would say it was *curious*. A dancing heart. He was sure it was due to the elevation of the ranch; they were higher than he had ever been. The air was thin enough that a good horse ride or walk left him a bit winded.

"It is the altitude," he announced.

"Huh?" said Segundo; he shifted his big feet and then resumed snoring.

On the far side of the property, Lupe stood among the small pines, watching Teresita's parade of children and beasts. He heard their voices. He watched her bang on the guitar like some cowboy. He wasn't smiling.

⁂

When the world changed, women and children were disinvited from the parlor. So was Segundo; Segundo was too crude for a gathering of gentlemen. Tomás had arranged for the great white men of the mountain to come; his transformation would leap forward, he believed. This was América del Norte, Los Yunaites Estates, and he was going to do things like a pinche American from now on.

Fortunately, Teresita was out in the twilight collecting herbs or talking to fireflies or bringing home orphaned bear cubs or levitating, Tomás didn't really care.

The room was chokingly blue with pipe and cigar smoke. Snifters of brandy and cognac glowed warmly on all tables. A great bowl of popcorn doused in jalapeño juice sat unattended, and a platter of beef quesadillas and salted jícama was decimated on the sideboard with a rubble of wadded cloths and tatters of tortilla scattered around it. Tomás waved about a morsel of elk sausage wrapped in bacon on a toothpick, as if he were conducting the opera of buff male laughter. Tomás had overheard his loggers calling these men plutes. It was oddly endearing. He tried out *pinches plutes* in his mind. The only thing missing was that damned Lauro Aguirre.

Two old boys passed the Sears catalogue back and forth and blushed wildly at the ladies' unmentionables. Dr. Burtch availed himself of a few more ambrosial elk sausages and washed them down with warm beer. The formidable Brit mine manager Ellis B. Twidlatch had laid his tall beaver hat on a chair and sat, knee-sprawled and full to bursting, with a rich pipeful of black Turkish baccy and a gleam of grease on his chin. When Tomás poured him a stout tipple of brandy, he cried, "Splendid!"

As was fashionable, the men had their hair parted in the middle and gleaming with pomade. Sir Twidlatch confided that his bride, Bunella, favored the marcel wave for her coiffure—"A bit of fashion she acquired in France." He cast a sly eye about the room. "One does pick up curious afflictions in Paris, don't you know!" The men laughed! They nodded and slapped their knees! Tomás put his hands on his gut and cried, "¡Chíngue a su madre!"

Silence.

Mr. Van Order had come uphill to buy lumber, and he was dead asleep in the corner, having consumed a pound of meat and a wide array of liquors. His peg leg extended into the middle of the carpet. Tomás bent to it and knocked sonorously.

"I not sell him that wood!" he announced.

Outbursts of guffaws all around.

Dr. Burtch had brought the Clifton banker C. P. Rosencrans, of the powerful California Rosencranses. Bucolic Morenci was vastly expanding the Rosencrans family fortunes.

The great man made a yearly visit to the mines in the company of his family, except for his beloved son Jamie, always too thin and feverish, who was twisted in agonizing fits at their Morenci home. Only six, he was already stick-legged and bedridden. Dr. Burtch was waging a noble battle to spare him what was starting to seem a certain death.

It was a great lesson to those men of the mountain that wealth and power did not always stop pain, did not dissuade death, did not alleviate the terrible midnight agonies of grief. It was an enormous mercy of Dr. Burtch's to bring Rosencrans to the parlor to laugh and forget his woes for an evening.

"Señor Rosencrans," said Tomás, pouring the great man a little thread of golden cognac. "Is to fix what ails us, no?"

"Sí," Rosencrans said, tipping his head politely. "Gracias."

"No hay porqué." Tomás beamed.

"See here," the grand Twidlatch said, "Tom!"

"Jes, Tweedly-yatch?"

"This Girl Saint of yours. Why, I never!"

"I never too," Tomás lamented.

"Yes, but as regards this Saint," Ellis Twidlatch insisted. "It must be a drain on you."

"Drain?" Tomás looked to Burtch. "¿Cómo?"

"Er, cuesta mucho?" Dr. Burtch offered. "Es mucho, erm, trouble-o."

Tomás slapped a burlesque hand to his brow and sank in a chair.

"Cheessiz Crites!" he said. "Tweedly-yatch! I lose everything for her. Twice!"

The men goggled at him and busied themselves with their snacks, smokes, and drinks. Much sad head-shaking. Van Order snorted and threw a kick with his good leg, lost in a dream of battles in Virginia. Matthew Lara, a teacher from Silver City, noted: "Just like a mule."

※

Guadalupe Rodriguez had found a cabin in Ward Canyon, on the outskirts of Metcalf. He had not earned enough money from Cabora Norte to pay for it, yet he had produced a mochila full of Mexican bills and coins. Money was money, even if it was greaser money, and the landlord reluctantly accepted the five hundred dollars' worth of pesos, though he charged Lupe another twenty-five dollars' worth for the bed and the pots. He threw in the pile of firewood and the kitchen chair. Lupe's cabin had three acres of land and a well, and aside from the outhouse being off plumb, it was in pretty good shape. He paid little Al Fernandez a silver dollar to bring him old papers from Clifton and plugged the gaps between the logs with wet, wadded strips of the *Copper Era* newspaper. It was a poor man's adobe, made with hot water, milk, flour, and shredded newsprint, the mix slopped into the walls where the caulking had peeled out over many winters.

He stole himself a hundred-pound sack of beans from the Urreas and brought it home on one of the wood-collecting donkeys that he borrowed. His chimney had birds' nests in it, and he set a huge fire and burned them out, sitting outside as the smoke filled the one room, not minding it, for it drove the field mice scurrying out, where he stomped them to death.

He carried Malichi into his clearing and slit his throat with a bowie knife. Deer weren't pets. Deer were meat.

He gutted the little deer and saved his heart, kidneys, and liver. He tossed the guts down the barranca behind his cabin—no need to inspire bears to climb up to his bedroom. He smoked the haunches and fried up venison steaks and chops. They were best when covered in white flour and fried in butter. He marinated the meat in wild blueberries. He ate like a wolf.

Later, he told Teresita that the fawn had been killed by coyotes. When she wept, he comforted her, pulling her close so she could rest her head on his shoulder. It was their first embrace. He smelled her hair—she had some sort of rose perfume. It made him tingle all over.

"It's all right," he whispered. "It's all right. Life is brief, but it is beautiful. Little Malichi waits for us. In Sea Ania. He is already restored."

"Oh," she sobbed.

He stroked her hair.

"I will hold you up," he said. "I will never let you fall."

Her nails dug into his chest.

His big hand felt the space between her shoulder blades. He pulled her tighter. He breathed her in.

She wanted to pull away from him, but she felt so warm.

He thought: Kidney stew and fried heart. Where could he steal some potatoes? He wondered if he could talk her into digging up some from the garden at her rancho for him.

"Shh," he said. "I am here."

※

C. P. Rosencrans cleared his throat.

"See here, Tommy," he said.

The men around the table—Dr. Burtch, Rosencrans, Tomás, and the formidable English mine manager Ellis B. Twidlatch—were all leaning forward, elbows on knees.

"Look," said Rosencrans. "It seems that this phenomenon—at least down below, in the flatlands, as you say—is costing you dearly. You have to convert this enthusiasm for Terry into capital."

"She will not work," Tomás lamented. "She will not *earn*."

"Why not?"

Well. This was uncomfortable. Tomás looked around for something to drink, but all the bottles were empty.

"You see, she, she, she made a promise to, to, to—to God. To God to not make money with the, the, you know, the milagros."

Rosencrans was a religious man. But he was a banker. He was a master of practicality. Business was measurable and sane. His was a world of amoral simplicity—and thus, invisible complicities.

"I make the money," Tomás said.

"Correct."

"She no make the money."

"No."

"We charge the patients the money."

"Charge them whatever you want. It's for her own good. For, my friend, when the powers leave her—and they undoubtedly will leave her one day—what will she do then?"

"I don't know. What?"

"She will turn to you." Rosencrans smiled. "And you will provide for her with your Consortium profits. You incorporate. Partners. But structured so that she can honestly say she took nothing. It would honor her, shall we say, religious beliefs."

"I love America," Tomás said.

※

Teresita dried her eyes. Lupe held her still, pressing her to his chest. He softly rocked her back and forth. They could hear the crickets, and an owl in the willows by the river called and listened, called and listened until another owl far downhill answered. The stars looked like white smoke above them. Teresita could almost see the world's rotation. And, like a small burning rim of a silver platter, the edge of the moon sizzled up through the leaves of the cottonwoods and looked into the valley. Her cheek was against his great chest; she could hear his heartbeat. He was all muscle. Over his shoulder, moving like small gray ghosts through the moonlight, reeds shuffled in the breeze beside the river, and ducks therein muttered softly, domestic details of their day traded in their nests. She pulled Lupe tighter. Oh yes. He felt that. He was feeling that all the way down his belly.

"You are the daughter of God," he whispered. "You are all-powerful."

"I have no power. The power is God's."

"You lie to yourself," he said, pressing against her. "Your power is yours. Inside you. I want to drink it. I want to lick up your power like water from a stream. Give it to me."

He frightened her.

"Your father is a clown," he said. "He is so jealous of you. Without you, he is nothing. Don't you see? You are the great one."

She pushed away.

"Your family? They are dogs."

"Stop."

"Look what he did to your mother."

She looked up at him.

"My mother? What do you know of my mother?"

"Everyone knows."

He moved his lips along her throat.

She whispered, "I must go. I have to go."

He said nothing.

He slid his hand up her spine.

She shivered like Caballito Urrea.

His hand reached her hair and pulled the ribbon until it came undone and her hair cascaded across the skin of his arm.

"I think," he said, "you will stay."

Thirty-One

TO HIS CREDIT, Tomás rejected the concept of the Medical Consortium. Once he was sober, he decided that sort of sham was a typical plute thing to do. Especially to his own daughter. At least, that's what he told himself. It was Gabriela who almost pulled his hair in outrage when he mentioned the plan, who sent him to sleep on the settee downstairs to ponder his infamy. In the morning, sore and stiff, he had repented of his sins.

The more he thought about it, the more tainted he felt. Plute bastards! Life wasn't always about money! He moped around until Gaby came down from their bed redolent of delicious scents and powders, her hair pinned above her brow in an intimidating prow and lacquered into a helmet that could crack a bad man's skull. She breezed past him and did not allow him to pull up her skirts as she strode into the kitchen.

He slouched out to the front porch and encountered the deeply offended Segundo, who whittled a stick and would not look at him.

"Did you have a nice party?" Segundo asked.

"Oh—" Tomás waved his hand. "You know how it is with those fellows."

"I don't know, boss. Why don't you tell me? I would like to know what decent *gentlemen* are like when they have a party."

Tomás coughed.

Gaby stepped out on the porch with a tray. A pot of Arbuckle's, a bowl of cream, a bowl of sugar lumps, one cup.

"Good morning," she said to Segundo.

"Why, thank you," he said.

"My pleasure. We are frying you nice eggs with chorizo, frijoles, potato wedges, and there is apple pie with cheese."

"Say! That's great!"

She brushed past Tomás and vanished inside without another word.

Segundo slurped his coffee extra loud and sighed as he settled his bones more comfortably.

"That Gaby," he said. "She knows how to treat a man."

Tomás shook his head, stepped off the porch, and wandered down to the bunkhouse.

"Boys!" he cried. "May I join you for breakfast?"

They shoved down the long wooden table so he could sit and eat among them. Lupe rose and walked outside. A tin plate with a stinking red mess landed before Tomás. They passed him a spoon.

"What is this?" he asked.

"Pooch!"

"What is pooch?"

"This!"

He sniffed it. He moved it around with his spoon.

One of his loggers said, "That's old bread boiled up with tomatoes. Put some sugar on it."

Tomás smiled wanly and patted the man's shoulder.

He rose and stepped outside and spit three or four times.

Maybe, he thought, they would all love him again if he threw a dance for them.

※

It was a grand soiree, old-Cabora style: Paper lanterns. A German polka band from far Benson. Great barbecued beeves. Sparklers for the children. Bonfires at either end of the open-air dance floor.

Before the event, the Urrea girls were in a frenzy. Dresses were held up and flung to the floor in a panic. Bonnets and scarves, rebozos and fans, flew around the rooms as the little ones tried to look big. The boys bathed reluctantly but cheered up when Tomás revealed new black cowboy boots all around, along with Mexican sombreros and tight black trousers.

In Teresita's room, Anita perched on the edge of the bed, and Teresita sat on the floor while Anita braided her big sister's hair. It was long and thick, and the braids were heavy in her small hands.

The door was closed and locked.

"And then?" Anita said.

"I don't know."

"Yes, you do know."

"I can't tell."

"Tell! I want to know! Tére! Tell me."

"It was so beautiful. It was so dark, but the moon came out, and the night birds started to sing."

"Ay."

"He held me in his arms."

"Ooh."

"He is so strong, Anita! Big strong arms."

"And then what?"

"And then—I can't! Then he...kissed me."

Anita screamed and fell over on the bed. They laughed and laughed.

"I had never kissed a man!" Teresita said. "Never in my life!"

"¡Ay, Dios! ¡Ay, madre!" Anita gasped. "What was it like? Tell me, tell me."

Teresita put her hands in her lap and thought.

"Well," she said. "It is a little soft."

Anita stared wide-eyed.

"A little scratchy from his stubble. And a little...moist."

"What!"

"It's kind of wet."

"From what!"

"It is his mouth, Anita. What do you think?"

Anita fell over again.

"Spit? Spit? No no no! Not spit!"

Teresita hung her head and massaged the back of her own neck.

She said, "It was a little like eating a mango."

"*No!*"

She was going to wear an Indian dress. A bright yellow skirt with blue and red ribbon sewn around it, with a white blouse off her shoulders and a shawl that passed behind her back and that she could drape over her forearms. She was dressing for her man. *Her man.* She knew he'd like it.

Teresita had Anita weave colorful ribbons in her braids.

Gaby tweezed her eyebrows.

Her man.

She could not believe how fast life moved, how quickly everything changed. In her hour of need, God sent her a miracle. And she had doubted. Thus was grace made evident. Even she, the least deserving, received manna in the desert. She was mad with ecstasy, and she didn't know if it was romance or religion, and she didn't care.

She could not contain herself, and rather than descend the stairs slowly, like a fine lady, she thundered down and leapt off the last three steps to crash onto the wooden floor.

Tomás, in his office, shouted, "Who let a buffalo in the house!"

She spun before the hallway mirror, trying her dance steps, working the tassels of her shawl. She could not stop smiling. She spun out the door and sashayed onto the porch. She looked across the yard and saw a disheveled man at the gate, sitting miserably on a small carriage. She raised her hand in a tentative greeting.

"Saint," he called. An Americano. "Please!"

She stepped to the ground and gestured for him to come forward. He jumped down, rushed to her, and took her hands in his.

"My name is Rosencrans," he said. "I am a friend of your father's. Please, I—" He closed his eyes. He was frantic. "My son. They can't do anything. Dr. Burtch."

"What is wrong with your son?" she asked in Spanish.

"Cerebral infection. He is dying. Can you help him? Please?"

⁕

Jamie Rosencrans lay abed, twisted in agony, barely able to breathe. When Teresita entered his room, he did not know if he was seeing an angel or not. She made his eyes pop wide when she came through the door, all rustling colored skirts and colorful braids. He was so surprised that for a moment he didn't notice the deep throbbing pain that poured out of the back of his head and twisted his body. His mother kept kissing the angel's hands. The room smelled of sweat and bread and urine. He made terrible choking whistles as he wrestled with the air.

"His lungs!" his mother cried.

"Yes, I hear."

"His whole body is going!"

"I see."

She came to him and smiled. Her eyes. They were so lulling. He lay and stared up at her. He himself looked like a starving angel to her. The little bones of his chest, the sad sugar bones of his face glowing through the skin nearly clear from the pain.

Teresita put her hand on his brow. He gasped. He arched his back a little.

"¿Duele?" she asked him.

He understood her.

He nodded.

"¿Puedes caminar?"

"No," he whispered. "I can't walk no more."

She nodded. She looked at his mother and father and said, "Please." She gestured toward the door. They did not want to leave the room. They were weeping openly, though Mr. Rosencrans was trying hard to hide it. "Please," she repeated.

They backed out. She closed the door. She sat on the bed with Jamie. The entire bed was wet with his sweat and his dribbles.

"Is bad, your pain?"

"Yes."

She smoothed his blond hair out of his face.

"Are you scared?"

One tear rolled out of his eye.

"No."

"Tired?"

"Yes."

She put her hand upon his brow.

"Do you know where you go when you die?"

He shook his head. He did not know what language she was speaking, but he could understand her perfectly.

"Do you know who I am?"

He shook his head.

"I am Teresita."

"Jamie," he whispered.

"Yes, I know."

She motioned with her hand for him to move over. He was able to scoot a few inches to the left. She lay a white towel on the wet spot on the mattress, and she kicked off her sandals and lay down beside him. She put out her arm and said, "Come to me." He nestled against her. She embraced him, brought his little face to her breast. "Listen to my heart," she said. He listened.

"I was dead once," she said. "Can you believe that, Jamie? I died. It was a long time ago. And I want you to know that death is not terrible."

"No?"

"No. Death is peaceful. It is only a door. On the other side—do you like deer?"

He smiled.

"Who doesn't like deer, Jamie? Right?"

"Right."

"Deer and grandmothers. They wait for you."

Jamie closed his eyes.

"I miss Maw-Maw," he admitted.

"She misses you. But she is in no hurry for you to get there."

She tickled him so lightly she barely felt it, but he did and he giggled weakly and almost squirmed.

"Hurts so bad, though," he said.

"Listen to my voice, Jamie. Can you do that for me? Can you listen to my voice? Listen to my heart? Hold on to me?"

"Yes."

"Can you smell the roses?"

"Yes."

"When I died and went to the other world, that smell came to me.

That way you know I am telling you the truth. Because people don't smell like roses, do they?"

"Father smells like tobacco," he said. "And sweat."

She laughed.

"Trust the roses, then. I was there for a short while. But I came back home. I had work to do. And do you know what that work is?"

"What?"

"I was sent back here to ease the suffering of God's little ones."

"Like who?"

"Like you, Jamie."

He was quiet.

"You can't do that."

"I can."

He was quiet again.

"Why?"

"I love you."

He put his arm around her.

"How?"

"By loving you. I just told you."

"Mother loves me. Father loves me. But I'm dying."

"Mother has not learned. I have learned."

They could hear a clock ticking outside the room. Teresita could hear Mr. and Mrs. Rosencrans listening at the door. Jamie's breath whistled.

"How is your pain?" she asked.

He paused, as if listening for it.

"Better," he said.

"Good." She laid her free hand on his face. She made a small sign on his forehead with her thumb. "Remember that death is not terrible. It is sad, though. What is sad is that we would miss you terribly if you left us now. We would all cry, Jamie. And I have to tell you that you will die. One day. Not today. Not tomorrow. I have looked into you and seen the sickness, and I am taking it from you and giving it to God. Let God have it! Let God put it into a worm or a beetle!"

Jamie laughed softly.

"That's silly."

"I have seen you are a good boy, and I know I would miss you if you died. So I won't let you die. I am a terrible woman! I am selfish! You are simply too handsome to die right now."

"Aw." He buried his face, mortified and delighted.

"Girls like me need boys like you in this world."

He smiled. He was so tired now. He felt like he was sinking through the bed, through the floor, sinking into the earth itself.

"I will let you sleep. You want to sleep now, do you not? Yes, I know. You can sleep now, Jamie, and you will wake up stronger tomorrow. You will dream tonight of hummingbirds. Go with them. I know you cannot walk now, but the hummingbirds will teach you to fly in your sleep. They are called semalú. Can you say it?"

"Semalú," he whispered.

"Good. You will wake up tomorrow. When you do, you must eat. Eat soup. Do you promise?"

He nodded.

"The day after tomorrow, I want you to sit up and hug your mother. In three days, I want you to get out of this bed and hug your father. Will you do this for me?"

He was starting to yawn.

"I'll...try."

"No. You will not try. You will do it. Say it."

"I'm tired."

"Say it, Jamie."

He smiled into her ribs.

"I...will...rise."

She kissed his forehead.

"Good boy," she said. But he was already asleep.

She went out to the hall.

"Three days," she said. "Better then. Three weeks"—she waved her hands before her—"healed."

Mrs. Rosencrans slumped against her husband and put her hand over her mouth.

Teresita said, "Lios emak weye."

She turned and walked out the door, thinking about the dance.

Thirty-Two

THE NIGHT BEFORE THE dance, Lupe staggered around inside his cabin as if drunk. But he was never drunk. His body was on fire. His mind was twisting in his skull in convulsive spasms. "I am wrathy," he muttered. "I am accursed." He stepped out into the cold night. He shivered, but not from the icy air—it was the fire. He threw his shirt to the ground. In each hand, he took up a belduque knife. The edges of night were blackening, bruised, poisoned with the eternal dark. Lupe whispered, "My Father hangs in the sky." No one heard or answered except for the owl, watching with yellow eyes. "I serve You." He clutched his knives and revealed them to the stars. "I serve. I am unworthy. I am incapable." He began his nightly fighting practice. He spun, thrust, slashed, jabbed. Spun, thrust, slashed, jabbed. Down low. Whipping his body erect. Low again. He absorbed the planet's energies as they flowed from Arctic to Antarctic. Magnetism coursed all down his body. He extended his arms out, a knife in each fist, and the icy dew collected on him, and his eyes saw nothing. Spun, thrust, slashed, jabbed. In the moonlight, the whirling blades gleamed cold white and silver all around him, blurred with his speed, like terrible wings.

Thirty-Three

"I HAVE NO HEART," Lupe told her.

The paper lanterns were bobbing in the breeze; paper banners and papel picado flags moved like colorful wings in the lamplight. Townspeople shuffled along, laughing and spooning, and the music was hilarious and bright—all tubas and accordions, drums and a trumpet.

Teresita had her arm through his. She thought he was being a vaquero, a macho, all bluster, all dark mysteries like all the boys she had ever known.

"Oh, you," she said, giggling. "I took your heart."

His jaw muscles rippled.

"Love, silly! You need to say pretty things to me."

"Like what?"

"Like 'Teresita, you have taken my heart. Teresita, you have overwhelmed my soul.'"

"I have no soul."

She sighed but wasn't going to let his mood ruin her night.

"Don't worry," she said. "I have enough soul for both of us."

He had dressed in his best black suit. He had strapped his Buntline revolver to his right hip, and it hung nearly to his knee; the bowie was on his left hip. He wore a gray Mexican sombrero.

"I haven't seen many of those since I left Sonora," she said.

"In honor of you."

That was more like it. At least he was making some effort. She would teach him how to speak to a woman.

She glanced at all his weaponry.

"Are we expecting a war?" she asked.

"Always."

But even Lupe was able to see his thunderous machismo was a bit amusing, and he smiled. He seemed embarrassed. She loved him for that too.

Anita tagged along behind them, and Lupe took his first dance with her. Teresita watched as he gently placed her feet on his black boots and swept her around the dance floor. Teresita laughed. She put her hands over her heart in a prayerful pose of devotion. She had laughed a million times at women acting like she was acting now, and she didn't care. The smells of popcorn and churros, carne asada and lemonade, filled the air around her. Al Fernandez was running around the perimeter in his railroad cap. Dr. Burtch managed a few awkward steps with his wife. They waved at Teresita. She laughed. Everything was so bright, so new. So funny. There was Segundo, squiring that fat girl of his as if she were the Queen of America. Teresita laughed again.

The first dance ended, and Lupe brought Anita to Teresita. The other children rushed in and surrounded Anita and bore her away in a controversy of whispers and shrieks. The band struck up a waltz.

Lupe bent to her in a small bow and extended his hand. Teresita tipped her head and took his fingers in hers. He spun her onto the floor and they danced, crashing into Segundo and Dolores only twice as they all circled.

※

Don Tomás Urrea arrived astride Caballito Urrea. He, too, was dressed in black. He wore his tightest pantalones (Gaby had been forced to cut a wedge in the back of them so they'd button over his gut). The legs of his pants gleamed along their outer seams with rows of silver coins. His belt was black leather with silver conchas. He wore his frilled white shirt and his tight black jacket cut high at the waist and embroidered with a shining scorpion on the back. Delicate red needlework etched the smallest red roses at each breast and at each cuff. He wore his twin .44s butts-out for fast cross-draw. His boots were brilliantly shined, and his spurs were miracles of gold and silver. He, too, wore a vast sombrero, though his was night black and worked with silver thread and had two small silver horseshoes affixed to the crown. He nudged Caballito Urrea into proud little sidesteps and dancing head bobs before kicking his right foot over the pommel, leaping off, and landing amid the dancers with his hat in his hand and a great shout of "¡Ajúa!" from him, Segundo, and the few buckaroos working out of Cabora Norte. It was a pure dose of real México, México Lindo, and he wanted to know how the cabrones liked *that!* He strutted. His chest extended beyond his gut. His pistolas squeaked and rattled in their holsters. He embraced Mrs. Burtch, shied away from Dolores, accepted three copas in a row of wine and tequila and whiskey, and he raised each in a toast to Clifton, to his Gabriela, who hid her face behind a fan—the vixen!—in the shadows beside the churro stand, to America itself. "¡Salud!" he bellowed. They clapped. They swooned. Tomás Urrea taught everybody what a man was: Soy todo un hombre, he explained to himself.

He said to Segundo, "It is good to be king, my friend."

"Must be," the pistolero replied.

"A lariat!" Tomás shouted, and as if by magic—or prearrangement—a worker stepped forth and provided the patrón with twenty feet of rope knotted in a loose lasso. Tomás removed his hat and placed it on Al Fernandez's head, on top of the boy's trainman's cap. He bowed. He commenced to spinning the lasso over his head. Whistles. Claps. Heels stomping. He whirled the loop of rope into a blur, then brought it down before him, spinning vertically now, forming a blurred window in the universe, and he stepped through the lasso and back. He skipped, he danced. The drummer took up the beat. Tomás hopped on one foot, whirled, sent the lasso dangerously close to the group of ladies, and whooshed it back so it passed around him like an ocean wave and was suddenly behind him. And up—they watched it rise and form a small tornado above his head. The rope extended to its farthest reach, and the open mouth of the lasso formed a perfect O in the air. With a flick of the wrist, with a dancer's grace, Tomás spun on his heel and dropped the loop over Teresita and cinched it tight. He pulled her, hand over hand, away from Lupe's side. She resisted, laughed, conceded, and rushed to her father. They clutched in a grand embrace as the populace shouted.

"Oh, Father!" She laughed.

He tipped his head to her ear and said, "Stay away from that bastard."

He released her and strode into the shadows, retrieving his hat from Al's head, throwing winks and nods. It was utter madness. If they had been carrying roses, the people would have showered him with petals. The shouting sounded like it would never stop.

"Yes, cabrones: What did you think of that?"

The Benson boys were perfectly happy to take a break when a group of local musicians appeared. The Bensons piled the beef and tortillas high. They guzzled wine punch and beer as the locals raised a ruckus with guitars, violins, and a bajo sexto; deeply nostalgic Hispanos tried to recall the old dance steps, the highly formalized Mexican ranchero pasos they had known as children. All the while Tomás and Gabriela commanded the center of the dance floor; he was all boot heels and ringing rowels, and she was all flaring skirts and high steps.

Teresita and Lupe walked around the outside of the crowd, murmuring about the moon and the clouds, about God and children. They both wanted children. Lupe dreamed of a small house on a cliff above the Pacific. He wanted to learn to fish. In his mind, tuna, lobster, and abalone were great treasures.

"Where will this palace be?" she asked.

He shrugged.

"Guaymas," he said. "Mazatlán."

"Then you will have to live alone," she teased. "For I cannot return to Mexico."

He nodded.

"Eso sí está cabrón," he conceded. He stopped and listened to the music. "California then. It doesn't matter."

California!

"My brother is in San Francisco," she said. "We could go there."

They walked.

"You think you're so much better than me," he said abruptly and disentangled his arm from hers and went to the sizzling taco brazier and snapped his fingers at the cook.

Anita was staring at Teresita.

"Where did you come from?" Teresita said.

"I was here." Anita scratched at a scab on her knee. "He's mean to you."

"Not always."

They watched him eat with his mouth open. But he was so handsome. He was so tall.

"Love," Teresita said, as if suddenly realizing it to her great surprise, "is not easy."

She went to her man.

⁂

His angers were brief. They passed like small storm squalls and were gone. He always made an effort to appease her after he'd erupted. In those moments, his kindness and grace were complete. His attention was tender and humorous. His affection felt incendiary, burning out of his eyes and illuminating her. He did not know poetry, but in those moments, he *was* poetry.

They took the floor. He held his hands behind his back, and he danced with crisp taconazos, his boots clocking like the hooves of stallions. And she dipped and swayed, holding the sides of her skirts up and out, at once joining him and evading him. He strutted like a rooster, and she was a dove shying away at the last instant. He came close—she allowed it. He tipped his face to hers and they circled, clicking their heels, until she broke away gently and smiled as she swirled her skirts. They formed blossoms around her, wings. He backed away, shied his great hat to the right, and moved around and toward her again. They ended the dance in a ritual embrace, and he snuck a fast kiss to her cheek as the audience applauded them.

She fanned herself as Lupe went to fetch her a glass of lemonade. Tomás appeared at her side.

"You danced!" he said.

"Of course."

"I didn't know you could dance."

"I have always danced."

"I never saw it."

"You weren't paying attention, Papá."

He crossed his arms.

How could he say what he wanted to say to her?

He was struck mute with the silence of every father of every daughter, that moment when the words cannot come, and what wanted to be said would forever remain silent.

Lupe came back and handed her the glass. He glared at Tomás. Tomás said, "I," and looked at the dark ground. He shook his head. He patted Teresita's arm. He took off his hat and said, "I am sleepy. It is time for bed."

She watched him retrieve Caballito Urrea from the cottonwood where he was tied. Tomás mounted the little stallion slowly, as if he were in pain. For a brief moment, in the gray light at the edge of the crowd, he seemed old. He slumped in the saddle. He looked at his hat, dropped it on the ground, and let the Apache war pony wander back downhill. Boys rushed in and squabbled over the great man's hat, but Segundo waded in and put the boot to their behinds and picked it up, dusted it off, and held it to his chest.

Teresita watched Gabriela watch Tomás slink away. Gaby turned and stared at her. She called the small ones, who protested but joined her. Together, they walked into the night.

⁂

And the house grew dark with the presence of Rodriguez. Even in his hut in Ward Canyon, he radiated his essence across the valleys and the field; his spirit slunk like a ghost through the pines and seemed to mock them from the corners, whisper poisonous imprecations in Teresita's ear. Tomás saw him etched in her face, saw him in shadows in the corner. Her tone of voice had changed—it was so subtle, perhaps only a father could hear it. Only a father could hear how his daughter's words lost a half tone of their melody and grew slightly clipped, slightly earthbound, shifting as a lover's voice does into the timbre and range of the loved one's. He could not bear the abomination of Lupe's voice flooding her mouth. The familial earthquakes had begun, and no one could stop the trembling of the bedrock, and no one could find a place to flee.

Teresita glared at her father, and he seemed ready to strike her at several moments during their days. She stopped eating with him and the others and locked herself in her room with romantic projects for Lupe, projects she wielded like a club to punish her family, who, she was certain, was betraying her daily. Lupe had told her they didn't want her to be happy, didn't want her to have love for herself. She was like a prize horse for them. They used her to attract attention and money and power. They were good for nothing on their own—they needed her fame to bring them into the eyes of the world. This is why they wanted to cut her off from God...and from him. They needed her alone and lonely, dependent on them. "You are a prisoner," he'd whispered.

And finally, irrevocably, the father and the daughter erupted. The family felt a terrible catharsis mixed with paralyzed shock. They knew it was coming. It had to come. They needed it to come, for the pressure in the house was as dense as an impending thunderstorm.

Like so many family battles, it began over nothing. It was ridiculous. Petty. And it immediately dragged forth slights and resentments, insults and disappointments spanning years. The earth ruptured during breakfast, after she had sullenly thrown herself into her chair and refused to look at anyone. "Ah," Tomás said, "the queen has deigned to join us commoners." They ate and murmured and thanked Mrs. Smith when she appeared with more amazements from her kitchen, and the whole time, Teresita heaved sighs of sorrow and disapproval, rolling her eyes when her father said anything. He felt it, felt every sigh like nails raked down his neck. Like all fathers, he elaborately ignored her outbursts and her mood up until he started to mock her—sighing in a false female voice when she did; slumping in his chair while casting ferocious hawk's-eye glances at Gaby to make sure his outrage was being noted. He raised his coffee cup in a toast: "To *love*."

She smacked her hand lightly on the table.

"What?" he said.

"Forget it," she replied.

Forks lowered. Eyes widened. Mrs. Smith peeked out at them. Anita blinked.

"Do you have something to say?" asked Tomás.

"Not to you I don't," she said.

He smiled. His face was red.

"Well, well," he said. "Aren't we vicious!"

She got up.

"Sit down!" he roared.

Anita jumped; Gaby put her hand on her shoulder.

"I don't think so," said Teresita.

"As long as you are in my house, you will do what I say."

"Or what?"

He rose.

"Gordo..." Gaby warned.

"Or you will find out," he said.

Segundo wandered in, looked back and forth between them, and walked out.

Reluctantly, shooting fire from her eyes, she sat down again.

"That's more like it," he said, not sure what to do with himself—he stood there feeling foolish for a beat, then sat. "We will eat a goddamned civilized breakfast with some goddamned manners and stop acting like savages," he proclaimed.

"Savages?" she said.

"Yes. Indeed. I refer to Mr. Rodriguez."

She busied herself with her spoons, moving them around, blinking back tears.

"I am having him escorted from the mountain," Tomás said.

She jerked in her seat.

"We've had enough of this romance of yours."

"Like you've had enough of God?" she snapped.

"Please," he scoffed. "Such drama."

"I love him!"

"You don't know what love is."

"And you do?" she said. She laughed. "Oh, yes, I see. Love is adultery with a waitress who could be my big sister. Thank you for that lesson, Pápi."

He jumped up and—everybody shrieked—went to strike her. She did not flinch. His hand flew forward, but he caught it in time. Pulled back. Just stood.

"Get out," he said. "Come back when you are ready to apologize."

She pushed away and went to the doorway and said, "I am not sorry."

Even though she was.

Thirty-Four

HELL CAME WALKING DOWN the mountain as the sun was clearing the peaks.

Teresita wasn't even out of her room yet—she was not even combed. She puttered in her room with the many newspaper articles about her that followers mailed her. It was amazing to her: places she had never heard of, and they were writing about her. She thought Lupe would enjoy them. She had in mind an album with these stories mounted to its pages and, perhaps, dried herbs and pressed flowers pasted in around them. She would give him her life, all in one place.

She shuffled the limp and yellowing pages, shaking her head. Where was Manitoba? Canada! She could not imagine it. And this, Fort Wayne, in a place called Indiana. Indiana! It must have Indians. She wanted to go there. Her scissors trimmed the stories.

Her feelings were a jumble. It thrilled her, and it aggrieved her, to see herself in the papers. She didn't know what to feel.

Anaconda, Montana? Portsmouth, New Hampshire? Newark, Ohio? Ah! New York! She ran her finger over the New York City news, as if she could read the English by touch.

She had to do something. Guadalupe was about to burst. She knew that. She knew it—any woman would know. His pain stung her.

They had walked down the mountain. He had held her hand, his fingers laced through hers. She felt safe. His arms were like stone against her shoulders, his hand was large, rough. The great pistola creaked on his hip, and the sombrero kept even the sun from touching her.

When they'd stopped in the tiny bosque at the entrance to Cabora Norte, he had swept her up and pressed his lips to hers. She kissed him back, hard, the way she thought he wanted her to kiss. His lips parted, and hers opened too. He breathed into her mouth. It was dizzying. His breath moved into her mouth and circled there, and she breathed it back into his. It was beyond anything she had imagined. They breathed into each other against a willow. And he pulled back her hair and licked and bit her throat.

She pushed his hand away from the front of her blouse.

"Teresa!"

"Wait, no."

He backed away. He stared off. He breathed hard.

"I want you."

"You have me."

He fell toward her and braced his arms on either side of her so she could not escape. She felt a bolt of fear for a moment. Terrible old dreams scampered down her body, and she raised one knee slightly.

"I want to be *inside* you," he said.

There was nowhere to go. Nowhere to look.

"Ay, amor," she whispered. "I know."

"You know?"

"I am sorry. My love, if I could, I would give you all of me."

"Show me! Give it."

"I cannot. Not yet. I . . . mustn't."

He dropped his arms and walked in a circle.

"It hurts, you know," he said. "If you are a man. It hurts."

She wrung her hands.

"I thought you said you *weren't* a saint."

"I am not a saint."

"Then allow me to love you like a man. Who will know?"

Her jaw were so tight they hurt.

"I do not know."

"I know!" he said.

He took both her hands in his.

"Come with me for a moment. I want to show you something."

And they hurried away from the rancho and made their way through the pines and the aspens, out past Lupe's cabin to a small butte that jutted into the Arizona sky like the rocky prow of some petrified ship. And when they stood out upon the point of the rocks, they could see all the way down, all the way to the orange and mauve and salmon deserts below, and to the cream-white playas wobbling in the heat, and to the violet and black Apache mountains beyond. They could see all the way to Mexico.

"Only I know you," he said. "Only I know your true power. Let me unleash it."

She stared at the world at her feet.

"Give me yourself here, now, and I will give my life for you. I will give this all to you." He spread his arms. "I will give you things you have never dreamed."

His hand closed on the back of her neck.

"The Witch of Cabora!"

He laughed.

"The world is yours. And you are mine."

"No, Lupe...I want to. Not yet."

"Take off your dress."

"I will want to. In time. I...promise."

He laughed without humor.

"I have nothing but love for you," he said. He put his hand on him-self. She looked away. "Do not be ashamed. This is in honor of you. Of my love for you." He leaned in and touched her cheek. "A man's love belongs inside his woman."

She put her hands out to his face and held both his cheeks.

"I am not ready," she said. "One day you will understand."

"Ready?" He tightened his grip. "I could sacrifice us right now. I could throw us from this cliff. We could be together forever."

She did not know what was happening. Was this love talk? Was this what men said to their women? Was this what true passion sounded like? Lupe was talking like some poet. She had never heard such things, even in her imaginings. She pulled back and strained against his hand.

"Please," she said.

He dropped his hand. He stepped away. He shook his head.

"When we are wed?" he said. "Will that make you ready?"

She blinked.

"What did you say?"

"I said, when we marry, will you be ready then?"

She was so stunned, she just stared at his dark shape against the sky. "Well?"

Finally, she managed to say, "Yes..." She meant to say more. To clar-ify. She needed to clear her head, at least. But she dared not speak.

"All right, then," he said. "But don't make me wait."

He nodded and tipped his hat to her and walked her back to the house, then left her to shake and replay every word a hundred times in her head.

⁂

Hell came clocking down the rail line in worn cowboy boots.

Tomás was sitting on the front porch, surrounded by his children. He rocked placidly, sipping his coffee. He had the deep-rooted fear of going barefoot that all Sinaloan gentlemen harbored: if you were barefoot, you were a pauper or an Indian. Not even in the house did they go discalced, but the sun was out and the boys had rubbed Tomás's sore feet and to hell with it.

He was telling them a tale of the gold mine near Rosario, Sinaloa—a fabulous place of mango trees and coconut palms, alligators and floods and bananas. In the children's minds, it was the Garden of Eden. With iguanas and snapping turtles.

"Your uncle Seferino," Tomás lied, "was wandering through the land, probably hunting a jaguar. Yes, it was a jaguar that had killed his…"

"Geese!" cried the littlest of the children.

"Silly," said Anita. "Jaguars don't eat geese."

"Right, Anita!" Tomás said, squinting at her. "The jaguar ate your uncle's goat!"

"Told you," said Anita.

"Uy, uy, uy," said little brother Paúl. "You think you're so special." He stuck out his tongue.

"So your uncle Seferino Urrea was wandering in the forest when he saw a monk. A very strange and eerie monk. All hunched over and mossy-looking. His hood hid his face in shadow."

"A ghost, I bet!" blurted Anita.

"Shh. So Seferino said, 'Hey, monk!' Something like that. But the monk hurried away, and Seferino followed him, and he was led into a cave. It's a terrible cave. Do you know why?"

They shook their heads.

"Because the cave looks exactly like gigantic human buttocks! ¡Nalgas tremendas!"

They burst out laughing, scandalized.

"¡Ay, Papá!"

"I'm sorry if it happens to be true. It is called Butt Mountain. Well, Seferino entered the cave and found the monk going deeper and deeper. Carrying a torch. He followed. They turned many times, down many corridors, and your poor uncle thought he would never find his way back out."

"Were there bats?" the littlest boy wanted to know.

"Were there bats! There were bats, my boy! Big black barking bats! Suddenly, Seferino came around a bend and found the monk standing before a huge pile of gold! Gold everywhere! Gold bars, gold coins, gold lamps! Spanish gold! And the monk turned to look at him, but beneath his cowl there was no face! Only a skull! And then the monk disappeared!"

He sipped his coffee.

"¿Qué pasó?" they cried.

"Seferino tied a rope to the biggest chest of gold and made his way back out, uncoiling the rope behind him so he could lead his friends in to collect the treasure. But when he gathered the men of the village and rode back to the cave—"

"The rope was gone!" Anita shouted.

"No. The rope was there. So they followed it. They marched in single file, deep into the ghost monk's treasure cave. But guess what they found. They found the rope—*sticking out of a solid wall of rock!* There was no way to get in to the treasure. And that rope, to this very day, dangles out of that solid rock wall."

He chuckled at the expressions on their faces, and he stretched out his legs and let the sun cook his toes.

"Good one, eh?" he said with his eyes closed.

"Who is that?" the boy asked.

And Tomás opened his eyes.

☀

He kicked open the gate and came through. His arms were across his chest, and his Winchester was tucked in them, forming a crooked cross with his torso. Tomás didn't know who it was at first—he had hacked off his hair. It was ragged and wild in the breeze.

"Go inside," he said, rising from his seat. The kids scrambled. Tomás reached for his pistols, but they were inside. Before he understood who this stranger was, he shouted, "Can I help you?"

Lupe whipped the rifle out and worked the lever. He walked forward, aiming at the center of Tomás's chest. Tomás laughed nervously. What a time to be without a pistola...or Segundo.

Lupe stopped ten feet from the porch, planted his feet, kept the rifle aimed at Tomás's heart.

If this pendejo thinks I'm afraid of him, he's a fool, thought the Sky Scratcher. He took up his coffee cup and insolently sipped and raised his eyebrows.

"I have come for what is mine," Lupe announced.

"Payday isn't till Friday," Tomás said.

Good one! he thought.

"Do not mock me, chingado!" Lupe warned.

Tomás dug in the corner of his left eye with one finger.

"Coffee's cold," he said and splashed it at Lupe's feet.

Lupe shook the rifle at him.

"She is mine."

Tomás put the cup on the table. He could hear the children crying behind him. Gaby was coming—he knew her tread on the wooden floors; he could smell her.

"I will have her! Now!"

Tomás sighed.

"Do you not think," he said, "that I have faced weapons before? Do you not think that men have tried to kill me a million times—all over my daughter?" He shook his head. "And now you? You? A dog-shit peasant, coming here like this?" He laughed.

Gaby stood beside him.

"Go away!" she shrieked. "Get away from my home!" She would have torn him apart with her own fingers.

"I take her or I kill you all. Don't make me kill you."

Anita shrieked.

"Go inside," said Gaby.

"You could not tie Teresita's shoes." Tomás sneered.

"She is mine. Give her to me or I kill her too."

"You idiot," Tomás said. "You goddamned worm."

He took one step down the stairs.

"Gordo, no," Gaby said.

"You need to leave here now."

"She is mine. I own her."

"Own? What is she, a cow? You own your own soul and nothing more, and sadly for you, I am about to remove your soul from you."

Lupe thought about that. He frowned. He smiled. He shook his head.

"I have the rifle."

Tomás glanced at the doorway, gestured with his head for Gaby to move back. She stood her ground.

"You leave my family alone," she shouted.

"Even without a gun," Tomás said. "Even with no shoes on my feet, I can beat you like a dog. I can kick the shit you call a life out of you."

Before Lupe could say more, Tomás sprang off the porch and kicked the barrel of the gun high; it went off in thunder, blowing a wedge of wood from the front of the house. Anita screamed. Tomás was sure he'd just broken his toe. But he kept moving, his arms coming down like lightning; he swung his right fist into Lupe's head and wrenched the rifle loose with his left as Lupe fell. "Did you see that, cabrón?" he taunted. "Did you see me beat your ass?" He raised the gun and struck and struck and Teresita burst out the door, shouting, "No! No! Stop! What have you done!"

The three stared at her—the father with the rifle raised like an ax about to sunder a log; the gunman splayed on his back, bleeding from his nose; the young mother willing to die to defend her home. The family tumbled out the door behind her. Everyone seemed suspended, spiderwebbed in the morning for a long moment.

Teresita broke the spell.

She shoved her father aside.

She fell upon Lupe, shielding him with her body.

"What?" said Tomás.

"How could you?" she shouted. "I hate you!"

"What?"

Lupe scrambled backward from the Sky Scratcher, hustled several feet away, and rose, pulling Teresita to him.

"She is mine, old man!" he shouted.

She buried herself in his embrace, weeping. Tomás could not believe what was before him. If anyone had told him this story, he would have laughed. It was more absurd than his ghost stories.

"Teresita, no," he said, smiling a little.

"I love him!" she yelled.

Lupe laughed at him.

"She is mine. I am taking her."

"Taking her? Where?"

Lupe jerked his head.

"They have a courthouse in this pinche town. I can find a judge."

Teresita looked up at him with her mouth open.

"This is a joke," said Tomás.

"Come to the wedding and find out."

"Teresa! I order you to come here this instant."

She looked back and forth between them.

"I am your father!" Tomás roared.

For just a moment, it seemed like she might come to her senses.

"You brought this . . . pinche to my door?" Gabriela accused. "This?" Gaby grabbed her own hair and pulled it. "He has come to rob you! He has come to drag you away!"

"This man is a pig," Tomás said.

Lupe turned to Teresita. He smiled sadly. His eyes were huge, wet. Blood stained his face from her father's blows.

"They do not know me," he said. "They do not understand what you have brought to me. This love."

He pulled her tight and looked bravely at the Urreas.

Gaby was beside Tomás. She put her hand on his shoulder. He still held Lupe's rifle—it dangled like an afterthought.

"No, Tére," she said. She shook her head. She tried to make Teresita smile, knowing in her heart she would never forgive her but trying to make this violence fade away. "Come on, Cúquis. This is not what you want."

Teresita was shaking.

"You!" she cried. "You are happy! You have your man! Why should I be alone? Why should you have all the love in the world?"

Lupe stood his ground, wiped the blood on the back of his arm. He spit—red spit.

"Lick that," he told Tomás and spun Teresita around.

Anita was shouting, pathetically, "Teresita! No, Teresita! Don't go!"

All the children were wailing and crying out, clutching at their father and mother, unsure what had just happened to explode their morning.

For a moment, Gaby thought Tomás would kill them both. She had seen his rages before. His face went purple. He elbowed her aside. He jogged forward and his finger went to the trigger, but she dragged his arms, pulled him, cried and shouted. She could feel him stiff under his clothes, wooden, trembling with anger.

At the gate, Lupe looked back and shouted: "You are welcome to the wedding!" He laughed at them all. "But bring us gifts, eh? Don't be cheap!" He turned away for a moment but turned back for a final taunt.

"Keep the rifle," he shouted. He snugged Teresita to his side and shook her at her father. "Good trade."

Teresita was confused, they could all see it. She was blinking like a creature in a trap. But she stepped through the gate with Lupe. She hurried away with him. And she never looked back.

Tomás dropped the rifle in the dirt.

He didn't care who saw him cry.

Thirty-Five

AS IF SIGNALED BY the eruption in Clifton, the Yaquis attacked the border again, sweeping out of the desert hills like furious spirits, wraiths with fire in their hands, assaulting Ojinaga, Juárez. They had learned things in 1896—not many wore Teresita's picture over their hearts this time—and they struck like Apaches, from ambush and arroyo, from high outcrops and in speeding runs through undefended streets, blazing and shrieking. But the Mexicans had learned things too, and they surged forth with massive numbers of riders and Rurales and mercenaries in killing waves, with American Gatling guns and repeating rifles, and their sheer numbers, their waves of horses, overcame the attackers and beat them to the earth, where they were shot and skewered and stomped under hoof and boot as the sacred Yaqui flag with its hummingbird on a narrow field of white fell into the bloody mud. It was Ochoa's revolution at last, but it was crushed before it began.

The Mexicans immediately accused Lauro Aguirre and sent agents across the river, as did the Americanos, but he had fled El Paso. Aguirre did not know where to go to evade these calamities. He knew nothing of what had happened in Clifton. But he knew there was refuge there, refuge among the family he loved second only to his own. Don Tomás

Urrea! The Lion of the Mountains! Teresita! The blessed Saint, Queen of Mexico, Queen of the Yaquis, Mother of the Revolt, Angel of Peace! So he sped away, sped west, trying to outrun night, trying to outrun the authorities. He would have to hide. He would have to creep like an outlaw. Always hoping for sanctuary, hoping for one last chance to inspire Teresita to ignite the world and cleanse it with wrath.

⁜

The silence took over the mountain as word spread from house to house—Teresita had married the terrible stranger. None could believe it.

But they had seen it, seen it with their own eyes. The tall man dragging her by one wrist as he strode uphill, walking the mile into town, and she, trotting, jogging, trying to keep pace with her groom. They saw him pound on the doors of the courthouse, saw him gesture at the guards, saw her try to pat her hair back, try to straighten her clothing and look respectable. Twidlatch called on Burtch, who sadly reported to Rosencrans, who rushed out to see for himself. But it was too late. Too late to change it, too late to voice opinions, for the deed was done even before the crowds had started to gather. Little Al Fernandez stood outside the courthouse and took off his cap when they came forth. She was weeping, but why, no one could say. Was she happy? Who would not be happy on a wedding day—even a wedding day as tawdry and melancholy as this? Guadalupe seemed to have forgotten she was beside him. He stood on the steps and stared at them. "What!" he demanded and strode away, heading straight for Ward Canyon. She was flushed, flustered. She looked from face to face. She put her hand on little Al's head, and she rushed after him.

"Was there a ring?" Mrs. Rosencrans asked her husband. "I never saw a ring."

Segundo and Dolores came up the street, but Teresita was already gone. Segundo rushed from person to person saying, "What? What?" As if he could not understand their words, as if they were all speaking

Chinese. He grabbed his little beloved and cried, "What has happened?" into her face.

"I don't know!" Dolores wailed. "She has gone insane, mi amor."

Teresita had gone quite mad. To them, it was unforgivable self-indulgence. This was all the women could think.

In the sepulchral Urrea house, the children sniffled in their rooms, threw themselves in their beds. Anita, betrayed and abandoned, hid in her closet and pulled her clothes off their hooks, burying herself in darkness. None dared come downstairs, none could face their father.

Even Gabriela backed away from him.

Tomás sat in the gloom, silent, feet splayed out, head hanging. He would not speak. He would look at no one. Gaby brought him slices of ham and thick slabs of bread with butter, but he did not look, did not stir. Just sat. Stared. Stared as the day turned dark, and the night overcame the room.

That night, people in Clifton ate cold suppers and gazed blankly out their windows. They expected terrible things. The night felt full of fear, but they could not explain why. It was only a marriage. It was none of their concern.

For years after, the people of Clifton asked themselves what they might have done. They asked what wickedness had come to their mountain. They asked if Guadalupe Rodriguez was even really a Yaqui at all. He was mad, they said, the devil, or one of his agents. But others said he was one of the assassins working for Porfirio Díaz, a spy, sent at last to penetrate the Urrea household and lay waste to it. They told themselves that it was exposure to her holiness that cooked his mind in his skull, that her light burned his thoughts to steam.

They did not know what powers manifested in Lupe's Ward Canyon, or how all these things came to pass. Tomás didn't know. Teresita didn't know. It could not be understood. But she, who had been waiting her whole life for a kiss, who had given everything to others, including her joy, had come in her moment of surrender.

In those last few minutes of dusk, when the tallow candles were lit, and the buttery color filled the cabin, he was silent but not unkind, not ungentle with her; she sat on his sagging cot and removed her shoes—she trembled, all nerves, all fear and regret, but bold with her decision to be a grown woman, to break free and claim her own destiny at last, with her husband—husband!—and she undid the buttons of her dress and stood before him, about to let it drop. He said nothing. He stared. He watched her and nodded to the things he wanted opened, dropped on the floor, and when she stood before him, he stepped to her, and she whispered, "My husband, my love," and he grabbed her hair and wrenched her head back and whispered, "You don't even smell like a woman, it makes me sick," and she knew she was about to die.

※

In the morning, Segundo found Tomás still sitting in the parlor.

He knelt beside the patrón's chair.

"Boss," he said. "Boss."

Tomás shook his head.

"Not this way, Segundo. It cannot end this way."

Segundo rubbed his chin.

"Esto está muy mal," he said. "It stinks bad, boss." He shook his head. "No good."

Tomás looked at him.

"It is her choice," Tomás said.

Segundo shook his head.

"Love," said Tomás.

"Ain't love. Ain't love, boss."

Tomás waved him away.

"We can do nothing."

"By God we can!" said Segundo. He had a little trouble rising. Oh, his back. His knees. But he made it up. He stood above Tomás and pointed at him. "I can go put a round through that little turd."

Tomás stirred himself.

"Everything I did. Everything I risked and sacrificed. Everything I lost for her. And they spit at me."

Segundo hung his thumbs in his pockets.

"Ain't easy being a father," he opined.

Tomás actually laughed.

"Indeed." He patted Segundo. "How right you are."

Segundo smiled his hideous smile.

"Right?"

"Right, my friend."

"I'll go kill him right now."

"No."

"One shot, right through the brainpan."

"Absolutely not."

Tomás rose stiffly.

"But you can do one thing for me."

"Name it."

"You could ride out there and see. Just take a look. Make sure my daught…Teresita is all right."

Segundo nodded.

"Claro que sí," he said.

"Down Ward Canyon."

"I know where it's at," Segundo said.

Tomás looked surprised.

"You don't think I wasn't watching him, do you?"

The patrón smiled. The amazing Segundo. They shook hands.

"Be careful," Tomás said.

"Me? I'm going to live forever," Segundo said, and he went outside and saddled a horse.

Tomás went out on the porch to wait for the news.

※

Segundo rode down the canyon and into Lupe's glen. At first, it was quiet. He sat on the horse and watched. The door of the cabin was open. Then Segundo heard Teresita screaming for help. Lupe stepped out of the trees to the side of the cabin with his left fist wound in her hair, dragging her across the ground. In his right, the immense revolver. Before Segundo could react, Lupe swung the pistol up and shot him off his horse. Segundo managed to squeeze off a round. Lupe fired again, kicking dirt into Segundo's eyes. The old man struggled to rise, and fell back and sighed.

※

Tomás heard the echo of the shots and knew what had happened. He had his guns and was running across the yard. He leapt on Caballito Urrea's back without a saddle and sped away. Even as fast as he was, there were already men from Clifton running out, getting mounted. They were moving. Tomás was in the lead.

He thundered into the canyon to the terrible sight of Segundo sprawled on the ground. He flew off his pony and crouched, pistol raised, but Lupe and Teresita were gone. He rushed to Segundo's side. The old pistolero lay staring at the clouds. Blood bubbled out of his chest, up high, well above the nipple. He was wheezing. He pointed toward Metcalf.

"Kill that son of a bitch," he said.

Tomás went hunting.

※

He could hear Teresita crying out, cajoling Lupe, shouting at him. Lupe was babbling—Tomás could hear it. Ranting. He started to run.

It was a quarter mile down the train tracks. Old ore tracks. He realized with a shock that he was still barefoot, and the cinders were bruising and cutting his feet. He ran from cross tie to cross tie.

Around the bend. There they were. Lupe had her. He was pulling her and slapping her, his gun stuffed in his pants. Shouting in her face. Tomás could hear the slaps.

"Why?" she was screaming. "Why? Why? What did I do?" It was

the most pathetic thing he had ever heard. He never wanted to hear such a thing again. "But I love you! Why? Why?"

"Cállese, perra," he snarled.

Tomás shouted: "Stop!"

Lupe halted, pulling Teresita down to kneel before him. He turned and glared at Tomás. He grinned. His eyes were wild, like some dog lurching in from the llano sun mad and foaming.

Lupe raised his gun. Tomás walked forward. Lupe thumbed back the hammer and fired. The bullet flew past Tomás's ear.

"Father!" Teresita cried.

"I am coming," he said.

Lupe fired; the bullet went wide. He stared at his gun. Tomás trotted. Lupe fired again; the bullet seemed to vanish. Tomás broke into a full run. He raised his gun. Lupe went to fire again and the chamber clicked empty. Tomás's pistol rose over his head as he leapt off the ground. He flew, he felt the wind in his hair, the fluttering of his shirt, and he came down upon Lupe and split open his head with a terrible overhead swing, all the weight of his leap and his rage and his great arm exploding the other man's scalp—blood hit Tomás's face as he tripped over his daughter and her attacker and they all rolled down the tracks and lay in a tangle.

Sobbing. Gasping. Tomás's chest hammering, his heart lurching inside him. Heaving.

She crawled from Lupe, too afraid of her father to embrace him. She moved a distance away and huddled there as the riders came to them. All Tomás could hear was her voice, muffled by her hands, asking "Why?"

Tomás stood. Men came running. Hands grabbed him. Hands struck Lupe, feet kicked his ribs. Ropes bound him. Men lifted Teresita to her feet. She looked at her father, tears all down her face. His feet were bleeding. His pistol was ruined. He threw it on the ground.

"Segundo is hurt," he told her.

It was an accusation.

He turned and walked away from her, and he did not turn back, even when she called to him.

※

Dr. Burtch withdrew the bullet from Segundo's chest. Tomás and many of his workers shuffled in the street, worried and drinking. Poor Dolores hiccupped through her sobs, and Tomás awkwardly comforted her.

They'd known when Burtch had inserted the tongs to grab the bullet because Segundo had shrieked, "More rum, chingado!"

Some of the men laughed.

Teresita had been dropped back at the house by the riders. Lupe, semiconscious and bleeding from many wounds now, was dragged at the end of a rope behind their horses, stumbling and cursing.

"Pig!" he yelled at Teresita as Gaby hurried her inside. "I should have killed you!"

Nobody knew what to think. Gaby locked the door, as if the lock could keep his voice out. The children hid. Mrs. Smith had stayed after work, and she sat in the parlor with a double-barreled 12-gauge in her lap.

Teresita was bruised. Her eye was black already, and the blood from her nose was crusted on her lips. Her eyes were almost silver with shock. She lay in bed shaking. Gaby cleaned her face with a moist cloth.

"What have I done? What have I done?"

Gaby blew out the lamp and left her alone.

※

Lupe's yowls were frightening. He was far down the prisoner's mine shaft, locked in the cell in the belly of the cliff. He ranted and gibbered and sent up noises like a trapped wolf's. People near the train station could hear him. They pulled closed their shutters. They kept their houses dark lest whatever was loose in their town find them.

Tomás stood in the street staring down into the black hole that was Lupe's chimney and window.

"Can you hear me, pendejo?" he called.

The howls never stopped.

"I have something for you."

He opened his trousers and pissed down the hole.

❉

Noon.

Clifton was utterly silent.

Not even crows made noise.

It was all wind and rattling weeds beside the tracks.

A lone dog clicked across the cobbles and vanished behind the Fernandez house.

Teresita stood in the street, sniffing the air. Not even cooking smells. It was as if the entire population had fled. No doors opened, no shades rose in the windows.

She looked at the cliff. The dark prisoner's hole stared at her like a blind eye. He was there — she could feel him. His heat seemed to pulse out of the hole. Tendrils of black and deep purple and sick red curled and evaporated in the sun.

"It was my eye that was blind," she said.

She walked toward it. He must have known, must have sensed her, because he began to yell again. His voice, now that the sun had risen, was small. Sorry and flat.

She stopped three feet from the hole and looked down it. Bars, rusted and stark. Beyond that, only darkness.

"Why?" she said softly.

"Because I hate you," he called.

She closed her eyes.

"Why did you lie to me?"

"Because it was easy."

He laughed.

"Because it was my duty."

He howled.

"Because! Because! Because! Do you want to pull up your dress now? Do you want to let me look? Let me look! I want to see it again! Back up to the window!"

She turned and took a step.

"Saint! Saint!" he challenged her. "Forgive me! You must forgive me now, right? Because you're a saint! Right?"

She walked away.

"Answer me! Right? Right? Answer me!"

She walked out of town.

Clouds burned like fire in the azure sky.

They were peach-, orange-, grape-colored far below.

It was like a garden.

Flowers in the sky.

Perhaps this was Sea Ania after all.

Perhaps she was dead.

Even God had turned His face away.

She deserved it.

She'd betrayed them all.

With nowhere to go, she just kept walking.

Thirty-Six

TOMAS MOVED SEGUNDO INTO his house. There, the wounded caballeros recuperated in the parlor, smoking and sadly sipping rum. They repeatedly played the new cylinder from Chauncey Olcott, "My Wild Irish Rose." Tomás was covered in bruises, but he didn't remember how he'd gotten them. His feet were swollen, and his left foot would never work right again. In the kitchen, Dolores and Gaby fretted while Mrs. Smith fattened them with biscuits and gravy.

Sheriffs had come and pried Lupe Rodriguez out of his hole. He was quite mad. He fought like a demon, cried that he could not be torn from his mother's womb, not by mortal men. They cuffed him and chained his hands to his waist and grew tired of his resisting, so they looped a rope around his waist and hauled him out with the help of a mule. He bounced and slithered up the chute like a bale of timothy.

They lifted him onto the mule's back and tied his feet together under its belly and led him shouting curses down the mountain.

Tomás saw in the papers that he had been found insane. The judge in Solomonville signed the declaration. The same sheriffs, not softened in any way toward their prisoner, transported him by iron prison wagon to the asylum in far Safford, where he was tied to a bed and kept down for hours at a time lest he tear open his own veins with his teeth.

The newspapers reported that Aguirre had been imprisoned for fomenting revolution or that he had fled, depending on the publication. Whatever his fate, Tomás thought, it served him right. All this ruination could be laid at Aguirre's feet.

And the newspapers said Teresita had been shot, perhaps killed. Bad enough the paper that gloated "Sainted Girl Beat by Hubby"—he threw that one in the fire.

People in Clifton were mostly circumspect. Many of them felt sympathy for Teresita and her family. But there were those few who had always said she was a witch. And there were others who, feeling now that she was not—from what they could tell—pure, turned against her, saw her as sullied and divorced from God entire. Talk circulated. It was a small town, after all. Sooner or later, the talk made its way around, and then started around again, changing and turning, darkening and building mockery in its heart. Those who loved her became silent, and in their silence, they felt shame.

It was not long until there appeared on the side of the barn, in red paint, an epithet that had been loose on tongues for days:

WHORE OF CABORA.

Tomás didn't see it. He never stepped outside. He barely ate, barely rose, did not bathe. He just played the maudlin cylinder and poured poor old Segundo small copas to drink.

※

She sat in the cabin. After all, she owned it now. Mrs. Rodriguez. That was rich.

She spent so much time on her knees, asking God to explain how she had gone astray, that her knees were bruised from the rough floor. But there was no answer.

The nights were long and terrifying. Every rustle of branches, every owl hoot or coyote yelp, convinced her that killers were coming for her. Or demons offering a darker sort of massacre. She pushed the door shut and braced the lone chair against it, tried to block it with boards. She did not eat—there was no food. Small deer bones behind the cabin, nothing more.

On the third day, Gabriela came to her with a bundle of her clothes and a covered pot of beans with potatoes and a stack of tortillas. She maneuvered her small wagon right up to the door and handed the goods to Teresita.

Teresita tried her old joke on Gaby: "Thank you, Mother dear."

But Gaby merely looked down on her with cold eyes.

Teresita grabbed her hands and cried, "I have sinned."

Gaby shrugged.

"I don't understand such things," she said.

"My father?" Teresita asked.

"Not well."

"Segundo?"

"Better than your father."

Gaby pulled her hands away.

Teresita asked, "Can I come home now?"

Gaby looked at her a long time.

She shook her head.

"No," she said. "Not now."

She shook the leads, and the horse trundled off.

⁂

The next day, Teresita heard the wagon again, she thought. She heard the snort of the horse, the crack of the wooden wheels crushing pine-cones. She hurried outside and held her hand above her eyes—since she'd been hiding inside all these days, her eyes were hurt by the sun.

But it was not Gaby at all. It was Mr. and Mrs. Rosencrans. And between them, small and thin and still pale, sat Jamie.

He struggled over his father's lap and dropped clumsily to the ground. He smiled at her, his skinny face luminescent as a candle in a clouded glass. He limped forward. She stepped to him and put out her arms.

He fell into her embrace and squeezed her waist.

"I can walk," he said.

"Bendito seas," she blessed him. She laid her hand on his head. "Handsome boy," she said. "Little man."

Mr. Rosencrans hopped down. He turned and offered his wife his hand and helped her to descend. The gesture was not lost on Teresita. They came to her, holding hands like young lovers.

"Thank you," Rosencrans said.

His wife kissed her cheek.

They stood like this for a moment, almost comfortable in one another's presence.

"You can't stay here," Rosencrans said.

"My father does not want me back," Teresita said, almost exhausting her English.

"Yes. So I hear. But I mean *here,* on the mountain. In Clifton. It's not healthy for you to remain."

"Where would I go?" she asked.

He looked at his wife.

"Well," she said. "We are leaving tomorrow. We return to the coast."

"Coast?"

"San Francisco," she said.

Oh! Teresita put her hands over her mouth. San Francisco!

"If I may," said Rosencrans. He withdrew a folded sheet of vellum from his coat pocket. He unfolded it. "I have a letter here from our friend Mrs. Fessler."

"A dear woman," said Mrs. Rosencrans.

"Yes." He read. "It seems her daughter, ah, Sally, is quite ill. Mrs. Fessler asks if we know you. She asks, in fact, if we might convince you to come to San Francisco—well, San Jose—and heal poor Sally."

"Isn't that wonderful?" said Mrs. Rosencrans.

Jamie hugged her tighter.

"No comprendo," Teresita said.

"You," said Rosencrans, "come with us. Tomorrow. On the train."

She dropped her head.

"No puedo," she said. "I have no money."

"Oh, Teresita," said Jamie. "We have money. Don't we, Daddy? Shoot—we have all the money in the world!"

The Rosencranses laid hands on her.

"It would be an honor," the wife said, "to take you home."

"Say yes," said Jamie. "Say yes."

Teresita smiled.

❆

That night, the dream awoke her. She heard puttering in the dark. She thought mice had gotten in again. Well, after the next morning, they could have the house. They could gnaw holes in the walls, and the skunks and foxes and squirrels and porcupines could come inside and destroy it. She would be gone.

A pot clanged. What a funny dream. She sat in the dark, listening. She fumbled and found a match and struck it on the rough wall and lit her last candle. She squinted.

An old woman stood in the corner with her back to Teresita. It wasn't frightening. Given all the monsters and fiends she expected in the dark, an old woman held no terror. Teresita had experienced these dreams before.

"Hello?" she said.

Huila, her old teacher, turned around and stared at her.

"Huila!" she cried. "You are dead!"

"Hmm," said Huila. "Tell me something I do not know."

She dragged the chair away from the door and sat on it.

"You have my pipe?" she said.

"Yes. In your apron."

"Give it to me."

Teresita rushed to the mound of clothing in the corner and withdrew Huila's pipe from her apron pocket. What a very odd little dream.

Huila lit her pipe and took a mouthful.

"Savory," she noted.

Teresita stared at her. Huila! Her heart was bursting with joy.

"Don't stare," Huila said. "Sit."

Teresita sat on the cot.

"You've had a bit of bad luck," Huila observed.

"I have failed."

"Failed at what?"

"Failed at my calling. My work."

"Really? One mistake is failure? Damn. It's a good thing I didn't know that."

Huila made smoke and watched it happily.

"Looks like sheep," she said. "Little puffs." She used the word in the mother tongue: *bwala*.

"I am so ashamed," Teresita said.

Huila shrugged.

"Ashamed of what?"

Teresita laughed.

"You are joking with me, Huila."

"Huila," the old one stated imperiously, "does not joke." She smoked and stared at Teresita. "When someone does something bad to another person, it is his own shame. Not his victim's."

"What are you saying?"

"Stop whining."

"Unfair!"

"Look," Huila said. "The American child was cured."

"Yes."

"The woman was cured who came with the poisoned womb."

"Yes, but—"

"Quiet. And you fell in love."

"I did."

"Women are stupid in love. Now you know."

Dios mío. Teresita rubbed her face. This was becoming a bad dream.

"Was he a good kisser?"

"Huila!"

"Was his little flute pleasing?"

"Oh my God!"

"Perhaps," the old woman said, "your job was also to remind everybody that men can be bastards."

"Huila!"

"Could be."

Teresita shook her head.

"I am going back to sleep."

"No," Huila said. "No, you aren't."

She leaned forward and put her icy hand on Teresita's brow.

"Now is the time for you to awaken. For the great work has begun. The world is calling you. You have learned you are not perfect. You are no different from any other person. But God still pours His power into you. No one can know why. Frankly, I am irritated with you. But God believes. He's strange that way. God believes in you. So wake the hell up and go forward. There is no time left for lazy moping. Not now. Child! If you were born to be a flood, you cannot insult Heaven by insisting you are a drought."

"What great work?" Teresita said, but it was morning, and she was lying on the cot, tangled in the rough gray sheet. The door was open. It had started to rain.

＊

Five hundred people gathered at the station to watch the little family and Teresita board the train. They raised their collars against the cold rain. Al Fernandez sniffled as he watched the Saint disappear into the train car.

They called and cried and clapped and waved their hats as the train pulled out. The whistle echoed all across the mountains as the engine's cloud of steam caused the people to vanish.

On his porch, Tomás listened to the whistle blow. His heart fluttered — it felt cold in his chest. He leaned on the post and listened. The sound of the train came faintly to him. Everybody that was left to him — his beloved, his children, poor Segundo and his Dolores — waited for him inside. Anita was inconsolable. Aside from her, Tomás had demanded, they were not to cry — not a single tear.

Farther down the slope, Lauro Aguirre paused to watch the train cut down and turn a long slow curve and then seem to be swallowed by the vermilion cliffs and the ragged trees. He rode into town and was baffled by the listless people wandering sadly in the rain. Aguirre pulled his hat over his eyes to keep the rain from his face and turned down the road to Cabora Norte.

When he reined in before Tomás's porch, the Sky Scratcher beheld him with no expression whatsoever on his face.

"You are too late," he said. "Our lives are over."

"Teresita?" Aguirre asked.

Tomás spit off the porch and glanced up at the rain clouds. He took the drops on his cheeks. He shook his head.

"Who?" he said.

He went inside.

He closed the door in his old friend's face.

Book II

TO THE SILVER SEA

Part IV

FAR AMERICA

That self-same Santa Teresa who has been worshiped as a guide from heaven by the Indians of Mexico on our southern border; who has been credited with miraculous healing powers; who was thrown into prison in Mexico charged with causing an uprising of the Yaqui Indians; who was banished from Mexico for the same reason; who has been the cause of uprising and bloodshed wherever she has appeared in Mexican towns or villages, and excited the fears of the authorities by the enthusiastic following her presence provided; who has gone about healing by the laying on of hands — as believers claim — until her fame has so spread that her presence in any place turns that place into a camp of sufferers flocked to see her; who was, it is claimed, the real cause of a bloody attack on the customs-house of Nogales, Sonora, Mexico some four years ago . . . ; who only last month was the occasion of another sensation in Arizona, when she was married on one day to a Mexican there, who on the next day attempted to shoot her — that self-same Santa Teresa is in California.

—HELEN DARE,
San Francisco Examiner,
Friday, July 27, 1900

Thirty-Seven

THE TRAIN ROCKED AND growled to a clanging stop. She smelled a change in the air. The conductor walked down the car calling, "Yuma! Yuma, Arizona!" She peered ahead, past the water tower and the bursts of steam billowing from the engine. Trees. White birds. Reeds. Mexicans. Arizona would always belong to the Mexicans.

She rose from her seat and rushed down the aisle and pushed out through the door. She could smell wetness. Mud. It smelled green after the relentlessly yellow scent of the desert. It was so hot, so brutally hot. There were no echoes—the heat had crushed all sound.

"¿Qué es?" she asked the conductor, pointing ahead.

He was standing out there on the platform of the train car enjoying a smoke.

"That's the Colorado River," he said.

His words came out in small gray puffs, as if he were on fire.

She jumped from the car and ran toward the river.

"Miss!" he called. "Miss!"

Her companions joined him on the small platform and watched her run.

"Poor thing," said the woman.

"I'll fetch her," said the boy.

"Don't got much time," the conductor warned.

The boy trotted after the Saint.

She stood on the bank above the great brown water. The sound of it broke through the heat—just the noise of it felt like a cool drink, a flood, the sound of the water pouring on her, into her, filling her. Two Indians fished from the bank and turned and looked up at her. She waved once. They tipped their heads to her and turned back to the

275

river. She watched a branch come near, pause, and shoot away on its way to Mexico.

Dragonflies rose from the shallows, languidly lifting and falling and sliding backward in the air. They hovered before her face and studied her.

"I have nothing left to say to you," she said.

The boy joined her.

The dragonflies swirled away.

"Why do they call it red when the water is the color of dirt?" she asked.

He squinted — he thought she'd asked where they were going in her fast Spanish.

"Yonder is California," the boy said.

It was all sand dunes. Far maroon mountains.

"West," the Saint replied, "is the land of the dead."

But he still could not understand her.

He took her hand and tugged her back to the train as the whistle blew and the water arm of the tower rose from the boiler's mouth and the engine chuffed once. They reached the steps and were helped up. The great machine recommenced its eternal stitchery as it mounted the bridge and rolled westward. The train's shadow wobbled on the water for an instant, like a surfacing catfish, before it was back among the sand dunes and gone.

※

And then they were in the Anza-Borrego Desert. They passed through Vallecito, that charred valley where the streambeds were long blankets of pale sand, and the old stage station squatted stark and lonely; few stagecoaches or wagons ever plied those roads anymore. A sunburned coot stood his ground on bandy legs and stared at them as they rushed by, casting him into the past as if he were a mirage. She saw a roadrunner. "Taruk," she said aloud, for despite all she would leave behind, the mother tongue was one thing she could not bear to lose.

She renamed the world as they went far from the People.

She put the words in the purse of her heart like small golden coins.

She saw a bird: "Wiikit."

She saw a small white butterfly: "Vaisevo."

She saw a jackrabbit: "Paaros."

She felt lonely and afraid. She whispered, "Sioka. Sioka. Sioka..."

They sped toward the great wall of the Cuyamaca Mountains, and the train for a giddy moment seemed as if it were going to explode against the stark cliffs before them. But no; it lurched and rose, surged up a long incline, and the slopes were suddenly covered with boulders, madly scattered, many-colored, round. They looked like the peanuts on the ice cream sundae Don Lauro Aguirre had bought her in El Paso.

She shoved El Paso from her mind. She pushed Lauro Aguirre away. He fell out of her mind in a scatter of newspaper pages and flying pencils and spun as if going down a long spiraling hole.

She stared at the rocks, and when she saw one fat boulder poised delicately atop a smaller boulder, she chuckled. It was her first laughter in days. The mountain was being humorous.

Her companions turned to her expectantly when they heard her laughter.

She pointed out the window.

"My father," she said seriously, "stacked those rocks. It took him a week."

They nodded and smiled at her, uncomprehending.

"Teta," she said, nodding to them. "Piedra."

She turned back in time to see trees as they skirted the south end of the high peaks. Great pines — first in ones and twos, then intensifying, and suddenly in a dark cool blur they ruled the landscape. Pines! She rose to her knees and gawked. Her eyes darted between the trees, stabbing deep into the valleys and glades. Oaks. She saw deer. She saw

Americans in red shirts. Horses eating great velvety meadows of moist grass. She saw sheep in a small pen. "Bwala!" she cried, pointing.

And over the hump and down, down, back to desert, but not for long. Manzanita scrub. Ahead, San Diego. Ahead, a baffling band of shadow in the coming dusk. She watched it, wondered at it. Until the sun moved faster than they did toward the western horizon, and the dark band lightened, from purple to blue, from blue to green. It peeked at her as she came around hills and topped rises. And then the sun struck it fully and it became a band of copper, then gold.

The boy leaned in. Pointed ahead.

"The sea," he said.

But they entered a valley, and it was lost from view.

⁂

The Saint had never seen such a place as San Diego. White buildings. Palm trees. Trolley cars. Bougainvillea and geraniums. Red buildings. Paved and cobbled streets in every direction. Horses, carriages, donkeys, sailors, children, dogs, wagons, flags, oleander, rose gardens, seagulls, pigeons, smoke, newspaper boys, gas lamps, musicians, ladies in great skirts with parasols, black faces, red faces, white faces, brown faces, yellow faces, hotels, tall buildings with sunset in their windows, red roof tiles, fountains, hobos sleeping on benches, strolling blue-uniformed coppers with helmets and swinging sticks, pepper trees, mosaics. Gray buildings with glass doors. She felt her heart hammering with excitement. She rushed from window to window as the train slowly inserted itself into the side of the city and made its way into the great old station, unleashing billows of steam that fogged everything.

Her hosts had arranged for them to spend the night in a downtown hotel, and a porter wheeled a cart with their bags into the station to be kept overnight for the Coastliner to San Francisco. They led her out to the docks, and she beheld the harbor with its gathered sails, its masts, its small tugboats churning the water, its pelicans. She put her hands to her face. The sea, the green sea, surged at her feet. She could smell it, smell its fish, smell its salt fetor. Oil formed rainbow swirls among the small tatters of paper and the raw sewage floating beneath her. She thought she could smell Japan. She saw sea lions farther out in the water, lounging upon clanging buoys. She shivered. She sweated.

They took her to a seafood restaurant on the dock and she stared numbly at the platters of crabs, oysters, fried clams. She was served a great braised flank of tuna on a wooden plank. She ate and ate until she thought she would swoon. Her host smiled as he watched her. He offered her a flagon of beer. She stared at it. Why not? All was lost anyway. She tasted it. It was terrible. Bitter. Yet bitterness was good; bitterness tasted of her own heart. The foam overflowed her mouth, and the bubbles burned her throat, but she drank it like water. *Do you see me, Father? Do you see me, Tom?* She laughed silently. She gestured for another.

"Gracias," she said.

It was the last thing she remembered saying.

Early in the morning, sick to her stomach and suffering from a spike being driven over and over through the side of her head, she rose from her bed and washed herself at the basin and dragged on her clothes. So this was how Don Tomás and Aguirre felt in the mornings after their great bouts of drinking. Father, it is not worth the pain. She pulled on her shoes and went downstairs quietly, sneaking out the glass front door so she could walk the cool shadows on Broadway as it went back to the water. Everything smelled like baking bread and horse dung. A drunk slumbered in a doorway. A prostitute smoked, leaning against a wall, and the Saint stopped and looked at her.

"Hola," she said.

"I only got this one," the prostitute said, flicking ash.

"No fumo," the Saint replied.

"No? You no fumar?" The woman stared back at her. "You need something?"

The Saint shook her head.

"Quiero ver el mar."

"The sea, huh?" the woman said. "That ain't the sea. That's just the harbor. It's dirty."

Teresita smiled at her.

"I'm bad company," the woman explained. "You don't want to be seen here."

"Sorry?" Teresita said.

"I'm what they call a soiled dove, dear. Get it?"

Teresita smiled, uncomprehending.

The woman thought for a minute, trying to remember her Spanish. She pointed to herself. "Puta," she said.

Teresita shrugged. "I am a saint," she said. "Es trabajo."

The woman laughed.

"It's a job?" she replied. "I suppose so, dearie."

She laughed again.

"¿Vamos?"

The Saint gestured toward the harbor.

"Jesus," the woman said. "What are you, loony?"

But she flicked her cigarette away and coughed.

"What the hell," she said. "I ain't doin' nothin'."

They walked down to the docks and watched pelicans open six-foot wings.

"Vaawe," the Saint said, gesturing to the ocean. She pointed to the sea lions. "Vaa loovo," she said. She raised her arms to the great pelicans and said, "Tenwe."

"Right," said the puta. "Whatever you say. You're the saint."

⁂

The train headed north on time. Her hosts had convinced the Saint to take a seat on the left side for the view. She was not disappointed. They left the city and entered hills, and soon the hills gave way to sea — real sea, open sea, a vastness of color. She had not imagined that water could have so many hues. The waves curled emerald and jade as they rose on the beaches, and the foam was white and hurt her eyes, the way it exploded with light. Dolphins surf-rode the riptides beyond the beaches. Fishing boats putted along the coast, and schooners were white and fast and riding curling bow waves as their sails billowed with sea wind. Small villages and port towns appeared and fell behind in bustles of color. Small islands. Confetti of gulls.

Before she knew it, they were in Los Angeles. It was bigger even than San Diego. Busier, madder, an immense dry scatter of a city. Chimney smoke and campfire smoke and cooking smoke and smelter smoke and factory smoke blew inland on the sea breeze and was trapped against the Santa Monica Mountains and settled in a vague brown pall over the basin. And with a lurch, they were back on their way, and they entered a dream of coastline, a rugged wildness of solitude and roaring waves, great rocks, twisted pines, surges and blowholes and ships and shorebirds and bays, great dark forests of kelp shadowing the water, flotillas of seabirds like small Spanish galleons where the water turned glassy. Just the smell of it made her sleepy, happy. It made her soft; it made her relax her tight posture and slump. Drunk again on the mere scent of such freedom.

Father, you never told me how beautiful the world was. Why did you not tell me what was outside the fence?

She blinked languidly, her eyelids moving like thick liquid. The coast became rock, then great blond swatches of grass above the waves. Trees were bent by the eternal wind into strange dream shapes. Her head dropped to her chest, and she jerked awake. Tall dark trees on one side, heaving blue-gray on the other. The sway, the surge, the sway, the surge...

And they were in yellow fields. Flowing vast meadows, farmlands. Grass. Dirt. Grass. Dirt.

Against her will, she fell asleep, her horror, her grief, her exhaustion pushing her down in her seat to a dreamless place of comforting rocking, lulling beats of the train's heart, her hand falling to the floor and bouncing softly there. Her companions covered her with the woman's shawl and gently lifted her feet to the seat.

※

When she awoke, many hours later, they were pulling in to the absolute astonishment of San Francisco at night.

Thirty-Eight

SAN FRANCISCO WAS FREEZING. Teresita had never been so cold. In her seat, she pulled her rebozo tight to herself. Shivered.

Nor had she seen fog. It formed a pliant wall outside the great doors of the station. All the clanging and banging and chuffing and whistling didn't budge the throbbing grayness at all. The steam of the locomotive seemed to rush out to rejoin its mother and cover the city.

Bleak. She thought the city was supposed to be colorful. Where was the balmy sea?

Mr. Rosencrans said, "Mark Twain averred that the coldest winter he ever survived was a summer in San Francisco." He smiled. He chuckled. She stared at him, shook her head.

"No lo conozco," she said. "¿Mark Buey?"

"Twain."

"¿Tren? Train?"

"No matter," he said, stepping away from her.

The station. Vendors sold hot nuts, and boys in kneesocks and caps hawked papers, and a violinist sawed away in a corner, coins in an upturned hat at his feet. There were more people bustling through the echoing space than there'd been in either San Diego or Los Angeles.

She saw few Mexicans, but many of the Chinese. Sailors, dashing in their hats, rolling along in hale squadrons. Coughing men, hunched and stinking of urine, shambled past her, dragging weary old feet and pulling tattered coat collars up to their ears. Bawdy boys in striped shirts snickered and skipped, one of them pulling off a companion's hat and tossing it to a third, all of them shouting "Hey-hey!" as they scattered, flipping girls' hair and blowing kisses to those they passed, including the Saint. Immigrant women in shades of brown kept their faces down and moved silent as a reproach.

A finely dressed woman in a yellow gown with a huge bustle behind had met the Rosencranses, and they conferred and gestured. Teresita stood as one mute. She felt as though they were bartering for her. She could have been a slave, or a shanghaied sailor about to set sail for an unknown shore. She had no idea who the woman was but sensed a sick child somewhere here, and that the woman in the yellow dress required Teresita's help to save the girl. She said to God: I put all my trust in You. The Americanos in the group turned and looked at her. A tall black man in a uniform with a shiny black top hat stood behind them, and the rich woman snapped her fingers and gestured. A servant came forward and smiled at Teresita, bowed slightly, and picked up her bags. "This way, madam," he said.

She followed him, nodding at all the strangers as she passed—did they know who she was? Did they recognize her? Had they seen her in the newspapers? She did not know. Her hosts reached out and touched her, light as leaves, as she passed. Jamie hugged her. She patted his head. She was gone inside, gone far away. She was running barefoot in the hills. She was walking along the banks of the River of Spiders, going up to Tomóchic. She no longer cared what happened to her. She would scrub their toilets. She would cook their eggs. Whatever her fate, she had earned it through her failures and mistakes. *Bless me, Father, for I have sinned.* This new exile was penance, she decided.

Perhaps she could make something of herself, earn money to send to

Clifton, as if she could ever repay her father for all that he had squandered on her enthusiasms.

The black man took her to a handsome carriage. She expected to sit atop it, beside him, but he opened the door and laid a small step at her feet and took her hand and assisted her in, onto its plush velvet-covered seat. He tossed her small bag into the covered bin at the back. Outside, between raveling curtains of fog, the city was a festival of twinkles on the hills. Lights blinked and shimmered everywhere—from lamps on corners, from windows, from burning barrels and small fires in alleys. Teresita stared at these lights and felt utterly lost—all those lives, and she adrift among them like a small leaf on the silver sea. Nowhere, in any direction, could she see a light that meant "home." Then, again, fog—and the lights were gone.

The fine lady, her hostess, came in after her, and the carriage creaked and settled as she mounted and fell to her seat in a cloud of fine powder scents. Her eyes were red from weeping. Her face was haggard. She reached across and grasped Teresita's hands. Her fingers were like ice.

"I am Mrs. Fessler," she said.

"Teresita."

They held hands.

"I am...*so happy*...you have come," the woman said. "And so grateful!"

The servant hove aboard, his seat above them squealing as he settled. He clicked his mouth, and the horse moved out smooth as a boat on a small pond. The streets shook and vibrated them, so their voices wobbled as though they were palsied.

The great woman's face went alarmingly red, then seemed to crumple. Her mouth fell open. She drew a shuddering breath.

And she wailed. She broke into sobs. She cried loudly, and snorted, and squeaked with choked outbursts. The horse clopped its hooves and the carriage lurched on. The fine lady blew her nose like a trumpet. She whimpered.

Teresita looked at her with tenderness.

She thought: Oh, be quiet.

⁂

It took them a good while to arrive in San Jose. They had pulled out of the bowl of fog in San Francisco as if rising from a tureen of mushroom soup. Over the lip, and now they were here. It was warmer. She could tell right away from the sound in the air that Mexicans were here. Mexican sound was different than American sound. Even the dogs in Mexican yards barked in Spanish.

They pulled up to the gate of a great house lit by gas lamps. She would see in the morning that the house was yellow, with white trim. Servants rushed down the front steps and swung open the creaking iron gates. The coachman opened the door and offered his hand to the fine lady first. Then he reached in for Teresita's hand and gently helped her down. He gestured toward the double front doors that stood open, the entryway fluttering with candlelight.

"Señorita," he said.

She bowed her head to him and walked up the steps. The maid was comforting the snuffling hostess. The staff looked at the Saint with their eyes full of expectation and hope. She saw no doubt in any face.

"Heal her!" her hostess cried.

Teresita looked her in the eye.

"I have not eaten for a day," she said.

The coachman, on the step outside, translated.

"Oh!" the great lady cried. "Help my child! Please!"

Teresita put her hand on her belly.

"Me duele," she said. "Tengo hambre."

"Yes, yes, certainly. We will feed you after you have seen to my girl."

She pointed inside and snapped her fingers.

"Now," she said. Small cotillion smile. "Please."

The maid showed her to the stairs and gestured for her to come.

Silent, the Saint followed her upstairs. It was the same story. It was the same illness as the little boy's. What was his name? She could not recall. Wasn't that odd? She sat on the bed, took the feverish hand, did the same thing she always did for every child, and felt irritated because she wanted some food.

Thirty-Nine

IT WAS ALL SO fast, yet seemed to take years. Everything that happened, happened in less than a year's time, though later, Teresita would think of it as a decade.

At night, she dreamed of flames and awoke more tired than when she'd lain down.

After the healing, the house felt like a jail. There was no subsequent plan. Nobody had really considered what to do with the Saint after her duties were complete. Certainly, they owed her. There was no doubt. But for how long were they expected to care for her? She had no income. It was more embarrassing than troublesome. Mr. Rosencrans certainly didn't have room for her in his house at the moment—his mother and father had arrived with towers of trunks and bags for a happy visit. Nobody in San Jose had the heart to put Teresita out on the street, but, really, enough was enough.

Perhaps her father would send funds, but the Saint knew she would not ask. It was awful for her—being tolerated. She left the house early in the morning and walked the streets of San Jose. It was bright, friendly, green. The farmers' market was vivid with peppers and melons; above were crows, gulls, and pigeons. Soon enough, her hostess's gardeners recognized her, and word began to spread. The Saint was ushered into many Mexican houses on the side streets of the city, given many cups of coffee, fed many bowls of pozole and plates of eggs and beans. It was a chore for her to return to the big yellow house. She tried to enter silently and sneak upstairs to hide in her room.

One of her few friends was Mrs. Castro, a neighborhood busybody who regaled Teresita with gossip. But she made gorditas that seemed to melt into butter as they were chewed. And her biscochitos were even better. And Mrs. Castro kept the most aggressive seekers at bay, bustling about Teresita like a terrier off her leash as they strolled. On some Saturdays, Teresita slept in Mrs. Castro's back room among her sewing projects and her trusty Singer machine.

"These hills," Teresita said, "are lonely." Mrs. Castro did not understand, but like all the mujeres of the barrio, she worked herbs and saw ghosts and revered the Virgin and kept holy water in a small bottle to absorb evil flung her way by brujas. She listened like a good student. This was Indian business. Her grandmother had been an Indian.

"¿De veras?" she said.

"No one speaks to the hills in their own language," Teresita said. "These spirits have been abandoned."

"Spirits?" said Mrs. Castro.

"The scriptures tell us," Teresita murmured, her eyes closed, as if she were walking in a dream and speaking in some trance, "that there is an angel given to everything in creation."

"Guardian angels?" whispered Mrs. Castro, offering her standard sign of the cross.

"Angels. They do not speak English." Teresita raised one hand as if in benediction. "Or Spanish. Learn the old Indian language of these hills. Go, then, and sing. The angels will hear you and rejoice. You will see wonders."

"Bendito sea Dios." Mrs. Castro sighed.

Teresita put her hand to her brow.

"I feel a little faint. It must be the heat. I will sit."

Mrs. Castro led her to a wrought-iron bench and sat her down and guarded her from any pilgrim who might come down the street.

The trance broke in the morning.

Teresita awoke to the delirium of a mockingbird, the coos of mourning doves, warm breezes lifting her lace curtains. The great house of her benefactress was otherwise silent. And she suddenly thought: San Jose! Why, she had lived in San José, Arizona, and now she was in San Jose, California. She was caught in circles within circles. How could she break the pattern? Unbroken patterns in life were merely mazes that led fools in circles until they died. She held Huila's old rebozo in her lap; she burned herbs in her abalone shell; she placed a glass of water upon her small bedroom altar. Gabriel's feather lay across it, along with a twist of sweetgrass and a bundle of sage, her crucifix, and her small totems. She preferred the Protestants' bare cross to the anguished Christ writhing on Catholic crosses. She preferred deliverance to pain. Aguirre had sent her a black Bible; its title in gilt shone: SANTA BIBLIA. It lay upon her pillow.

She dug in the drawers of the small desk in her room and found paper and pencils.

⁂

To:
Sra. Juana Van Order

From:
Your Teresita
In exile

Oh! Beloved Juanita!—

How my heart longs for you and our hours of delightful laughter now that I find myself a prisoner in this lovely place. It is all very comfort-

able, all full of the most expensive objects and the fattest beds in the world. The señora is friendly, but I am intruding on her. I don't know what to do.

I am sick of being told what to do. I am sick of others dictating my actions. I am tired and I am unwilling to be a mere passenger in my life. Yet... Please, tell me, what should I do?

I laugh at myself....

Perhaps one of your boys could come—I cannot understand any-thing anyone says to me.

✳

No! Weak. Pathetic.

She stared at her letter through tear-blurred eyes. They weren't tears of self-pity or sorrow. They were tears of sheer rage. It was useless. She sounded like an idiot. Her bald-faced stratagem was absurd: *Perhaps one of your boys could come.* Like requesting a mail-order bride.

Huila whispered in her mind, *A woman in trouble does not need a man to save her, child—she will only have to save him in the end.*

Walking that maze.

She crumpled the page and threw it away.

What she really wanted to do was write to her father. But she could not. She believed he would not accept any letter from her. And what would she say?

Perhaps she could send the fugitive Aguirre one of their famous cryptic notes from two years ago:

Damn it!

Perhaps, simply, *No.*

That would suffice.

Forty

CLIFTON HAD BECOME so quiet—or was it only the ranch? Gabriela felt like a nun in an empty church, almost afraid of her own footsteps, as if their resonance on the wooden floors would somehow shatter the mourning silence.

And poor old Mr. Van Order had died in Solomonville. That didn't add to the happy times. Tomás was too bereft to even respond, and Gabriela had sent perfumed cards of condolence in his stead. She had also shipped some flowers to Juana, but they had wilted before they ever got to her.

Tomás voted for McKinley in the presidential election after hearing of the "full dinner pail" doctrine. He had lost money in stock market panics and bad investments, and Republicanism—with its echoes of La República Mexicana—appealed to him. "William Jennings Bryan?" he baffled Gabriela by shouting. "Debs? Please! Por Dios."

In spite of the landslide victory of his candidate, doom seemed to dog his steps. He hated the news every day; the American population had swelled to seventy-six million. Soon there wouldn't be a place for a man to stand. And worse, immigrants poured in by the millions. Why, just that morning, an editorial stated that nine million foreigners would enter the county by 1901. He wrote letters demanding that the borders be closed, that the European trash be stopped from sullying the Americas any further. Germans, Italians, Irish, Chinese, the Hebrews—all taking over his country. It was getting so that a man could not hear good old Spanish anymore.

Bubonic plague in San Francisco! He rattled the pages. Would it kill Teresita? He consumed the stories of dead Chinese immigrants in hotel basements.

He turned the page and learned that the life expectancy for an American male was forty-seven years.

"Jesus Christ!" he cried. "I am already dead!"

Smoking made him cough.

Even music depressed him. The latest wax cylinder to come was a ghastly thing by some pendejo. It was called "Boola-Boola." Tomás threw it in the fireplace.

He asked Gabriela, "Has a letter come from Teresita?"

She had to say, "No, mi amor."

And the next morning: "Any word from Teresita?"

"No, chiquito. I'm sorry."

"A telegram?"

"No."

"Do you think it's the plague?"

"No, no. Don't worry."

"The plague," he said. "It is passed through fleabites. You don't think she's in a place with fleas, do you?"

"Ay, chiquito. No! She went with fine people. Good people. Muy ricos."

"I would hate for her to be bitten by fleas."

It broke her heart. It made her angry. Damn that Teresita!

She finally scolded him one morning after hours of his fretfulness.

"Gordo!" she said—her affectionate term for him. "Why do you not write to her!"

"Oh, no," he replied. "No, no. That would not be right. She wronged me. When she asks me for forgiveness, then I will answer her. I will grant it, of course!" After a moment, he said, "She doesn't want to hear from me."

Damn them all. Gaby was sure enough tired of this moping around. There was work to be done. There were chores to do. Even Anita was apparently paralyzed, and lay upon her bed wistfully playing with dolls or reading Teresita's old books. For hours! Why, when Gaby was a girl, she was up every day before dawn collecting eggs, shoveling cow shit, gathering fruit, or plucking peapods off the vines. And damn that Lauro Aguirre, who had hidden in their house from some nonexistent Texans who were allegedly intending to carry him off to prison.

Indeed, Aguirre spent his days in the stifling shadows of Tomás's parlor, sipping tea and staring at the floor with his compadre. They acted like they'd all been shot by bandidos! And the only one who had actually been shot, Segundo, worked like a man of twenty in their absence.

Then, as if it were nothing, Aguirre left for his stinking Texas, and Tomás grew more hollow, alone in his dark office. Before him, on the table, medical books open to the plague chapters, all of them heavily annotated and underscored, and a collection of colored pencils scattered all around. His reading glasses were atop his head. One red pencil tapping softly.

*

The various businessmen in town had not forgotten the Sky Scratcher. All those barons the workers called plutes — by God, they had enjoyed some times at the Urrea spread, and now they sent invites down to the house. But Tomás was uninterested in hilarity, or business, and this appalled them. Just like a Mexican, they said, to be so lazy he can't even stir his stumps to make a dollar. And so they did forget.

Except for the great industrialist Twidlatch. El Tweedly-yatch, as Tomás had called him, had a plan. He mounted the train in the morning and chugged away with his sights set on distant San Francisco. Land of opportunity. Gold Coast. Home of piles of glittering gold and pots of coin. Home of the legendary Saint of Cabora. He headed west in great good cheer.

*

Tomás awoke, gasping. It wasn't the first time. It started with the sensation that he had swallowed water and choked on it. He jerked and coughed. His chest felt as though a great stone had been laid upon it. His shoulder felt like he'd been shot. He reached out for Gaby, but she was already downstairs, attending to her duties as wife and mistress of the rancho. Bless her. Bless her heart! Beloved Gabriela! Just as well. Why alarm her? The pain. The pain! He clutched the sheets in his hands. He groaned. He could take it. He was Tomás Urrea. Pain? He laughed at pain. But he did not laugh—he cried out. With great effort, he stifled his cries. Only the weak, Tomás reminded himself, whimpered. He lay there sweating and panting until the pain dulled. He knew he would tell no one. No, he was not weak—he wasn't going to crawl off to Dr. Burtch asking for help. Indigestion, he told himself. Even though he rarely ate. That was his problem. All this sorrow. All this fasting. *By God, he'd eat.* He'd eat fried pork and eggs and chorizo. In a minute. As soon as he could get out of bed.

Forty-One

MISS HELEN DARE KEPT her auburn hair braided and tightly coiled at the back of her head, held in place by two ivory chopsticks crossed through a tooled bit of leather suggesting a lotus blossom. She had a difficult time working her straw hat around that and pinning it down. There was always hair trouble when she was in a hurry.

She hustled from the editorial offices of the *Examiner*. She was almost late, but she'd resigned herself to the fact that reporters were always in that state. And she still had to meet her recalcitrant translator before she rushed to the Saint's abode. Teresita had arrived in San Jose to some acclaim among the Mexicans of the city. Helen checked her notes. *Twenty-eight yrs old—Saint of Cabora—healing—Indian uprisings—Clifton AZ—San Francisco—Medical Consortium promises her she won't make money here. (?) Provides home, provides vittles, takes money for "upkeep." (?)*

Miss Helen Dare was tired of all the local-color stories she was assigned. Her editors believed these pieces required "the woman's touch." This Saint assignment, though one more in the tiresome series, at least had some real news overtones.

Hers was a small sorority. Newspapers were still a boys' game, and women reporters were scarce on the ground. But if any city would allow a woman to succeed in a man's world, it was San Francisco. She smiled as she tucked in a few loose strands. Not far from Union Square, her friend would be waiting on the corner. She watched for his lanky form in the sidewalk throng. He spoke excellent Spanish from all his cantina-crawling and bandido-chasing. They had to get all the way to San Jose before noon.

The bustle of Market Street amused her. The rattling cable car moving inexorably toward the bay. The mad scramble of newsboys and pedestrians, and the few comic auto cars. Chaos seemed to reign. She wondered if the Girl Saint had seen this crazy parade yet.

※

The house was white. A two-story wooden Victorian-style cottage with deep purple trim. Its shutters, doors, and filigree were all ripe as wine grapes. It was hardly the most lurid house in the San Francisco area, but it was hard to miss. Hard to forget too. This was, of course, part of the design. Atop its roof, a golden rooster weather vane struck an imperious pose.

The house sat in the middle of North Seventh Street, number 235. A small home with olive trees stood to one side of it, and a business sealed off Teresita's view of the other end of the street. Tomcats everywhere. Teresita had been amazed by the modernity of the house—it had an electric buzzer on the front door, and a simple button push made the inside of the building buzz like a rattlesnake's rattle, if the snake had been twenty feet long. And beyond, on the cross street, an electric streetcar passed every fifteen minutes, one of the very cars that would carry Miss Helen Dare to their appointment.

Among the associates, the house and the scheme within it were known as Twidlatch's Folly. He could afford to laugh along with them. True, the rent was prohibitive, but the profits were steady and handsome. The other members of the Medical Consortium shared the costs of the Saint's needs, but as landlord, Mr. Twidlatch was able to take a higher percentage of the overage. If Rosencrans had been involved, he would have overseen a bank account in Clifton, some recompense to her father and the family ranch. But Rosencrans wasn't involved, and the Urrea clan was far away.

The contract had been a masterpiece of fake sincerity and bogus piety. She didn't have a lick of El Inglés. She signed in faith, since Twidlatch had been a friend of her father's. Sometimes when he was in his cups, he boasted to his comrades, "I own the Saint of Cabora."

She believed, at first, that profits were being banked to repay her father. Her own needs were minimal. She wanted her debts — those that could be paid — to be squared. It was only later that she understood that there was no money going back to Clifton.

Today, pilgrims were kept at bay. It was important to have the house relieved from siege for this newspaper story, under control. Teresita was rested and well fed. Sweepers cleared off the steps and swept the sidewalk clean — even horse droppings were taken away from the brick street and deposited around the corner. Poor children carried the dung to their grandmothers' vegetable gardens off the alleys behind the street. There, chickens scratched still, as if these yards were small portions of Sonora, where people ate cactus and grew their own tomatoes and fried brown eggs fresh from the straw piles beside the outhouses.

The porch awaiting Miss Dare was plain — wide enough to take believers in single file and to hold two chairs to flank the queue. Teresita's minders — paid by the Medical Consortium — sat there all day, guarding the door and regulating the clients.

Two painted Mexican flowerpots rested on the rails. One held white geraniums and the other held red ones. They made the Saint happy, but also set the tone for the Mexicans who shuffled about before the steps, awaiting their conferences. The Consortium had learned quickly that they were the most trusting yet suspicious of all the people. Mexicans needed some suggestion that they were safe or at least on friendly ground. Mexicans never felt at ease until they saw something Mexican.

The picket fence was close to the front of the house and afforded no real room for a garden—it was mostly yellowing grass and some scraggly ivy, though one rhododendron bush lent a festive air to the sidewalk and porch.

Teresita had requested canaries, for some reason. Why not? The Consortium put cages of canaries on the locked back porch. It was glassed in and held one small swooning couch, on which she often slept after insomnia had kept her moving like a wraith from window to window, staring out at the silent streets lit pale yellow by the gas lamps.

Canaries. They sang all day, from before the sun rose and into the afternoon when the sun began to fade. They sang so incessantly that when the Consortium allowed Teresita to go to the farmers' market, she could still hear the birdsong in her head. She didn't know if her bodyguards heard these songs too. They did not speak to her.

She made small nests for the yellow birds out of tea strainers and cotton. At night, she covered their cages with her shawls. She would stare at them when she was alone, after her day's work, and think, If only I had the wings of a bird, I would fly away and be at peace.

※

Helen met her friend on the corner. He was working at the *Californian* and the aptly titled *Wasp*. He stood in the sun, tall as a lamppost and thin, his carefully tended curls piled atop his head, and his great mustache jutting to either side of his face. Like stingers. He wore no hat.

"Girl Saint, eh?" he said by way of greeting. He leaned away from Helen as if being pushed by a gust of wind, his hands going helplessly to his chest. He was infuriating. But he was a fine translator. "An Indian, no less."

"She happens to be Mexican," Helen said.

"Delightful," he replied.

"Shall we?"

"We shall," he said, offering his arm as they set out to meet Teresita.

Ambrose Bierce. She smiled. His great body knocked into hers as they rolled. Women said they could feel him from across the room when he entered a door. He smelled vaguely of bay rum and rich tobacco. She didn't know about feeling him from a distance, but now, as he radiated heat beside her, Mr. Bierce had her full attention.

For the entire swaying, rattling ride, with transfers to two green cars, they said little. Bierce jotted notes in his small notebook, ideas for stories that Helen had seen—ghastly things she didn't much care for. He smoked. She cadged a thin cheroot from him and drew critical stares as she lit up and blew smoke into the aisle.

San Jose.

Bierce noted, "Ah, the Pearl of the West."

"Oh, you," she replied.

When they saw the house, Bierce muttered, "Three cheers for subtlety."

"Hush," she scolded.

Twidlatch stood in the street in his absurd beaver top hat. Parked at the curb was a gleaming 1901 Oldsmobile Runabout with the celebrated curved dashboard. Bierce leaned in and took a gander. It smelled of leather. "Next year's model!" he called. There would be no auto cars on a reporter's salary.

"It came by rail," Twidlatch announced, rocking up on the balls of his feet.

Bierce sucked at a tooth as though a bit of pot roast were stuck there and turned away.

Two hired apes stood on the steps of the porch. Rules of all sorts came at the reporters in a cascade. No questions about finances, for example. No exiting the house with the Saint. The Great Man in his tall hat kept stating "I must insist" after every demand. Bierce had earlier been bored by the entire enterprise, but now that this hideous toad had accosted him with his Britishness, he was raring to go up the steps. He wished he had brought his derringer as well, for this bloated autocrat could use a good peppering. All through the lecture, Bierce kept looking over his shoulder.

A Mexican matron with gray hair and eyeglasses stood resolutely in the middle of the street, braced as if facing a stiff wind. Her apron revealed old stains of mole and chicken blood that had not washed out over the years, and in her hand she held a drooping bouquet of cilantro as if she meant to flog the Englishman with it.

"Is this the Saint?" asked Helen.

El Tweedly-yatch coughed out a single humorless laugh.

"This is the irksome Mrs. Castro, apparent sheriff of Seventh Street."

Mrs. Castro put one finger to her eye.

"Los estoy observando, cabrones," she said.

Bierce had a slight cough of his own.

"You are obviously in good hands," he offered.

The Englishman shrugged. He turned them away from the implacable matron and introduced them to an oily-haired impresario.

"Mr. Suits," he announced.

"J. H. Suits," the gent said, bowing slightly.

"That suits me fine," said Bierce.

"Really, Ambrose," chided Helen.

"I am the Saint's personal manager," Suits told them. "Here to answer any questions."

Helen took his hand.

"Pleasure," she said.

"Perhaps, this...gentleman here," Suits said, "would care to stay outside with us as you chat with Saint Teresa?" He offered a small case of cigars.

Bierce looked around.

"Awful lot of beef gathered to control one li'l Mexican gal," he drawled.

"It is our duty to protect her." J. H. Suits exhaled.

"Mr. Bierce," said Helen, "is my translator."

"Ah."

"Excuse us," Bierce said, pushing through. "Deadlines, don't you know." As soon as he'd sensed they didn't really want him to see the Saint, he wanted very much to take a peek.

Helen smiled at the gents and followed him to the door. They tussled a bit to see who would be first to enter, but Helen moved him aside. "It is my story, after all," she said, elbowing him.

The front room was spare. Wooden chairs and an oval carpet. "Brussels," she noted with approval; he shrugged. Carpets? Could anyone care about a carpet?

A waiting room. Uncomfortable chairs lined up along the wall with sad little stains from the heads of the hopeful leaning back against the wallpaper. Votive candles flickered on small dark end tables.

"La Santa," said Bierce, "needs to watch these candles unless she wants a conflagration."

He stroked his whiskers and squinted slightly.

"Apocalypse," he noted, "always follows outbreaks of holiness."

Teresita opened the inner door and smiled at them. The scent of roses wafted out. Helen took her hand. Bierce raised his eyebrows and seemed as if he were ducking a thrown shoe.

Helen Dare already saw her own words streaming through her mind: *She came to meet me with a soft, swift, gliding step, a slender outstretched hand, a soft-spoken Spanish greeting—tall, slender, flat-chested, fragile....* Bierce noted that Miss Helen had already fallen in love with the Saint. He preferred rounder women. Well, actually, skinny women were quite fine too. But sinners were definitely better than saints. Hell—all women. As long as they weren't idiots.

"Eh?" he said.

"Pásen, por favor," the Saint repeated.

They entered—Bierce doffed an imaginary hat. He moved his upper body around as if it were on springs, inspecting every corner of the room. She regarded him with a vague grin — he reminded her of her father. He was tall enough. He hitched his dark trousers at the knee, flared open his coat like wings, and sat down and crossed his legs. He stared at the standing ladies and crossed his arms. They looked down at him. He sighed. He rose again.

"By all means," he intoned. *"After you."*

"Gracias," Teresita said.

. . . Beautiful, black-fringed, shining brown eyes and a grave sweet smile, Helen wrote in her mind.

They took seats on the settee across from him, backlit by a window that revealed the side of the neighboring building — a brick establishment that featured a leering mural of a moron holding up a bottle of elixir and grinning. TAPEWORMS! it proclaimed.

She sat herself down beside me with her long slender hands together on her knees with the perfect ease of perfect unself-consciousness.

Helen shook Teresita's hand. Bierce bobbed his left foot impatiently as if he needed to run around the block. He yanked his notebook out of his inner jacket pocket and licked the point of a pencil. Nodding sagely, he wrote: *Early one morning in 1872 I murdered my father — an act which made a deep impression on me at the time.* He laughed out loud.

"Great literature, ladies!" he announced, replacing his notebook close to his heart.

"My rude companion," said Miss Dare, "is the notorious newspaperman Ambrose Bierce. He is a terrible man."

"Oh?"

"They call him the wickedest man in San Francisco."

He shrugged.

"The oldest, perhaps," he mumbled.

Still, Bierce was delighted to be translating such dire comments about himself.

"He published a scandalous book," Miss Helen confided. "It was called *The Devil's Dictionary.*"

"Are you familiar with the devil?" Teresita asked Bierce.

"We are drinking companions," he replied. "I regularly cheat him at poker."

"Is he a sore loser, sir?"

"He cursed me with these good looks," said Bierce, leaning back and wickedly stroking his whiskers.

Miss Dare said, "They call him Bitter Bierce."

Bierce translated as if announcing a dukedom.

Teresita turned back to him.

"And are you bitter, Señor Bierce?"

"As gall," he said.

He beamed.

She nodded and leaned toward him.

"You could chew sugarcane," she suggested.

"Eh — what?"

"Or perhaps a dose of algerita. Chop the root with an ax and soak it in water. I'd say three to five drops a day under your tongue. Good for the liver... Forgive me, but you look like a drunkard."

"Indeed!" he said, warming to her immensely.

"Try biscuit root. Biscuit root, drunk in corn liquor. It will cure the effect of drinking...too much corn liquor."

Helen Dare stared at them as they laughed.

"Anything I should know?" she said.

"Mere preliminary rounds for the great boxing match," he replied.

"Eres un borracho, y eres sangrón tambien," she said.

"By God!" Bierce said. "I am rude. Quite right! It is my best feature. You refresh me, Santa, I must declare. Oh. And when I say *God*," he added, "I mean of course if there were such a critter."

Helen cleared her throat.

The interview began.

※

Bierce was unmoved by so much hooey. Miracles and the like. The revolutionary part, the shooting, that appealed to him. He was not only a newsman but a war hero. Most of the concerns of the good citizens of San Francisco seemed so much foofaraw and spume to him. He had tasted true life, raw and pungent, and he had no interest in niceties and shared illusions. Teresita's limpid dark gaze moved him somewhat, he would admit; she had a certain bovine blinkiness to her—though deep inside, he thought of her as deerlike, but that appalled him and he refused to entertain the poetry of it.

Miss Dare excused herself for a moment, and Teresita showed her to the excuse-me. Helen really needed time to scratch her notes as fast as possible before they faded from memory. It was best, she had found, to take notes out of sight to keep the flow of information in the actual interview free and unfettered.

When Teresita came back in the room, she offered Mr. Bierce tea. He shook his head. She sat.

"What do you think of my story?" she asked him.

"The company is bearable"—he sighed—"but the discourse makes me want to jump out a window."

"Oh my."

He grinned, pleased with himself. He fondled his whiskers. He bobbed his impatient foot.

"How do you like California?" he asked.

"It is...bearable," she said with a small smile of her own. "But the discourse..." She shook her head and blew air through her lips.

"Ha!"

This Saint had some bark on her.

He leaned in.

"There is one thing you must beware of," he warned.

"What is that?"

"Vampire bats."

"Excuse me?"

"Vampire bats. They are everywhere. They come at you and keep on coming, slashing with razorlike fangs. You can't feel the sting until you are exsanguinated! Your manager will find you bloodless and pale on the ground." She blinked. "Why, I was with a farmer across the bay in fair Oakland. They must carry ax handles for protection! The swarm came at me. If I hadn't had a hoe, all would have been lost!"

Teresita stared.

"They came at me. Wave after wave. I beat them and beat them. It was hideous!"

Helen Dare came back in the room.

He sat back, crossed his legs, and nodded darkly at Teresita.

"Did I miss anything?" Helen asked.

"We were simply discussing natural phenomena," said Bierce, smiling warmly. "Say, Santa—how about some of that tea?"

✳

"When you awakened, after this...this trance you mention," Helen said. "You could heal?"

The canaries tossed bubbling music in the air behind them.

Teresita nodded.

"When I cured people, they began to call me Saint Teresa." She smiled, blushed. "I didn't like it at first, but now I am used to it."

"Yes," offered Bierce. "Everyone calls me Saint Ambrose. It is a burden."

"Hush," said Helen.

Teresita continued, already aware that one ignored Bitter Bierce's outbursts—he was mostly amusing himself.

"Some said I was a saint, and some said there was an evil spirit in me. Some have come to examine me and said it was in the blood or the nerves. But I feel it was given to me by God. I believe God has placed me here as one of His instruments to do good."

She smiled at Bierce.

"Perhaps you too, Saint Ambrose."

"Heaven forfend," he said.

"But this Consortium," Helen said. Teresita glanced toward the door, her brows knitting a bit. "They are making money off you, are they not?"

"The power to do good makes me happy and grateful. I have no wish to be paid." She shrugged. "I have no care for fine things or fine houses or *money*."

"Then you are unique in Christendom," Bierce noted.

"You would like my father," Teresita said. "He too is a foolish man."

Bierce sipped his cold tea and worked his eyebrows at her.

"But the Consortium..." Helen insisted.

Teresita waved a hand impatiently.

"I refuse no one who needs help. Yes? Sometimes, I know, people come to me because they have curiosity but no faith. If they are sick, I try to cure them. I try not to have the same negative feelings toward some people as they have toward me. Sometimes I feel the power that is in me bounce back at me when I send it to them. But I try again."

"The Consortium assists in this?"

Teresita poured herself more tea and dropped in two lumps of sugar. She sipped and stared at Helen over the rim of her cup.

"Holiness," she noted, "is expensive."

The silence after that was long and heavy.

The women turned and looked at Bierce. His head had fallen back. He was snoring softly.

"Perhaps," said Teresita, "another topic would be more of interest to your readers."

Helen Dare let the Consortium go.

"May I ask," she said, kicking Bierce's foot. He snorted awake. "What malady was it that so affected the Rosencrans child that you healed?"

She was hoping for a mystical response, some real Indian zinger to cap off her story.

But Teresita simply replied: "Cerebrospinal meningitis."

Helen was taken by surprise and sat back with her eyebrows raised.

Teresita grinned.

"You think it is magic," she said. "This is my science."

She extended her hands.

Helen declined to touch them.

꙳

As he took his leave of Teresita, Ambrose Bierce paused at the door.

"Santa," he said. "This sincerity routine of yours. It works."

He nodded out toward Messrs. Suits and Twidlatch and their pis-mires and mugwumps gathered on the steps keeping an eye on the house and the street and the reporters.

"My advice to you, however, if I may be so bold."

"You may."

"Take charge of this rabble."

He nodded once, turned away, leaned back.

"These donkeys of yours could use a little gelding."

"Gracias, señor," she said.

"Snip-snip," he called as he tumbled down the steps and burst into the afternoon.

"Farewell, Mr. Bierce," she called.

"¡Adios!"

Why, Mr. Bierce had brought her the most pleasure she had enjoyed in a long while.

Teresita stared at her minders, closed the door before they could come to it, and quietly turned the lock.

Forty-Two

THE STORY APPEARED ON July 27 to some acclaim. It certainly upped the ticket purchases for the Consortium. J. H. Suits had Teresita scheduled down to the hour: Up at six, breakfast and ablutions until seven. Quiet time until eight thirty. Clients from nine—an hour earlier than before—until five, with a half-hour break for lunch.

Supper at six. Six days a week. She was "free" to walk out on Saturday mornings—accompanied by guards. Otherwise, she was kept inside. She was open to a sign, she felt—she was thinking of a coyote, a wolf, a lion. Hummingbirds or ravens or dragonflies or a spider. Any sign would do. Until then, she would do as she was told.

And what about Buenaventura? Surely he would come for her. Perhaps he'd see the newspaper story. But Mrs. Castro's investigations finally brought news of that. Fast Johnny Urrea had gone on to Virginia City, seeking gold. With that, Teresita lost her smallest hope that she would be set free.

But in her quietest hours, she imagined her father, her father and Aguirre, each taking a cognac in a large snifter with Mr. Bierce. And she knew what they would say to her. Huila would say it too. They would tell her: *Set yourself free.* And Huila would whisper: *You already had your sign.*

※

Bierce remained intrigued by Teresita for a while, but both he and Helen, in their competing newsrooms, forgot all about her after September 8, when the Galveston hurricane hit Texas, killing eight thousand people. Unlike Dare, Bierce welcomed devastation. Ah, death! Telegrams arrived in a steady flow; Morse code keys ticked and tacked, and Bierce drank a toast to every dead corpse.

Both reporters missed the small story that would have brought them narrative gold, a small bit on an inner page of September 24's *Oakland Tribune.* But who read Oakland's papers? No one did when whole city streets in Texas were lost in the Gulf of Mexico.

The unseen headline read: "Santa Teresa Causes Litigation." The relentless Mrs. Castro had marched into the police station and demanded that Mr. Suits and his henchmen be arrested for unlawful imprisonment, illegal confinement, and white slavery. Lieutenants Newsom and Burciaga had gone to the scene, and as soon as the minders on the front porch leapt the rail and ran into the alley, the policemen had turned on

Suits and clubbed him to the ground. Why would people run if they were not guilty? Mrs. Castro waded in and kicked Suits firmly in the culo. The coppers stormed up the steps and broke down the door—its old wood gave way and the hinges burst free, dropping the door at an angle and revealing cowering Mexicans in the waiting room. Shrieks, cries of alarm.

Teresita came forth from her healing room and put her hands on her hips.

"It wasn't locked," she said.

☀

Suits spent several days in custody. Unrestrained, Twidlatch, who had a stark terror of spending time in gaol, found good tickets on a train bound for Portland and then Seattle. There, he entertained propositions to engage in the ferry trade, finding a tempting investment opportunity in the refurbished Vashon Island line. He was out of the saint business and better off for it. It didn't hurt that he had also taken Suits's profits. He told himself Suits had God by the tail—and despite this setback, there was always money in that.

☀

When Señor Suits, along with two large and ominous associates, crept back to the house with purple shutters a week later, he found the door replaced. Mexicans had brought a fresh unpainted pine slab and mounted it. In place of bodyguards, Mrs. Castro stood in the middle of the porch and wagged an accusatory finger. "What is your business here?" she demanded in English. Suits hadn't known she could speak English.

"Er," he said. "I would like a word with Saint Teresa. Please."

Mrs. Castro went in. A moment later, she emerged. She gestured.

"Enter," she said.

"Boys," Suits whispered. "Keep an eye on the door—I might need rescuing."

They chuckled as he went in. Mrs. Castro followed. "I translate," she announced. He only murmured, "Yes."

Teresita sat in her small kitchen, near her canaries. She had a steaming cup of tea on her table. She looked at him, sipped some tea, placed the cup carefully in the saucer.

"Sit," she said.

He sat.

"Remove your hat, please," she said.

He did.

She crossed her legs and bobbed her foot — Mr. Bierce had taught her that.

"Well," she said. "Things did not work out the way you'd planned."

She sipped her tea.

Suits said, "I meant well."

"No. You did not."

Suits craned around and looked at Mrs. Castro.

"Change is coming, Señor Suits," Teresita said.

Mrs. Castro delighted in translating his name back to him, making it Spanish. Señor Trajes, she called him. The women laughed. It wasn't friendly laughter. Mr. Suits did not feel that a white man needed to put up with uppity greaser women, and later, at the bar, he would tell his confreres that he hadn't done any such thing. But now he cleared his throat. He stared at the floor. When they laughed at him, they shrieked like crows.

"You, I think," Teresita said, "must be very bad."

He affixed a look of misery on his face.

"I have lost everything," he said. "I have only sought to care for you and, and, the holy work you do. I have children."

Teresita smirked.

"I enjoy your sincerity routine," she said. "It almost works."

Mrs. Castro delivered this line like an ice pick in the ear.

The canaries were apparently rioting in their cages.

Suits nervously glanced at Mrs. Castro again.

Mrs. Castro said, "She could kill you with her eyes."

"Excuse me?"

"Her *eyes*. Her *eyes!*"

It had never occurred to Suits that all the miraculous-power rigma-role might be true.

"Mr. Suits," Teresita said. "I am sitting here. Not in that corner."

He turned back around. He was very confused. He could smell her. He wanted to open a window. The roses.

"You have lost nothing," Teresita said. "Nothing! It is I who have lost everything." She drained her cup. Mrs. Castro rushed to refill it. The room was dark. The shadows were rich brown and deepening. "You have your country. You have your language. You have your friends, and, if you aren't lying, you have your children. You have your *business associates*. What do I have?" She placed her hands on the table and examined them. "You?" She smiled up at Mrs. Castro. "I have Señor Suits. What a blessing from God."

"Cabrón," Mrs. Castro muttered.

"I did my best," Suits protested.

"You did your best to steal from God," Teresita said. "If you care to confess, go find a priest."

Suits couldn't get a handle on this conversation.

"What can I do?" he asked. "To...rekindle...our...arrangement."

"What do you propose?" she said.

He cleared his throat. "My associates in the Consortium are reason-able men. Professional men. They represent, er, *clinics*. Medical clinics, you see? They seek to post illustrations of you to, ah, attract the Meskins."

"I see."

"They'd pay us a fee for that."

"Hmm." She thought of her father. This income—she owed him, did she not? She could not return, not yet. And she could heal, even from afar. She could heal Tomás's heart, heal her corruption. Collect-ing alms.

And this was unforgivable too—but the idea of seeing more of this gaping nation was deeply appealing. After all, was this not a country of people for whom return to their homelands was not an option?

"And perhaps you would be willing to appear at events. Public, let's say, events. Lend your blessing, so to speak," Suits continued.

"There is money in this?"

He laughed.

"Why, yes, I'd say so."

He was squirming, loosening his collar a bit, his hair oil dripping and showing around his ears in greasy little rivulets — Teresita watched him melt like a candle.

"Give me a cigar," she said.

He goggled.

She snapped her fingers.

"Come, come," she said.

He dug in his coat and produced his slim case. He snapped it open. She took out a cheroot, bit the end off, and spit it in the corner. He was alarmed when she pulled a match out of her skirt pocket and struck it and lit the cigar and turned it as she fired the end thoroughly. She drew in a fat mouthful of smoke and blew it into his face.

"From now on," she said, "things will be different."

Mr. Suits could only bow his head.

"How different?"

"As different as I want them to be," she said.

"Ladies don't act like this," he whined.

"I am not a lady!" she said in her heavy English. "I am the Saint of Cabora!" She said it like a stage name, more mercantile than sacred, aware of Suits's desires. She did not believe it, had never believed it, but would use it now, a magician's misdirection.

"Her eyes, estúpido," Mrs. Castro warned.

"This is your problem, not my own," Teresita said.

"All right. What are your demands?"

"I wish to continue healing the sick," she proclaimed.

"You will remain with the Consortium?" he said, astounded.

"If I break my contract with you, can you assure me there would be no litigation?"

"Certainly on my part, there would be no lawsuit. However, my partners..."

"Exactly what I thought," she said. "I was foolish when I signed that paper," she added. "I am not foolish now."

Here it comes, he thought.

"First, I do not wish to stay here. And I no longer wish to see you."

"I—"

"Ever."

Hell, he thought, I ain't all that bad!

"And when did you hope to blow?" he asked.

"I would like to have left yesterday."

"You're barking at a knot there, sister," he said.

"Mr. Suits," she admonished, "speak clearly."

"Ah. That order would, ah, be difficult. But we'll get things square with the bosses as soon as we can. We'll have us a grand tour. Don't worry."

"I am not worried," she said. "Not anymore."

⁎

By October, she was in the redwoods, celebrating her birthday. She took a basket of bread and cheese and apples into the groves and sat among the mossy hollows. Her assistants waited at the carriage until she was through. She was unfailingly polite to them, but she never addressed them informally, never offered them a glimpse of her thoughts. Only once, on the ride to the big trees, did she make conversation: "Did you send five hundred dollars to Mrs. Castro?" she asked. The old woman had cried when she left, but Teresita had gone on into the world. If this Consortium had her bound by contract, she would use them to take God's power to all of America. Let Aguirre's revolt take root. She thought she might enjoy meeting Queen Victoria one day. "Have you been on a ship?" she asked, but none of her assistants answered her.

Redwoods were so old and huge they swallowed sound and made weather.

The operation rolled north to Astoria, where she slept in a sea-themed cottage decorated with fishing nets and dried starfish. She was enraptured by fishing boats, and the foggy melancholy beaches eased her spirit. No one knew her, so no followers hounded her. She was free to consort with sea otters and a fox that exited the rain forest and stared at her on a long beach cobbled in round stones like colored eggs waiting to hatch pastel birds.

※

The Columbia River Gorge was painted in washes of mist and water-color and stretched so far her heart could not bear the distance. Portland was busy roundabout with schooners and skiffs, freighters and comic tugs. Antic trains roared with rusted voices beside its waterways. She healed the people at a small revival in the Mexican quarter. She donated the roses she was given to an orphanage.

She met Eskimos in Seattle, down from Alaska and lounging near the lumber skids to Puget Sound. In Boise, she met Urreas—a good Basque town. Walla-Walla, Yakima, Enterprise, Lostine.

Mormons in dry northern Utah came to see her and listened to her handlers' tales but declined any healings. In Nevada, she looked for Buenaventura but never found him. Reno was baked bare as old bones. Wild horses charged down the yellow hills on the road to Virginia City. Her handlers drank whiskey and beer in the Bucket of Blood, and she ate her first Chinese food there. She mistook the pepper pods in the kung pao for beans and put in a good long time gulping lemonade after that. She slept in a haunted hotel in Gold Hill that resonated late at night with the cries of children who weren't there.

On that leg of the tour, she ministered to a miner who had blown off the fingers of his left hand with a bad dynamite charge in a cat hole.

⁂

"I will require two thousand dollars a year," she'd told Suits. "Not profit. Not for me. You—that is your own business. See what God says about it. I have simple needs, and I will not rely on you to fulfill these needs. I will take care of myself."

"Done."

"I will have an assistant."

"Done."

"And I will have a family member or a family friend join me as soon as I can. I will not be subjected to untoward company, behavior, or advances, and I will not—ever—deal with the Consortium alone."

"Agreed."

"Our contract is complete in 1904," she'd said. "After that, my dear Mr. Suits, you are welcome to accept God or reside in Hell. It is no concern of mine."

"Can we shake on it?"

"I'd rather not," she'd said.

⁂

Everywhere she went, she was followed by swirling flocks of newspapers. Her handlers collected them, made press packages of them, forwarded them to cities ahead of the procession. Clippings piled up in the mochila she kept. She didn't care about them. She remembered how foolish she had been in Clifton—making albums for Rodriguez.

She recoiled as if from a slap. No. Thank you. Not that, not today. She put him far from her thoughts. Back down his forlorn mine shaft.

She grew more devout the more trapped in hotels she became. There was no going out among the plants for her. There was no climbing hills to hear Itom Achai call to her. There were no deer songs. In fact, she was deeply alarmed one morning to find that she could no longer recall the word in the mother tongue for "deer." She wept in frustration. Then she went to her knees and prayed, rosary beads moving through her fingers like pebbles rolling down a stream.

The men in the Consortium treated her with respect. No one laid a hand on her, or made an untoward move toward her. They became her team. The four centurions. Mr. Smith, her fussy assistant; Elias, the tall longhaired gunman who handled her security; Van Belle, her driver and the true mystic in the bunch; and top-hatted Swab Dave, the fixer who could arrange any kind of deal in any city. They never saw her laugh, never heard her joke. If you had told them she had been a singer of bawdy corridos in her youth, they would have been stunned and doubtful. Only after she had locked herself in her room at each hotel did they go to the cantina and bend an elbow. It was whiskey for them, though their salary was tight and they often drank busthead from the cheapest barrels, which left them sore and blurry in the mornings. They took women to their rooms and told them stories of the Saintess before they bought their pleasures and in the mornings were often stunned to find their soiled doves asking for her blessings and prayers. The four men had to keep their faces still at those moments, and the gals were professional enough to ignore them. Each day, it was like the night before had never happened.

And on.

Teresita met with a gunfighter in New Mexico who had fed poor Mexicans and was there to receive her blessing. He knelt and she laid her hand on his head like a cool cloth.

"They have not caught you yet," she said.

"Not me. They will never catch me."

"But they will kill you if they can."

He grinned.

"We all die."

She nodded.

"I will see you there," she said.

He rose.

"Do you still sing serenades?" she asked.

He tossed his long black hair back and smiled.

"Only to the loveliest women," he said.

He kissed her hand and strolled away.

"What are you looking at?" he said to Teresita's bodyguard.

"That was Bunbury," she said. She smiled. "Of the Iberians."

"Who?"

She wiped her eyes and said, "I will rest now."

And she saw Wyatt Earp speak in a candlelit theater in Denver. She rode out twisters in Oklahoma on her way to Kansas, where another set of twisters ate the edges of the town where she cowered. Cheyennes rode out to meet her wagon near Montana's border. She saw Shakespeare in Helena and didn't understand anything but the drama of Lear in his distress, which did not require language, after all.

She yearned to see Chicago and its vast lake. They had the tallest buildings on earth in Chicago.

"Later," she was told. First, they had to go south and east. The Consortium signed a contract with St. Louis, Missouri. Many sick people there were clamoring for her attentions. San Francisco, of course, had been named for Saint Francis. But who was Saint Louis? She thought he must have been French.

"We can stop?" she asked.

"We can stop."

"I want to stop."

"Don't worry."

"I am tired."

It was to be a four-month engagement and a sure bet for the Consortium. St. Lou was going crazy with the approach of the Louisiana Purchase Exposition—a World's Fair expected to bring more than ten million visitors to the city.

She felt like a burned building. And who could she talk to? Her world was made up of armies of strangers.

When she wrote to Juana Van Order, her only request was huge, she knew—but it was time. She did not trust those around her. She did not trust El Inglés. She asked her old friend to send her fair Harry, her old beau, to translate for her.

※

When she saw the Mississippi River, she sat on the bank and cried. It took some work to see the water, for the bank was crowded with boats, and they formed a wall of freighters that banged together, bow to stern, with a loud cracking sound. But as if out of a book, a riverboat hooted and paddled against the current, white as a gull. The Consortium agents could not get her to rise or to stop weeping. So they stood about unhappily, keeping any well-wishers at bay. "Let her cry," someone said. "Women do that."

"The Mexicans," said another, "is emotional."

But she couldn't cry for too long; it would be bad for business.

※

There were already signs. The Consortium had noted the protests in Utah first: Mormons wanted her out for preaching false doctrines. In Denver, Mexican-haters and Indian-shooters rumbled ominously in the background of her events. And here, suddenly, there were signs. Held up by a skinny preacher and dark-dressed women. OUT MEXICAN WICH. The Consortium tried to bat these placards down. SATANS BRIDE GREASER HERETIC. But the preacher made himself scarce when the tall pistol man who kept the Saint secure waded toward him through the gathering bodies.

Trailing Teresita, a line of jostling girls and swaggering boys and dogs and hunch-shouldered men and drunkards and fat women moving like sailboats, and no matter what city they visited, somehow the people knew she was there and came to her bearing flowers, cameras, food, roses, infants, wounds, blood, white eyes, cakes, and tears. She signed pages torn from Bibles, signed shirts, signed bare arms with drooling fountain pens, signed the faces of half-broken dolls. The assistants and the minders could no longer smell her—she was like spring when you lived in it; you became unheedful of the scent of the garden. The pilgrims, they seemed to take her in with their very breath and they could pull holiness into their flesh and feel it hot and redolent in their own darkness.

And it was after supper, well after supper, after ten that night, the Consortium aghast with dread and frustration, when she appeared in the lobby of the Planter House on Pine Street and ignored them except to note, "It is a big pile of bricks, is it not?" They worked on that translation among themselves. She strolled to the desk to collect her key to the suite where she would reside—it was in her contract, this new living in comfort.

Suffering did not, in spite of what she had once believed, improve holiness. Suffering did not increase sacredness; it only distracted from it. God did not deliver grace any quicker to a peon in mud than He did to a millionaire in a penthouse—it was simply that the millionaire, though greatly more in need than the peon, did not notice grace when it came. Why would he? Cigars, whiskey, grand beds, and gold wallpaper were all more visible than God. You could put your arms around a bawdy woman, but you had to intuit the Holy Spirit. No. It was all mud. Some mud was more glittery, that was all.

She was through with hunger and discomfort. If she was going to live in the constant fire of the shrieking, jostling, hungry, desperate public, she would sleep well. She would eat well and bathe well.

The deskman handed her the key. And he handed her a folded telegraph slip. She opened it and smiled. Laughed. Crumpled it and tossed it on the counter and ran up the stairs. She actually hiked up her skirts and ran.

Forty-Three

AND SHE WENT TO great Union Station alone.

She had never seen a castle, but Union Station looked like what she imagined a castle should look like. It loomed over Market Street in towers and minarets, its great doors showing a vast space within. The fountains outside were full of water-spouting Greek gods, or were they Romans? Perhaps they were some sort of angels. Whatever they were, they were muscular and seemed alive in the spray. She was in love with them. She took a seat on a bench and meditated on the rainbowed waters as they formed arches in the air.

Everything was brighter that day. The scent of the river was as fresh as summer. Little birds in swirling chubascos attacked the streets and dove upon the dry horse droppings to liberate oats and flakes of straw. Butterflies swept in from the hills beyond the city and the prairies beyond the river. She stood and spun in the street, forgetting she was the Saint of Cabora. Just Teresita. Just a happy young woman. Just for an instant.

She planned furiously in her mind. She made mental lists and crossed out everything on them as soon as she imagined them. She worried over her hair and her dress. Plans upon plans flitted like these butterflies.

She could no longer think of what a friend was. She had lost so many friends, so much family, that she had put aside such absurd things as companionship. She exiled Huila, her sister Anita, from her mind. She exiled Aguirre, Chulo and Gabriela and her old friends from Cabora. In her mind, she sent Tomás out into the hills to walk alone; in dreams, he called her name under storming skies.

Now. She brushed her front for the tenth time. Patted her hair. Licked her fingertips and smoothed her brows.

She wore a tight jacket of a shiny deep gold hue over a cream blouse with a throat ruffle. Her brown skirts flared out from her hips and swept the floor, but the flare was modest. Teresita did not flounce. She wore laced brown boots that added an inch to her height, and she had her hair pinned back and boxed in a smart little hat she had found in the oddly named Misfit Clothing Parlor on Olive.

She walked inside the station and caught her breath for a moment. It could have been a cathedral. The arc of the high roof was gilt, full of detail up to its white cap—so much detail she didn't think she could make it all out. Electric lamps with three white globes of light each rose from the floor on black iron posts. And the great face of the clock at the far end was held up by either two ferns or two great feathers. She remembered Gabriel's feather. Perhaps it was a cathedral.

Teresita saw stained glass. If she had seen it in San Francisco, she had not paid attention. She had not seen such a play of light and color before. Three nymphs, sitting before a low wall, lounging in some kind of ethereal sunlight, hills visible beyond. The sparrows that had invaded the vault of the station just added to the illusion. It was as if their chirps were coming from the magical glass, birdsongs made entirely of light.

A man bumped into her and broke her reverie.

"Hello," he said.

She moved away from him, cross that he had disturbed her.

He hit his leg with his newspaper and moved away.

On the street, and in the green streetcars, men collided with her. People seemed to recognize her, and smiled at her or whispered and gestured with their chins and eyes. But with these lone men, she felt as if she were being hunted. Often, handsome gringos presented themselves to her, blocking her passage so she had to step around them. She closed herself to the world and moved along.

A blind man asked for coins, but she was distracted and went by without even noticing him.

※

The train was an hour late. She ate boiled peanuts and drank hot coffee. She puzzled over the *Republic* newspaper. The announcements echoed and she didn't really understand them anyway.

She craned her neck and peered at the grand clock face. It was pale and fat as the full moon. And its hands went slowly around and around, passing her hour. She fidgeted. She worried. She pulled on white gloves, stared at her hands, and decided they looked foolish. She pulled the gloves off by taking the middle fingertip of each in her teeth and pulling. The etiquette of Cabora would not have allowed that! It made her happy. She threw the gloves in a black waste can.

She stepped outside to the platforms. It was her habit to take the sun when she could. No one out there even glanced at her save the porters, who might have ushered her back inside but were busy laughing and poking one another in the ribs. Great hilarity. She closed her eyes and sat on a bench and listened to the music of their play.

Then, great swoops of pigeons, a distant whistle, a clanging bell, and a plume of steam, white and bursting, from the scrubby trees and crab apples out along the tracks. And here it came, clanking into the echoing huge shed. For a moment, she thought she would retrieve her gloves.

She stood and brushed her skirts and struck a pose and waited. Demure, but open. Excited, perhaps, but not overly so. Poised, she would say.

Poised, yes. For Harry.

※

The big engine rolled in, all frenzy and bellows. Steam burst forth and made twin clouds, one on either side, and the train staff went to the doors and put down small sets of steps and helped weary travelers down and dragged heavy bags to wagons. Porters blew whistles. Three bells rang. Shouts.

All was tumult. A storm of faces and bodies and coats and hats. A fat man in a floor-length coat being berated by a fat woman dragging her coat on the ground. Teresita craned her neck, stood on her toes, moved back and forth on the platform seeking that bright red-cheeked visage of her silly would-be beau. People bumped into her. Men eyed her and tipped their hats. A limping gentleman passed, trailed by two Negro porters hauling a heavy cart overloaded with valises. She impatiently stepped aside, watched for Harry's bright eyes and sunburned hair, and she smiled thinking he would have a cowlick when she saw him and chided herself to stop being silly—he would no longer be a boy, after all. He'd be a man now. He might even have whiskers. She might not recognize him. Why, he could have been the fat man in the big coat! She smiled. Oh, where—where?

A tall character in a tawny camel overcoat and a pale gray hat blocked her way. This again. She put a hand on his upper arm and politely shoved him a little.

"Excuse me," she said.

He did not move. Some dark fellow with her father's mustache. She glanced at him: what an insolent American giant. He was smiling at her. She shook her head. This is not the time for such idiocy, she thought.

"Not now," she said in her best English.

"Ma'am?" he said softly.

His voice was quiet, almost a whisper. It made her look up again. He gazed steadily at her.

He wore a dove gray homburg with a wide satin band. He removed his overcoat and hung it over his arm. His vest was black corduroy, and his watch chain looped across his chest. His jacket came down to midthigh and matched the hat, though its lapels were black. A small red pocket handkerchief peeked from his chest pocket. He had a black riverboat gambler's ribbon tie knotted at his throat. His mustache was abetted by a small triangular patch of whiskers under his lower lip. His face was slender; his eyes like deep pools of black water with diamonds in the bottom of each. They were etched in the corners with laugh lines.

He doffed his hat — his hair was dark, parted on the left.

"Hello, sweetheart," he said. "Been a while."

"John?"

He grinned at her.

"The one and only."

"John Van Order?"

"You were expecting Harry?" He looked wounded, then grinned some more. His grins looked wicked, she was already noting. Like the joke was on the world, not John Van Order. "Sorry," he said. "I'm afraid Mother would never send her Harry to live with a divorced woman."

"Excuse me?" she blurted.

He held his hat in one hand and regarded it for a long, silent moment.

"Mrs. Rodriguez," he said. "You have made a damned mess of your life."

He put his hat back on. Regarded her with a cool gaze. His eyes never left hers.

She drew herself to her full height. She was indignant, ready to defy him.

But she found herself smiling and blushing.

"True," she finally said.

They laughed.

"You scared me for a minute," he said, bending to pick up a small carpetbag. "You had that fightin' Indian look in your eye."

"Things," she said, "have made me... fierce."

"Sweet little you?"

She punched his arm lightly.

"It has been hard for me!"

"Oh, no doubt."

They were speaking Spanish, glorious, colloquial ranch Spanish that she hadn't been free to enjoy for a thousand years.

He glanced around. People were looking at her. "Things get a mite complex when you ain't looking." In English.

"¿Qué?" she said.

"Está cabrón," he explained.

She cast her eyes down. John Van Order. Ay, Dios.

"It is so good to see you," she said.

"Not many pards in the Saint business?" he said.

"Pards?"

"Amigos. Cuates. Camaradas."

She smiled. Frowned. "Not many," she said.

His eyes were at half-mast and he smiled slowly, half nodded.

"I do not understand what has happened to me," she said. She shook her head. She moved her hands. He watched. He noticed she was nervous. "I think I have made mistakes. But"—she breathed in, looked up at him, brightened—"I am taking charge of my life."

"'Bout time, eh?" he said.

"It is harder than I thought."

He said, "I can help you with that. I have a little experience in the hard part."

He took her hand; without thinking, she laced her fingers through his.

"I have a hankering for a cup of coffee," he said, and they walked through the station together.

❋

They found a small white table in front of a bistro far enough from the windborne fountain spray that they wouldn't get wet. They sat on uncomfortable iron chairs and they bent to fat white cups of steaming coffee thick with cream and cinnamon. Early afternoon tipped over to dusk, and still they sat. Streetcars periodically drowned out their voices, and they simply sat looking at each other till the cars passed. They leaned toward each other again; they laughed. John slapped the table and pointed his finger at her as she held her hands in front of her face.

Passersby tipped their heads, some of them laughing too behind their fans or newspapers at what they took to be young lovers so giddy at the table. John ordered more coffee and a plate of biscuits with honey in a little pot. It didn't take long for pigeons to swirl down around them and commence their preening, gurgling circuits on the sidewalk. Both of them tossed crumbs to the sooty doves and shook the table with laughter and small shouts of exultation.

"Any word from Robison Field?" he asked.

"Who?"

"The St. Louis Cardinals! Patsy Donovan? The home-run king?"

"Baseball!" she could be heard to cry by those across the street.

"I guess you don't know about the Browns either," he mourned. She stared. "American League?" he offered. She shook her head.

"After seeing you play," she said, bright-eyed, "the sport was ruined for me."

"Aw," he drawled. "Shucks."

"That was not offered as a compliment."

John jumped from his seat and threw his arms in the air and Teresita laughed so loud it could be heard all the way to the fountains, and the pigeons exploded in panic but were drawn back by their magnetic greed to the small ingots of biscuit falling to the bricks.

Teresita noticed his hands shaking just a little as he sat back down. And the long distance in his eyes. For all his laughter, his eyes were sad. It had never occurred to her that John Van Order might be a sad man. Or was she simply making him sad in her own mind? Tomás would have said she was already imagining a healing. What would Huila have said?

"Your hand," she said, as she watched his cup rattle on its saucer. "It is trembling."

He smiled self-consciously, put his hands in his lap.

"Do I make you nervous?" she asked.

He shook his head, disappointing her.

"Naw," he drawled. "I'm used to you."

He squeezed his hands together.

"Drying out," he said quietly.

She had imagined that, perhaps, possibly, he would offer a piropo to her—some gallant thing about trembling before her beauty...something.

He said, "I had some...times in Chicago."

"Times?"

"...difficult times." He nodded at her as if beseeching her to change the subject. "I made a mess of things my own self," he said. "A little drink. Bad things. You know."

The waiter came out with a fresh pot and filled their cups again.

"Very kind," John said.

"My pleasure," he replied and went back inside.

"I do not know," she said. "But I can imagine. There was drink in my house." She left it at that.

The gaslights were sputtering and starting to fire up as lamplighters raised their smoldering punk torches to the glass enclosures; the whole boulevard seemed to be blinking and sparkling as if fireflies had formed twin parades that stretched into the distance.

"I had a little tussle," said John. "The bottle." He tipped his head to the side. "It was not my friend."

He smiled ruefully.

She sipped her coffee and stared into those eyes of his.

"You are better now?" she asked.

"Mother hopes so," he replied. "Hey, now," he said. "Don't you go trying your yerb spells on me."

"One has to be willing to be healed for it to work," she noted mildly.

"I'll do it on my own, thank you very much," he said. He raised his cup in a toast to the city. "Ladies and gentlemen: John Van Order!"

She ate some biscuit.

"You know," he continued, "I dreamed of—oh, what? I dreamed of the good life. I always wanted to be a city slicker. Never got to New York." He put down his coffee and crossed his arms. "That's the only city in the world. They say the whole thing's made out of money!" He smiled. She watched. "Didn't you want the good life?"

"No." She shook her head. "Maybe a little." She dabbed at her lips with her napkin. "Yes."

They laughed again.

He leaned toward her and confessed: "I inherited money when Dad died."

"Oh, John!"

"Lost it all."

"Oh, John!"

"Cards, whiskey." He wasn't foolish enough to say *women*. "Schemes. Seemed like a plan at that moment. All gone now."

"John!"

He nodded.

"Can you believe it?"

He looked away, overcome with remorse.

"Fool," he muttered.

She put her hand over his.

"You know what they say. He who does not run around like a fool in his youth will run around like a fool in his old age."

He tipped his head.

"They also say," he replied, "unlucky in gambling, lucky in love." He huffed a little through his nose.

"Are you lucky in love, John?"

"Never been in love," he said.

He stared until she looked away.

"At least not that I ever admitted."

She sighed.

"My, this is good coffee," she said.

When they stood to leave, he grabbed his little bag.

"Mr. Van Order," she said. "Where is your luggage?"

He looked at the bag, shrugged. He gestured at his fine outfit. His satchel.

"This is about it," he said. "Got my razor, my brush, and my mug."

She took his arm. Felt the gunbelt against her hip as she pressed close.

"I see you brought your pistol," she noted.

They headed through the first pool of streetlight and into the shadows in between.

"I thought I could pawn it," he said. "Buy us a steak."

Their laughter bounced back at them from the storefront windows until they reached the corner and disappeared from sight.

Forty-Four

HIS HAND WAS SHAKING when she took it in hers. The falling night brought a chill, but it wasn't cool enough to make a man shake. He seemed unsteady—as if his balance had slipped a bit. She was certain he had not been drinking. They stood outside and looked up at the foggy smear of the Milky Way as it made itself more visible with incremental blackness surrounding it. She leaned against his great chest. He was so tall, the Sky Scratcher.

The rancho was shut down. The workers' bunkhouse stood empty except for a family of skunks that had made it their own. For some reason, Tomás had refused to have them shot. On some nights, Gabriela spied him out in the meadow, surrounded by their jaunty erect tails. A convention of varmints, he called it. "My only true friends."

The lumber operation was still running, but only just. Segundo was doing manly duty as the manager, but his legendary cowboying and top-hand exploits did not prepare him for administrative duties. Gaby and his little Dolores spent many hours at night wrestling with the ledgers. Tomás no longer showed interest in these matters. "All these numbers," he said, "give me a headache." As long as they had enough money in the bank to keep them from the poorhouse, he was satisfied.

He often asked himself what he had left to prove. Nothing. To whom would he prove it? Nobody.

A shooting star fell copper to the west.

"Tomás! Tomás!" she cried. "Did you see it?"

"Sí, mi amor."

"Wasn't it pretty?"

"Sí."

"How do you feel?" she asked.

"All right."

"Would you like to eat?"

"Not really."

The Sky Scratcher could once eat a side of beef and drink a barrel of beer. He had lost interest in riding too. Most of their horses were gone—sold off to the neighbors. She told herself that men of a certain age slowed down. Hips grew sore, bones more brittle. But she caught herself. Though it seemed that fifteen years had passed since Teresita's terrible abduction and rescue, and her banishment from the mountain, it had really been a short time. Tomás was not an old man. Far from old. He just acted old.

She wrapped her arms around his waist and pulled him in tight.

"We got a letter from Juana Van Order," she said.

"Oh?"

"She had news of Teresita."

"Oh?"

The moon was making itself known now, and its glow was erasing some of the Milky Way from sight.

"And what do you hear of the living legend?"

She jerked at his waist in friendly admonition.

"Teresita is well. You know how she is."

He blew air through his nose.

A laugh? She smiled. A laugh!

"Healing the sick," she said.

"Our Lady of Perpetual Compassion," he said.

"Now, now."

"For strangers."

He coughed up a bitter little laugh.

"Juana says she has sent her son to help her," Gaby reported.

"A son?" He pulled away from her. "Which son?"

"Well, it's that older one."

"John?" he shouted. "The Saintess is living in sin with a drunken criminal?"

"Ay, no seas así," she said. She hated it when he was in his impossible mode. "John is no criminal."

"A lout who squandered his livelihood on gambling, whiskey, and whores," Tomás replied. "A fine companion, I must agree."

"Gordo." She sighed. "Teresita cannot speak English very well. You know that. She asked for help, and Juana sent help."

He stepped away and looked toward the bunkhouse—his skunks weren't awake yet. Ah, to be a skunk! That was a life!

"Another miraculous healing is at hand, no doubt," he said.

He walked toward the porch.

"I will sit," he said.

She followed him.

"I am so proud," he noted, "that my daughter is living in sin with a sot."

He spit. For a moment, he reflected that whiskey, gambling, and whores could be found on his own résumé. But that was not the point.

She stood on the steps and peered up into the deep gloom of the porch. A match struck and his face flashed orange, his eyes staring cold at her as the cigarillo tip flared, then the light went out. The stink of smoke.

"Sometimes you make me wish I had gone away with her."

She frightened herself—she heard the words escape her mouth and it was too late to stop them.

He took a drag of his smoke, blew it out, coughed.

"Be my guest," he said. "Leave."

Gabriela went in the house and softly closed the door.

Outside, Tomás Urrea let tears slip down his cheeks and drop toward his flailing heart.

Forty-Five

SHE EXPLAINED HER SITUATION as they walked. Her duties and her entanglement with the Consortium. He was appalled she would agree to work for no money. What kind of a confidence scheme was that? Some of the dirty dealers and cutpockets he'd known in Chicago called men like those in the Consortium sharpers. Damn holy girl, he thought. A fool.

"I need you to help me with English."

He said, "You need a mite more than English, if you don't mind my saying."

He tipped his hat at ladies they passed, kept wary eyes on the men.

"I don't need a man to rescue me, if that's what you're thinking."

"We'll see about that, Mrs. Rodriguez." He smiled at a group of schoolgirls. "How do, ladies?" he asked. They giggled. "Teresita," he said. "I'm a rougher cob than those muchachos running your show. It might be just what you need. I'll be there if you need me."

"Gracias," she said.

Teresita thought he moved like a stalking cat. Gliding through the world, watchful, still, about to explode. She remembered how the buckaroos back home had all been known by nicknames: El Piochas, El Guasas, El Rubio, El Emba, El Chino Cochino. And she found herself thinking of John Van Order in this fashion. In her mind, she called him El Tigre.

The pianist in the lobby warbled "Bird in a Gilded Cage." John thought that was appropriate as he collected his key and watched the hired zookeepers gather around Teresita. "Obliged," he said to the deskman and tapped the key on the counter. He wondered if she even realized she was in prison. Hell, no, she didn't know it. She'd been in prison back in Arizona too. He clenched his jaws in anger, watching these characters jostle her.

"Where have you been, Terry?" her assistant Mr. Smith was saying.

She had told him of these four men of the Consortium—Smith, the gunman Elias, the fixer Swab Dave, and Van Belle, her driver—but John did not approve of their familiarity or physical nearness.

He cut between Smith and his three compatriots as if he were riding a little cow horse and had placed himself at her side before they knew he was coming.

The Consortium employees fell back a half step.

"And you are?" Mr. Smith demanded.

"I'm Jesse James," John replied. "And what business is it of yours where she was?"

"Pardon me?" said Smith.

"You heard me, pismire."

"¡Ay, John!" Teresita said.

He cut a glance at her to suggest she remain quiet.

"You're a bit bold for my taste, friend," Elias offered.

"Ain't talking to you, Daniel Boone," said John.

He was still gazing into Smith's eyes as if seeing something strange through them, something inside Smith's skull.

"But if you insist on injecting yourself into this conversation, I will offer you my full attention. And it won't be no neighborly chat," said John.

Van Belle guffawed, and Elias gave him a dirty look.

"You're no kind of white man, are ye?" said Van Belle.

"White enough to put you in your place, mule skinner."

Now Elias laughed at Van Belle, and Swab Dave hoped there'd be a fight he could watch, being bored by all this holiness bidness.

"As for you," John said to Smith. "You're crooked."

"I never!"

"I can smell it on you."

"Well!" Mr. Smith looked to Messrs. Elias, Van Belle, et al. "We care for Terry's well-being."

"I don't believe that is your role in this endeavor any longer."

"Pardon me?"

"I'd say your job is to fetch us water when we're thirsty or breakfast when we're hungry or to wipe my boots when I step in shit."

"I beg your pardon!"

John put his hand on Teresita's arm.

"I'll be watching out for Miss Teresita from here on in. You will be addressing her formal-like. None of your familiarity. You are her employees. A little show of respect is required."

She didn't understand a pinch of what was being said, but she knew anyway. El Tigre was magnificent. El Tigre was ten feet tall.

"Glad we cleared that up," John said.

Elias and Swab Dave traded looks and stepped back. It was only a job, and not that good a job, and they were too smart to engage in needless dustups. But Mr. Smith, sheaves of telegrams from Mr. Suits burning in his pockets, was frantic. Bold as a bureaucrat, he blustered and filibustered and made the error of putting his hand on John's chest.

John looked at the hand, looked at Smith, grinned, pulled back the hem of his coat, and revealed his holstered revolver.

"I keep five beans in the wheel," he said, "and one chamber empty. Don't make me clear leather, Mr. Smith," he said reasonably. "Unless you fancy early retirement."

They formed a tableau.

"I don't mind walking away with four beans left. I ain't a hoarder."

Smith looked at the Consortium centurions. *Beans?* Elias shook his head slightly. Smith stepped away.

John smiled at the gathered representatives of the Consortium in a collegial fashion. It scared them all to their boots. He tipped his hat.

"Night, boys," he said. "I'll enjoy my room now. I feel a touch drowsy. And hungry. How about you all round me up a steak and some potatoes." He took Teresita's arm. "Ma'am," he said, as if they were strangers. "Oh," he said over his shoulder. "I'll have my trousers laundered."

The Saint and the Tiger strolled away and ascended the great stairway.

"Good night, now," he called. "Say your prayers, hear?"

She laughed into his shoulder.

"Cabrones," he whispered.

She fell against him—it was delicious and dreadful, scandalous.

"Were you really going to shoot poor Mr. Smith?" she said.

"I ain't shot this pistola ever," he said.

"You!" she said. "Are so bad!"

"But I'm handsome," he replied.

"That is debatable."

He put his hand over his heart in mock sorrow.

"I thought," he accused, "you were supposed to be a saint. Why are you so mean?"

She shrugged.

"I cannot lie," she said.

His room was next door to hers. He bid her a chaste good night when he saw her in. He went to his own room and immediately opened the connecting door and stepped into her room. She was surprised, but not that surprised.

"Admit it," he said. "I am the handsomest man in St. Louis."

She nodded somberly.

"I admit it," she said. "However, that is not saying much."

Mr. Smith, scandalized, listened to their laughter through Teresita's locked door.

❋

Teresita managed to maneuver the laughing El Tigre back out the connecting door and then she threw the lock and tossed herself into her bed and kicked her feet in the air. He was such an idiot! She rolled over. She laughed into her pillow. He was so bad! He was so pretty.

Poor Harry, she thought. Having to compete with that. She thought she would write to Juana right away, but got no further than the idea.

Smith had gone to bed, so now she was the only listener. She heard the room-service waiter knocking on John's door, and the rattling of the cart as his steak was delivered. And one more thing, but one she didn't hear: John slipping the man a few coins to bring him a small bottle. "Just to help me sleep," he said. The server nodded and winked and quietly glided out of the room.

Forty-Six

MR. SMITH DROPPED a silver dollar on the counter of the telegrapher.

SMITH TO SUITS / URGENT / SAINT BROUGHT IN PISTOLEER / ARRIVE HERE SOONEST.

✳

Their first few days together were tremendously satisfying. They descended to breakfast each morning, a bit too early for his taste. But copper pots of coffee and platters of buttermilk splatter-dabs topped with blueberry compote cheered him. He took great rafts of bacon or sizzling links of German sausage on his plate. She enjoyed berries or melon bits sculpted into the shapes of flowers. One morning, the chef carved her a swan of apple, melon, and peaches. The Consortium lurked in the background, vigilant and fretful. Mr. Smith had assigned Swab Dave to spread folding money around the staff to ensure that word of the adjoining rooms not leave the hotel. For the sake of business, rumors of someone's having midnight trysts with the Saint would not do, and these two were costing the company a small fortune. It was clear that Mr. Van Order, for example, had no intention of procuring a job.

Teresita was blind to them. She had not laughed so much since—well. Cabora? Before? Since the old Santa Ana rancho in Sinaloa? Since she was seven?

El Tigre was an awful, awful man. She made sure to keep the door locked between them, though he had taken to scratching at it and making pathetic meowing sounds late at night. "Go away!" She'd laugh. "You are insane. You are an idiot."

"Good night." He'd sigh through the wood.

"Do not bother me again!"

After a few moments of silence:

"Meow?"

These days were also times of meetings and confabulations between them. Of strategy arguments and long sheets of fancy hotel paper with figures and destinations scratched and crossed out. Walks in the night with endless arias of Van Order's ambitions ringing in Teresita's ears.

Their breakfasts were a refuge from their constant debate. Afterward, however, Teresita became busy with clients and newspapermen. The reporters gathered in the lobby; John had never seen anything like it. The little girl from Arizona grew taller, sedate, as dignified as a living statue of some kind of Roman goddess. He sat near her, not allowed to be in any way familiar, and translated their questions and her answers. She seemed false to him in those moments—indeed, he was pretty sure the whole saint thing was all a fine scam. Just more snake oil for the pan. He'd seen some world-beater scams in Chicago, and this one was as sweet as they came. What he couldn't understand was why Teresita wasn't rich. Where was the money going? There was surely money—he'd look around the hotel—damned loads of it. He wanted a bit better than to eat it up in pancakes. Even charging new trousers and starched white shirts on the Consortium's ticket did not begin to bring him recompense.

And it was a bore. These reporters, whether from New York or Mexico City, all asked the same questions. How did she do it? Mr. Smith and Mr. Van Belle ushered these pissants in and out. Elias lounged around on a red velvet couch and smoked, looking at John with the same skeptical squint John had on his own face.

When did you first realize you had these powers? Are you a saint? Why do you suppose God chose you for this work? What can you tell us of Indian uprisings in your name? Are you the Queen of the Yaquis? Can you tell us a bit about your husband's violent attacks upon you in Arizona?

John thought it would be funny to mistranslate, and it was only his feelings for Teresita that kept him from doing it. *Yes,* he imagined telling them she had said, *I asked the Indians to kill everyone, especially the white people of St. Louis. They're coming now.* The reporters didn't understand why John laughed sometimes.

After the morning's interviews, Teresita was taken across town to a rented hall where she attended to the halt and the lame. Before she could leave the hotel, however, there was always a small gauntlet of fanatics to pass through. They hugged her, kissed her cheeks, offered papers and photographs of her for autographs. An ugly old picture of her standing awkwardly beside a chair and surrounded by flitting cherubs appeared. "Where did you get this?" she asked the woman. "It must be a collectors' item now." She signed everything. John had no interest in any of this. He'd seen plenty of that in Arizona. It made him queasy. He didn't understand it, and he didn't know whether he could believe it or not. He would be happier in her company if she weren't some kind of lady pope—though, of course, in that case he'd have to do more than eat above his means and relate her stories in English to those desperate for a narrative. He should be with her, but he just couldn't do it. Besides, these pilgrims were mostly Mexicans come up the river to work on building the World's Fair. Gypsies—that and

Indians and mumbling Missouri plowmen who didn't need to speak. They all could point to their sores, tears in their eyes.

Sometimes these believers, having stumbled upon him before Teresita had escaped the hotel, asked for his autograph. As if his very nearness to Herself imbued him with renown. He would gladly sign their papers with a flourish: *Yours, Baron Ephemeral von Yarb.* Yet as she moved onward, John could feel himself being forgotten. By the time she neared the doors, it was as if he had never come to her at all. The distance between them multiplied until he was left in the lobby, discarded.

Only Elias was left there with him.

"What the hell," he finally said on the third day.

"Pardner, I been asking myself that for months now," said Elias.

John had never seen anything quite like Teresita, he had to admit. The way she loved those people. At the end of the day, her hands and skirts were filthy, and she smelled, smelled of poverty. He had made a deal with life that he'd not smell that way again. But there it was, painted across her body by the sweating unbathed kneelers, the wormy kids, and the haggard ladies. Overlaid on that was the cigar stench of the rich, the curdled perfumes of their wives and daughters with their expensive bellyaches, pennies and double eagles and limp dollar bills going into the coffers at the door.

What the hell, indeed. He liked his li'l Saintess just fine. Liked her face, the way it lit up in wicked humor when he said some japery. Liked her hands. Liked her slim build and her ripe-looking bottom.

And he liked her potential—liked feather mattresses better than hard ground, boardinghouse bunks, and haylofts. Liked them a great deal more. He liked the thought that he could bend the Consortium to his will and deliver them to Manhattan.

The night he went to kiss her good night, she cried.

"No, please, John," she said. She was afraid. She felt that slip, that slide into heat and tingles she had felt with Rodriguez. It was terror so profound she could not express it. No, she could not. No, she would not. She hadn't the strength for more of it. Or the heart. Not now. Not again.

But John was funny. And John kept the wicked away from her. And John took her hand to help her over puddles in the street, brought her a single flower at breakfast, told her she was pretty as maple trees in October. And though she did not know what that meant, she knew how lovely those words sounded.

"You don't care for me?"

"I do."

"Be mine."

"Let me think."

"Go on, then," he said, opening her door for her. "You think. I'll be here in the morning."

She looked at him in that way he liked, from eye to eye.

"The last time," she said. "I . . ."

He touched her lips with one finger.

"Go on, now. I ain't mad." In their country Spanish, *estoy* had become *'toy*.

She went in and closed the door.

He laid his forehead on the wood and sighed.

Out to the street.

He busied himself with discovering rhubarb pie and Busch beer— not, fortunately, at the same moment. The thought of that made him turn light green. He risked his last fifty dollars in a card game down by the river, and he walked away with a poke of $546. He felt flush, and enjoyed the overcrowded docks. Hogshead barrels, cursing sailors, geese, runty dogs, and strolling whores. Great hilarity, he found, along the west bank of the Mississippi.

He got back to the hotel after everyone had gone to bed. Even the piano was abandoned. The lights were turned down low. Dawn was already sneaking along the prairies. He crept into his room. He lay on the bed and sipped from his hidden bottle.

He stared at the connecting door.

Somehow, its white paint felt like a rebuke. He sipped. He kicked off his boots. How could she scold him in her sleep?

He blew her a rueful kiss and closed his eyes.

※

She rapped on the door in the morning, as she did each day.

"Are you decent?" she called.

She unlocked the door and peeked in at him. She didn't seem angry. She didn't seem amused. She didn't seem anything.

He sat on his bed in a sleeveless undershirt, pulling his boots on. He stood, his braces falling to his sides.

"Hey, bunkie," he said.

"Buenos días."

"Seeing you," he said, "completes my morning."

He smiled at her.

"Oh?" she said, coming in and fingering the watch on his desk.

He stepped to the wardrobe and withdrew a stiff white shirt. It had so much starch in it, it looked like a thin slat of wood.

"It's my boiled shirt," he said.

He worked his arms into the resistant sleeves.

"That shirt," she noted, "looks more fried than boiled."

He chuckled.

"I swear," he said, choking a bit as he fastened the collar button. "You're as fresh as a breeze in a garden." He was giving it his cowpoke best. What the hell—it was the kind of line that worked on the girls in the cantinas.

She tipped her head.

"Gracias," she said.

He tucked the tails in, drew the braces up, and squared his shoulders; he took up his vest, watched her watching him as he did up its three buttons.

"Are you mad at me?" he asked.

"No," she said. "Not until I hear what you were doing last night."

She handed him his watch. He started winding it. "Then I might be mad at you." She was angling for a sophisticated mature woman's tone. It would have been worth a chuckle or two on the vaudeville stage.

They tried on their roles as she went across his room and out into the hall through his door. He followed. Thus he met the rumpled Mr. Suits.

※

They sat in the farthest corner of the dining room. Teresita and John took a booth, and Mr. Suits sat in a pulled-up chair on the side. Teresita sipped grapefruit juice. John and Suits downed epic drafts of French roast chicory coffee.

"This mud's stout enough to hold up a fence post," Mr. Suits quipped to his own profound amusement.

He wore a dented bowler and needed a shave.

They stared at him.

He turned to Teresita, whose hands were upon the table, wringing each other like wrestling badgers.

"Terry," he said, "you got my men boogered."

She looked at John with an eyebrow raised. "Confused," he explained. "Beat."

She looked back at Suits.

"And?" she said.

He did not want to be here, but business was business. His men had reported John's worrying interference. All right, sure, the Saint was still under contract. But this could slow things down, bog them up pretty good, John being made of fairly stout mud himself.

"I come all the way out here to consider your conditions." He raised his hands. "Fully understanding we reached a consensus once before. This here is a whole new game."

"I want nothing, I told you," she said.

He sighed. Drummed his fingers.

"How do I parlay with a saint?" he asked John.

"She answers to God." John shrugged.

"You a churchy man, John?"

"Of occasion."

"What do I do, sacrifice my oldest son on the altar?"

"That's funny," John said, and translated for her. She did not smile, simply stared at him. He busied himself with his coffee.

"I'll be honest," Mr. Suits said. "You make me jittery sometimes."

"Yes," she said.

John came to his rescue: "Teresita requires her two thousand dollars a year."

"My God, man, that's exactly what she's getting." He sneered. "You do realize the average salary in America is four hundred a year. I'd say we've been generous. So. Why am I here?"

"Me."

John sat back and smiled so wide his eyes crinkled.

"I require a touch more worldly recompense than she does."

Suits drew his pencil and notebook from his pocket and sat there shaking his head.

"Where'd you learn that one?" He snorted. "A book?" But he licked the pencil.

"Begin," he lamented.

⚜

It wasn't such a bad deal, really. Of course, nobody in the Consortium would be happy with it. But John pointed out that it was better for its members to meet his demands than to receive the nothing they would earn if he took Teresita back to the old frontier; better for the group to satisfy him than to deal with the lawsuits he would bring against the Consortium, which he thought he could win, what with the organization's criminal record of white slavery and all. And besides, with him around with his pistola, they could fire a centurion or two, balance things out somewhat.

A load of new clothes and a good fat regular payday and some custom-mades for his feet. Not bad. It was the hotel rooms that would cost 'em. That and the relocation to New York City.

"Looks like you found the golden stew pot, Mr. Van Order," Suits grumbled. He ordered a whiskey.

"Early drink, Mr. Suits?" Teresita said.

"Kentucky breakfast," he muttered.

He looked at her for a long while, then consulted his notes.

"I can do all this," he said. "Sure. I'll sort it out." The drink came. He sipped once, then tossed the whole shot back. "That'll work," he noted.

John bit his lip.

"What we have to prepare for," Suits said, "is all the scandal."

"What scandal?"

"Your enemies have engaged in, shall we say, tawdry stratagems already. This here situation can only degenerate into calumny and loose talk."

John squinted at him. He shook his head a little.

"You want to chew that one a little finer, Mr. Suits?" he said. "We don't follow."

Suits reached into his jacket and withdrew a ragged bit of newspaper.

"This here," he said. "From right here in St. Louis. Regardez le horseshit right there."

John took it.

It was an advertisement promising that Teresita would pay ten thousand dollars and furthermore deliver five thousand armed Yaqui warriors to any man who would marry her.

She leaned over and looked at it as John fumed.

"Kind of insulting, I'd say," offered Mr. Suits.

"Inflammatory," said John.

"Makes Terry look like a crazy spinster and a renegade besides." Suits wiggled in his chair and glanced around for the waitress.

Teresita said nothing. She had been attacked before. She didn't even waste time wondering who had placed the ad. Warriors? What warriors? Men and war, that boring refrain. What really stung her was that someone thought that she had to pay a man a fortune just to marry her. Am I so bad? Am I so damaged?

"I didn't know you had enemies," John told her. Had he forgotten her history? Mexico? Revolution? Ghosts? Apparently he had, though he'd never been much for looking back on events, large or small.

She looked at Suits and shook her head. Who would have paid for such a proclamation?

"I am surrounded by darkness," she said.

John stared at her.

"Makes you look bad, Terry," Suits reiterated, gesturing for the waitress to bring him another shot. "People don't like women acting up. Perhaps they're dry-gulching you in the press to queer your play. Unless it's true." He grinned nervously. "You got Yakis waiting out there?"

"That's ridiculous!" John said.

"Maybe so, maybe so." Suits received the shot glass and sniffed it. He took it in and felt it spread through all his aching muscles. "That'll work." He sighed. He retrieved the advert, smoothed it, folded it, and put it back in his pocket. "They'll discredit you at every turn. That's the game. The heart of man being a dark sombitch and all."

They'll.

"Better a shamed face than a stained heart," Teresita announced.

"Well put!" Suits yelled. One whiskey shot too many, Teresita was thinking. "But look here. You two lovebirds..."

They both snickered.

"...whatever you are. You two livin' together? Travelin' together?" Suits sat back, crossed his legs, shook his head. "Say good-bye to the saint business. It's a dirty scandal, and your enemies are going to make the most of it."

He put his hand out and touched her wrist.

"You are a Mexican," he reminded her.

John would have popped him one, but he was thinking about what the man had said. By God! The weasel was correct on that point: they were going to fall into scandal.

"Well, Suits," John said. "We're in a pickle, because I'm not leaving."

"We have formed a...consortium," Teresita told him.

Suits stared at the table, arranged his spoon.

"Funny," he said. "Witty."

"Business," said John. "Nothing personal."

"I see," Suits replied. "It will seem personal indeed to your followers, pardon me for saying."

"What would you have us do?" asked John.

"Far be it from me to tell you to hobble your ambitions," Suits said softly. He looked John in the eye. *I've got your number.* He smiled a tight little smile devoid of any warmth whatsoever.

Before John could say anything, Teresita spoke.

"Then say we are married," she said.

"What?" both men blurted.

"Release the news to the papers. John and I were married. It was a joyous event. And they can keep their opinions to themselves."

The men sat and gaped at each other.

"I think," John said, "I might join you in a drink. If my bride doesn't mind."

She sat back, smiling mildly.

"You are a grown man, mi amor," she said. "You do not need my permission to drink."

John tipped his head to her and winked at Suits.

"That," he said, "is what I like to hear."

Forty-Seven

MR. SUITS WAS so persnickety after his breakfast that he marched to the lobby stiff-legged and fired all four centurions and kicked them out of the hotel. If there'd been a dog about, he would have put the boot to it too. He tossed the morning pianist a nickel to ease his mood and requested the tune about Captain Jinks of the Horse Marines. He and the pianist sang it with gusto: "'I'm Captain Jinks of the Horse Marines, I feed my horse on pork and beans, and often live beyond my means, I'm a captain of the a-army!'"

This goddamned Saintess and her cowboy pal would no longer be his concern; after he finished the business of this morning, he'd be on a train back to San Francisco and his little candy shop. To hell with the whole dirty business of holiness. He'd quit the Consortium and live in peace. He imagined the sign he'd put in his window: NO MEXICANS OR INDIANS.

"Your ride has arrived," Suits called into the dining room, wishing the day were ending instead of beginning.

They were greeted by David Rowland Francis. It was quite the coup for the Consortium, this event, and it was intended to remind her of the power and connections the group enjoyed. The trip had been planned days earlier, and its timing was now off, but the visit was still worthwhile. Mr. Francis was the former mayor of St. Louis, the former governor of Missouri, and the current president of the World's Fair. Cameras clicked and blew light at them as they all shook hands. John noted Francis's shoes—cream and brown and slick as ice. Every thread of Francis's suit announced his position. John was embarrassed by his own clothes—he'd thought he was dapper, but this governor made him feel like a ragpicker.

"It would be an honor to introduce you to the site of the Louisiana Purchase Exposition," Mr. Francis said. His teeth were perfect. "Shall we?" he said, gesturing with his ivory-colored hat.

They went to his Packard auto car as if in a dream. It had a canvas top like a prairie schooner held in place by spidery iron legs that folded down in a cunning fashion to expose the passengers to the salutary Mississippi breezes. The car came to life with a bang after a stout spin of the crank by the chauffeur. Its motor made a jolly racket, going *bucketta-bucketty-bucketta-bucketty*. Everything seemed slow. Cameras.

Applause from a few gathered. WITCH on a placard. They mounted the green car with its liveried driver in his brass buttons and silly cap. Mr. Francis offered John a cigar; they reclined in the leather seats. "Robusto or figurado?" Francis asked. Ah, Cuban, sweet and brutal. John accepted the flame and chewed a mouthful of smoke.

Teresita was all excitement and glory. She exulted every time Governor Francis pointed to some new golden detail on one of his fat buildings. John — uncommonly, the one who looked for the unseen — saw beggars in the alleys between these behemoths, saw a cart horse with a bum leg being lashed, limping along with a teeming cart of refuse dragging behind. Dogs lit out after the puttering auto, barking and trying to bite its wheels as Mr. Francis tipped ash over the side and regaled them with the most elegant talk John had ever heard. Teresita placed her hand on John's knee. Mr. Francis glanced at this. John moved his knee. He would have to teach her to dissemble a bit. Play the cards tighter to the belly. Sometimes, she went around as open as this Packard.

"Aren't you happy, John?" she said.

"Oh, I'm happy," he said, tossing her a smile and patting her hand. He turned to Governor Francis and came up with a translation. "She is exulting over your fine city, sir," he said.

Francis beamed.

And there it was before them, this massiveness: the World's Fair a-birthing. Cranes and smoke and tumbling herds of workers below, overflown by birds in huge numbers on high, banging and hammering and shouts and whistles. The great exposition's bay had been dug; scooped canals led from it, visible through the gates and the gaps in the walls. The water in these was green. Indians in canoes paddled back and forth, and small electrical launches puttered between them.

"Isn't it marvelous?" Governor Francis cried, excited as a boy by his grand folly.

They leapt from the halted car, and the governor lit out at a fast clip, waving his arms excitedly. John dawdled a bit, watching. Francis and

Teresita paused to sign autographs, to pose for pictures hugging strangers. John stopped well away from the white gates and regarded the rabble. A ragamuffin in striped shorts and a dirty cap stood near him, peering in at the tumult.

"You goin' in?" he asked the boy.

"Cain't do it."

"Sure you can," John said. "Who's stopping you?"

"Don't got no money, mister."

"Son," said John, "I never had a red cent. Look at me now."

The kid sniffled and stared.

"C'mon," said John. "Let's stroll."

The kid followed him through the gate and nodded to the various coppers and roustabouts standing in his way.

Over here was the fast-rising Festival Hall, soon home to the greatest pipe organ on earth, said to be as loud as Creation Day itself. Along the other side rose the Colonnade of States, leading to the dining halls. Frantic sputters announced the awakening of the four white-water fountains out in the bay. In the west, through the columns of the Colonnade, a cascade began pitching water down a stepped facade. The spiderlike object in back was the two-hundred-and-fifty-foot festival wheel, so recently a sensation in Chicago. The great statue by the bandstand was of the patron saint of St. Louis, France's King Louis IX. Neither John nor the kid was impressed. Teresita noticed the boy and smiled at him.

"What's them mountains back yonder?" the kid asked Francis.

"Those would be re-creations of the Tyrolean Alps." Francis beamed.

"Whar's them elephants?" the kid demanded.

Francis snapped his fingers and gestured for an assistant to take the bothersome little tramp to the paddocks. John winked at the kid, who doffed his floppy cap and vanished forever.

"So many wonders," Teresita said. "It is overwhelming."

"Miss," the governor said, "when construction is complete, and the whiteness of the exposition is reflected in the bay, it will be the most beautiful place on earth. Why, there will be Indians from India, and American Indians from the untamed West in the Apache village. The whole world will converge."

"Apaches?" she said.

"Indeed."

"Where'd you get the Apaches?" asked John.

He wasn't comfortable with Apaches around.

"Why, Mr. Cody will provide them."

"Buffalo Bill!" John cried. He laughed. "Well, I'll be dogged."

"There are several of his representatives here now," Francis said. He glanced around and confided, "A trial run, you might say. You can't keep the Indians away from the ice cream stand, though."

"Ice cream?" said Teresita. "I love ice cream!"

Francis looked at John and raised an eyebrow: *See what I mean?*

He took her arm.

"Follow me," he said.

❊

John would have preferred a beer. As they approached the white-and-pink ice cream pavilion, by God if he didn't see a bunch of flat-footed Apaches lounging around, as advertised. Teresita surged toward them, but he managed to take hold of her and steady her down a bit. Francis was their business for the day, not the savages.

They swept into the chilled ice cream parlor.

"Electrical," Francis boasted.

"I love ice cream very much," she said.

Francis smiled like an indulgent father.

"Never tried it," John confessed.

"We have many amazements on display at the exposition," Francis announced. Teresita looked out the window at the Apaches. The governor gestured to the paper-hatted fellow behind the glass cabinets.

"Behold," said Francis. "The ice cream cone!"

"Hell," said John. "They had those in Chicago."

"But did they have them in waffles?" asked the governor.

John whistled.

"I didn't see no waffle cones. If I'd come across that, it might've made me fatter."

Pistachio! Teresita attacked hers like a little chulo. John gripped his drooling waffle and sniffed the ice cream. He poked his tongue in suspiciously. "Sweet!" he said. He smiled and started licking straightaway. Teresita took a small spoon from the container and continued to eat her ice cream from the waffle.

"You can eat the waffle," Francis noted, licking ice cream from his whiskers.

"You're defeating the purpose," John whispered to Teresita.

She ignored him, looking out that window. Those Apaches gathered out there in the shade were looking back. They appeared to John like little prairie wolves on the llano.

He was alarmed when she dropped her unfinished cone in the trash can and wandered out the door.

"She is interesting," observed the governor.

"Always something new," said John.

The men followed her out, the bell above the door tinkling merrily as they left.

She stood in the sun, shading her eyes. A bandy-legged warrior walked over to her and looked her up and down. He had a red rag tied about his head.

"Not as festive as the Sioux," Francis noted. "Desert men."

"Know them well," John said. "Never cared for them."

John bit his waffle.

The Apache nodded at Teresita.

"I thought it was you," he said. "I didn't trust my own eyes."

"I am happy to see you again," she said.

He nodded.

"The Creator must still care for my People."

They shook hands.

"Venado Azul," she said. "You do not look a day older than you did in Arizona."

He smiled.

"I was already a thousand years old," he said.

He glanced at the white men with their drooping, leaking waffles.

"We like that ice cream too," he said. "If we knew these refugees had ice cream on their boats and wagons, we might have given up sooner."

He coughed once; she recognized it for a laugh.

His friends sat on the white chairs and craned around and stared at her. She raised her hand. They nodded.

"How is the Sky Scratcher?" Venado Azul asked. "Still drinking that vino?"

"I have not seen him," she said. "Life pulled us apart."

"I know how that is," he said.

She touched his arm.

"And you? Your people?" she asked.

He toed the ground. She noted he wore deerskin slippers. He puffed air through his lips, as if a wind had taken his people away.

"We came here. It is a job." He shrugged. "The world ended."

"The world ended and yet here you are at the World's Fair."

"Somebody else's world."

They laughed sadly.

She kept looking over his shoulder.

"You see him," Venado said.

"Yes."

"Do you care to meet him?"

She fluttered a bit. She touched her hair. "Dare I?"

"He'd like it," Venado said. "He likes saints." He looked over at John and Francis. "He might go a little rough on these white men, though."

She glanced back and giggled.

Venado took her arm and led her to the squat dark one sitting heavily and munching his waffle. He had vanilla on his lips. He crunched the last of the waffle and carefully cleaned his fingers and lips on a cloth napkin. One of the other warriors took it from him and folded it and set it on the glass table. The old man looked up at her. She felt fire and snow course through her. She trembled upon connecting with his eyes. The oldest eyes in the world. The eyes that had seen everything in this life and many things in the next. She felt deep terror, and she felt the profoundest love. This old man, steeped in holiness and blood. His face was cragged and severe. He looked like he had never laughed in his long life.

He put out his hand to her.

She, for the slightest moment, felt that she should fall to one knee and bend her head and receive his benediction. But she realized he was reaching out to shake her hand. Did one take this rough blunt hand so easily? This hand that had smitten so many enemies?

She took it. He shook, three times, hard, and let her go.

His voice was deep, full of rocks.

"Hi," he said.

She almost laughed.

Venado Azul looked down with more love on his face than she could comprehend.

"The Yawner," he said.

"Is that his name in your tongue?"

"Goyaalé." He nodded.

She put her hands before her heart and smiled at him.

The old man smiled back, glanced at his companions, and chuckled. They all laughed. He looked back up at her and tipped his head. He put out his hand again.

"What does he want?" she asked.

Venado grinned.

"Twenty-five cents," he said.

A bit confused, she dug in her little bag. She produced the quarter and handed it to Venado, who handed it to the Yawner. The old man took a creased white card and a pencil from his pocket and slowly wrote on it. He handed the coin back to Venado and said, "Ice cream."

Venado shook his head and went inside the ice cream parlor. The old man handed Teresita the card and said, "Autograph for you. Saint."

She carried it away, and only when they were in the car again, heading back downtown to the hotel, did she hand it to John. John unfolded it and glanced at her. He looked down at the card.

It said:

Geronimo.

⁕

In the hotel lobby, after Governor Francis had left them to grand flourishes of gratitude on their part and magnanimity on his, they sat on a love seat and watched revelers gathered at the piano singing endless refrains of "Meet Me in St. Louis." John was moody.

He asked the bellman to arrange for a pair of iced cobblers to be brought to them. The drinks came on a silver tray: sherry, shaved ice, orange juice, and sliced fruits, with a cherry atop the ice. She looked at him quizzically.

"A wedding toast," he said, raising his glass.

She smiled and tasted her drink. It was sweet. It was good.

She watched him focus on the singers, a lost, faraway look on his face.

"John?" she said. "Why so quiet?"

He took another sip, then held the glass in both hands in between his knees as he leaned forward and stared. I was just wondering, he thought, why the world is so sad. But he said nothing.

She put her head on his shoulder. They sat like that for a long time. When the music ended, he took her hand and accompanied her upstairs. At her door, he took her shoulders in his hands and turned her to face him.

"Mrs. Van Order," he said. His voice was so soft, she could barely hear it. She looked up at him, from eye to eye, taking in his entire face. "I need to kiss you now."

And he did.

Part V

NEW YORK

New York, Feb. 23 — Santa Teresa, the Mexican Joan of Arc, who was accused of inciting the Yaquis to revolt and who later astonished the Pacific States with her alleged healing powers, is here . . . .

She says she possesses magnetic powers that will cure the lame, the sick, and the blind. Her chief power lies in the great, dark eyes, demure and unsophisticated in conversation, but aggressive, intense, lustrous like a metal mirror when fixed with piercing earnestness on the patient whose hand she is clasping or whose brow she is touching with her magnetic fingers.

— WASHINGTON, D.C., DAILY STAR,
February 23, 1901

Forty-Eight

TOMAS HEARD FROM Juana Van Order that the children had
wed—at least, that's what she told him the newspapers said. He crumpled her letter. And he had heard, just one day before, from Lauro Aguirre, no less, America's professional expert, that it was being reported
that the couple would pull up stakes in St. Louis and move their operation to New York City, though his account had not included any matri-
monial details. New York City? That great Moloch that belched fire
and smoke and consumed its own young? Brutal nightmare of dark alleys and alien tongues? Why, as far as he could tell, it was worse than
Mexico City—a place, he noted with pride, he had managed to avoid.
Horrors.

Oh, and—married?

He was so stirred with ill ease by the news that he decided to mount
a horse for the first time in months. A man had to get up in the hills to
think this kind of thing through. He stormed through the house, tossing objects out of boxes, unable to find his spurs.

"What are you doing?" Gabriela cried.

"Going out!"

"What has happened?"

He held her arms in his great hands and peered into her face.

"Teresita has married Van Order," he said.

"Harry?"

"John!"

"¿Qué?"

"Sí. Teresita es una Van Order," he mourned. "Y se va a Nueva York."

"¡Nueva York!" she hollered, moved more by his hysteria than by her
own feelings in the matter.

355

He released her and stomped around as if he'd never entered the house before.

"But," Gabriela cried, "she's not even divorced!"

Tomás stopped and pondered, and then turned to his beloved.

"Gaby," he reminded her. "I am still married to Loreto."

As if this were news to her, she cried, "Oh my God!"

Her impression of Teresita as a spoiled madwoman only deepened.

Segundo, who was in the kitchen, so busy stealing biscuits from the tin and dipping them in the butter pot and then dousing them with honey that he missed Tomás's brief appearance, wandered out, trying to lick the gold drops from his mustache.

"¿Qué pasa, boss?" he said.

"Looking," Tomás said as he sent tablecloths sailing from a chest, "for my"—he kicked a chair—"hijos de sus pinches madres *spurs!*"

Gabriela smiled in spite of herself. She hadn't heard her Gordo unleash a good healthy ranch curse in ages. That's my Gordo.

"Aquí," Segundo drawled, pulling open a drawer of the china cabinet with one finger. The fabled spurs lay in there with discarded screwdrivers and pocketknives and a handful of arrowheads and some carpet tacks. By God! Tomás glared at Segundo. That old son of a whore was lazy even when opening a drawer!

Tomás sat and strapped the spurs on and enjoyed, for the briefest moment, their ringing.

"Don't snag the carpet, mi amor," Gabriela said.

He gritted his teeth.

He leapt to his feet and fought through the wave of dizziness and rushed out the door.

Tomás was discovered standing there staring at his empty rancho.

"¿Dónde están los caballos?" he demanded.

"Don't have lots of horses left," Segundo said.

"¡Quiero un caballo, chingado!" Tomás yelled.

"All right, all right. Don't rupture yourself," Segundo said. He'd never moved fast in life, but now he moved like a snail in the rain. He had his thumbs irritatingly thrust into his belt and he strolled toward the old barn.

Good Christ, thought Tomás, am I as old as he is?

"You coming or not?" Segundo drawled.

Tomás marched like a federal soldier. His eyes bored into Segundo's back. Insolent bastard. He would talk himself right out of a job any day now.

"Not much but these nags," Segundo noted. "There's a damn owl-head pinto over there won't never be rode. That's just dog food, that one."

The horse was moon-eyed and suspicious.

"I'll take care of you later," Tomás said, pointing in its rolling eye. "There isn't a horse born I can't tame."

Abashed, the horse turned its head and nibbled a blackfly bite on its haunch, but it kept a worried eye on this towering pendejo.

"Got this grullo over here."

"That horse is blue," Tomás observed.

"Nag's got some zebra stripes too," said Segundo.

"Bring him."

Tomás cast about and found an old McClellan saddle on a stall railing. It was dry and cracked, but he didn't care. He hauled it down and slammed it on the grullo. The horse filled its gut with air when Tomás went to cinch the saddle and was deeply offended when Tomás kneed it hard in the side and knocked the air out and pulled the strap tight.

"I'm in no mood for a smart horse today," he warned.

The grullo blew air through its lips and jiggled its mouthpiece and grunted when Tomás climbed aboard.

"Want company?" Segundo asked.

"Hell no."

Tomás trotted out of the barn and nudged the blue horse toward the gate, accelerating like a motorcar. They parted a sullen knot of black-and-white magpie cows. Through the gate.

"Think I care?" muttered the wounded Segundo. "I got biscuits to eat, you cabrón."

He wandered toward the house, but the boys leapt up from behind the porch railings and *pow-pow*ed! him with their fingers. He clutched his chest, staggered in a circle, and fell with one leg in the air. They ran to him and jumped on his stomach, shrieking like the unleashed minions of Hell.

※

Tomás galloped into the trees and across the meadows and into the dry rocks and he kept thinking about how much the saddle hurt. He didn't remember saddles hurting down *there,* his thighs burning from being forced so far apart by the horse's body. He thumped the horse on the shoulder and said, "Fat bastard!" He wished he had thought to bring a hat — now that they had cleared the trees, the sun was awfully strong. It hurt his eyes. And suddenly his ass was sore. This horse was reconfiguring Tomás's nether parts.

He reined up and brought it down to a saunter and had some disagreements with the grullo about whether to halt, but he finally convinced the blue horse and they came to a stop. He dismounted, lost his balance, and fell over and rolled down a small hill. Not showing its amusement, the grullo busied itself with savory remnant grasses that appeared between patches of snow. Snow! Tomás realized he was in a crusty little ice patch and was slowly getting soaked.

He crawled and got to his knees and struggled to his feet and trudged up the slope that was longer going up than it had been going down.

He fell on a flat rock and sat there, absorbing the heat like a lizard. He rested his forearms on his knees. The blue horse came over and nudged him with its nose.

"Don't try your wiles on me," Tomás said. "It's too late for that now."

It butted him again and stared at the side of his face.

He reached over and stroked its long old lip.

"Aren't we a pair?" he said.

※

Later, he sat in his study, aching all over from the ride. He didn't let anyone see he was sore, but he could barely stand up straight, and his legs were wobbly, and his undercarriage was as tender as overripe plums, and his back hurt. He must have wrenched his shoulder on that impromptu downhill expedition.

He lit his oil lamp and packed a pipe with aromatic tobacco. It was like smoking candy, but the refined chappies uphill were all pipe suckers, and he was not going to be outperformed by them. He'd show them sophistication.

He lined up his ink bottles and pulled a fancy cream rag sheet and studied his quill and then dipped it in the brown. He'd heard Rosencrans speak of New York a while back. He bent to the letter. The pen scratched, and, honestly, it put his teeth a little on edge. Those kids wouldn't know their hats from their asses in a place like that. Why, his little girl would be eaten alive by all those gangs and crooks and scoundrels and immigrants.

He didn't approve of John Van Order, but John was a generous distance beyond Mr. Rodriguez in value. He pondered: Did this not make him and the delicious widow Juana coparents? Was this one of those plural marriages the Saints of Deseret had engineered for themselves? He'd have to look into that. Juana Van Order was, no doubt, still a fine girl, sweet as pastry. He might yet have a few pokes in him. He sighed and shook his head.

To the letter, with the full fire of his attentions! Cajoling, arguing, shaming, demanding. It was a classic Tomás Urrea production. He blew on the ink and folded the letter and slid it into a heavy envelope. It was good. By God. He could still write a letter even if he couldn't ride a horse.

He pulled open his bottom drawer with his boot tip and bent, grunting, to withdraw an amber bottle from the files. He sat back and enjoyed the small sea sound of the gold cap coming unscrewed and the rolling fingerlings of scent cutting under the pipe smoke. He tipped the bottle and felt the color burn in his mouth where his gums were raw and sore. It stung. He winced. But when he swallowed, it hit his belly like his own mother's love. One more, he told himself, and it went down smoother than the first. He puffed the pipe and smelled the edible smoke and enjoyed the liquor fumes coming back up his throat to join it on his tongue. He was in a world of benevolent essences, in the air and in his body. One more! He took a longish pull and gasped in delight.

The clock struck midnight before he knew it was late. He had been sitting there like a brain-fever patient, happily smoking and staring into the dark. He tapped out the glowing plug of tobacco and put the bottle away and blew out the lamp and creaked to his feet.

Gabriela would be up there in their bed, deep asleep. He went to step up on the stair and found his leg wobbling and weak. The front of his thigh refused to support him. Oh, well. That wouldn't work. He was so lamed up he didn't imagine he'd be climbing those stairs. He looked up. To be honest, she just snored anyway, snored so loud she kept him awake. He shrugged one shoulder and wandered to the front room and stretched out on the small couch. His feet went up on the arm, but he didn't care.

New York.

Who had ever heard of such a thing.

Why—

But he was already asleep.

Forty-Nine

AFTER MR. SUITS LEFT St. Louis for far California, Mr. Smith wormed his way back into a managerial position. Field agent was his commission title, since he was the only Consortium member with personal experience in dealing with the formidable Van Order dreadnought. In telegrams, the clients were referred to by code. Teresita was the Soprano, for she was now handled like a prima donna of the stage, if not a diva; John was Wild Bill, for in spite of his pretensions, he appeared a swaggering cowpuncher and possibly a shootist. In fact, none of these men could tell what he was, except that he was Herself's partner in intractability. "Highfalutin calf wrestler," Suits had called him as he departed.

Names. It hurt John's heart, afterward, by dawn light, when they lay naked in the snowy sheets, stunned and afraid of what they had done, still wet with each other, already wondering what tomorrow and the next year and the years thereafter might bring, that Teresita called him companion.

Companion? Not lover? Not darling? Not even John could know what that word *companion* meant to Teresita. He might come close to understanding her solitude, her years of exile within her own life, but who could really understand such a thing? Teresita herself barely understood it. In her mind, she and John had been united, at least by history, since they were nineteen. She kissed him, yes. And she kissed those years as well — those years and that connection to him, no matter how tenuous, for she knew no connections but the most ethereal. She had learned that life on earth was a dream, and not always a good one, and that the morning would come and she would awaken into death and she would be among her lost ones and the deer of the flower home and she would wonder what had happened to her and why it had happened. And she knew that God would never answer her.

Teresita and John's delights were in small things. Shy turning from each other, his glimpse of her bare back as she bent away from him to retrieve her clothes, his using the sheet as a wrap to hide himself from her. Her freed hair swishing back and forth across her milky skin, the curves of her side, her arm covering her chest and her hair hiding half her face—her one visible eye regarding him with a joyous gleam. His hair standing on end from the pillow, and how he had no idea he looked insane.

For a moment, clothed in night, they had been free and laughed and cried out and moaned. They had swum in each other, waves of every year and every yearning and every loneliness and every sorrow breaking over them, crashing around them. She felt herself held tight as a fist, and felt that fist pried open by pleasure. For her to open the buttons of her dress for him, how she shook, how she had to silence all the dread warnings and cries of outrage welling within her and seeming to whisper from all around, the act of faith it took for her to see him before her, see his bare chest in that low light and not think that again an unexpected beast would burst forth, some devil would take this man and twist his face into the countenance of a wild dog, and the blows, the cries, the blood would come again. It made her cry. And John felt like he was lifting into the air as she felt like she was sinking below the earth and he opened his eyes to make sure she hadn't sent him floating in the air with one of her Yaqui spells. In that swoon, the smell of roses faded, surrendering under him, to the smell of flesh and woman and sweat and honey. Slowly, it eased back as they slept, their arms and legs entwined, her hair over his face, in his fists, in his mouth. He could not get her close enough. He wanted their ribs to interweave and hook them together. Then, as he started to snore, he kicked away from her and took most of the bed like a slumbering bloodhound. She scooted to the edge of the bed and lay on her side and fell asleep smiling and dreamed of a small hummingbird—a hummingbird too small to be seen whose body was made of sky and whose wings were made of words.

When they were robed and combed in the morning and seated at their tiny round window table with tea and toast and melons and sweet cream, they fumbled, they looked at their hands, they laughed, she wept — not sobbing, simply slow, rolling tears that she didn't even seem to feel. He wiped them from her cheek with one finger, sore afraid that he had come into her world and violated the temple. Surely the likes of John Van Order did not lie in the bed of a saint. Though his faith waxed and waned and he never could get the truth of the situation bucked out to his liking. Some days, she was just his silly little girl from the Arizona backcountry.

"Are you upset?" he asked.

She shook her head.

"Did I hurt you?" he asked.

She reached her hand across the table and put her cold fingers over his lips.

She stared into his eyes.

"You must," she said softly, "love me."

She pushed her fingers hard against his mouth to keep him silent, then rose and went into the bathroom and closed the door. He heard water running. He studied the pattern of the tablecloth. He drummed his fingers.

"Love," he said, trying that unfamiliar word to see how it felt on his tongue.

❧

John started a ledger of her wonders — he forced himself to attend her healings. He translated for the Scandinavians and Germans. That was a dance, all right — their twisted lingo having to make sense to him in English first before he could roll it over into español for her. Former rebs and border ruffians limped in, their ancient gnarly limbs busted and wrenched by relentless hardships. Irishmen and Scotsmen with their alien accents. Hell, Texans were hard enough to understand sometimes.

John noted each farmer, immigrant, widow, orphan, laborer, river-boat man, whore, salesman, copper, Mexican, Catholic, Indian who came in. The Baptists stayed away and some of them maintained a hostile vigil. "Satan seduces through beauty!" one preacher cried. "He was the morning star! He was an angel of light! No woman can withstand his wiles! God shall not suffer a witch to live!"

Teresita went to him.

"Brother," she said.

"You're no sister to me!" he cried.

"Why do you assault me?" she asked.

He held his black Bible before her face and shook it.

John stood behind her, translating this pig slop. He'd be damned if he could understand why she attended to this kind of rabble. He'd heard about the secret powers of his beloved; he wanted to see her paralyze a shouter or two just for his own entertainment.

"This holy book," the preacher told her. "This holy scripture rebukes you."

She nodded. Smiled. Raised a hand toward him. Here it comes! John thought excitedly. But she only talked.

"You can stack two thousand Bibles on an ass's back," she said. "And he would still be an ass."

John really enjoyed that.

She went inside.

John stepped up and made his revolver visible, but the gospel sharp was not afraid to go to his great reward and only doubled his shouting when he was threatened.

※

September 12, 1901 — Healings and Appointments
Mrs. Lindstrom .... gout
Mr. Pettigrew .... carbunkle

Indian male.................................. bad tooth (sent to dentist)
Vilma S .... whore maladys
Bob-Bob Trews .... blind (inconcludid)
Gaitan Garcia............................... dead (bad luck there!)
Anon.. undisclosed, but it hurt
Molly H .... with secret child (17 yrs. Old)
Helga Buckter .... lady trables
Sixteen orphants........................... barkin cough
Miss N Cangemi .... just prayed

※

"Sometimes," he said, "they don't come for nothin' other than to pass the time."

"People in America are lonely," she said.

"They just want to pass the time, do they?"

"They want to be with me. I do not ask why."

"I know why I want to be with you, darlin'," he said. "But why do they? No disrespect or nothing."

"I make them feel better."

"Feelings, eh."

"Feelings matter."

"Feelings are for little girls and kittens. I don't think about them much."

"One does not think about feelings, silly. One has feelings."

"I feel like a drink," he scoffed.

"Do I not give you feelings, John?"

He smiled.

"You do. By God but you do."

She rubbed his knuckle across her lips.

"You make me happy," she said. "That is a feeling…and a healing too."

He put his lips on her lips. Their mouths stuck together in the tenderest way, and pulling them apart was as delicate a thing as either of them would ever feel. They took the moment, eyes closed, in silence, to note it.

"I swear," he said at the end of that kiss. "I don't know how you do it."

The hotel lobby was shady and quiet.

"Do what? Kiss?"

"Well, that too."

He raised his ledger of wonders.

"This here."

"God does it through me," she said.

"Isn't that pious."

"What do you mean by that?"

"I didn't see God in that room. I saw you in there, and I saw a bunch of shuffling sad cases is what I saw."

"God," she said, exhausted and slightly bored, as if she were a schoolmarm explaining again the same mathematics problem she had explained to generations of uninterested children, "cannot be seen."

"What good is He, then?"

"God is seen through the evidence of His presence."

"That's rather handy," John said with a cocked eyebrow. "God's there because you say He's there. These are" — he sought the right words — "extravagant claims indeed, Mrs. Van Order."

John believed in God — maybe not in the church version of God, but he accepted the idea. What he was having trouble with at the moment was the thought that the woman he was tussling with at night was representing the presence of the Lord by day. Could you be naked in front of God? Well, if you wasn't Adam and Eve?

"Through His effect, He is known," she said. "Not seen directly."

"How do I know it's Him then?"

"If you have the eyes to see, you will see the evidence."

"If I believe God's there, I will see God?" By God! Was that declaration sufficient?

God would be a great poker player, he thought.

They were seated at a quiet lamb-chop dinner. She didn't like lamb and remembered he'd tried to fool her into eating it the first time she met him. She spread the mint jelly on her toast and busied herself with the roast potatoes and the green beans. He watched this and shook his head. His gal was too skinny by far. He'd have to get her to eat some beeves if she was ever going to round out. Get some color. Lately, she was pale as a lunger, seemed wan. It was these healings of hers, he was certain. Those shuffling peons and dirt farmers. Whatever she was doing to them, they were suckling her dry.

"Did you not see the evidence today?" she asked.

He took a good long swallow of beer.

"Okay," he offered, trying out this newest exclamation heard at the docks. "I saw something. I see it every day."

"Well?"

He shrugged.

"Sweet...heart," he said, uncertain about how to make those words tumble into conversation. "That dead fellow..."

"Yes?"

"He stayed dead."

She smiled and tried not to. She blushed. She shrugged.

"It doesn't seem given to me to raise the dead," she noted. "However, in those situations, I minister to the family and try to send them into their lives with peace."

"They had old granddad in a cart like a fire log!" John said. "Lucky the coppers didn't see that."

"Stop," she whispered. "You're so bad."

"Tell me I'm lying!"

Her uneaten lamb sat in a small bay of grease like a burned island; the waiter took it away.

"May I have tomato soup?" she asked.

"Certainly."

"Gracias."

"I am cursed with practicality," John confessed.

"You think me false," she said.

"Nope," he said. "Didn't say it, didn't mean it."

"Why do you criticize me?" she asked.

"Not you. I'm with you, not nobody else. It's this whole...thing...I can't quite feature. Maybe that's my test of faith, as you might put it. But, look—if you'd been able to grow my pop a new leg, then for sure I would believe it and kneel to you."

"No, no, no. Kneel to God, do not kneel to me." She patted his hand and looked at him sadly.

"You admire these electrical lamps," she said, placing her hands flat on the table.

"I do."

"What powers them is invisible. You can't see electricity. You can only see its effect. Light."

She smiled. Spread her hands before him.

"This is what God is like. You never see Him. But you see what He produces. You see what He causes to ignite and burn."

The soup arrived. She floated small crackers upon it and bent to the bowl. He sat and watched her. He rubbed his temples. God the electrician was beyond him right then. His skinny gal was something to ponder, though. He might not be able to track the divine by the light of day, but John could feel God when they made love. There was no way to broach that in polite conversation. It sounded crude, but it was the least crude thing he had ever thought. He sat on that one.

He smiled at her through his headache.

"Time for more beer," he said.

※

No one ever entered their suite except for maids and waiters. Thus no one knew that he tossed shirts in corners and she picked them up and folded them. No one knew he liked to lie on the bed with his boots on and that she scolded him every time. No one saw where he liked to kiss her—along the soft hinge of her jaw, just beneath her ear. Or where she liked to be kissed—on the forehead, a child's kiss, a kiss she had never felt. It sent shivers down her back, and it filled her with an illusory warmth, a nostalgia for tender years that had not happened.

Perhaps intruding observers would not have been so shocked at their nakedness if they'd seen the couple late at night, lying spent and sweated, her head upon his bare chest. Oddly, Teresita felt most pure when she was with her new husband, most free, most herself.

Or would they have been more shocked by her whispered confessions and pleas? When she gripped him fiercely and said, "If I could, I would quit"?

His great hand on her spine—how it curved, how elegant and long it felt in the dark. He admired the way it led his hand down to the swelling of her hips and her bottom.

"Don't quit yet," he advised. "We aren't there yet."

"Aren't where?"

"Why, New York." He patted her rump. How friendly it felt. How comfortable. His. "Quit after New York."

She nestled against him and dared to imagine the sin of retiring.

"New York," he murmured. "You won't be sorry."

He waited till she was asleep. He extricated himself from her arms and rose silently. He dressed in the dark and picked up his boots so he could put them on in the hall. He bent to her and kissed her dear, troubled face. He put his lips to her earlobe. She squirmed and laughed in her sleep. He touched her face. Before he went out, he opened her bag and fished out a few dollars. Just one drink. One drink, or two. And a game of faro or poker. That would do it. He let himself out and sat in the hall to pull on his rose-stitched high-heel custom-mades.

"Buenas noches, Mrs. Van Order," he said.

※

SOPRANO AND WILD BILL NEW YORK SOON / LIVING AS MAN AND WIFE / IF DISCOVERED DISASTER / ADVISE.

※

SMITH—MUST AVERT SCANDAL / DIVORCE SOPRANO SOONEST AVAILABLE / WILL ARRANGE THIS END / WILD BILL FEND FOR SELF?

⁂

BRING SOPRANO TO LOS ANGELES FOR DIVORCE / DIST
COURT DIVORCES EASY / TRAIN NY AFTER TO MEET COWBOY.

⁂

GREASER RAIL UNION STRIKE LOS ANGELES / WILL KEEP
SOPRANO AWAY FROM MEX / IMPERATIVE GO SMOOTH AND
NO NEWS.

⁂

SOPRANO FINDS TROUBLE BY NATURE / BRACE SELFS.

Fifty

FINDING OUT SHE'D be in the west while he faced their destiny alone
put John Van Order in a blue funk for a while. But it couldn't last. Not
with New York on the horizon. New York! With its smoking towers and
its epic streets, its rivers and harbors and parks and industry, New York
of the avenues, of the dances in Harlem and the bridges to Brooklyn. He
had seen it all in books and magazines. He had dreamed it as a place of
laughter and music and perfume and none of the stink or the dirt or the
chickens in the poor shadows or the hard times that crushed workingmen to the cobbles. There was no gloom in his head yet.

In an old-books emporium, he found a volume that brought him great
joy. He tried to share passages with Teresita, but it was beyond her understanding, and there was no way to translate his delight into her languages.
It was a slim volume: *Vocabulum: Or, The Rogue's Lexicon* by New York
City police chief George Matsell. And although the idiom of the gangs of

New York had surely evolved since the book's appearance, in 1859, John was certain that phrases would remain current among those in the know. He studied it and laughed and cornered her with trivia all day.

"Do you know what the New York criminal calls a man?" he said.

"No."

"Bene cove! Isn't that rich?"

"Ay, sí."

"Bene cove," he marveled. "How about what they called the madam of a whorehouse?"

"Why would I know that?"

"A cab-moll!"

"Mira nomás."

She reminded herself of Gabriela, of the way she indulged Tomás and deflected his outbursts with a sweet distractedness that allowed him to believe he was impressing her while not overly burdening her mind or taking her attentions from her own thoughts.

"You know what a nose is?"

She was packing her trunk.

"No idea," she muttered, thinking: Do I need heavy stockings in Los Angeles?

"A trunt!"

"Amazing," she offered.

Ah, this was going to be the life for him. He lay back on the bed, his boots dirtying the quilt. He was going to meet the bene coves and give 'em the fam grasp, gripping their flappers like a real foxey foyster.

"I love the study of languages." Professor Van Order sighed.

"That's nice, mi amor," she said.

※

Their day of parting was coming, but like all lovers, they ignored it as long as they could. Her birthday arrived, but she refused any presents. He celebrated it with a small ginger and raisin cake with buttercream icing in their room. For that one night, she agreed to sip rum.

He knew he had to go ahead to find their digs in New York. There was no time to spare. And she, if she was going to preserve her good name and if she was going to be his woman in the light of the world—she was convinced she was his bride in the eyes of God already—she had to register her papers in court and be freed of the nightmare of her past once and for all. She could barely remember Lupe Rodriguez, had forgotten much of his face, and she wanted his name erased and burned. As did the Consortium.

The pilgrims were fewer now. The high society people of the city had been to her and faded away. The local newspapers were no longer interested in her. These four months had felt like years. Whole lifetimes had happened to them.

Freed from responsibilities, Teresita and John spent their last days together in the city roving. They tried the new frankfurters in their crispy buns. They ate the celebrated World's Fair hamburgs, which John could not get enough of, while Teresita found the grease of the meat vaguely nauseating. One of John's new bene coves owned a rickety Ford, and he drove them across the bridge to far Illinois. There wasn't much over there, but they made a show of marveling at the rich black soil farmers showed them. They met the black men of East St. Louis, John unable to prevent her from holding every Negro hand extended to her; if he wasn't careful, she'd launch some new crusade to heal every colored person in America. They ate pork cracklin's and remembered delicious Mexican chicharrónes. The flivver puttered them out to the haunted Cahokia Mounds, and Teresita was amazed that pyramid builders had once walked these very plains.

A hot-air-balloon ride at the fairgrounds scared both of them out of their wits. But once they were as high as the crows that circled them demanding to know what they thought they were doing, Teresita opened her eyes and laughed. It was joyous. Flying at last. Like Huila!

They saw an opera and didn't understand it. They caught a barrelhouse piano show in a smoky theater. John tried to play a banjo and sounded very bad. She couldn't stop laughing.

Try as he might, John wasn't able to wrangle an elephant ride for his beloved, which was all she wanted on that last day. But, no, nobody at the exposition would allow it. He even offered the bastards twenty dollars.

"I have disappointed you, Teresita," he said.

"I hate to say this, Mr. Van Order, but I may never be able to forgive you."

"What if, Mrs. Van Order, I scrub your back tonight?"

"Ooh," she said. "But that's no elephant ride."

"Sadly true, my dear. But there's other fine rides at the Van Order Exposition!"

"¡Qué malo eres!" she cried, pleasing him no end.

He smiled and laughed.

"Take me home," she said. "Now."

"Watch me do it," he replied.

⁂

One burning candle made the room dark orange. Its weak light wobbled, as if the walls were bubbles that were changing with the breeze. Shadows breathed in and puffed away from them.

He wanted her beside him. Naked. Just to lie there. He wanted to feel her close to him. And there she lay, on her back, arms relaxed at her sides, frank and open to him. He reached over and laid his hand on her belly. It was so soft. Shadows within shadows, circles within circles, he had no words for it. Touching eternity right there. He felt her belly rise and fall with her breathing.

"Why roses?" he asked.

She sniffed the air.

"Can you smell them?" she asked.

"Yep."

"I'm sorry."

"No, no. I like it."

She moved closer, rested her head upon his solid arm.

"I don't know why," she said. "It just happened."

"Wasn't one of them saints called Teresa too? She smelled like roses."
She nodded.

"Roses are holy, I guess." He yawned. "I was always partial to the sweet pea myself."

"John! You like flowers?"

"I don't know one flower from the next. You'd have to ask my mother about flowers."

"The Yaquis," she said, "use rose petals to represent God's grace."

"How about that," he murmured.

He put his hand on her hair and felt its shine through his fingers.

"Like your hair," he said.

"And I like yours."

"Like my whiskers too?"

"Your whiskers are a bit prickly."

"Hey now!"

"Like kissing a porcupine."

"I can't do without them whiskers," he said. "You'll have to suffer."

She laughed, curled into him.

"I love your whiskers," she said.

"All right then." He rubbed her side with his big hand. Ran it down to her hip and cupped her pelvis, then ran it back up to her ribs and over to her arm and down to her fingers. "It's a good thing you like them — I been thinking of growing a beard. Maybe down to my belt."

"¡Ay, no!" She gasped, and he pulled her over on top of himself and laughed into her mouth.

They lay there breathing against each other.

"You know what?" he said.

"What?"

"I'm sorry for all them things . . . all *those* things that happened. In your life."

She was quiet.

"I'm sorry you been through that."

She absentmindedly scratched at the hair on his chest.

"Thank you," she said.

"Makes me mad," he said.

"Me too," she finally said.

"Aw, Mrs. Van Order."

"Yes?"

"Nothing. I just like hearing the words."

They blew out the candle.

⁂

Under the blankets, she said, "I don't want to go."

"I don't want you to go," he said.

"I must."

"It's for the better. You know it."

"I know it."

"We should stay up and watch the dawn," she said.

"That's exactly what I was thinking just as you said it."

"Oh, John." Silence. "John?" He started snoring.

She turned away from him, still in the refuge of his arm, and closed her eyes and tried to ignore the perturbation of worry and exultation rushing across her brain like a horse race. Faces, names, places, voices, fires, guns, animals, faces again, and faces, faces, faces.

As the sky burned pink at its bottom hem, she rose and attended to her belongings one last time.

⁂

At Union Station, he saw her to her car, a nice Pullman appointed with gilt lamps and a porter who showed her to her compartment. It held a bunk and a seat in a small space. Tight accommodations, but plush. He'd never ridden in a berth like that. John checked that the door locked. "You'll watch her like your own?" he asked the porter as he slipped him a twenty-dollar gold piece. The porter slid the coin into his vest pocket and tipped his head.

"You can count on me, sir," he said.

"Feed her good."

"I shall."

"All right then."

"We pull out in twenty minutes. Sir? Ma'am?" He tipped his cap and moved on down the narrow passageway.

John got Teresita squared away and felt her tears wet his shirt as he held her. He was startled by a bit of a sniffle on his own part. Toots from outside and small sobs against his chest and calls from the crew and a small lurch as the train tried to leap out of its paddock early. John kissed her, then she kissed John, then John kissed her and turned to go but spun back and kissed her again. How was that for a fit farewell, he thought.

"Stay out of trouble," he said.

"I will."

"Promise."

"I promise."

"At the least sign of religious revivals, assassins, pilgrims, Mexicans, Indians, you get out."

"I will." She looked up at him. "And you do the same."

"Me? I never get in trouble." He really believed it.

One last embrace.

"Don't join no revolutions," he said. And, as he stepped away: "Or start any!"

She watched from her window as he trotted down the platform beside her until the train accelerated and he reached the end of the elevated walkway and windmilled his arms so as not to fall off and suddenly she was watching the city and the far exposition whirl away and before long, the blurring rippling Missouri hills came along like green explosions.

※

He walked.

He stepped into a small bar called Homer's around the corner from the station. It stank of spilled beer and fried peanuts. A collapsed old lout slumped at a stool by the far wall like some pile of filthy laundry. Riverboat men drank and joshed one another on the other end. John was interested to see a urinal trough running along the bottom of the bar behind the low brass foot rail. The brass was stained green and brown. There was that stink too. The barkeep stopped wiping the bar with his wet pestiferous rag and smiled up at him.

"Whiskey," said John.

"Nectar of the gods, mate," said the barkeep, uncorking a smudged brown bottle.

"You Homer?" John asked, settling on his stool and planning a long siege.

"Aye."

John took a sip and wrinkled his nose. What was this weak donkey piss?

"Homer," he said, "I think you baptized this bottle a time or two."

"I never watered down no drink in my life," said Homer.

"Ha!" cried one of the boatmen. "That's rich. He baptized so many bottles they oughter call him the pope!"

Homer grabbed the shot glass away from John and tossed the whiskey on the floor.

He selected a Tennessee bottle and poured John a new shot.

"Tell me I'm a crook now," he said.

Ah. That was like a mouthful of sunshine. Rolled on down, making soft music all the way.

"That's better." John nodded. He tipped his hat to Homer.

"What's your name?" Homer asked. "Now that we're intimate and all."

"Why, my good man," announced John, "my name is Benny Cove!"

"Well, Benny," Homer said, "how's about another drink and one other for me for all my troubles?"

"Whiskey," John said to the room. "Good for what ails you and for everything else too!"

They toasted him and he toasted them and Homer poured and John started throwing 'em back, two, three, five, seven shots.

⁂

The agony in his head when he awoke in the alley, covered in scraps of spoiled food and barefoot, could have been from the whiskey, or the swollen egg on his brow, or both.

He didn't know what time it was, morning or noon. His pockets were turned out and his watch was gone. His pistol belt was lying four feet from him, its holster empty. He managed to heave to his knees and felt the scum of the alley sinking into his trousers. He rose, slowly, swaying, and bent over and vomited on his own shadow.

He tumbled out of the alley and passersby did the old-reprobate two-step and cut wide divagations around him and went on their way, clicking their tongues and shaking their heads. He was blurry, at best — his eyes did not pick out the squabbling gulls flown up from Louisiana, nor did they feature the pigeons beyond their leaflike blowing at the wobbling end of the street.

He minced to the door of Homer's and found it locked. He pounded on the glass, but no one answered. Children in the street laughed at him. He righted himself and combed his hair with his fingers. "Where has my damned hat gotten to?" he asked.

It was a long transit to the hotel, akin in his mind to the journeys of mountain men of old trudging barefoot through savage prairies as red savages whooped and unleashed hordes of arrows as they marched. Coppers turned to him as he passed and found him so grim in his debauch that they merely shook their heads and didn't roust him for a vagrant. It was funny to them — another victim of the ol' docks.

The hotel lobby caught its breath, aghast, when all gathered therein turned and beheld his staggering from the door to the desk to the stairway and gone. Only after they heard the door of his room slam did they begin to mutter and snicker and complain and gossip. The piano recommenced its endless tinkling concerto of sentimental favorites. Bustling ladies with parasols and fat children hurried through like mother quails. Mr. Smith, sitting in the easy chair closest to the fireplace, watched the whole sad performance and laughed quietly into his handkerchief.

He was already composing his next telegram in his mind.

WILD BILL, he was thinking.

OUTGUNNED.

Fifty-One

JOHN COULD HAVE PUNCHED Mr. Smith right in the mouth for his smug smile. But he didn't dare upset the applecart, not with Mrs. Van Order gone. There was nobody there to protect him, and here he was, having to beg.

It was a good thing his tickets were already bought; he was all in. It was a fix — but he told himself it was just a patch of bad luck, he'd had them before, plenty of them, and he'd work his way out of it, and he'd get it done before Teresita met him in the great city. Hell, he still had his coat and his jacket, and he'd tied on his old gambler's ribbon tie. He also had some shirts and some new charcoal-gray trousers to replace the ruined alley-smeared old britches he'd had to throw in the trash can.

When he took inventory, it was columns of plusses and naughts. Yes, he wouldn't have to go naked. But he was clean broke. He had his finer things that they had bought over the last three months. But he was already wearing his old worn-out boots, and he hated to take the journey so tragically shod. That, he was certain, was no way to enter Manhattan, but he'd make do. Still, he needed some folding money and a hat. He figured correctly that there was no chance Mr. Smith and his godforsaken Consortium would buy him a new pistola. But there was a long journey ahead of him, and meals, and drink, and poker. And he couldn't enter the great city without enough in his poke to buy a fried egg. How would he make rent?

Mr. Smith was barely able to contain his laughter as John hung his head and concocted tales of woe and need, hoping to stir his stony heart, but without the Soprano there to back his play, Wild Bill was a trembling sot with rummy boiled eyes and quivering fingers. A rat-faced wheedler hoping for a few more tens in the pot.

"Not so high and mighty now, are we, Mr. Van Order?" The jape thrilled Mr. Smith all the way to his feet.

John stared at his hands because he knew that if he looked in Mr. Smith's face, he'd launch over the table and throttle him on the spot. And then what would he do? So he accepted the lashings of Mr. Smith's mirth and hoped to have the chance some fine day hence to perforate him with a well-placed shot—what his penny-dreadful dime novels called a blue whistler.

Ultimately, it wasn't nearly enough money, but John was in no position to complain. He took the cash and tucked it into his inner pocket and buttoned his jacket. They sat there, neither one willing to break the spell of mutual contempt. John could not open his mouth to say anything—certainly not thank you. Mr. Smith could not bear to end the utter joy of seeing the shit-kicking waddy with idiotic pretensions squirm in perfect misery and shame.

Finally, John said, "Say, Smith, you goddamned penny-pincher, will you stake me for a new hat?"

Calling Smith that gave John back some small uptick of pride.

Mr. Smith handed over a further twenty-dollar bill, just to show he could and could have given more if he cared to, and left the table lest Wild Bill ask him for a horse too.

※

It was fall, and cold, and he had not thought to buy an overcoat. His old camel-hair number would have to do, though it was not built for river winds. He fooled them all by doubling his undershirts and then wearing two shirts over them, and his jacket, and the tan coat buttoned tight. Better to look a little fat than to look cold. He could stand on the top deck watching the monstrous river roll, watching the banks in all their tiresome detail spool out behind, watching the smaller boats falling away as they chugged relentlessly into the north. If he looked fat, people would assume he had prospered. If he shivered, people would assume he had not. He couldn't hide his battered boots, but perhaps they'd think he was a cattle baron made rich by his epic cattle drives from the border to the Midwest.

The stateroom in the upper reaches of the paddleboat was all white. Mr. Van Order took great pains to mingle with the rabble down below, feeling the obligation to represent the Saint in her absence. But he was also seeking games of cards, for the boat's official gambling rooms were a tad rich for his taste, and the buy-ins to the games were for stout constitutions, and he would have lost much of his walking-around money against the weighted wheels and doctored dice in that red velvet plushness. Still, a few hands of five-card stud while sipping sweet rum, smoking black cigarillos, and smiling grandly at the stunning bar girls was irresistible. He actually won a round or two and upped his poke by two hundred dollars. He swaggered, he strolled—he was back! Benny Cove was rampant upon the earth.

The relentless rolling surge of the boat disagreed with him. The whapping of the paddle, as if some giant beaver were pushing them along with its flat tail, lunged the vessel forward, and the roiling waters rocked the craft back and forth. Mr. Van Order's first breakfast, a conglomeration of waffles and sausages, had him vomiting over the rail halfway through. He managed to clamp his new Montana-style hat to his head and hoped he'd not been seen. He spent the rest of that morning in his room, seasick and praying for mercy.

※

Luckily for him, it was only a three-day trip, beating against the tide, and he was soon on solid ground again, standing at the Illinois border.

He could feel the earth swell and recede beneath his feet. When he took a step, he rocked and lost his balance. One of the stripe-shirted river scum off a longboat laughed and told him he had some malady called sea legs.

"Ain't been on no ocean," John quipped.

Idiot.

He made his way toward the train station. It wasn't easy. He could haul his own case of shirts, but there were also three cases of Teresita's and a couple of hatboxes. Damn it—the tips were going to kill him, all these bastards pulling carts for him. But he was damned if he was going to drag wagons through the street for himself. There was a limit.

He didn't notice when a box, a smaller one, fell from the stack on the wagon and lay in the street. The box that contained Teresita's crucifix, her shells and her herb bundles and Huila's apron. He rumbled along beside the wagon, cobbles shaking the whole awkward collection as a burly young Italian fellow pulled like a mule.

The box lay on its side. Later, at sunset, a child found it and cracked it open. He tossed the herbs on the ground, pocketed the cross, and held up the apron. It had some shotgun shells in the pocket. An old pipe. The kid put the pipe in his back pocket. A pocketknife! He stuck that in his pocket too.

He folded up the apron and placed it over his shoulder. He kicked the box up and down the alley until it was collapsing. He kicked it into the river, and it commenced its journey back to St. Louis. Maw was going to be happy to get a new apron.

※

John purchased two beef and onion sandwiches and three apples, put them in a sack, and bought himself a little bottle for those nippy nights. He tipped the Italian to muscle the bags onto the train and was delighted to find his berth. He didn't have no state car like Teresita, but he did have a cozy bunk in the wall of a hallway. Wasn't tall enough inside to roll over, but he didn't mind—he liked to sleep on his back or his belly and there was a curtain to help with the light. When he inserted himself, he imagined he was some ancient pharaoh in a crypt.

This time, the rolling and the rocking eased him. Solid ground was where a man belonged. He was yawning before they reached Chicago. He was asleep by Indiana.

He slept late the next day, awakening several times to people bumping into his sprawled legs and arms, the conductor roughly tucking him back in until further slumber was impossible. John slid out of his bunk and stood on aching feet. Sleeping in his boots meant his feet—which tended to swell at night—hurt pretty bad. But there was nowhere to put his boots if he took them off, and he'd be dogged if he was going to let somebody steal these too. He cleaned up in the washroom at the end of the car, scrubbed his face, and dried it on his shirttail. Combed his hair. Cleaned his teeth with tooth powder on the end of his finger. He put on his hat and made his way down to the seats at the windows where he could smoke and stare. What the hell was that out there? Ohio? He scoffed. Ohio! Maybe Pennsylvania. Rubes in little black buggies? He wanted to shout out: *Friends—you plow them onion fields! I'm going to New York City!*

By the second morning, he had begun to smell a bit tart, but he was all right. He was sore, though. Sore and sour. The sandwiches had gone a little green, and he had to toss the second one. The apples and the bottle sustained him.

He felt like he was choking in the train cars, like one of them fishes all canned up in an airtight tin. He wanted to get out there and breathe in some of that fabled eastern air, that Atlantic breeze come all the way from France, or Greece, or wherever. He wanted the west to fall away from him like one of his tired old dreams.

For the first time in his life, John Van Order was entering his destiny.

And, after more hours of cramped discomfort, growing dread and excitement, restlessness and leg cramps, he could be forgiven—when he first caught sight of New York throbbing in the distance—for crying out "Good God!" and turning his back.

❊

Silent exultations of horror and excitement.

This place, so massive, so clangorous and dark. He was made small, finally, invisible, helpless. He stood in the great station looking up at its vaulted heights, much taller than St. Louis's. And the crowd was faster, hunched into the day, hurrying with serious intent. He was knocked aside three times as he stood with his tumbling cartload of cases. He lost his great hat once. The first of two hundred New Yorkers called him Tex.

John drank the last of his bottle, and a blue-backed copper in a police hat tapped him with his nightstick and said, "None of that here, Tex. This isn't the Wild West." Called Tex twice in ten minutes; he was appalled. Did they not see his fine camel coat?

He stared at the hustling chaos. All those feet in all those leather soles making that clacketing racket on the marble floors. They had bowlers and top hats and caps and ridiculous flat straw hats and some Germanic businessmen's hats and a couple of louche slouch hats, but no sombreros in sight. A few brave souls went about with no hats at all. John stared at a chappie over there with a beret. French son of a bitch.

Nobody anywhere wearing a cowboy hat.

He couldn't find a free porter, so he pulled his wagon along himself, indignant, burning with embarrassment. The doors out of the station and to the city seemed a mile away, and they appeared to retreat before him as he struggled. The cold made his eyes water. He squinted and turned his face away. He bumped into a paperboy yelling: "Booker T. Washington visits Roosevelt! Negro in the White House! Get it here! Get your paper here!" The boy turned on John and snapped, "Jay-sus! Watch it, Tex." The boy veered away, hollering with a limp paper over his head: "Booker T. dines with president! Get it here! Riots in the South!"

John banged out the double doors with his back to the street and pulled his wagon with him. He turned and beheld. The city: A wall of brick before him, cutting off light. Streams of human bodies rushed by on the street, confabs in every language whipping around his head with the wind. He couldn't even hear any English in all that babble.

A little black boy was dancing for pennies in the street, his brothers slapping their thighs and knees in a crazy rhythm. A shoeshine boy toting a stained box stood and watched them, laughing. Somewhere beyond, John heard an alarming clanging, as if giants were tossing huge sheets of steel from rooftops. Fine gents in tall hats came along in a tight formation, five of them in a wedge, talking money and smoking and wielding shiny walking sticks like batons with which they conducted the mad ballet around them, cutting through and storming away before John could offer 'em a howdy. Horses drew flat drays like river barges. Skittering little black cars hopped around like june bugs. Everything barely missing every other thing. John saw right away that each corner was a test of survival skills.

Here's what he didn't expect to find: he didn't expect to find that the city smelled like horse turds and mule squirt. Why, the street before him was jammed with carts—tall carts loaded, as far as he could tell, with refuse. Broken tables and old chiffoniers. Nags pulled these wagons and went every way in the street, parted by the rumbling, bell-abusing trolley cars. Those spindly little motorcars stalled and sputtered, blowing klaxons at the horses that balked and stomped and unleashed steaming avalanches of crap in the gutters. There were far more of these contraptions here than in St. Louie or Chicago. Where was the music? He had thought the city was alive night and day with festive concerts and dance ensembles hosting cotillions in the many parks. And he couldn't get over these boater hats. The more he looked, the more he saw these hats. He'd be dragged to Hell before he put one of those clownish rigs on top of his head; let 'em call him Tex all they wanted.

Some mad dog in a long frock coat stepped up to John and demanded:

"Wer, wenn ich schriee, horte mich denn aus der Engel Ordnungen?"

"Back off, bindle stiff," John said, pushing him away.

The shoeshine boy stared up at him.

"Need a shine, mister?" he said.

"Nope. Not now."

"Them boots looks like shite," the kid noted.

John looked at his poor old boots. They felt, at the moment, like his only friends on earth. He looked at the kid. The kid didn't have a coat, only a tattered cardigan. He was shivering.

"Is it always this cold in New York?" John asked.

"Nah." The kid shook his head. "It gets colder'n this." He sniffled. "You want the shine or not?"

"Right here?"

"Mister. Where else we going to do it?"

The kid shook his head as John raised his foot to the shoe-shaped top of the box and rested it there. He spit and worked his brownest brown polish into his rag and got to it. John stood, feeling like a heroic statue, feeling the cold move along his bones. He found himself missing his little Saint.

John observed an old man in a heavy black frock coat and a black hat, a long white beard and a long curl of hair hanging by each of his ears, and some kind of rebozo ends bouncing out from under his coat.

The policeman from inside the train station came out and observed them.

John, remembering his beloved Matsell crime lexicon, said to the kid: "Twig that copper, lad. He's peery at us."

"Tex," the boy said, focusing on the boots, "talk English, all right? This is America now, not no 'nother country."

Glancing up, John found a distant streak of sky; it looked like a trout stream in a canyon had somehow been upended and hung above his head.

He made a silent vow to himself: As soon as he made his way through this frightening maze and settled somewhere, got the bags unpacked and the heater turned on for Mrs. Van Order—who wasn't used to the cold of a city—he would head out and find some bene coves to pal around with, and he would get so drunk he couldn't see a hole through a standing ladder.

Fifty-Two

THE VOICE SAID, "Mr. Van Order?"

John had stood there with his polished boots, unable to move, staring out at the hubbub and blocking the flow of pedestrians until irate New Yorkers kicked his feet and waved their hands and pushed him back against the wall. He didn't mind. He felt safer there, and the wall was warm from the sun sneaking down the canyon to it. This right here, he was realizing, this whole New York episode, was the longest of long chances, and his odds were looking paltry. When the voice spoke, he was startled and expected anything—even one of Teresita's angels.

He turned and regarded a gent in a blue suit and straw hat. Everyone was wearing them. Oh, well, John thought, the hat is gaining on me.

"Mr. Van Order," the man said again. "They said I would recognize you."

"How do," said John. "Who said?"

"The Consortium." The man fished out a yellow slip from his pocket. "I received a telegram."

"I'll be dogged," said John.

They shook hands.

"I am Dr. Weisburd," the gent in blue said.

"Doc, hey? Well, I am delighted to make your acquaintance, Doc. I was starting to think I'd made one of those calamitous decisions you hear about."

The good doctor smiled.

"Would that be your first?" he asked.

John laughed.

"Now that you mention it," he drawled, happy to have encountered the right audience again, "I almost made a bad decision back in 1899. But I decided against it."

"Smart move."

Dr. Weisburd tipped his head and extended a hand.

"I have a wagon down the block waiting for you. Perhaps we can find a helper."

He put his hand over his head and snapped his fingers. A porter appeared as if by magic, calling: "Sir!" Dr. Weisburd nodded toward the wagon and headed out, followed by the cart—a two-man parade. *Snap your fingers.* Van Order took mental notes. It was going to be tough figuring out the play in this burg, but he'd do it. He told himself there had never been any doubt.

"We'll get you settled in your new digs," Dr. Weisburd told him.

John basked in autumnal light.

"I appreciate the Consortium arranging this for me," he said grandly.

The doctor coughed softly.

"I'm afraid this is all about Mrs. Van Order," he said. "I assume you are seen by my associates as a house servant."

John maintained the blandest face possible. He told himself it didn't matter. He'd show them all. Who cared how he got into his penthouse? The point was that he was getting into a penthouse! In New York!

"New York!" he cried.

Dr. Weisburd watched him.

"Indeed," he said.

"Cold, ain't it!"

"It is a bit brisk, yes."

John almost busted his neck with all the craning around he was doing. Dr. Weisburd was kind enough to divert the driver from his itinerary to afford John a view of the harbor and Lady Liberty beyond, off the lower Manhattan shore. "Isn't she a sight," he said. The doctor grinned as if he had built her himself. He pointed to her left and intoned, "Ellis Island," as if that meant anything to John. Smoke-belching ships crowded the waters. Self-important little tugs rushed about. "Don't that beat all," said John, just to have something Tex-like to say.

They wheeled around and got back to the main drags and wended their way up to Broadway and worked the varied boulevards to head east. It wasn't lost on John that he had come all this way only to be lugged through the streets by a mule. In his mind, the city had been all airships and Fords and elevated trains moving through silver towers.

"Streets paved with gold!" Dr. Weisburd announced, as if reading John's mind. But John wasn't a fool. It was probably easy to read his mind. He reined himself in a little. It wouldn't do to play the hick in a place like Manhattan.

"So," he said. "You're a real doctor."

"I am."

"The Consortium has gone legitimate, eh, Doc?"

Dr. Weisburd turned to him.

"Were they not before?" he asked. "I had been told they were a respected medical concern in the West."

John smiled, patted his shoulder.

"Now that you're aboard, things will look up," he said. "Let's just say they had their shady moments."

The doctor looked concerned.

"Did they behave dishonorably?" he asked.

"Honor had nothing to do with it."

This was not what Dr. Weisburd had been told.

"I joined in," he said, "strictly to further the medical works of Saint Teresa."

"How'd you join?" John asked him.

"Why, I made the thousand-dollar donation, of course."

John sputtered. Those dirty sons of bitches. Partnerships!

"Are there many of you, Doc?" he choked out.

"Perhaps a thousand across the country."

"I'll be double damned," John announced.

He was feeling growing dismay. They didn't head into whatever glittering gulch of fine hotels he'd imagined. They didn't clop along the edge of Central Park—wherever that was. He looked around, his heart sinking into his gut.

He noted that both the clangor and the magnificence were receding. The buildings grew lower, and turned to wood, and became scarcer. There came a tall church on the right side of the street, the tallest building in this part of the city. Beyond, by God, he saw a farm of some kind, and the cobbles ran out and the street turned to dirt and mud. The wagon shuddered as it lurched down into the clods and mud smears. Dogs. Trash.

"Where are you taking me, to Russia?" he quipped.

"East Twenty-Eighth Street," the doctor replied. "Right around that corner by the church."

They turned the corner and parked in front of a row of small redbrick and brownstone buildings, three stories tall and backing onto a bit of woods with a creek and some pasture beyond.

"It is not a penthouse," the doctor said apologetically. "But for now, it will do."

It was a wooden building, narrow, with bay windows bulging out over a small portico: 110 East Twenty-Eighth Street.

John jumped down. Mud. Jesus Jumping Christ.

"Yep. It'll do," he said. What else could he say?

They went in and climbed the stairs and found a stuffy brown room on the second floor. But it was furnished. "A painter below you and an opera singer above," Dr. Weisburd said as he pulled open the curtains and let the sun in. John tried the couch. It listed to starboard. He'd have to put a book under that corner. Their bedroom was on the south side, and its windows let in warm light. If he craned his neck, he could see the spire of the church. Kitchen and commode were on the north side.

"That way lies Lexington," the doctor said. "If you follow Lex all the way down to Twenty-Third, you'll find my office. Right on the corner. You're in luck—Saturdays, the farmers set up their stalls right there and sell produce."

"Wonders never cease."

"Why, that street can carry you right straight to your dreams."

What a booster was Doc Wise Bird.

John grimaced a small smile of faux enthusiasm.

"If I walk that way, Doc, can I see all them fancy addresses where I thought I'd be livin'?"

The doctor tipped his head slightly.

"This is New York, Mr. Van Order. We got you here. It's up to you to realize your own ambitions."

He clapped John on the back.

"Millions have."

John looked down at the dirt street.

"How 'bout that," he said.

The driver came grunting and banging up with the first trunk.

"Is this move on me, or on the Consortium?" John asked.

Dr. Weisburd was about to tell him it was all on him, but the look in Van Order's eye stopped him. The man was suspicious. Foolish in his posturing. But afraid. It came off him in waves. The doctor was moved by his raw humanity.

"It would be my pleasure," said the doctor, "as an associate of the Consortium, to cover this expense for you and Mrs. Van Order."

John smiled sadly.

"Why, thank you."

He put out his hand.

They shook as the second trunk started its slow way up to them.

———————※———————

Later, he hung his Montana rancher's hat on a peg and walked downstairs to escape the dark boxes in his dark rooms. John had been alone before, but not like this. He strolled down to "Lex" and looked both ways. Yonder lay some kind of wilderness, and hither he saw civilization, lights. A few blocks ahead, he saw a tendril of cooking smoke angling away from a sidewalk bistro of some sort. He was starving. Why was he reluctant to step off, back toward the great city? He stood on the curb, his foot hanging in midair over the dirt of East Twenty-Eighth. Laughter came from an open window above him. A woman's voice, answered by a man's voice, singing "I Love You Truly." The window slammed shut. John turned. With a sputter and a bang, a Pierce Motorette sped by, kicking up little dirt clods, its driver waving distractedly at his witness as he wrestled the wheel to try to keep the vehicle from crashing into one of the shuttered shops lining the sidewalk. A couple strolled by, and the man murmured some European babble to the woman.

This wasn't so bad. He could do it. He shrugged his shoulders against the chill and followed a scruffy little dog across the road and down to the diner, where he looked in and spied, through the steamed window, families and workingmen hunched over bowls of noodles with red sauce poured over them. He saw bottles of red wine. Smelled garlic and cheese.

He opened the door, stepped in on creaking floorboards, and did his best to start his first night of his new life.

Fifty-Three

DON LAURO AGUIRRE SAT on the stony ground at the corner of State and Brooklyn in Los Angeles, California, with smoke rising from his hair.

"I, of course," he said, "fully apologize for this unfortunate development."

Teresita sat in the dirt next to him, her dress scorched and smoking, like his hair. They watched the bungalow across the street burn down. It was a warm night—it had been a hot winter. Firemen scrambled from their wagon-mounted pumpers and tried to throw weak streams of water onto the flames.

Teresita was especially interested in the way the rose hedges around the house caught fire and burned.

"I'm used to it," she said.

The chimney wobbled, tipped, caved in through the roof in a huge eruption of sparks.

"Oh my," she noted.

"Did you lose everything?" he asked.

She pulled out her folded divorce-settlement documents. The corners had burned off, but otherwise, they were intact.

"Not everything," she said.

"Ah. The troublesome Mr. Rodriguez."

"Gone for good."

A fireman walked over with a tin cup full of water.

Glass shattered across the street. Agitated Mexicans gawked. Some curses could be heard above the amazingly loud roar of flames. So much noise from such a little house.

❄

She would always remember Los Angeles as a kind of unfocused dream. The long train ride, passing as it did through Missouri and Oklahoma and stopping here and there in wide plains and desiccated desiertos. Into Texas, where they pulled up in Amarillo, and a place named Yellow that was, all about, surrounded by yellow seemed perfect to her. She was sitting inside her secure little pod watching the train crews outside and the hunched travelers passing her narrow door when she saw a familiar form go by. Bolts of emotion! What? Not possible! She threw open her door and cried, "Don Lauro!" And with great cries of his own, he swam upstream against the toiling bodies of Texans to reach her.

"My girl! My girl!" he kept saying as he hugged her.

His Vandyke had grayed at his chin, and his hair had thinned, but he looked very much the same.

She pulled him inside her compartment and cried with joy, both of them blurting "What are you doing here?" at once.

They laughed.

"You first!"

"No, you first!"

"After you!"

"No, I must insist!"

So she told him of her trip to Los Angeles to the district court and her divorce.

He, of course, had revolution on his mind. The rail strike was looming. Mexican rail workers were trying to join the union, and the railroad had brought in union busters. Goons! To assault and beat these paisanos. He told these tales in hushed tones lest the railroad employees overhear him and throw him from the train.

"Oh?" she said, a dangerous gleam in her eye. "They need help?"

"Now, now," he said. "Caution is in order."

"I can help them," she said.

"I, of course, would welcome your participation, my dear. However, I would urge restraint. At this stage, your effect could be incendiary! And," he intoned ominously, "they have ears everywhere."

Who was he kidding? When had any Urrea ever shown restraint in any matter? Aguirre sighed—Here we go again, he thought. Yet—yet. He immediately imagined the new era about to be born. Surely, divine providence was afoot.

After Teresita's catastrophe in Clifton, Aguirre was wary of the endless revolt as it pertained to her. He did not know how best to proceed. Was he Aguirre the revolutionary or Uncle Lauro caring for his young ward?

She asked, "And my father? Any word?"

He smiled at her sadly.

"He is...well. Tomás is great. A giant." He patted her knee. "Sad, but well."

"Sad, Don Lauro?"

"Still mourning you, my dear," he said. "And..." He tipped his head. "We all age."

"I should write to him."

"You should."

"But what would I say?"

He thought a moment. He shook his head.

"That," he said, "I do not know."

They changed the subject as the train lurched out of the Amarillo station, allowing them to busy themselves with comments about the sad, burned landscape.

It would have been indecent for Don Lauro to stay overnight in her cabin, so of course he slept sitting in his seat toward the back of the train. In the morning, though, he rejoined her. They enjoyed sweet rolls and a carafe of coffee the porter brought them. They spent the long approach to Los Angeles recalling past glories. It seemed Aguirre's network of radicals had procured for him a bungalow in East Los Angeles, and he would not hear of Teresita adjourning to a hotel—not with such a trying court appearance looming! Besides, he knew if he had the Saint of Cabora in his headquarters, not only would the rail strike succeed, but he would have willing interviewers lining up at his door. Perhaps she might be moved once again to write a column or two.

※

The rail strike stretched out as long as the pleasure of the court in the matter of *Rodriguez v. Rodriguez.* Anti-union thugs came into town from Bakersfield and clubbed Mexicans with ax handles. Teresita won her case. And three firebombs hit their bungalow one late January night at eleven o'clock. Nobody ever learned if it was an attack on Aguirre and the union men or on the Saint.

Aguirre, ever the gentleman, bought her fresh clothes for her journey to New York. Agents of the Consortium, in a panic that their client had almost been burned up in the arson, rented her a fancier railcar and stationed two detectives on the train to watch over her. Teresita was surprised to feel disappointment that Mr. Suits did not appear. She had gotten to the point where anything at all from her past—anyone who wasn't dead—was full of golden and innocent morning sunshine.

As they stood in the station waiting for the departure hour, Don Lauro held the *Los Angeles Times.* The headline read: "Saint Teresita Burned Out."

She said, "I do not think I will mention this to Mr. Van Order."

Don Lauro thought for a moment and replied, "Let us not talk about this with Tomás either."

"Done."

They shook on it.

"Uncle Lauro?" she said.

"Yes, dear girl?"

"I think I may be a bad person."

"Nonsense!"

"I have been selfish."

"How so?"

"I told the Van Orders I needed a translator…but I understand English."

"Oh?"

"I am not stupid! I have been here long enough to understand it. I just wanted someone between me and the patients."

She hung her head.

"Perfectly understandable, Teresita! It's called self-preservation!"

"Why should I be preserved?"

He stared at her.

"Surely you are not serious."

He put an avuncular arm around her shoulders.

"Buck up, Joan of Arc," he said.

She smiled sadly.

"Uncle Lauro?" she said.

"Hmm?"

"I asked for someone to come because I was lonely."

Before he could respond, she hopped aboard, and the train moved out, heading north this time, north and west, heading for the Rockies and the plains, the ghosts of the buffalo and the great rivers, rolling it seemed for a year as she lay in her bunk reading a scandalous Argentine translation of *Sister Carrie.* She had not encountered such behavior or ideas in books before.

Lauro Aguirre had meant to say: *Sometimes God is not enough.*

She rolled and rolled until she came, like John had before her, into the great city. Joining the hundreds of foreigners flooding its streets. Migrating in the wrong direction. Coming, unlike her fellow travelers, out of the west.

Fifty-Four

IF NOT FOR the Consortium, John would have missed her train. One of its messengers woke him by loudly banging on his splintery door until he was roused from his painful slumber on the floorboards in the living room. He had such a shock that his little Saint was coming to him that he rushed about and tripped over the small rug still bunched from his sleeping and fell to the floor, cracking his forehead and raising another dull purple egg where the last one from Homer's bar had so recently receded. Blurry-eyed, he fumbled his way into the bathroom and ran hot water into the claw-foot tub and sank there to ease the ache out of his bones. When he realized that the house was a mess and remembered that she did not approve of messes, he leapt from the bath and staggered about trying to dry himself and clean at the same time. There was no food in the house. No flowers. The bedclothes were not fresh. And there were not enough of them. His blankets were tatty, old, brown. No quilt, no bedspread. He was aghast at himself. What had he been thinking? Where would he take the rubbish that overflowed from the bin? He threw open the back window and tossed the garbage into the black and gray snow behind the building. It was full winter, and John did not appreciate the neighbors' wet feet and the icy mess they left at his entry. He watched the clock as he banged around naked and frantic. The radiator thumped and gurgled as if demons were crawling up the pipes to eat him alive. It was the worst day of his life.

Tomás Urrea's letter to Mr. Rosencrans had set in motion an invisible avalanche of events that were already transforming the landscape without either the Soprano or Wild Bill knowing anything about it. Rosencrans had written to one of his plute compadres, a Mr. Sloane, jefe of a great Yankee oil conglomerate. Thus did the news spread quickly among his social circle: a new sensation was on its way to the glittering tors of Mannahatta. A Saintess, no less. A lady revolutionary! The elite had already dined with the great José Martí. They had attended soirees with Mark Twain and found him an amusing fellow. Now they were eager for this new oddity to arrive, vetted as she was by Rosencrans and the partners in the Consortium.

When the train came steaming from the west, it was met by a gaggle of fine capitalists in their capitalist hats. Even Mrs. Vanderbilt joined the receiving line. It was a splendid turnout—so splendid that John stood away from them and watched from the shadows. These bright, witty people, exuding rich scents and richer laughter. A laughter as exclusive as their million-dollar hats. Nobody he knew laughed like that.

He brightened when he saw his little Yaqui queen step off the train. Her hair was shorter. He would never learn it had been burned. She wore Los Angeles high fashion—all white, with white lace at her chest and throat, and white fabric boots peeking out from under the long hem of the dress. He was stunned. He had never seen her look more like an angel. Or a damned snowbank. And he knew she would freeze in New York.

Oh. No, she wouldn't. Mrs. Vanderbilt immediately opened a great box and presented her with a shining fur coat that seemed to swallow Teresita whole. John thought she looked like she'd been et by a griz.

The plutes and bankers swarmed her before he could make his move. By God, they almost lifted her off the ground. Them rich sons of bitches feed like vultures when they catch a whiff of the meat, he thought. They bowed and patted and he could see them give her limp little dead-fish handshakes, all the women wearing gloves so they couldn't even feel Teresita's hand if they wanted to, and the men with their bellies and their ridiculous walking sticks and tailed coats bobbed and strutted about like turkeys in a barnyard.

And then they swept her away before he even called out a hello, and he was left there standing in the station wondering what had happened.

※

Under the deafening El tracks, in the sleet-blown cold black wind, walking fast.

He trailed them to Fifth Avenue, where they welcomed Teresita into an establishment with gold frames on its windows and where liveried swells guarded the door, and inside, men in tall white mushroom hats stood before leaping flames, and waiters in red and black and white stiff shirts moved like small boats on a lake. John stood outside in the cold, leaning on the wall. His breath fogged the glass and blotted out her face. It was still sleeting. John started to laugh. "Could I make a more miserable appearance?" he asked. Ice granules caught in his hair and melted on his face. His boots had holes in them. The first thing he'd get now that Teresita was home was new boots. And an overcoat.

He wiped away the frost and watched. They treated her as if it were the World's Fair and she were a monkey or a jaguar in the zoo. He sneered at them with all their manners and hankies.

Inside, it was a forensic triumph. The gentlepeople of New York handled her with extraordinary care. They prodded her and collected impressions of her responses without her ever knowing. They could barely communicate with her, though she understood them fairly well. They affected blank stares at her accent and relied on a young friar from San Juan, Puerto Rico, who attended the luncheon to gamely translate the nine hundred quips, questions, requests, and bons mots flying around the long table. Teresita was their savage princess come from strange eldritch realms to grace them with new sensations. Oh, yes — they could smell the roses! They were nervous with the hope that she was either a true healer or a fraud. Either one offered delights and sensations.

Caviar...no. She found out immediately that caviar was not for human consumption. Salad with leeks and chilled asparagus with crumbled goat cheese and garlic croutons. That was better. Soup came in a boat-shaped tureen and had clams and potatoes in red sauce. She moved the clams around with her spoon, hoping it looked like she'd eaten a few.

She was handsomer than they had imagined. She gave evidence of excellent table manners, though they noted with wry eyebrows that she did not know the difference between the salad fork and the main-course fork. And she moved the soupspoon toward herself instead of away from herself, which was not how a lady of real breeding would do it. But she did chew with her mouth closed, which was a welcome sur-prise to them all. They felt their standing in the world reasserted with her every bite.

Teresita had never met a Puerto Rican. She was fascinated by the young priest. The way he said words seemed precious to her, how instead of saying *carne,* "meat," he said what sounded like *calne.* The gathered jewels and fine linens and hat pins and earrings and tall hats and cravats did not much catch her eye. She had seen all that before, all that future rot and dust, all that vanity. One woman had a great pin in the shape of a spider, and its parts were made of gold and gems. Teresita liked that and she wondered if the woman was a curandera.

The fine people were all pleasant, but she barely heard their talk. She watched the mouth of the priest, watched him form what to her sounded like phantom sounds. In New York, she was noting, Spanish was a foreign language as well.

Cornish game hens dressed in buttery brown coats of dough arrived, the birds lovingly placed drolly in rice and steamed carrots, as if abed.

"Tiny turkeys!" she exulted, and when the priest translated her words, the gathered minions laughed, not altogether kindly. Their eyes caught a certain sparkle when she revealed herself as a naïf.

To her right sat a lovely sixteen-year-old dewdrop of a girl with honey-colored hair and green eyes. She could have been whipped up of meringue. Teresita could have scooped out a taste of her with a spoon. The girl was a Hungarian princess, a Deszilly, though this meant noth-ing to Teresita. She wanted to say, *Oh? Your Highness. And I am a saint.* But she reminded herself that she was not a saint, at least not to the

Catholic church. She smiled. The priest smiled back. At a table removed from the main party sat Dr. Weisburd and his small family. His long-haired wife and their daughter, a poet. He watched Teresa with his dark eyes, at once sad and amused. One of the bankers, well in his cups— rum toddies all around to cut the chill!—noted Teresita watching the Weisburds. "He's a Yiddisher," the fat man confided.

Teresita turned to the priest.

"He is not welcome at this table?" she asked.

"There is a certain social structure," the priest noted. "Constraints."

"What of you and me?" she asked.

He smiled. He sipped his white wine. He lightly touched his clerical collar.

"We are the entertainment," he said.

Teresita laughed. They clinked glasses in a private toast. The gathered great ones felt a surge of dread. What if the exotics were mocking them in their obscure languages? But Teresita dazzled them with her saintliest smile, and they calmed down.

She turned in her seat and raised her glass to the doctor and his family as well, toasting them from a distance.

Chocolate truffle cake with looping battlements of frosting looked like small cathedrals stolen by giants.

The coffee came in dollhouse cups you could use for thimbles.

It was all so exquisite.

※

The aristocrats burst out of the restaurant and formed great steam-blowing cadres around her. They had brought in the finest taxi—a rumbling little Cadillac. They helped her in and stood waving her off with shouts and huzzahs. It chugged into the weather making *ahoogah* klaxon cries.

Dr. Weisburd was the one who saw John shivering in misery against the wall.

"If we hurry," he said, "we can catch her. Come on, Tex."

He waved toward his own carriage. Doc was old-fashioned. He had a horse pulling the rig, and a bundled driver looking like some mythological hulk in skins.

"Hey, King David," John said. "Don't call me Tex."

It was slow going. The sleet was really pounding down now, sliding out of the sky at a sharp angle. John peered out, trying to see her through it. He didn't say another word. The doctor's family traded many looks and the poet daughter laughed but her father kicked her foot and shook his head. She managed to choke back her amusement.

John jumped out before they reached East Twenty-Eighth and said, "Thanks, Doc. I'll pay you back someday."

"Think nothing of it, T . . . John."

John looked into the storm, ice already covering his eyebrows and whiskers.

"I must have rocks in my head," he said and vanished into the heaving gray air.

She was standing in the vestibule looking at the names on the three mailboxes. John had forgotten to put his name up. She had a small bag and a larger valise. Most of her things had burned, but he wouldn't know that. He burst in the door in a swirl of cold wind. She turned and stared at him. They didn't move for a moment. And then she was in his arms.

"Where were you?" she cried.

"I was right there."

"No, you weren't!" she said.

"I was. I was." He patted her back. "I couldn't get to you. I watched you, though."

He squeezed her. Mr. Somers opened his door and looked out at them. He was the painter. His room was crowded with easels, and the happy smells of linseed oil and paint came out around him.

"Bill," said John, "meet my wife."

Bill shook her hand and insisted on carrying the heavy bag up for them.

"Bill gives me books to read," John said.

"Dios te bendiga," said Teresita, putting her hand on the painter, who ducked his head and smiled and combed his beard with his fingers and headed downstairs again with a wave.

She didn't even look at the rooms. She stared at John.

"I watched you eat," he said. "I was outside the whole time."

He felt small, forgotten. Overwhelming sorrow hit him. This wasn't the way he'd imagined it. His eyes brimmed. What the hell. How embarrassing.

She dragged his shaggy head down to her chest and rocked him, standing there as the storm threw itself at their windows.

※

Days and days.

New York City leapt at each dawn with grandeur, maniacal energy that overcame the visitors and crushed them before noon. The sky shrieked, the land hammered around them. But warmth briefly returned, and they prowled. They crept the tumbledown blocks at the mouth of the three Brooklyn bridges. She was mad for the great bridge itself, and she made John walk across it often, stopping to admire its cables above and the dark water below, antic with tugs and ferries. They stood in the tenement shadows all up and down the East Side, they ran from rain squalls and cutpockets in the tumult of Broadway, they discovered the new pizza pies in a narrow brick-walled oven of a building, and they inevitably wandered the Chinese streets, where Teresita touched the hands of her beloved old Chinese monks and grandmothers. John took her to see the Flatiron Building—called the Fuller—as it was growing out of spindly bars of metal, already looking like the most beautiful building she would ever see. A brisk walk down Lexington and a turn on Twenty-Third to the corner of Fifth Avenue. That slender mystery triangle cutting through the city like a magical little ship.

Days and days.

On their first bright morning of falling snow, she stood at the window, puzzled. "John," she said. "Someone on the roof has cut open his pillow and is shaking out the feathers!"

But warmth returned quickly and melted the down.

As they strolled in the great park watching prams full of babies rattle down the shaded paths, John, with a flourish, presented Teresita with a small yellow package.

"Juicy Fruit!" he said.

She took a stick of chicle from the pack and quite enjoyed it.

From boats that circled the fat south point of the island, they beheld the clamor, the mass, the heavy splendor of the great machine—its million scurrying ant-people coughing and shuffling along its many paths like the ghosts of the Indians long dead and buried under cement and brick. The far mouth of the Hudson revealed itself from the deck of the boat like the bright golden gate to some better world, a western vista of hope and light beyond the immense tumult. John meant to ride up that river to see what was there. Someday.

Teresita was used to being pummeled by bodies now—San Francisco, St. Louis, Los Angeles—it seemed that everywhere, everywhere, men built hives like wasps and swarmed there. It seemed so distant to her that she had once wandered abandoned deserts gathering plants. Were there plants in New York? She had to look twice.

"Immigrants everywhere," John said. "Italians come on German ships. It's crazy here. Greenwich Village is all tenements."

"Oh?" she said, not knowing what such a village could be but eager to get to the villagers and start to heal them.

"There are tunnels," John said. "They are building a subway."

"Subway?"

"Trains that go underground!" he cried out like a little boy.

Teresita suddenly recalled the days when her father had argued over the scientific marvels in Jules Verne novels with Lauro Aguirre before they had ever ridden trains.

The shores of the island were not high, not noble, but low, crowded, bristling with dead docks and collapsing warehouses, rogue trees bursting magically from the cracked creosoted wood of the quays. Water all around. Massive forces of water: water underground, water before and behind, water simmering under streets in mummified sarcophagi of buried creeks and streams. Teresita felt the surge and throb under her feet. And the islands—islands all low and dark with clotted trees and heavy with ghosts.

Wall Street, that old avenue of the ruined city wall. Back when the city was a fort. Ruins of a lost culture—how fast cultures moved! How recently did the canoes of the native hunters circle the island! How recently the meadows hereabouts had small lakes and populations of deer and bears, where now buildings and theaters stood. Where once wooden farmhouses faced deep woods, then brick and wooden flats and wooden hospitals crowded those former cow paths and hunting lanes and the farmhouses already forgotten as the flats tumbled to the brownstones and the Chicago-style tallness reaching for the sky that had never changed, a sky that could have been seen by the most ancient resident's eyes as familiar…when the smoke and glare abated after midnight. What kind of a place was this where the sky remained steady and the land changed like storm clouds? She could feel the layers of sound and voice in every neighborhood, Five Points so dense in its buried music she could almost not breathe there.

But the power, the power of it. The island and its outliers were like an armada. Manhattan itself an engine, infernal in its pulse. It pulled the earth toward sunrise out of sheer exuberance. Just stepping out their little door exhausted her.

Days and days.

When they returned from venturing down to the block between Thirty-Fourth and Thirty-Fifth Streets to visit the new Macy's department store, she was so exhausted that she went to bed without supper. The aristocrats apparently kept different hours than the working classes, for they sent cabs for her at night to deal with gout and carbuncles, sore backs and mysterious female agonies. John was left at home.

Mornings could be slow, as he slept off his comfort from the night before.

Out their back window, she saw foxes. She saw deer. She saw shadows that paced north, then south. East, then west toward her. Then away again. Sad shadows, hungry and confused, shadows that could not find the water, shadows that could not find the old walking paths that had been torn out of the living soil and replaced with stone.

They ran downstairs when it was hot inside their rooms—Bill Somers liked his heat on high—and purchased tall glasses of the new syrup tonic Pepsi-Cola. The bubbles made her sneeze. John tried to hide the long string of small belches the tonic inspired.

She opened the curtains only to greet New York's daily magnificent sunrise, exploding out of the sky as if God Himself had chosen this city for His blessings. Later in the day, when the shadows appeared, she shut the curtains. On most days, she was out the door, on her way to an appointment, joining all the million other workers deaf to the sounds of the ghost island. And John, with his headache, carried her coat for her.

※

"What did you do in Los Angeles?" he asked one night.

They lay in their narrow bed, smelling the opera singer's garlic wafting down from above. Pigeons shuffled and cooed on their small window ledge. John hated them, but Teresita fed them crumbs. He wished he had his pistola.

"Nothing, really," she said into his ribs. "Court."

"I can't believe I haven't asked you yet."

"We are so busy."

"Is it busy like this in Los Angeles?"

"It is busy, yes, in a lazy way. Don Lauro kept me away from too much craziness."

"Don who?"

"Don Lauro! You know Don Lauro."

"Nope. I don't know no Don Lauro."

"Lauro Aguirre," she said.

"I never met no Lauro Aguirre," he insisted. "He was in Los Angeles?"

"I stayed with him," she said.

"What do you mean, you stayed with him?"

He was growing stiffer beside her.

She patted his chest.

"Now, now," she said.

"Don't 'now, now' me," he said sharply. "What do you mean you stayed with him?"

"John! Don Lauro is like an uncle to me! He is my father's best friend in the world! I have known him since I was a girl!" He said nothing. "I stayed with him. Yes! We had a house."

"Jesus," he said. "You had a *house?*" He laughed bitterly. "Ain't that rich. Poor Johnny out here missing his woman and she's in a house with some old goat having a high old time."

"John!"

He rose. He paced. He stared at her. He shook his head.

"John?" she said.

"I cannot believe you," he announced.

He grabbed his coat and hat.

"I don't understand!" she cried.

"You should have told me," he said.

He went out and slammed the door and galloped downstairs.

"I'm going for a drink!" he called.

Days and days and days.

Fifty-Five

THE WALDORF-ASTORIA HOTEL lobby was a cavern overcrowded with pianos and settees. They entered and were swept up by handsome swells and powdered ladies in sashed dresses that trailed the floor and revealed huge bustles in back that made them seem to be oceangoing schooners with sails made of eggshell-colored silk. Their hair was lifted in gleaming buns and pierced by chopsticks. Some carried fans and all worked sly little shawls off their shoulders. They tittered and whispered and swept Teresita away like a squadron of angels swooping down upon a sinless girl on Judgment Day. Wrists jingling with silver baubles hanging off charm bracelets—small Eiffel Towers and steamships, palm trees and cable cars, camels, pyramids. John was left behind in the company of a crazy granny from Long Island named Effie Woodward who had appeared in Indian garb complete with headband and eagle feather. She was trailed by her sultry and exquisitely bored daughter Louise in a vast hat with small straw flowers arrayed on its great wings. Effie took his arm and followed the flood of ladies into the deeper recesses of the labyrinth where humid scents of food permeated the excellent great rooms, and warbly sentimental music played incessantly— immigrants in tuxedos and profoundly greased skullcaps of dark hair sawed away at fiddles and breathed through clarinets; one drub-drubbed on a stand-up bass and another brushed a small metallic snare drum while melancholy saxophones and a single muted trombone gave background voice to a melody sung archly into a megaphone by the skinny gigolo in white who occasionally turned and conducted the entire maudlin combo.

Teresita sat at the head table and apparently didn't need any damned translator at all, as John could plainly see. So what else had she kept from him?

He smiled at Effie, who occasionally shook her eagle feather at Teresita and droned on about hidden Lemurian masters, the secrets of Atlantis hidden beneath the sphinx in Cairo, and the powers of the great line of mystic Indian chiefs of which Teresita was a descendant. Here he was, stranded with Pocahontas. Already, he noted, Teresita was throwing her hands up when she laughed, lifting her palms in what looked like surrender. The powdered faces around her didn't open their mouths to laugh—they pulled the points of their upper lips down to their lower lips and worked their shoulders up and down as they surrendered with their hands.

"Aho!" Effie said, extending her rather tattered feather toward Teresita.

"Aho!" John concurred. "Damned right, Effie! A-holy-o!"

Effie rattled her feather again.

"Yippee-ti-yay," he muttered into his glass of white wine. Pink salmon lay on his plate, surrounded by some sort of purple vegetable. John munched a bread stick. He was thinking about some good bloody beef. He signaled a waiter.

"Got beer?" he asked.

"Sir," the boy said and walked away.

Sir? What kind of answer was that? Was that yes or no?

"In your previous lives," Effie asked, "who were you?"

"Goddamn, madam—one life is more than enough for me!"

Louise snickered.

Effie produced a small leather pouch and spilled colorful stones and a bone on the table and stared at him meaningfully.

"Do you see what I've been saying?" she said.

"Of course," he lied.

To his great shock, Teresita was ushered upstairs to a guest suite after supper. She looked back at him and mouthed *Sorry.*

"Fame, dearie!" chirped Effie. She had pulled an aromatic bundle of sage from her bag. "Shall I smudge you?"

"Maybe next time," John said.

"You could use a good job," Effie announced. "How about you come to my antiquities store in Washington Square and learn to deal treasures?"

"Job?"

"You can't just sniff around after the Saint!" Effie cackled.

His beer never came.

"Excuse me," he replied, heading after Teresita, but the suited gents intercepted him and hustled him to the door. They had waved down a car to take John back to the ol' homestead. "Sure you won't mind, old boy!" They guffawed and blustered. One of them thrust a white package at him and said, "Here—take some food!" He tossed the sack aside as he was hustled out but managed to grab a bottle of port.

"Time to skedaddle," he told the driver. He drank from the bottle as they drove along, the driver narrowly avoiding several crashes on dark corners. They passed a dray horse that had been broadsided by a little truck—both of them lay on their sides expiring loudly in the backlit fog that was starting to creep down the street.

When he went upstairs, he found a letter tucked into the door. Heavy cream paper wrapped around a long white feather. Feathers again! What was it with feathers lately? He opened it and shook his head and tossed it on the floor.

"Wonderful," he said.

It purported to be from the angel Gabriel. Welcoming her to New York. Congratulating her for keeping true to her duties to God. He had no idea that Teresita and Gabriel were correspondents from way back, but he wouldn't have been surprised to find that out.

John hunted for some fresh matches and his bag of tobacco. He rattled around in the flour tins to find some folding money. As he walked out for the night, he stepped on the letter. Gabriel had warned again of doom coming to those who did not heed God's call. On the street, John thought he should have thrown the letter away. Later, Teresita would prove him right.

⁂

The hot bodies crowded around him in the little bar he found on Second Avenue. "She can't be known," he said, bending an elbow and downing his third shot. "I know her better'n anybody, I reckon."

"Have another, Tex," said the barkeep.

"Think I might," he said. "But, fellas, I'm telling you, she can't be known. You look at her, and she's a mystery."

"Ain't that the truth," said one of his new pals. "About all of 'em!"

Haw! The boys nodded and guffawed. Women! By God!

"I married me a German gal right off the boat," confessed the barkeep. "Try that one on for size. Can't understand a damned thing she says." He tipped a slug of amber into John's glass. "But she keeps the bed warm and boils me a pot of red taters every day!"

Uproar. Fraternity. John bought the next round for all his bene coves.

"To Tex!" they bellowed.

It was the best he had felt in a week.

⁂

Teresita came home from the Waldorf a changed person. John was sitting in the shadows with his legs extended, reeking of whiskey and smoke. He just stared. She was now attended by noise—the skirts and underskirts and clattering bracelets rattled like turkey feathers. She took up twice as much space in her new dress. Her hair was sculpted atop her head, and a ridiculous little black hat was pinned there at a jaunty angle. It reminded John of a boat on a wave in some painting of ocean storms.

The grandes dames had remade her in their image. For the longest time, he had fantasized such a scene, fine clothing on his little Yaqui. Lifting those great skirts. But now that he saw it, he felt like laughing.

Worse was Dr. Weisburd, standing behind her all wet-eyed. Damn it. Another sucker in love with the Saint. The doctor placed a small stack of white boxes on their table and kissed her on each cheek. He tipped his hat to John and trotted downstairs.

"He kissed you," John said.

"That is the style," she announced.

"He kissed you twice."

"Everyone in Paris kisses each cheek, John," she said, an expert suddenly in the world of high society. "New York City is the Paris of America."

Snooty.

He smirked.

First Don Lauro, now the Wise Bird. He wasn't a fool. Teresita and her men.

"I see," he said.

She busied herself removing her spiderweb shawl and folding it carefully.

"What's this stuff?" he asked, gesturing at the boxes with his chin.

"Oh, John! They showered me with gifts!"

He massaged his temples with his fingertips.

"And they sent this for you," she said, handing him a small case.

He popped it open. A gold watch and chain nestled in red velvet. He lifted the watch and swung it in the dull light.

"Do you like it?"

"Sure." He put the watch away. "Who wouldn't."

"Perhaps we could get it engraved."

"Perhaps."

He checked his glass — it was empty.

"Say," he said conversationally, "have you done any healings lately?"

She was distracted with her boxes.

"Healings, mi amor?"

"You know — that thing you do that makes you a saint."

She glanced at him as she fluttered out the pale silk petticoat she was holding.

She smiled.

"Mrs. Oppen had a terrible toothache," she offered.

He nodded.

"Mrs. Oppen," he noted.

He got up, walked to the kitchenette, poured himself some water from a pitcher.

Staring at the wall as he drank, he said, "Have you seen any immigrants lately?"

She stared at his back. She went to the couch and sat. She unpinned her little hat and put it on the table.

"Didn't think so," he said, coming back and sitting down. "So busy with rich ladies and hats."

He chuckled.

"You have a ministry of stylish hats!"

He yawned loudly.

She crossed her arms.

"Why are you so angry with me?" she said.

"Angry? Do I look angry?"

"Yes."

"Not me! I'm a happy cowhand. I ain't got a thing to complain about. Hell, I got a roof and three squares. Even got a indoor crapper just like real people. I think I'll get me one of them fancy straw hats so I can be just like your friends."

"John!"

"John!" he cried, mimicking her.

He smiled.

"Our first fight," he observed.

"You are impossible!" she cried.

He sat back in his chair and sighed.

"Not worth talking about," he said. "Everybody changes. You aren't any different." He paused. Picked at the chair arm. "After all," he said.

She gasped.

What was happening here?

The air inside the room felt like it weighed hundreds of pounds.

They were trapped in their seats, staring at opposing walls. Unable to stir. Unable to speak. Whole landscapes, crowds, nations churned in their minds.

"Have I changed?" she asked.

He laughed once: Ha!

"You know, my father is a great rancher—quite refined."

"Yep. Your father. Thought he was better than everybody. I didn't care for that."

This was news to her.

"You wish you were my father!" she snapped.

He glared at her.

"Bullshit," he said.

"He might have hired you, John," she said, "to milk his cows or to brand his horses. But, really"—she shook her head and laughed a little, theatrically—"I have tried—very hard—to make you a gentleman...."

"Christ!" he shouted. "Listen to yourself!"

He flung himself around in his seat.

"You can't be serious! You? The barefoot Indian girl? It is amusing to hear such talk from you."

He sat back and looked away from her, red in the face, stung, muttering imprecations against his fate and all fancy people. Teresita, his betrayer.

Her hands shook. She studied his boots, for she didn't want to look at his face. All her life, she felt, was going to play out like this—a slow river of mud burying her until she suffocated.

She collected herself.

She cleared her throat.

"Is this not what you wanted?" she asked. "Did I not give you the life you wanted?"

He turned his head and stared at her.

"I gave you New York," she said. "I only came here for you."

He opened his mouth, but nothing came. He blinked. He lifted a hand slightly.

"I would have gone home to my family. I am nobody's daughter now. But I am here with you."

She nodded as if to herself. She pursed her lips.

"Perhaps we can no longer talk," she said. "We used to talk."

"I'm . . . sorry," he replied. "I—" But he didn't know what he meant to say or what he was feeling.

"Maybe tomorrow," she said, rising.

"No!" he cried, reaching for her. His head was spinning. Had he been wrong?

She stood looking at the floor.

"John," she said.

She turned her head a little and looked at him from under her brows. "I am with child."

She went to the bedroom and quietly closed the door.

Fifty-Six

DID SHE NOTICE THAT as her sorrows increased, the scent of roses faded from her skin? John had noticed that much when he told her, "This ain't a fairy tale, Teresita. This is real life. And we are in the middle of it." She smelled of sachet, lilac, sometimes powder. Rarely, sweat. But the roses were hard to smell—he had to go behind her ears, right where the hair sprouted from her tenderest skin. He didn't often get there these days.

They struggled, as many couples must. Rupture and reunion. Accumulating wrongs hidden tenebrously in the deepest shadows where they refused to be defined, just radiated their pain outward to poison the smallest moments. She grew gravid with her first child, and he was fascinated with her extending belly, with her protruding navel and the mysterious dark line that appeared running down her abdomen. How her breasts suddenly became large. He marked it all and delighted in it. Yet...

She told herself she had been selfish to dream that she could be happy. It was not her lot to live in comfort and joy. Not when so many of her People hung still in dead Mexican trees, when so many of them lay scattered in terrible arroyos all across the desert. Was she being punished? she wondered. Punished for joy? For wanting a life that did not involve sacrifice and nothing but?

When John wasn't there, she found Mr. Somers a kind neighbor— he helped her up the stairs, and he went to the corner market and the farmers' stalls and brought her apples or milk.

One day John tossed another egg-spackled plate in the sink and turned to her and said, "How do I know that's not Weisburd's baby?" She cringed, knowing that those words a woman would not recover from.

After he had gone on his tortured rounds, she pulled up her shawl and braced herself along the railing and went downstairs to the street. The contract with the Consortium was finally reaching its termination. The men wanted to sign her up again, but she knew she would not. It was over.

She hadn't felt God stir in her for...weeks. Months, perhaps. She hadn't heard Him speak, hadn't sensed Him in her prayers. When she prayed.

It was so hard to remember anything. This roiling child within her. She told herself that the movement of the baby inside was the kick of God Himself. But it was not the same, and no mystical talk would fool her. Magical? Yes. But all flesh and blood. There was no Holy Spirit dancing up and down her spine. The distractions were huge—duties she had attending to the fine people who still presented her to one another as if she were a famed actress from the gaslit stages on Broadway. The endless chess match with John. Her headaches were tremendous.

Prayers—at night she forgot because she was so weary. In the mornings, she often overslept and missed the ritual completely. And frankly, kneeling was becoming out of the question. She realized she hadn't been in a church since El Paso, perhaps. She couldn't remember any churches in between there and here.

Mr. Somers had rhapsodized about the stunning new cobalt-blue window in the Marble Church, around the corner. She had seen the church many times, of course, the tall steeple and the baffling sign in front: COLLEGIATE CHURCH. What did that mean? Certainly not Catholic. But a college church? What college? Atop the church, a rooster on a stick, turning in the wind. She had never seen a rooster on a church. Somehow, it felt comforting.

She walked to Fifth Avenue and turned and went a block to the corner of Twenty-Ninth Street. The mud of Fifth was being bricked over now as the city spread like lava, eating the scant woods and small farms at this end, rolling ahead toward the shores of the island. Many carts rushed around the bricklayers and jounced into the dirt beyond, casting up puffs of dust that choked everyone. Teresita paused for a lull in the great flow and stepped into the street, waddling a bit, holding up her belly. She took the proffered arm of a gent on the other side and rose to the curb as a skronking goose of a jitney wobbled by on spindly wheels.

They were not far from Penn Station, and the traffic was at times jammed to a halt all around it. This was not as bad a day as some. Perhaps the station had not yet disgorged its first travelers, she thought.

The church appeared empty when she peeked in the door. She stepped in and was greeted by a warm roll of notes from the organ. Someone was in the loft, practicing, and though she did not know the hymn, "Filled with the Spirit's Power," it was pleasing. She looked around. No holy-water founts. A bare cross above the altar. Ah, she thought—Protestants. Christ risen, not suffering. Well, that suited her fine. She could use a little ascendance now.

She walked into the pews and stared up at the Tiffany window. Yes, she saw the blue. Moses and the burning bush. The flames were deep cobalt in the morning sun. It was quite entrancing. She sat and breathed.

"God?" she whispered. "Here I am."

A rector came forth carrying a huge key. She blinked. The key was four feet long!

"What?" she said.

The man nodded to her.

"Big clock," he noted.

She craned around to see a big clock on the wall.

"Yes," she said.

He heaved the great key up and inserted it in a keyhole that could have held a possum. She started to smile. He regarded the whimsical key.

"I see," he said. "Yes. It is comedic!" He grabbed the key. "Well, watch this!"

He put his knees and back into it and turned the key with great ratcheting clicks.

"Must!" he grunted. *"Wind! The clock!"*

She started to laugh.

What a strange little moment.

For a few seconds, the key didn't want to come free, and he wrestled with it.

She laughed harder.

He looked over his shoulder at her and grinned.

"Blasted key!" he said.

It popped out and he staggered back and hurried away.

"Did you come for the window?" he asked and then vanished through the narrow arched passageway at the far end of the church.

But she couldn't have answered anyway.

The sharp pain that bloomed in her abdomen as she laughed made her bend over and gasp.

And so her daughter's journey into this life began: suspended between time and laughter.

Fifty-Seven

SURELY, TERESITA THOUGHT, her powers had abandoned her.

God Himself had abandoned her.

She lay in Bellevue's maternity ward crying out in pain. Someone, comforting her, had babbled that it was the most modern such lying-in ward in the country, perhaps the world. Modern? She yearned for hot tea, a bundle of soothing herbs, and the hands of Huila herself. Not all this echoing white porcelain and cold metal. No. *No!*

She heard herself bellow: "I want a *banana!*"

Why was she not able to work her medicine on her own body? Why was she not able to do for herself what she had done for hundreds of others? She wasn't thinking well at that moment, but when she could think, she realized she had not brought a little one into the world since before St. Louis. Perhaps she had forgotten how. Perhaps she was without powers.

She was mortified that she was going to pee all over the bed. Or worse. And all these Americans watching.

¡Ay!

¡Ay, no!

Calm, she told herself. Calm. What did she say to those expectant girls in their huts? She couldn't remember. If she could only remember, then by God she'd make some progress.

¡Ay!

"I want to get on my knees!" she shouted.

The nurses did not understand her. They patted her hands while holding her in place. She was starting to fight. The doctor peered down at her.

In English, she said, "Knees... please... now, cabrones!"

She didn't even feel guilty about cursing. To hell with them all. If Tomás were here, they'd hear some ripe words.

The doctor looked at the nurses and grinned a little. They raised their eyebrows. Indians, they were thinking. Mexicans. Raising a fuss. Squatting like animals. He nodded, and they tied her wrists to the rails with cotton straps.

"You're a tetch combative," he said. "This will keep you from hurting yourself."

She stared at the straps.

"We will have our baby the modern way," he said as he strolled out.

She was breathing like a trapped coyote.

Oh, there was certainly no smell of roses in that room.

Whole nations of pain.

She said to her child: "Why are you trying to kill me?"

She said to God: "Why are You absent now?"

She said to Huila: "You did not come to help me, damn you!"

It turned dark. The dark went on for a few weeks. She cried and shouted. She actually slept, but the sleep was demented, hot, full of monsters and fires. Then it was growing light. How fast was the night in New York? Eternity and a minute were indistinguishable to her now. Still, her body clenched in bone-cracking waves of hurt.

She told God she needed help. But God knew. God knew it all, didn't He? Even cats, dogs, cows—all mothers struggled in torture. She had not given it its due. She had too easily erased the suffering and never imagined why the suffering was part of it. *God knew and didn't care.* Worse, God had made it that way.

"Why do You hate us?" she asked the empty air.

God did not answer.

"Agua," she demanded. She was beyond asking politely. She was beyond being the Girl Saint. If she could have gotten her hand free, she would have scratched the nurse's wan smile right off her face. The nurse brought a steel cup to Teresita for a gulp. And another. In between swallows, Teresita smiled drunkenly. She drooled. She grunted. Now, she thought, now I understand. I understand. I don't care to understand. I get the notion — it is clear. God? Help? Oh, she had not prayed much since arriving in New York. Now, hypocrite that she was, she was begging for help.

Well, why not?

Why in the *hell* not!

She laughed. The nurse mopped her brow. "You're doing great," she said.

"I was in prison once," Teresita snarled. Her hair was sweated to her face. Her teeth were white and savage. "It was worse than this!" Her English was suddenly perfect.

"Yes, dear."

"You think I can't do this?"

"No, dear."

To keep her mind off the pain, Teresita recalled her dramatic arrival at the hospital. The church rector had fetched the organist. The organist had summoned a groundskeeper. The groundskeeper had pulled a wagon out from around the corner on Twenty-Ninth and bundled the expectant mother in the back and hustled, standing in the box and shouting, all the way to First Avenue, pulling up to the imposing Bellevue towers in a state more frantic than Teresita's.

No John. No sign of John. John had no idea. John was out in the city somewhere. "John," she said, trying it out. "John! John! John!" She thought somehow he would sense her call, feel summoned. But he was not a Yaqui. Not an Apache. He was not even her father. Damn him. Damn them both. Damn them all. "John!" Oh, it hurt so much that she was dreaming while awake, seeing Huila and Cruz Chávez against the wall, arms crossed, looking dour and shadowy. Of course they were shadowy. "They are dead!" she announced to the doctor.

"Yes, Mrs. Rodriguez," he said.

"No, no," she gasped, but they ignored her.

Then came the blood.

⁂

Dr. Weisburd had found Teresita in her room, and he had arranged for flowers to be delivered. Little Laura, slightly yellow from birth jaundice, with a scrunchy monkey face, lay swaddled and snuffling in a wicker bassinet beside Teresita's bed. The mother was still weak from blood loss, but she would be fine.

Dr. Weisburd maintained a respectful discretion, and when it was time for Teresita's bloody cotton pad to be changed or for the baby to nurse, he stepped from the room and allowed the nurses to attend to the female details. He didn't understand the profound emotion Teresita inspired in him. It wasn't romantic, of this he was certain — well, perhaps in the poetic sense. But he had never once imagined, for example, his lips on hers. Nor had he imagined her bare breast. He walked the halls. This, he told himself, was why he stayed out of the room at such moments. He was a gentleman, and a married man. Discretion was called for.

This is where John found him, out in the hall. John had dark circles under his eyes, but he remained dashing in his own way. Dr. Weisburd would have liked to be as rangy and dangerous. He would have enjoyed great whiskers like that. He would have enjoyed wearing a cowboy hat too. He had never even ridden a horse. Every time he saw John, he blushed.

"Where is she?" John demanded.

"Room three-twelve," Weisburd said.

John looked at him for a long moment.

"You been in there a lot, have you?"

"I am a doctor."

John smiled, patted him on the shoulder, went to the door. He looked at Weisburd and winked. Stepping in, he removed his hat and gawked down at the baby.

"My God," he said.

"Do you like her?" Teresita asked.

"I guess she's yellow," he said.

"It will pass."

John stood stiffly beside the bed, holding his hat before his belly. He reached down absentmindedly and tugged on Teresita's toes. The baby yawned in her sleep.

"Look at that," he said. "Little bug."

"Do you want to hold her?" Teresita asked.

"Aw," he said, grinning shyly. "I figure I'd break her if I tried."

"I'm glad you're here," she said.

He stared at the baby and avoided her eyes.

"Well, of course," he muttered.

They both chose to ignore the topic of his not appearing for the birth itself. An unspoken negotiation. Nobody would win the debate, so they let it drift into the shadows, hoping it would vanish in the past, but knowing it would not.

The infant started to fuss in her little bed. Fretting, moving her little yellow fists around in front of her face. Pouting and gurgling.

"She's going to cry," Teresita said.

"How come?"

"Hungry, John."

"Oh?"

"I must nurse her."

"I can leave," he said, moving away.

"Leave?" She laughed. "Why?"

He shrugged.

"Isn't it private? Nursing and all?"

She opened her top. He stared. "You have seen me a hundred times," she said. "Fetch her."

John dropped his hat on the bed and rubbed his hands together as if to dislodge imagined trail dirt. He wiped his palms on his trousers. Grimacing as if the infant were made of solid lead, he scooped her up and held her like a medium-sized ham hock. Why, she didn't weigh nothing at all. He laid her on Teresita's chest and stood back as if there were a gusher coming that was about to knock him off his feet. His eyes were wide.

"Is that real milk?" he asked, astounded by every single detail of life.

"Yes, silly."

"You sprung a leak on the other side," he noted.

He decided to sit down. This was too much. She took pity on his delicate constitution and covered her other breast. He fell into the one chair and averted his eyes from the wet stain on the front of her robe.

She lay smiling faintly and the baby suckled.

Someone in the next room kept coughing—long rasping sounds of despair.

This ain't for me. Hospitals, he thought.

"What're you calling her?" he asked, squinting as the little mouth continued its greedy assault.

"Laura," she said. "I've named her after Lauro Aguirre."

"Ah," he said.

He was stung. He thought she might name the girl Juana—after his mother. Or himself. He stood, retrieved his hat.

"Well, I've got to skedaddle. Got to attend to some business. I've been laboring down to Mrs. Woodward's furniture shop. Very interesting, let me tell you." He made a muscle. "Making good wages. Why, I sold a mirror from France to the mayor of Trenton! King Louie looked in it, they say."

"Stay," she said.

"Got to go."

"Don't leave."

He stood above her, caught like a moth in a web. He couldn't move. He turned and looked out the window. The great city waited outside. It was hungry for him—he could feel it. Its million rooms and ten thousand alleyways waited for his return.

"It isn't how I thought it would be," he said.

She watched him.

"What isn't?"

"Anything."

Teresita was so tired. Her whole body ached. Her breasts hurt. Her back hurt. Her nether parts stung. Her feet were freezing.

"She's asleep," she said, gesturing with her chin.

John took little Laura from her and laid her back in the big rocking cradle, where she looked like a little cake in a picnic basket. He leaned down and gave her a chaste peck on the cheek. "Sleep tight," he whispered.

He looked into Teresita's eyes.

"Good work, Mrs. Van Order," he said.

His voice was choked.

"What's wrong?"

"I'm just happy," he said.

She had a sad smile on her face.

"We thought it would be easier," she said. "Didn't we?"

He sank his chin to his chest.

"I haven't been too good at this," he said. "Was the other one...Was Rodriguez...Was he meaner than me?"

"Oh, John."

"Ain't kidding."

"Yes. Yes, John. He was meaner."

"Have I made you happy?"

"Yes."

His eyes were wet.

"Come here," she said.

"What."

"Just come here."

She opened her arms to him.

He stepped to the bed, meaning to give her a small hug and be on his way. But he bent to her and kept coming until he was lying beside her. She wrapped him in her arms and pulled his head to her damp hot chest. He started to talk, but she said, "Shh," and stroked his hair. She felt him relax against her. And then he began to cry.

She lay there too tired to feel anything, thinking: What have I become?

Fifty-Eight

TYPHUS HAD BROKEN OUT in the town. Mice and pack rats. It hopped from house to house, went into the mines and was belched back out like invisible smoke, catching the workers and their children. Shivers, fevers, ugly rashes. Coughing and incontinence. Some went mad before they died, and the doctor kept busy going from sad house to sad house, too exhausted finally to be frantic.

And when Tomás came down with it, all they could do was have a bed installed in the parlor so they wouldn't have the stairs to contend with. Besides, there was a small fireplace there, and he could be kept warm, though he fussed and complained endlessly about the stifling heat. Tomás appreciated the stupidity of it—he had been hiding his crumbling health for several years. And here he was struck down by a simple pauper's disease.

"The plague," he said. "I have the plague."

The children were kept upstairs in an effort to prevent their catching the fever. Poor Gaby—she mopped his bright red brow and wrung out his soaking bedclothes. The doctor suggested she wear a mask over her face, but if she did there was no way to breathe when she was struggling with Tomás. She dragged him every morning from the sweat-drenched mattress and propped him in a chair with a quilt tight around him, where he blinked like a baby owl. She stripped the soiled and wet sheets and turned the mattress over. It was stained yellow—she would burn it when he got better.

It was a wonder she didn't catch it herself, but that was how the outbreak happened. It picked out a member or two of a family and spared the rest. Or it wiped out all in a house, sometimes leaving one infant alive. No one could predict where or how it would fall.

The mountain was silent, as if waiting to hear who next would die.

⁂

"Teresita could fix this," Tomás said. His teeth chattered. He thought he was cold in the burning hot room.

Gabriela was upstairs, asleep. She had been working with her eyes closed, dreaming on her feet. Mrs. Smith had become mother to the children, since Gaby was now mother to Tomás. The smell of sickness was so regular in the house that she no longer sensed it at all. When she climbed the stairs, she actually bent at the waist and helped herself up with her hands—rising, she thought with bitterness, like a barn cat.

She had finally asked Segundo to care for Tomás, since only Segundo was strong enough to carry him around, to bathe him, to put up with his endless rage at being so weak. Frankly, grief and fear tired her out much more profoundly than the constant physical struggle to save Tomás. There were no medical answers—no treatments. Just patience. Faith.

"I got you, boss," Segundo said, lifting Tomás in his arms and laying him in the deep tin tub of hot bathwater.

"¡Cabrón!" Tomás cried. "You have boiled off my huevos! Are you making huevo soup?"

Segundo grinned and chewed a toothpick.

"Naw," he drawled, "you still got your balls. I can see them in there."

Tomás made the water shiver in the tub.

"I'm cold," he said.

"I got it."

Segundo brought a kettle in from the kitchen and poured hotter water in the tub.

"Feel better?" he said.

Tomás lay back.

"Ah...yes. Gracias, Segundo. What would I do without you?"

"Shit," Segundo said. He sat in a chair near the tub and opened the newspaper to look at the drawings. "You wouldn't have made it this far," he noted.

"No." Tomás was looking down at his sad ribs. Gray chest hair. How did that happen? "No, definitely not."

They chuckled until Tomás started coughing.

"I could send her a telegram," Segundo offered. "She could heal you."

But Tomás had fallen asleep.

※

Segundo wrestled him out of the water. He was limp and steaming, dripping on the floor. Just like a big baby. Segundo didn't know what to do with him, so he laid him on the end of the bed and quickly threw a towel around him and rubbed him brusquely. Tomás mumbled complaints but didn't awaken. His hair stood straight up on his head, but Segundo was damned if he was going to comb the Sky Scratcher's hair for him. He yanked a nightshirt over the boss's shanks and pulled the covers down and manhandled Tomás farther up the bed and laid his head in a nest of fluffy pillows. He pulled the blankets back up and let them fall and remembered his own mother tucking him in at night. He paused and smiled, thinking of it. How she'd lay him in the narrow bed with his older brother and his little sister. How there was one thin blanket they shared. How the sister slept between the brothers, and the brothers fought a tug-of-war all night to get more of the blanket. But that wasn't what made Segundo smile. It was his mother. How she'd sometimes take the blanket and say, "In the night, the dew falls down!" And she'd unfurl the blanket above them and let it settle. How they'd laugh! And she'd pull it off and say, "But later, it begins to rain!" And she'd unfurl it over them again. How they'd squeal! And the third time, she'd pull it off and say, "But then, when you least expect it, it starts to snow!" They'd all call it out with her. And the blanket would snow down on them in the gloom of their little hot bedroom. Segundo smiled and shook his head. Maybe they were in Heaven. He tossed a couple of aromatic logs on the fire and drew a second quilt over poor old Tomás and watched his eyes move under their lids.

His face was drawn. His breath was rank. The rash had chewed him up, crawled up his chest and around his throat and onto his face. Segundo thought he was dead at several moments during the night, but then Tomás drew a sucking breath and went on dreaming.

Segundo himself drifted off at about three o'clock. The relentless ticking of the clock had seemed to grow louder during the night, louder and deeper and wider until he fell into it and was knocked out by its echoes. He dreamed of Cabora and its many horses, kicking and fussing in the chair until the gray seepage of dawn light from the windows prodded his eyelids open. He regarded an empty bed.

He jumped out of his chair.

※

In a corner of the room, where they had shoved Tomás's desk to make room for his bed, pens and sheets of paper were scattered. Segundo squeezed past the end of the bed and looked at the papers.

Dearest Teresa

said one, but it was scratched out. The next:
Daughter

Then:
Querida Hija

※

All abandoned.
And the last sheet:

My Beloved Teresita, Daughter —

Before you throw this letter away, let me tell you

⚜

But there was no more than that. Ink everywhere. Segundo saw Tomás's slippers under the desk. The fool was wandering around barefoot.

"Got no sense," Segundo muttered.

He stepped out into the hall. The house was heavy with sleep. He could feel Gaby and the children above, still deep in their dreams.

"Boss?" he whisper-called.

The front door was ajar.

He grabbed his coat and hurried out.

There was a faint trail through the dew. Tomás had gone out to the barn.

"Damn fool," Segundo said.

He hopped down and walked across the grass.

"Boss," he called.

The barn door was standing open. He stepped inside and squinted. The blue horse was in the corner, bent down.

"You in here?" Segundo said.

The horse looked at him and blew air through its lips.

Segundo went to it and found Tomás sitting on the ground with his back to the stall upright. He was pale. Like porcelain. Segundo had seen dolls in Gaby's cases that looked exactly like Tomás looked now. He had wet himself at the end.

The horse was worried, looking down at the body and moving its ears back and forth and bobbing its head.

"Oh no," Segundo said.

It hurt his knees to get down with Tomás. He rested his hand on the blue horse's flank to get down. He peered at the Sky Scratcher's face. His eyes were closed. He looked peaceful. At least there was that.

His hair was still a mess.

"Oh no," Segundo said again softly.

"Hey, now." He ran his fingers through Tomás's hair, trying to comb it down.

"Let me fix that for you, boss," he said. "Let me fix that."

He spent a good half hour there, sitting quietly. He took off his coat and put it around Tomás because he looked so cold, even sitting in hay. The blue horse shied away and went into its stall and turned its back.

Then Segundo went to the house, wondering how to fetch the family.

Part VI

GOING HOME

I may be approaching darkness, but I am not yet blind.

—Teresita's last interview

Fifty-Nine

HAVING A CHILD had really rounded Teresita out, John noticed. She had curves and hips, and her body was soft, just the way he liked it. All those sharp edges had been tucked away. He even enjoyed her belly, which gave her fits. She felt that the red lines etched in her flesh made her look like a map of the desert with dead rivers scrawling over the landscape. She called it "my paper belly" and "my baby-map," which made John love it more. It felt like a secret of womanhood, something his mother never told him.

The fine ladies in her social circle bound her in corsets and fancy webworks of silks and satins that formed impenetrable buttresses underneath her clothes. She became in public a kind of dainty warship with a firm prow like an icebreaker and an aft deck that could withstand storms. But at home, when the nanny left, and when they had a few scant hours together as Laura slept, and after the painstaking chore of unpinning, unbuttoning, unwrapping his bride, John fell to the pale landscape of her body, his white flesh settling over her tea-and-cream-colored form like an early snowfall.

They were utterly alone in this new world, the three of them. There had been no word from anyone out west in over a year. John often thought of writing to his mother, but he wasn't the writing type. He engaged in many dreams of walking up to her door in Solomonville and waiting until she opened it. Perhaps carrying his daughter in his arms. Just to see the look on her face. He imagined the look of shock and then realization as she saw little Laura, then the joy and tears. It was how he went to sleep on many nights.

Teresita too—when she wasn't concerned with the doings of her ladies, or the uptown balls, or the upkeep of John and Laura—spent time in reveries of Clifton and her lost family. Consortium money was still coming in, and residual fees from her various commercial appearances came their way. John had managed to put a good sum in the bank as well. And he had put away most of his own allowance. They were almost... wealthy. She had time to dream of home.

It seemed they had been away for only months, though it had now been a few years. She'd always meant to express her feelings to Tomás in a good long letter, that good long letter everyone means to write. She went over drafts as she lay beside John, kept awake on most nights by his cataclysmic snoring or Laura's endless snuffling, bellowing, grunting, fussing. Teresita's head tossed on pillows that always felt too hot; she sought the cool space on the pillowcase. She fretted. Jesus Himself had said to let tomorrow worry about itself, but she worried. She ate herself from the inside with worry. She felt as though she lived in a fever.

John himself was sometimes awake, kept from sleep by his little Yaqui queen's oddly delicate snoring. He hated the way her nose went *whee,* and her lips popped softly. He put his pillow over his head and turned his back to her on those nights. He thought again about his mother. He honestly didn't know if she was aware she was a grandmother—though his brother Harry had probably beat him to it. In the mornings, he watched his poor little Yaqui bend to the writing desk, trying to compose a note to her father.

Family was a big joke on everybody.

John told himself that he could do without any of it.

Teresita saw his ambivalence. All new mothers knew what their husbands felt, even if they told themselves they didn't. She could smell it. She could see it in his movements. Sometimes he enjoyed fatherhood, but often he looked upon Laura with a kind of detachment that broke Teresita's heart as much as it angered her. When he dismissed the child, she wanted to throttle him. Laura snored in her pen, big and already starting to utter words when she dragged herself upright by pulling on the furniture. Now when Teresita and John fought, they fought about their future. About family. She wanted to go home; he wanted to stay. He was drunk on the city as it drank him and finished him, sip by sip. She wanted to take her daughter to her father and Gaby and Segundo. She wanted horses and herbs and aspens and pine trees.

"It is over, John."

"What is over?"

"This. New York. All of it."

"You're crazy."

"I am not crazy! Don't you ever call me crazy!"

"You're crazy as a doodlebug!"

She threw a pillow at him.

"Terry!" he cried. She hated that. *Terry?* "We're just about to crack this town!"

She stared out the window at the oncoming Atlantic weather and sighed.

"You never even took me to the ocean," she said.

But some days were good.

※

So it went, circles, the lone edge sharpening.

"Don't you miss your family?" she'd asked.

"Family?" he scoffed. "Hell no." He was reading his paper. It was a bad time to interrupt him, but she didn't care.

Another time.

"I miss mine."

"A lot of good your father and his high-and-mighty family have done you."

"I need to fix what happened."

"You never will is my guess."

Another.

"I did him wrong," she had cried. "It is my fault we are apart."

"Oh, come now." But the paper took his attention.

"I await God's judgment on the matter," she had said.

"Mrs. Van Order," he had replied, affecting a fine uptown accent, "you are a fool."

He thought he was being funny. She did not find it amusing.

"And you are a drunkard," she had said.

"That I am!" he'd boasted, rattling the paper. "By God I am!" He had tossed the paper on the floor. She'd bent to pick it up, her every movement ripe with reproach. "You bet."

And then.

"I want to go home."

"Home? What, Arizona?" He blew air through his lips. "They will laugh at you."

"Let them laugh."

He opened another paper. How many newspapers did he have? He was like a newsprint magician, pulling things out from behind his buttocks.

"You can't leave here," he said, shaking out his pages like someone's grandfather. "You're famous. What will all your admirers do without you?"

"I am hardly famous."

"Honey." He put down the paper. "Who lives with you? Who knows you better than anybody else in the world?" He pointed to himself. "Rich bastards take you to fine suppers. People ask for your autograph, reach out to you as you pass. They take your picture. Nobody does that to me. I'd call that famous."

"It means nothing," she said.

He tossed the paper on the floor. She went and picked it up and added it to the sheaf in her left hand.

"You know," he noted, "you love it. You love being famous."

"John!"

"You, you go around," he said, raising his hand in a beatific posture, "distributing your fame as if it's some kind of blessing." He tapped imaginary people on their heads; he waved and smiled. "You dish out fame like you think that's healing everybody!"

"That is not true."

"That is exactly true."

She turned her back.

He laid his feet out before him and relaxed into the chair.

"This saint routine got too big for the rubes and cowpokes in Arizona. Don't you get it? The Indians are as dead as the buffalo. There's nothing out there for you now."

She tried to be present. Tried to hear him, John, and not her father. She was so tired of all of it. Tired of herself. Miracles. Perhaps the miracle was her own child. And the rest? She turned her eyes to him and tried to read his lips because her ears were roaring.

"You were so busy becoming an American you can't go back," he declared. "You don't fit no more. New York is home now."

"You are married to this city!" she yelled. "Not me! Those people out there are your family!"

He said, "You was Queen of the Yaquis, and now you think you're the Queen of America."

"Stop it!" she cried.

"I won't let you abdicate that throne, girlie!" he said. "Not now."

Laura snorted awake and started caterwauling.

"I am the queen of nothing," she said.

Laura yelled louder.

John stood and stared into the crib.

"Nice," he noted, fetching his hat and nodding to the apocalypse raging within the wooden cage.

"At least," he said, "nobody out there yells at me."

He stepped toward the door.

"Oh?" she said. "Leaving again?"

"The atmosphere is a touch rich in here." He sniffed.

"The master of the timely escape," she observed.

"Adios," he said brightly.

"How manly," she said. "Running from a woman."

"How saintly of you," he said, pausing at the door. "Why don't you go out and heal someone."

"Like you?" she shot back, lifting the baby and trying to bounce away her crying.

"Mama, Mama, Mama, Mama," Laura added to the conversation.

"Excuse me?" John said from the landing.

"I don't heal anyone anymore," Teresita replied. "Didn't you notice? Your little problems engage me night and day."

"You don't heal nobody," he said. "Truer words were never spoke."

Before he could say anything else, she closed and locked the door.

He called through the wood, "Well, I guess you'd better get back with God and fire it up again, my dear. I know you like money to buy all them fine dresses."

"Someone has to earn money," she said.

"As if I won't," he said.

He snarled, laid a fist against the wood, but did not pound. He grinned savagely. He adjusted his hat. He hadn't even told Teresita he had left Effie Woodward's antiques emporium. Oh, well.

"Praise Jesus," he muttered as he trotted downstairs and hustled toward the city.

☀

Laura lurched around the apartment like a drunken sailor. Teresita had a headache. She was still nursing but trying to convince the big toothy child that a nice warm cup of milk or cool fruit juice was better. Her nipples were sore, bitten and chewed. She cleaned up the rooms for the thousandth time. She stopped what she was doing and looked at her daughter. Laura had climbed atop the chair and stood with her arms in the air.

"How's she do that?" Laura demanded.

Teresita laughed.

They shared a bowl of sweet potatoes mashed with butter. They watched little brown birds out their back window. Teresita changed Laura's diaper and placed the offending cloth in a lidded bucket. They crawled on the floor acting like rabbits. The nanny came in the afternoon, in time for Teresita to prepare herself for her evening appointment in Gramercy Park. After she consulted with the lady there, she and John were going to take a carriage ride up to Harlem to watch singers at a new supper and entertainment establishment. It would be a fine evening. She went to her wardrobe to select her dress, and she stopped for a moment and looked around her bedroom. Still brown, still sad. But comfortable. Like an old shoe. Not in any way the equal of the glittering rooms where she did her work now.

Then she stopped, silent, and stared.

No herbs. No cross on the wall. She took a cream dress from the padded hanger; the gold material that wrapped the wood was rich with lilac and heather scents. She held the dress before herself, smoothed it against her bust. She paused again. She looked over her shoulder. As if someone were watching her. But of course, no one was there. She turned and looked again. John's scuffed and beaten boots beside the bed. But no altar.

She blinked. Where was her altar? She'd always had an altar. Huila had taught her that much.

Where were her objects? She had no idea. It bothered her. The fact that she hadn't noticed they were gone bothered her more than their absence. She looked at the clock. She didn't have time for this. New York City ran by the clock. There was no dawdling. She thought: Manhattan *is* a clock.

But where were her herbs? She had always hung herbs from the rafters. There were no rafters. And where would she find herbs in New York City? She stood in the middle of the room and stared at the floor. She raised her hand to her brow.

"Who's there?" she said, whipping around. The room was cold. No one stood behind her. "Huila?" she said.

"What, Mama?" called Laura.

"Nothing," Teresita said.

"Ma'am?" called the nanny.

"Nothing."

Teresita closed her bedroom door and leaned her head against the wood.

She could not remember the last time she had touched soil with her feet. She could not remember when she had last put her feet in free running water. She had not pulled a fruit off a tree or ridden a horse or prayed in a sacred spot. Were there sacred spots in New York? Wouldn't people just laugh at her if they found her talking to trees? Collecting seeds from plants with her old apron?

Where was her apron? Huila's apron. Where was it?

She let out a small cry. She tore open her small chest and threw the rebozos out. No apron. Rebozos! When had she last worn one?

The apron was not in the closet, nor was it in any of the drawers. She spun in place. What had she done with it? What had she done?

"Huila?" she said.

She looked under the bed. There was nothing. She didn't even have a photograph of her father. She had nothing but expensive clothes and buckled shoes, hats and ribbons and hairpins and stoles. Nothing that mattered. No shells. No bones, or seeds, or branches with leaves.

She slowly sank to the bed and sat there in the dread afternoon light.

She slid forward to her knees.

"I have failed You," she whispered.

Silence lashed her.

"I have betrayed You."

The silence was punishing her.

"I am no one now."

The silence was complete.

"Please," she said. "Please." Outside her door, Laura laughed in her perpetual state of grace. Teresita's head bent all the way to the floor. "Please."

But it was time for her to go. Her knees didn't want to allow her to rise. All she wanted was to take her daughter under the covers and hide in a nest as if the last twenty years had not happened. As if they could be little sisters — she wasn't ready to be anyone's mother. Anyone's wife.

She had even failed at being someone's daughter. If she only had wings, she would fly home and be at rest.

She stared into the mirror.

"People once believed you could fly," she told herself.

Now? Only Laura. Only little Laura would believe her if she told such a story.

She closed her eyes.

She turned away from herself.

She laid out the clothes and undressed and pulled her silks from the drawer.

She began to enclose herself, pulling the bindings tighter and tighter.

꙳

John wandered around Red Hook taking in the accents and the smells as dusk dragged the sky over him like a blanket. He'd downed three or four flagons of lager, and his attitude had lightened. There wasn't a faro game to be had anywhere. It had sprinkled, but no real rain had fallen. He clocked along humming a little tune, laughing at the kids rolling hoops down the street with sticks, the myriad piebald street dogs scattering like trash in the wind, all of 'em runts — boys and mutts. He was walking back to Manhattan. Why not? There was some sport to be had at the west end of the Brooklyn Bridge.

The bridge. How many damned times had Teresita made him walk that? The cables looked like spiderwebs to her, and those Indians liked their spiders. He guffawed. He hiked. He meandered. He had no particular place to be. He didn't remember their fight. Poles and Russians bumped into him. "Watch it," he said. "Whoa, hoss!" Hunched and dark and lost in their coats. Lovers strolled around him, pausing and hugging and cooing at each other. He smiled upon them, blessed them. He was ruler of the earth. He dallied halfway across the bridge and produced a flask as if by magic and pulled a sweet ounce of whiskey down his throat.

Behind him, a voice said, "That'll do."

Recognizing the phrase, if not the voice, John scowled around.

"By God," he said, "if it isn't Mr. Suits."

Suits looked a little moth-eaten. Even his bowler hat had a couple of rough spots.

"How about a snort?" Suits said.

John handed him the flask. Suits nursed on it.

"Steady now," John said. "Don't drain the bastard."

Suits handed it back; John shook it. It was empty.

"Damn it, Suits," John complained. "You ain't been here but one minute and you're already stealing me blind."

Ignoring his rebuke, Suits said, "How's the Girl Saint business?"

"Thought you'd retired," said John, now noting the presence of Elias the nine-foot-tall pistolero from St. Louis. "I see you brung Goliath with you," he commented.

"Brought David too," said Suits.

There he was: Swab Dave, the arranger, in his felt top hat.

"Why, girls!" John crowed. "We're having a reunion!"

Suits took his right elbow. Elias waded in and took the other.

"Shall we?" Suits asked.

"Where to?" John said.

Suits shrugged.

"We'll find a place. For a brief chat."

They walked him down the long slope of the bridge.

Sixty

SUITS AND JOHN SAT in a dismal corner of a stinking café in a narrow alley amid clouds of smoke. John nursed a big cracked mug of coffee. Suits had a glass of watery root beer. Elias and Swab Dave lurked outside the window, their faces distorted by the grime and the cheap glass into carnival masks.

"I was asked to intervene in your affairs one last time," Suits said. "Seeing as how the Saintess is about to run out of her contract."

"How was your retirement?"

"Pleasurable enough, John. Far as it was from you."

"Haw!" John toasted him with his chicory-bitter coffee. "What are you offering?" he said.

"What do you want?"

"I'm not the problem," John replied.

Suits fiddled with his hat, scooting it around on the table. "What's she want?" he said. "Herbs?" He snorted.

"Suitsie-boy," said John, "you'd have to talk to her about that. She has a powerful hankering to head on back to the mountains and rusticate."

"Meaning?"

"Meaning Mrs. Van Order might be just about done. Played out."

"I see." Mr. Suits took a sip of his tonic. "She's dispirited."

"I'd say."

"Beyond argument?"

"She's firmed up on the plan."

"Is she persuadable, though? That right there's the question."

"I think," John confessed, "this has all been too much for her. The city, motherhood."

"Yourself."

John drank some coffee.

"I was never no Fourth of July picnic."

Suits finished his root beer.

"Let me ask you," he said. "Did you ever see her heal anybody?"

"Heal?" said John. I'm not about to betray her, he thought. "Like grow a leg?"

Suits shrugged.

"I saw some things that was curious," John said. "But I never saw no dead rise, if that's what you're sayin'."

"I'm not saying nothing," said Suits. "Just asking."

"Asking if she's a fraud."

"Didn't say that."

"Didn't say nothin' else either."

John finished his coffee and slammed down the cup.

"Hell, Suits," he said, "how am I supposed to know? You'd have to ask an Indian, I guess. Is it real? She thinks so."

Suits nodded.

"She's the boss," he said.

In his jacket pocket, Suits had a letter. He had carried it all the way across the country. He didn't know what to do with it. The notice of Tomás's death would definitely end their chances to sign Teresita up for another year. Hellfire, the Saintess would be up and gone to kneel at the grave of her daddy. He couldn't blame her. He wasn't a monster. Not exactly. He slid the letter across the table to John.

John read it and sighed. He shook his head.

"She finds this out now," he said, "and we can all kiss New York good-bye."

"I have an idea," Suits said.

⁂

Teresita rubbed sage oil into the shoulders of Mrs. Dashiell. She massaged the great lady's shoulders, digging her fingers into the muscle. "You have grief," she said. *Jou hob griff.* She could feel it, sorrow etched into her back. Deep regrets clenched tightly in her neck. The oil felt hot under her fingers, warmed by the skin. It filled their noses. Teresita thought it made Mrs. Dashiell smell like she was about to be cooked in an oven with some potatoes and onions.

This was stupid. When was the last time she helped a mother bring a child into the world? When was the last time she healed a truly sick person? All she seemed to do was ease gout or rub sore shoulders for rich people.

In her mind, over and over: I have failed You. I have betrayed You. I am no one now.

The whole time that she was hunting down shames and disappointments in her client's body, she was feeling her own throb like a splinter inside her. Her father. Gaby. Her sister Anita. Segundo. She thought of the good people of Clifton. Of her followers. Of the Indians in the hills and the desert. The People. She had come so far from her roots. So far from her home ground. Now, she was no longer a rebel. No saint. She was a mother, a wife. And she wondered how far she could go if she kept walking farther and farther from the dry desert path.

She smacked Mrs. Dashiell.

"Hey!" the lady yelped.

"So sorry."

She squeezed and pulled and smoothed and pressed. She had always squeezed and pulled and smoothed and pressed.

When she was done, she said, "You will go to bed tonight and weep. You will cry for a time, but do not be concerned. It will pass within an hour, and you will sleep in peace."

Mrs. Dashiell went to rinse off the aromatic oils, and Teresita was brought a pitcher with warm water and lavender soap to wash her hands. Rather than go to Harlem, she just wanted to go home. She wanted to lie with Laura and wait for John to come home.

Why didn't she rub his shoulders with sage oil? How could she be kind to strangers but act cross with her loved ones? Why didn't she find his ancient pains and rub them free?

She excused herself from Mrs. Dashiell's party and accepted a carriage back to East Twenty-Eighth.

She would wait up for John. And when he came home, even if he was drunk, she would greet him with a long embrace. She would lead him to their bed, and she would pull the boots off his feet and pull the shirt over his head and lay him back with his head on the pillow.

And she would tell him she was carrying his second child.

⁂

"Darling!" John cried, entering the apartment like a gust of wind. He waved around a small bunch of flowers he had bought off a cart.

"Here," she called from the bedroom.

He peeked in. She was under the covers, her bare shoulders showing. Laura was snoring away.

"Here I am," Teresita said.

John smiled.

"Sorry," he said.

"Me too."

"I didn't mean to be so tetchy."

"It's all right," she said.

He showed her the flowers.

"Got these for you," he said.

"Take off your boots," she said.

He did it very fast.

Later, as they lay there, he said, "I'm going to take you to the sea tomorrow."

She buried her face in his neck and smiled.

"John?" she whispered. "I'm expecting."

"Expecting what?" he asked.

Then he realized, and he had the presence of mind to praise her and coddle her and act enthusiastic while his mind raced, trying to find the angle now—trying to calculate how he could manage the situation.

⁂

They stood at the docks in lower Manhattan. Laura goggled at the world from her pram. Stink and gulls. Great bulks of ocean liners weeping rust. Teresita watched a poor little turtle that had come down the river bobbing disconsolately between vast black hulls, looking up at them from the churning water.

"I thought we were going to stand on the beach," she said.

"It's the ocean, isn't it?" he said, having a high time watching rich sons of bitches walk up the planks to the ships.

"How'd you like to join them?" he asked.

The looming ship before them let out a bellow: *bah-woot!* It echoed around them, shook their innards. John burst out laughing.

"Don't you love it!" he yelled.

"It could be yours," said a voice off her left shoulder.

Teresita turned her head and beheld Mr. Suits looking like he'd grown a thin layer of mold on his face. He wore a green checkered coat that bore a smudge down one lapel.

"You," she said.

"What a delight," Suits intoned. "To see you again."

She turned to John.

"You!" she said.

"Hear the man out," he replied.

Laura looked up at Suits.

"Who you, ugly man?" she said.

He ignored the child.

"Behold the luxury liners of the White Star Line," he said. He scratched under his chin, causing some loose flesh depending from it to wobble. "These fine ships are going to England! Imagine that!

"You too," Suits proclaimed, "could be boarding one of these fine ships!"

She stepped away, wheeling Laura's carriage.

Suits raised his voice.

"As the Saintess, you could go abroad and meet royalty! Miss? Don't they call you queen?"

She walked away.

"One more year with the Consortium! What do you say? We'll send you to Europe! Meet you a king!"

She went on down the docks and didn't look back.

"Damnation, Van Order," said Suits. "She don't get easier to deal with."

John pulled his flask.

"That she don't," he said.

Far from them, Teresita smiled. She didn't want to hear any more plots. She was fully in the glow of God's mysterious power.

Venado Azul stood there smiling at her.

＊

He was in a black suit with a small top hat and a frock coat that hung well below his knees. He had replaced his deerskin slippers with shiny black boots.

"Saint," he said.

"I am so happy to see you," she said.

"I see you there and it makes me smile," he replied.

"What are you doing here?"

He nodded to the great black wall of ship before him.

"Buffalo Bill has bought us tickets on this big canoe, and we're going to row it to England to make believe we're killing each other for the king and queen."

He shrugged.

"It's a job."

"Indian!" Laura shouted. "Indian!"

He looked down at her.

"Hello, small one," he said. "She looks like your father."

Teresita beamed.

"I married too. A white woman," Blue Deer admitted.

"Oh?"

"She comes from Indiana. Fast-Horse Cathy. A sharpshooter."

"Bless you both."

"She's on the boat."

They stood there, pleasantly silent. White men, Blue Deer thought, needed to fill up every moment with chatter. Sometimes, silence was more comfortable. Come to think of it, Mexicans were babblers too.

He cleared his throat.

"I am sorry," Blue Deer added.

"Sorry? About what?"

"About the Sky Scratcher."

"What about him?"

"All of us mourn him," Blue Deer said. "When he died, a great warmth left the world. Made us all feel cold."

She could not hear. She turned. Behind her, small and shadowy, Suits and John stood drinking liquor and laughing. They looked her way and froze. They knew from looking at her that she knew.

Her hands went to her face.

She fell.

John ran. He ran toward her as fast as he could. But he knew no matter how fast he ran, he would never be able to catch her.

Sixty-One

SHE WAS SO TIRED. She was already sick in the mornings. They'd all expected her to take to her bed when she heard of Tomás's death, but she did not. She could not. She had responsibilities. And just as Laura's birth had not stopped her from doing her work, her father's being gone would not stop her now. It was a question of discipline. No one would ever again see her cry. Not even God. She had decided to go home.

To Clifton.

But Mr. Smith's men were not as willing as the Consortium to let her simply waltz off. Not with that fat roll of dollars they knew she must have with her. No, there was no way they'd let her carry off enough money to feed them and buy them drinks and boots and coats for years.

She grimly went to work in the finest clothing John had ever seen.

She had become white as a New York maven—creamed and powdered. Her hair was luxuriant, treated with steaming oils and set in thick crowns. She wore gloves to her elbows and twirled a small parasol. Her heeled shoes lifted her almost as tall as he was with his boots off. Her lips were painted and glistening as berries, her eyes lined with kohl, and her eyelids blushing with copper or blue powders. Her brows became thin arched structures denoting endless surprise. Her cheeks were now rouged, slight tints of her old brown on her new white face making it look like she'd been pinched or like a cold breeze had licked her skin. Her nails were pink as little seashells, and her legs were silken, relieved of all trace of hair.

Mr. Suits had already placed items in the press reporting that the Girl Saint was going abroad to be received by royalty, but it was all a folly. As soon as she finished her last rounds of New York activities, she was through. She was going home. She could think only of her brothers and sisters, could dream now only of repairing her ties with Gabriela. She would have her next child in the west. Away from cities. She would lay flowers on her father's grave, and not John, or the Consortium, or that Satan Mr. Suits would dissuade her.

Elias and Swab Dave caught John in Greenwich Village near a tenement building. They rushed him backward into the shadows of an alley that seemed to be hosting a convention of cats. They slammed him between the walls and punched him in the gut and left him on his knees.

Teresita knew the next child would be a girl as well. She could feel it, the way the little bean turned inside the oven of her belly, the way she settled and stretched just like Laura had. The gas and the endless peeing hadn't started yet, and Teresita planned to be in Arizona before any of that began.

John pleaded with her.

"One more year?" he said.

"No."

"I am not done here," he said.

"But I am."

"Look at yourself!" he cried. "You've become a fine lady! You wear little straw hats and white stockings."

"I never meant to be a fine lady, John."

"Aw, now, sweetheart. You yourself said you're no saint."

"I am not a saint. You said that I am."

He hung his head.

"You tell the world that you heal the sick."

"God heals them, not I. I am God's instrument."

He smiled.

"Really," he said.

"Yes, really." She stared at him. "After all you've seen, do you doubt me?"

"What have I seen?" he said.

She just looked at him.

"I have nothing to say," she said. "I am without words."

Teresita had agreed to wear a new Gibson-style dress for a small gathering on Park Boulevard. John called it the beauty competition. Though it was true that the best-dressed lady of the event would win a small ribbon, it was all for charity and general amusement. Nothing major. But it was her last commitment. After that, her contract ended and her connection to New York was broken and she would go home.

She got her things together.

"I will be back late," she said.

"Win that ribbon."

"I will."

She kissed Laura on the head.

She paused at the door and said, "I am sorry you never saw a miracle."

She walked down the stairs.

John said to Laura, "I guess I have to pack our bags now."

Laura said, "Drink me!"

He poured her some apple juice, then got out his flask and slugged down a few.

✳

Teresita returned home at ten o'clock. She had been a sensation in her dress and her magnificent hairstyle. Black lacquer chopsticks held the bun in place, with small pearls in cunning woven settings that looked like drops of dew in her hair. She did not feel lovely. She did not feel happy. She smiled because she had become an expert in smiling. She thought of her father, of how her father would both disapprove of this dress and desire to see it on Gaby. She smelled like lilacs. She could no longer smell roses at all.

She carried her gilt and purple ribbon in her hand. *Queen of New York.* How funny after everything. She didn't even say farewell to her friends. She had trouble remembering all their names. Their faces were already fading from her mind as if covered by snowflakes.

Men stood in the shadows down near Lexington when she left the cab and opened the front door. The vestibule was dark, cold. She climbed the stairs, feeling the unbearable heaviness of the new child dragging her spine back down. Her body simply didn't want to climb another stair. Her high heels hurt her feet. The bindings and corsets and stockings made her hot and itchy and sweaty, and she wanted it all off.

John was not home. Poor Mr. Somers from downstairs snoozed in John's big chair, and Laura was balancing her new teddy bear on her head. The bears were all the rage, and Teresita had ordered this one all the way from Germany.

"Hello, Mama," said Laura.

"Why are you still awake?" Teresita said.

"How does she do that?" Laura shouted.

Teresita shook Bill Somers awake and thanked him with a kiss on the cheek and sent him back down to bed.

She locked the door and carried Laura into the bedroom and laid her in her crib.

"You're too big for that," she said. "Time for a big-girl bed."

Laura held up her bear and made it dance in the air.

Teresita pried the shoes off her feet. She had a blister on her right foot — the stocking had worn through in the shoe, and little tatters had rubbed on her smallest toe. She pulled up her skirt and detached the stockings from their hooks and peeled them off like dead skin. She rubbed her legs and sighed. Her feet in her hands felt cooked and tender.

"Stinky feet!" Laura commented.

"I am the Saint of Cabora," a baritone Teresita intoned. "My feet smell like flowers."

They giggled.

"Mama stinks," Laura said.

Teresita pulled the chopsticks from her head, careful to catch the pearl webs before they fell to the floor. She shook her hair loose, and it fell heavy on her shoulders. She gripped it in both hands and fanned it out and scratched her scalp.

The dress fell like heavy crepe to the floor and she stepped out of it and let it lie. It formed a small battlement — looked like a one-woman prison. She undid her underthings and set herself free and dropped a loose nightdress over her head and slipped her feet into sheepskin moccasins and twirled her hair into a braid.

※

Teresita was ready for home. It was over. She was finished. She could feel it in her body. Home. As she folded her clothes and stuffed her trunks, as she sang to Laura and lit the candles and the gas lamps, she thought of home. Of the flowers she would plant on her father's grave. New York had been like her first beer — she'd thought it would taste sweeter.

"Arizona, Mamá?" Laura asked over and over, as if tasting a new candy. "Arizona?"

"Yes, sweet pea, yes."

"Papá too?"

"All of us in sunny Arizona." She was distracted with her packing.

"Sunny!" Laura shouted, clapping her hands.

The crash of the splintering wood startled them and made Laura scream. Elias and Swab Dave surged through the door as Teresita rushed to the crib and grabbed her wailing daughter. The men stood there panting from the rush and the door-busting.

"You had to be trouble," Elias said. He was rolling up his sleeves. Swab Dave laughed a little. He took off his hat—blond hair fell past his shoulders.

"Get ready, girlie," he said.

"Get out," Teresita replied.

"Give us the money," Swab Dave demanded. "Maybe we'll leave."

"What money?"

"You're so cute," Elias said. "What money, she says."

"You are scaring my daughter."

"Shut yer yap and give us the money or we'll take care of your daughter too."

Laura craned her neck around and stared at him.

"You're bad," she said.

Elias moved toward them, and Teresita held up one hand.

"I am warning you," she said.

The two men looked at each other and laughed.

"Shit," said Elias, and came for her.

Teresita felt it from her feet. It was a tickle and a burning. It was a thump that rolled all the way up her skeleton. It was a wave that came from some invisible sea and crashed into her hands and eyes. She felt her hair fly as it burst from her.

"¡No!" she said.

She didn't shout. She was firm. Not loud at all.

Both men were caught in midstep and became wooden. Their hands up. Their eyes wide. They squeaked and made horrible spastic faces, and drool flew from their lips and they fell to the floor and twitched and gargled and quivered at her feet.

"You," she said, "do not threaten my daughter!"

Laura looked down from Teresita's grip and pointed. She laughed.

The men hammered the floor with their heels. They frothed and mewled. It was horrible to see.

Teresita grabbed a heavy coat and a blanket for Laura and rushed past them.

Suits stood in the doorway, blocking it with both arms.

She didn't even give him a chance to speak.

The wave hit him so hard that dust burst from his clothes and he was shot backward down the stairs and crashed to the floor.

Bill Somers, in his nightshirt, rushed out of his apartment and shouted, "What the hell is going on here?"

Teresita ran downstairs, feeling light as a deer.

Laura was whooping.

They ran into the street.

Laura shouted, "How's she do that?"

And Teresita started her journey home.

Sixty-Two

MAGDALENA VAN ORDER URREA was born in Juana Van Order's ranch house in Solomonville, Arizona. In attendance were Dr. Burtch from Clifton, Juana herself, and a reluctant Gaby, who had not yet forgiven Teresita for destroying everything she held dear. Love prevailed, however—Tomás would not have forgiven her for ignoring Teresita at such a moment.

Outside, ancient Segundo sat in the wagon with his rifle across his aching knees and wept slow tears. He wept easily now—the death of Tomás had rendered him melancholy and regretful, and his hands shook with tenderness and his eyes sprang tears at any sign of beauty, sorrow, or impermanence. He cried when trees were felled by great winds. He cried at first snows. He cried at births and weddings and Christmas Eve. Why, Dolores had caught him holding yellow baby ducks and weeping. He had become gentle in his old age, and he'd kill any son of a bitch that mocked him.

John sat inside the house, dizzy. New York was still filtering out of his veins, and he was powerful sick from it—his head ached and his feet twitched. At night, he still heard klaxons and screaming El brakes instead of crickets and coyotes. Mama Juana fed him and he ate every bite. She brought him olive and chicken tamales, and he jumped on them like a barn cat on a mouse. Eggs fried with nopal cactus; he ate them with six tortillas. Beans and charred beefsteak and onions? He sopped up the grease with rough chunks of bread. He drank bottle after bottle of Mexican beer, and he didn't care if it was warm.

Teresita lay in the back room with the new babe, bleeding and weak. Gaby sat with her and they kept the door shut. When the letter came from the Consortium, John knocked and stepped in sheepishly and read her their apologies: The Consortium members in no way condoned nor had any foreknowledge of the dastardly actions independently undertaken by Mr. Suits et al., and they extended their sincerest wishes for a speedy recovery from such trauma, etc., etc., and looking forward to the day when she could see her way clear to reinstating their mutually beneficial arrangement, the terms of which—but of course!—were absolutely negotiable.

She held up her hand to stop him.

"Please," Teresita said, "take that fine letter and place it in the stove and light some kindling with it."

He stood there, not knowing what to say.

He decided on: "Right. Okay."

He went to his mother and changed the subject.

"Mother," he said. "All these fellows around here wear guns."

She laughed.

"Why, don't they wear pistolas in New York?" she said.

She sat in a gray wooden rocker on the porch. He joined her and squeaked along beside her in his own chair. The loose boards of the porch sounded escalating and receding notes like the slats of a marimba as the rockers agitated them.

"You can't be carrying guns around in the city," he said.

From the wagon, Segundo's primordial raven's voice squawked, "This ain't no city."

"Where's your gun?" Juana asked.

John watched a roadrunner strut from east to west as if he owned the ranch. It took a couple of minutes for him to appear, waggle his tail, stroll along casually, and then disappear in the Spanish bayonets growing in the distance. All he needed was a big cigar.

He said, "I don't know."

※

"You never married John," Gabriela Cantúa said.

Teresita lay back against the pillows, weak and feverish.

"No."

"The people here know that."

Teresita shrugged.

"We are married in God's eyes."

"How do you know?" Gaby asked.

Teresita was stumped.

"One just . . . knows."

Gaby raised her eyebrows and let them drop—they would have made a thump if it were possible.

"They say your daughters are bastards."

Teresita shook her head.

"Not all of them say such things."

"Enough of them do."

Magdalena slept against her mother's chest.

"They said the same of me," Teresita said. "There are no bastards. We are all God's daughters. Our parents only borrow us for a season."

Gaby resented that—she had definitely not borrowed her children!

Teresita was serene. She was letting go of the tangled branches of her days, letting their fruits drop to the ground. She was not apathetic, but she had become detached. She could have floated out of the bed on a slight breeze. She didn't like to look at Gaby because the light was showing through her. It leaked through all the gaps in her body.

Everybody was becoming clear. It was very strange, yet did not alarm Teresita. If they passed between her and the sun, she could see thin light threads burning through them. She could see the shadows of their bones. Everybody glowed pink. She supposed they would continue to clarify before her eyes until they were like soap bubbles, almost invisible and revealed only by the swirls of color cascading across their surfaces.

"We are mostly empty space," Teresita said.

"Excuse me?"

"We are only made of light."

"I see."

Gaby did not see, but she was used to Teresita's half-mad proclamations.

"How interesting," she said blandly.

The room was quiet. Laura was out in the parlor, endlessly rearranging Juana's many buttons from her sewing boxes. The baby's body between the two women made infernal noises, as if she were some overheated little machine. Some of these noises were so rude and so startling that the women forgot their sorrows and laughed out loud.

"My God," said Gaby.

"I think this one will grow up to play the trumpet," Teresita said.

After a time, Gaby said, "Ay."

Teresita listened to the clock ticking.

"Ay, sí," she replied.

"Pues," said Gaby. "Mira nomás."

"Qué cosas," Teresita agreed.

What else could they say? Such things, indeed. How many million women had gathered in the rubble of how many histories and sighed, *Oh, well. How about that?*

"They say that coming home was a retreat," Teresita said. She reached out and grabbed Gaby's arm. "But I will tell you the truth. I failed when I found fame. The higher I climbed, the farther I strayed. Wait. Just listen. Don't speak. Not yet.

"I failed. I failed, Gaby! I made a hundred, a thousand mistakes! I thought I was doing the right thing. But I lost my way. Huila warned me that we wander off the path, and I thought I would never do such a thing.

"Everyone is gone! Everything is gone! Because of me!"

She cried. She rubbed the tears from her eyes angrily, with the butt of her palm.

"Coming home is not my failure. Leaving New York is not my retreat. Coming home is my triumph." She paused for breath. "Do you see? I am a mother now. I am not anybody's daughter. I am nobody's saint. I am walking back to the road, and all the illusions of that life are gone. I despise them and I despise her."

Gaby stared at her. It wasn't the first time she didn't understand Teresita. She had always been on some other level from the rest of them. Gaby was still not certain that Teresita wasn't simply insane.

"Who?" Gaby asked. "Who do you despise?"

"Her," said Teresita. "The Saint of Cabora."

Gaby gasped. She made the sign of the cross.

"That's a blasphemy," she whispered.

Teresita laughed. It was the best laugh she had had in months. She laughed until her eyes were wet again, and she laid Magdalena down and wiped her eyes with the edge of the sheet.

Gabriela, confused, patted her on the shoulder and got up and let herself out of the room. "Bendita sea Dios," she muttered, crossing herself again, just in case.

᙮

All the fancy Manhattan clothes went to Juana and Gaby. Teresita saved the parasols for Anita, because she knew her little sister would love such frilly things. Laura sat with Gabriela in the back of the wagon on Mama Juana's quilts and pillows. It wasn't much, but it would be a start. Teresita sat atop the wagon beside Segundo. She cradled Magdalena in her arms and covered her with a rebozo. They looked like a peasant family searching for farmwork on the haciendas of the desert.

John had refused to leave his mother's house.

"I don't wanna," he said.

"But, John," Teresita said. "We're going back to Clifton."

"Not me."

"We're starting a new life."

"Don't make me."

"We're leaving."

"Ain't gonna."

What was he, a child?

"But you will join me later," she said. "Join us."

"Sure, yeah. I reckon I'll mosey on up in a day or two . . . you know."

They looked in each other's eyes.

She touched his cheek and turned away. Ah, John. Almost entirely clear. With her back to him, she could remember only his eyes.

Juana showered her and the girls with kisses and tears.

Segundo kissed none of them, but he did cry. He shook the traces and the mules hove to and groaned onto the dirt track that cut across the llano and bent to the hills that cut into canyons and creaked slowly into ridges that followed the old Spanish trail up and up, trailing Coronado's conquistadores and the shadows of Apache riders and the endless etching of hawk-wing shadows and darting ephemeral glitterings of dragonfly flight, up out of cactus to scrub oak to pines and spires and waterfall trickles and patches of breeze-drunk yellow flowers. Wanderers coming down the trail stood aside and watched her pass, silent. Some of them took off their hats and stared. Others spit or looked away and patted their burros and waited for the damned wagon to get out of the way. No trumpets. No heralds. No honor guard. "Bye!" Laura called to them as they rumbled past. "Bye-bye!" None of them waved.

⁂

Segundo had used part of Teresita's inheritance to secure her a snug little house across the street from her old co-adventurer Al Fernandez. Al was tall now. He no longer wore his railroad engineer cap, but he did carry chests and quilts into the house for her. Laura walked beside him, matching her footsteps to his as best she could.

Teresita wanted to do one thing, and one thing only. She wanted to kneel at Tomás's grave and confess to him, tell him all the things in her heart, say to him those things no other person alive or dead could ever hear or know. The most secret things a daughter can confess to her father, hoping he could somehow hear and understand them.

But first things first: she had to go to the Urrea house and see her familia. Segundo waited for her to brace herself and change the baby and fuss for a moment before she was ready. She remounted the wagon and they set out. She carried the parasols like rifles. When the wagon pulled up to the house, many small faces peered out from the doorway and the windows and Teresita descended and stepped up on the porch she had left a hundred years ago.

"I am home," she said. "Forgive me for being gone."

And the door swung open.

⁂

The next morning, as they all slept, she crept out of the house and found a blue horse in the barn and saddled it and rode through the dew grass and out the gate and up through town and onto the Morenci road and up past the mine roads to Shannon Hill. She tied the blue horse to the fence and walked past the spot where she and Anita had first spoken to Rodriguez. She knew Tomás was at the far edge of the cemetery, in a double plot that had been laid out for him and Gabriela. There was not yet a headstone, but there was a plaque with a plot number and the rusting letters u*r*r*e*a and a low iron fence around the grave and the flat space beside it. No one in sight. Dead paper kites rattled in the electrical lines like crashed fruit bats. The wind made forlorn noises as it topped the hill and sped toward the canyons beyond.

Teresita stepped over the fence and swept weeds and bits of paper off his grave with her foot. She knelt at his head and whispered, "Hello, Father. I have come home." She stretched out on the sun-warmed soil beside him. She laid her hand on the ground above where his heart would be and stroked his chest through his five feet of cover. "Father," she said, "it is a beautiful morning here. You would like it. Did you know you have a blue horse?" She laughed a little, as if she'd heard him exclaim in his usual fashion, *Seriously! Blue!* She closed her eyes and laid her head on the dirt as if it were his shoulder.

"Ay, Papá." She sighed. "Please forgive me."

And she related her story to him as the sun rolled along and the day turned on its axis into cool blue afternoon.

Sixty-Three

"MAMA USED TO SMELL like roses," Teresita told Laura. Anita knelt behind the child, braiding her hair. Teresita was down on her knees in the middle of the oval carpet, and Laura had her hands on Teresita's face, rubbing her cheeks. "And Mama healed the sick like that."

Laura laughed.

Dolores bustled around carrying bundles of herbs and sweetgrass braids from the parlor to the kitchen. They had rented the building next door to the Greenlee Printing company. Its wide porch was crowded with comfortable chairs and hanging baskets of geraniums and nasturtiums. Don Lauro Aguirre had made his last journey to Clifton to bring Teresita supplies from the curandera store in El Paso. He'd brought her a mysterious hanging flower called a fuchsia, and it immediately drew hummingbirds to its exquisite meteor showers of blossoms.

He sat outside with a pot of coffee and was still watery eyed over his compadre Tomás Urrea's passing. It seemed that the world was dying all around him. Mexico was bleeding. His comrades grew old and weak or were imprisoned or shot. And the legendary Sky Scratcher was gone from the earth. It was one thing to know the news and deal with it from a distance, and quite another to be here in the great man's shadow. It was...visceral was what it was. He was disconsolate and couldn't even face a quick visit to Shannon Hill to pay his respects.

"What anhedonia!" he proclaimed, imagining Tomás scolding him for his absurd vernacular. He stifled a small sob.

"Mama had thousands of people come to see her when she lived in Mexico," Teresita explained to Laura.

"What did they want?" Laura asked.

"Me."

"Why?"

"I do not know."

"Silly people," Laura said.

Teresita smiled. She shrugged.

"Not so silly," she said. "Maybe Mama was silly." She sat back. "I forget."

Inside, where they were, it was all comfy little couches and chairs and potted plants and children's art on the walls. Teresita had hired Dolores and the famous Mrs. Smith to help her. Upstairs, three bedrooms had beds for clients. She rose from the carpet and watched Segundo and Al Fernandez hang the sign by the front door so it faced the street but did not impede access: CLINICA TERESITA, it read. Segundo had painted crude but fetching roses and hummingbirds on the wood in an elegant French style. Teresita was sure the morning glories she'd planted by the front steps would swarm up the posts of the porch and make a fine frame for the sign.

Cedar incense burned in covered dishes designed to look like little adobe houses. Laura loved to peer in their small glowing windows and imagine the tiny people living inside, having warm little lives. Teresita touched her daughter's head and went to her office back beside the kitchen. This would be her consultorio, where she could examine her clients and apply her potions. She had a slight cough that didn't want to go away. She smiled—perhaps she should prescribe a tea for herself.

None of them knew how far word of her return had traveled down the mountain. There had been no press interest, at any rate. No reporters following the river up the steep road to see her. No photographers. And no pilgrims to speak of. Some down below felt that she had been revealed as anything but a saint. What saint cohabited with gringos and had babies? Others had heard that her powers had faded along with her scent. The Americans posited dense psychological theories to explain her saintly affliction. Delusional, they said. Both the miraculous period and the fading of the miracles. The Mexicans argued that her soul itself was used up and gone. No one asked the Indians, but they would have said, *She's tired and bored and doesn't want to do it anymore.*

But Teresita was perfectly happy among her leaves and twigs. The clinic did not smell like Burtch's offices, not of chemicals and camphor, but of dried flowers and sage, of mint and tart berries and cedar smoke, vanilla beans and cinnamon. She coughed and thought that perhaps some rose hips with honey would feel good in her throat.

She caught herself singing.

She had never sung in her memory, except when she played guitar for the buckaroos back in—well, it felt like a century ago. It made her smile. "Ay, Teresita," she said aloud. "Cómo eres." She had never talked to herself out loud much either. She sat with herself as if with an old friend. She hugged herself as she pulled a shawl tighter—the mountain could be brisk. "Let's have that tea," she announced and urged herself out of the chair. "Come on, old woman," she told herself. She was thirty-two years old. On the outside.

❈

Gabriela walked up to the clinic and beheld a line of men lounging lugubriously while the women worked inside. John Van Order had appeared from somewhere, and he completed the coalition of louts rocking like great-grandfathers: Aguirre, Segundo, Al Fernandez, and John. She shook her head. Gaby knew that the only real man in the world had died. And look at what was left!

"I will never marry again," she said, clomping up the steps.

Segundo, swiping Aguirre's coffee, muttered, "Say what?" but the rest of them were deaf as they stared at the sunlight creeping across the street.

Gaby withdrew a portfolio from under her arm.

"Teresita," she called. "I have brought something for you."

Teresita came out with her tea.

Gaby handed the portfolio over, and Teresita placed her cup and saucer on a small table and opened the flap and looked upon a photograph of her dead father laid out on the table in the rancho's front room.

"That's him," Gaby noted. "Lying in state. I thought, since you missed the funeral, you might want this."

Teresita's head spun, but she didn't know if it was from grief or shock or from her cough.

"Thank you," she said.

"He was tall," Gaby said.

They stood there.

"Well," Teresita finally replied. "That he was."

They went to Teresita's consultorio and put the sad picture on her desk, turned away from the room so that only Teresita could see it.

Teresita sat down at her desk. "Gaby?" she said. "When all those people came to Cabora, those pilgrims? What was it like?"

Gaby said, "It was horrible."

"It wasn't beautiful?"

"No. It was ugly and disturbing. All those dirty hopeless people. That smell. All of them frantic to touch you."

Teresita rested her chin on her fist.

"I thought it was beautiful," she said.

"I suppose you would," Gaby said.

Gaby walked out of the room. Teresita stared at the door. She made it move an inch, then another. It swung shut very slowly and she stared until she heard the latch click. She sat calmly in the shadows.

⁂

John had been sulky. He had always had a surly streak, but Arizona had put him in a right state of pique. He knew Teresita didn't like him to smoke in her clinic, but what the hell. He held his skinny black cheroot in his teeth and hung his thumbs in his dungaree pockets and slouched like a melting candle. He still hadn't been to their little house up the street from the church. Mostly, he pouted around in Solomonville, telling tall tales to his mother.

"How's that baby of ours?" he asked.

She sat at her desk watching his ashes drop to the floor.

"She's fine," she said. "You should see her." She smiled. "I believe you have seen her, haven't you? Once?"

"Jesus, Terry," he said.

He said it like his bene coves had said it in New York: Jay-zuz.

"You love me, though. Right?" he said.

She breathed out through her nose.

"I will always love you," she replied. "You know that."

He sat down, crossed his legs. There was mud on his boot. She hoped it was mud. It was dropping small bits on her carpet.

"Ain't that a relief," he said in English.

He ground out his smoke on the sole of his boot. Teresita reached across the desk and took the stub from his hand before he dropped it on the floor along with everything else he was dumping there.

"Hey!" he said, as if he'd just had an idea. "How about that Don Lauro? He's a real caballero."

"A fine man," she agreed.

"A bit of a buggy boss, though," John confided. "I bet he can't ride no horse worth beans. It's a miracle he got all the way up here on his own."

She drummed her fingers on her desk.

"What are you getting at, mi amor?" she said.

"Why," said John, all wide eyes and clear features, looking like the pure-hearted boy he never was, "he's fixing to go back down to Texas. In that wagon. I'm worried."

"Worried."

"He don't even carry a belly gun. Hell—bandidos, Indians, who knows what's out there."

"I see."

She glanced at the picture of her father lying on the table, his boots on and his great whiskers pointing at Heaven.

"And you would go with him, to guard him on his adventure."

"Can I?"

"You are asking my permission?"

"Well, yes."

"Are you not a grown man, my love? Can you not just tell me you intend to go on this journey?"

She did not add: *The way Tomás Urrea would have done it.*

John slapped his knees and smiled.

"Okay then," he said. "We're agreed on it."

He sat staring at her. She sat staring at him. She could not remember what he looked like naked.

"Can I borrow some money?" he asked.

He was startled when she fell back in her chair and laughed.

⁂

She cried when they parted. Don Lauro caught many of her tears on his lapels. He patted her on the back and stared at the peaks and ordered himself to remain dry-eyed. Everything was wrong. Everything awry—the revolution should have freed the Mexican people by now, and his dear Tomás Urrea should be sitting in the gubernatorial palace of Sonora watched over by an honor guard of ferocious Yaqui warriors, an unassailable force for good ruling the new north—La Frontera de Oro. Yes! The Golden Border! But now none of it would ever happen. This warrior queen appeared to be happy… puttering, playing nurse to miners and peasants. What had happened to her greater healing? He shook his head. Revolution indeed: a circle back to where you started. He placed a chaste kiss on the crown of her head and climbed aboard his wagon.

"Adios," he said, holding on to her hand.

"Lios emak weye," she blessed him.

He nodded, let go of her fingers.

John cried. He cried because he knew he wasn't coming back. She knew it too. Laura stood on the clinic porch crying, "Papa! Papa, come back!"

"I haven't left yet," he said.

But he and Teresita both knew he was already far gone. He was in her arms, yet he had passed beyond the curve of the earth. He was already invisible.

He stepped to the porch and said, "Laura, you take care of your mother and sister. I'll bring you back some candy."

"Bye, Papa."

She stood, stoic as a medicine woman, with heavy tears rolling down her face and falling from the edges of her chin.

He mounted the blue horse. He had Segundo's massive rifle that he'd liberated so many years before from Mexican assassins. Segundo stood with Laura and put his hand on her head. "Cabrón," he muttered.

John cocked his hat and looked handsome and led Aguirre's mule down the cobbled street and out of their lives forever.

And Teresita coughed.

Sixty-Four

EVERYONE AND EVERYTHING that had touched her had been only a tide of some unseen ocean. Things rolled up her, over her, and she thought she would drown, but they always receded. The tide always ebbed. And all those many who had come to her, those men and women and children and old ones and spirits and dead bodies and warriors and infants and mothers and widows, washed away. They were mere foam that agitated her until some passing moon drew them back to blend with the great darkness beyond.

She happily emptied her chests. She emptied her boxes. And she emptied her mind. She had her daughters now, and they were the only ones who could still keep out the light. The girls were perfect and small and holy and hers. They were solid in the world that had begun to float away.

Segundo stopped her one morning and asked her, "Can't you heal no more?"

She shrugged.

"I do not care to try," she said. "This is a new century. Let doctors do God's work."

She put canaries in her own house because she remembered the sound of them with joy. She burned vanilla-scented candles and ate chocolate cake and drank the thickest foamiest teas with the heaviest cream because it made her happy. Bits of quartz and paper wasps' nests lined her windowsills. A coyote skull brought to her by Al Fernandez sat on her bookshelf. As much as she ate, she slowly thinned out again. The curves John loved melted, and her old bones started to reassert themselves. She coughed and the cough became wet and chronic, and one cool morning she found pink splatters in her handkerchief.

Her work was not through—the clinic did slow but steady duties among the weary and the injured. Those she couldn't help with poultices or teas or smoke, she sent to Dr. Burtch. She had nothing against pills.

She walked down the hill to the Catholic church in the early mornings and lit candles for her dead. She sat in the silence and locked eyes with Jesus on the cross. "We understand each other," she told him. "Not all crosses are made of wood." He seemed to agree.

As her body wore out, she used a cane on achy days.

Anita found her standing in the cobbled street one morning, barefoot, feeling the egg-shaped stones with her feet. Eyes closed. She was pale as her beloved candles. Her lips were red. Anita thought it was from the blood.

Teresita was smiling.

"Sister?" said Anita.

Teresita put her finger to her lips.

"Listen," she said.

"To what?"

"To silence."

Teresita smiled and tipped her head back to catch the morning sun full on her face.

"I can hear ten thousand things," Teresita whispered.

"I don't hear anything."

"That is because you never listened, child."

Teresita opened her eyes.

She raised her hands and blessed the planet.

"Thank you, world," she said.

That afternoon, it began to rain.

⁂

The San Francisco River that charged through town was a moody companion. It was too rocky and precipitous for a good swim, but it gave up fishes in its shallows and respites, and it coughed up rainbows on hot days. Everyone in Clifton knew, though, that it was prone to buck out of its banks in snowmelt season or when the southern monsoon clouds made it up to the peaks to be scraped empty of rain; it liked to flood and seemed to take actual pleasure in carrying off porches and miners, mules and auto cars. People saw it as a character in their history, an outlaw perhaps. It never struck a bargain.

And in that last year, it pitched and swept into the town and splintered walls and drowned dogs. Teresita's house was up the slope and stayed dry—the girls were upstairs with Segundo and Dolores—but the clinic took a big hit; waves churned up the porch and tossed the waiting room's chairs against the wall.

And though Dr. Burtch had ordered Teresita to stay inside, warm and dry, she could not. Paisanos were being flooded out of their homes. She went into the storm and the bellowing waters and sandbagged and dug and carried children and saved goats. She fell in the water and was fished out by the Calvillo brothers. Belief in her had waned in some people, but not among them. The elder Calvillo insisted they had found her because she had sent blinding beams of light out of her eyes that led them through the flooded woods to save her.

She spent two miserable nights shivering beside the heroic rescuers and the pick-and-shovel brigades come from the mine trying to build levees in the face of the icy inundation. When the waters slowed and rolled away from some homes, the miners carried her to her house. She was soaked through and burning with fever, and she seemed to be made of little broken sticks and black cloth, her hair falling and dripping and brushing the muddy ground.

꙳

There was nothing to do but take her in the wagon to the Urrea rancho outside of town. Segundo laid her in the back amid quilts and pillows. Dolores and Gaby fetched the girls in a little carriage, and they all made their way out of town. Ten or fifteen people stood in the street and raised their hands to Teresita, took off their hats. She smiled at them, waved her hand. They could hear her coughing.

Dr. Burtch had Teresita installed in a back bedroom, away from the family.

"Consumption is a terrible malady," he told them. "It could contaminate you all. It's best to keep her comfortable and keep your exposure to a minimum."

Segundo didn't care. He sat in a chair off to the side of her bed and kept his pistola at hand, as if he could shoot the Grim Reaper if he showed his bony face. When Teresita needed clean cloths to catch her bloody sputum, he fetched them and tossed her soiled cottons into a fire lest any fanatic appear seeking relics.

"Don't let them come for my bones," she said. Her face was white and burning, yet strangely holy. He could not look at her without crying. "Don't let them dig me up."

"Ah, cabrón," he said softly. "That's crazy talk. You ain't dying."

"We are all dying."

"Not me," he said. "Didn't I tell you I'm living forever?"

They smiled at each other.

She closed her eyes.

"But, Segundo," she mumbled. "Wouldn't that be terribly lonely?"

She drifted to sleep.

※

Anita became the little mother to Laura and Magdalena. They had a visitation schedule. It was best in the mornings, after Segundo and Gaby had cleaned Teresita up and put some of her old New York face paint on her to make her look less cadaverous. Dr. Burtch made the girls maintain their distance, perhaps the cruelest part of the entire ordeal. All they wanted was to hold their mother. But they could not. Still, Laura would break loose and jump to her mother's side and hold her hand and rest her face against her mother's chest. Dr. Burtch could not bear to force her away too quickly, so he allowed her to dawdle on some mornings. Little Magdalena peered out of her blanket wrap like a ferocious little owl, wondering who all these people were.

A newspaper had run "Saint of Cabora Near Death" on its front page, and incredibly, pilgrims filtered uphill. Several of them confessed to Gaby, "We thought she was already dead." They brought gifts: serapes, potted lemongrass and cilantro, chickens, holy water, gold coins. One old man from Silver City brought them a chunk of Tomóchic's charred altar, scavenged after the massacre of her followers. They set glasses of water on the steps of the farmhouse, burned candles. The porch became a small shrine.

"They're going to burn down my house!" Gaby complained, not at all willing to allow another siege of pilgrims to overwhelm her life.

Occasionally, Teresita accepted visitors—they had to stay as far from her in the room as possible. These visitors made Gaby and Segundo believe Teresita was actually improving. She sometimes showed vigor and sat up in bed and even sipped chicken soup with lemon.

She told a reporter from Guaymas that she had dreamed vividly since becoming ill.

"I have visions," she said.

"Hallucinations," he corrected.

"Visions, I said. I am not delirious. I can speak clearly."

He wrote in his notebook: *Hallucinations.*

"What did you dream last night?" he asked.

"I dreamed of San Francisco. My favorite city."

"What did you see?"

"I do not understand it. I saw a great crater, full of fire and smoke. The city was gone."

He smiled a little.

"And you believe this is—what—prophecy? Are you sure?"

"I may be approaching darkness," she said, "but I am not yet blind."

Segundo poked his head in the door and said: "You. Out."

Teresita made the sign of the cross over the reporter's head.

※

She slept. She seldom awoke. She coughed in her sleep. Segundo wiped the blood off her chin. Her breathing was a ghastly, bubbling thing. No one wanted to hear it. Gaby actually found herself praying that God would take her and end her suffering.

And then came the morning. They all thought it was over. She woke and called weakly for her most beloved to join her. But not the little ones—they were not ready for it. So Gaby and Anita and Segundo stood in her room and looked down on her. She seemed to glow. Segundo thought she looked like sunlight breaking through white feathers—her skin looked like a dove's feathers to him. Her eyes were cradled by purple shadows. She smiled and looked into a corner of the room. Gaby turned her head to look, thinking some spider had settled there, but there was nothing.

"I love you all," Teresita said. "I know you love me."

Segundo started sobbing immediately.

"You old lion," she said.

He blew his nose.

"Hold my hand."

He stepped forward and cupped her fingers in his big calloused paws.

"It is almost night," she said. "And I must sleep. Don't mourn me. And don't forget me. I will not forget you." She squeezed Segundo's hand. "I will wait for you all. We will be together again."

She closed her eyes and sighed and they thought she had died right before them, but then she opened her eyes and looked at each of them.

"I cannot sleep yet," she said. "Someone is coming."

"Who?" said Gaby, but Segundo shook his head a little. She was clearly slipping away and starting to drift.

"I will meet the next visitor, please. And forgive me, because then I will...sleep."

She reached out to Anita and took her hand.

Gaby and Segundo stepped out of the room and wiped their eyes.

"Damn," he said. "I hate to see that."

They walked to the front of the house, and there they found a tiny white-haired woman waiting on the porch. They just stared at her.

"I have come," the woman said. "Take me to her."

Segundo shook his head in resignation — Teresita and her strange ways.

"It's witchy," he said.

They led her to the back of the house and she stepped in the door and stood looking down at the Saint.

"I am Cayetana," she said.

Teresita smiled up at her. Little Cayetana, La Semalú — the Hummingbird herself. She had left shortly after Teresita was born, had not been seen since. Teresita had felt her shadow all these years, had sensed her far away, knew she was not dead. Saw her on some nights, during her most vivid dreams. And here, on the long unlikely mystery road, she had come back. None of those present would ever stop wondering, would ever miss an opportunity to tell the story of the Hummingbird's return.

"Oh, Mother," Teresita said. "I saw you coming."

"Will you forgive me?"

"I will!"

"I was a bad mother," she said. "But I am here for you now."

"Mamá," Teresita said.

Anita backed out of the room as Cayetana Chávez sat on her daughter's bed, and Segundo and Gaby took her away from the room because they did not know what to make of this last miracle. They sat out in the parlor and listened to the women laugh until night fell.

Sixty-Five

WHEN SHE AWOKE, her gathered family was all asleep.

Dawn was warming her end of the house. Her loved ones were scattered about her in poses of sheer exhaustion. There was dear old Segundo, splayed out in the comfortable chair in the corner of the bedroom, knobby knees spread wide, old beaten cowboy-booted feet fallen open at an angle. He was snoring like a rusty engine, and his knuckly hand lay upon the pistola in his holster. His whiskers had gone white, but his face remained the aged and ageless warrior mask it had always been. She smiled. Segundo had already been a hundred years old when he was born.

She could see his dream. It wafted all around his head like incense smoke. He was younger—she could tell because his whiskers and hair were all black. He wore a black leather vest, and he had an immense pistola at each hip. They had ivory handles. And his plump little wife had made him raisin tamales, hundreds of raisin tamales. The steam from them filled his dream with the scents of cinnamon and corn dough, and he was eating. Eating and eating. Coffee flowed into his huge cup as if from a waterfall. Segundo grunted once, shifted in his seat, and chuckled in his sleep. She watched him smack his lips.

She smiled.

On the bed, her own mother lay across her legs, face turned to one side, sleeping peacefully. Her little face was softened by age, its surface covered with small wrinkles. The corners of her mouth were loose, puckery, like cooked fruit. Teresita could not tell if the shadowy creases there had come from too much laughter or too much sorrow. She reached out and smoothed hair off her mother's lined brow. Wiry with gray.

She hooked a stray curl away from the old woman's cheek and put it behind her ear. Cayetana didn't stir. Her breathing was steady, oceanic. Teresita could feel it against her knees.

She did not realize how lonely she'd been until Cayetana came into the room. Teresita almost didn't mind dying if it brought back her mother. There were no words for it—indeed, there were almost no adequate emotions. She watched her mother's slumber and thought about God's strange humor, that the happiest moment of her time on earth was among her last.

And there, on the floor, poor Gaby sat, reclining the top half of her body against the bed. She was snoring slightly. Her hair was still a great cloud. Full of curls, full of life. No wonder Tomás was so in love with her. Her skin was like coffee with much heavy cream stirred in, and cinnamon, and vanilla. Gaby was still delicious.

A cat came in and hopped up on the end of the bed and stared into her eyes.

"Are you the only one still with me?" Teresita asked.

The cat jumped off the bed, stretched, and went under Segundo's chair.

Teresita looked around for Dr. Burtch, but he was gone.

The girls, her daughters, were in their own rooms. Her little sister Anita was caring for them, sleeping at the foot of their bed. Anita, who would walk through blizzards and wildfires for her. Teresita did not want the girls to sit at a deathwatch. It was better for them to read and play with their dolls. She did not want them to remember her like this—weak, skeletal, spitting blood. Teresita could see them through the floors of the house.

Bloodied cloths lay in a wad on the bedside table. The terrible porcelain bowl where she spit up clots had mercifully been emptied while she slept. Of all the horrors of this illness, it was that bowl of blood that most filled her with dread. Its ugliness, the fact of it, erased all illusions.

She stretched. Yawned. She actually felt better. She reached for the brush and attended to her hair. Why, she was refreshed by the sleep she had enjoyed. A sleep free of coughing or fever. No dreams either.

The windows were open. That was rare. They kept her bundled and safe from drafts. But the scent coming in was so rich. She breathed it in deeply—the curtains billowed in the breeze. It even felt a bit chill. It was as refreshing as a drink of lemonade. Clean. All the mountains sent their aromas to her: pine, hay, honeysuckle, chimney smoke, horses. Were there flowers at this time of year? She could smell them. Sweet peas. Geraniums. Roses.

She sniffed her arm. No, it wasn't her. It was from outside. Real roses.

The sun was bright out there. Birds sang. Oh! She closed her eyes and listened. Jays fussed. Crows joked. Doves murmured. Little songbirds chittered madly into the distance. She heard the kissing sounds of the hummingbirds. A dragonfly whir that suddenly brought to mind the desperate *thwap* of El Paso's doomed ornithocopter.

She heard the door latch click.

The door swung open, and cottonwood fluff drifted in. It looked like warm snow. The sunlight was blinding as it rushed through the doorway. She was confused for a moment—didn't that door open to the hallway? She'd thought so. Wasn't she on the second floor of her father's house? Had she forgotten that it opened to the outside world? Perhaps she had been moved to a cabin in her illness. She frowned. Perhaps she was in Segundo's cabin and didn't even realize it. Her mind was still cloudy. She shook her head slightly. She massaged her eyes with one hand.

Huila stepped into the room. She wore her old dress, her ancient apron. She had a rebozo over her head, but she took it off and draped it over her shoulders. She smiled at Teresita, put her hands on her hips, and said, "Well, well, well."

Teresita smiled back at her.

"I am so happy to see you again," she said.

"Ah, child," said the old one. "How could you think I would not come to see you at a time like this?"

She came across the floor and took Teresita's hand. Teresita put the old one's knuckles to her lips. Her hand smelled of cilantro and mint.

"They're all asleep," Huila noted.

"Yes."

"It has been hard for them."

"Yes, Huila."

"Still, I don't appreciate laziness. There are chores to do."

Teresita laughed.

"¡No seas mala, Huila!" she scolded. "You cannot be mean to them. They have cared for me. They are tired."

"Hmm," said Huila. "Do they think we are not tired? Here I am, dead, and I'm still working!" She shook her head. "Work, work, work. Oh, well. If you were born to be a grinding stone, you can't complain when they crush corn on your back!"

Teresita laughed again.

"Ay, Huila," she said.

"Come," said Huila, tugging her hand.

"I cannot," Teresita replied.

"Why not?"

"I am ill."

"Are you?"

"Deathly ill."

"How interesting." She tugged. "Get up."

"But I am weak."

"Not really. You are not your body. You were never ill. It was ill. It has nothing to do with you."

Teresita stirred.

"It certainly felt like it did," Teresita complained.

"Nothing personal," Huila replied.

Teresita snorted.

"That's what you say."

"Come, now—I haven't got all day." Huila stopped for a moment and looked around. "Well, actually, I do."

They laughed again.

"Huila, ¡cómo eres!"

"I am tremendous," Huila conceded. She tugged Teresita's hand harder. "Up!"

Teresita slipped her legs out from under her mother. Cayetana never stirred. She swung her legs over and contorted herself to get around Gaby. She managed to rise without bouncing the bed. Not an eyelid fluttered.

"I don't want to wake them," she said.

"No. They have to awaken on their own."

Huila raised her eyebrows meaningfully as she helped her up.

"How do you feel?" she asked.

Teresita closed her eyes, took a breath.

She opened her eyes.

"Better," she said. "I can breathe."

Huila nodded.

"Come," she said. "I have something to show you. Outside. Don't look back. Just come outside with me."

They stepped to the door, and Teresita reached over and laid her hand on Segundo's brow.

"And my girls?" she asked.

"They will be fine, child. Let's go."

They walked into a brilliant spring morning. Teresita felt a little weak, but not as weak as she had felt yesterday. Her feet were bare. She always liked that. The ground was covered in damp, thick grass. Teresita's hem was immediately soaked with dew. The grass felt luxurious against the bottoms of her feet.

"Feel good?" the old one asked.

"Oh, yes."

"Better than that sickbed."

Teresita nodded.

They were looking all round them at columbines and foxgloves, daisies and cosmos. Sunflowers, morning glories. Wild irises were purple, yellow, and white—butterflies that erupted from the blossoms looked like more blossoms suddenly animated.

"Strawberries!" Teresita said. "We should pick some."

"Later," Huila said.

She ushered Teresita through the garden and out under the trees. The shade here was cold, vivid with ferns and mushrooms and gossamer with billowing spiderwebs.

"I always loved the aspens," Teresita said.

Huila said, "They're a bit precious for my taste."

"Look how they tremble in the breeze! They look like coins in the light."

"Focus, child," Huila instructed. "Come."

They stepped through the trees and were hit again by glorious sunlight on the edge of a great precipice.

"Behold," said Huila.

Teresita looked up, above the trees, above the peaks, and gasped.

"Do you remember this?" Huila asked.

"I do," Teresita whispered.

"I have shown you this once before."

The sky was full. Every part of it taken up by a shining silver globe. Mirror-bright. All of them spaced exactly the same distance apart. Receding into the infinite distance. Hundreds of pure silver spheres. Thousands. Each globe shimmered with blue from the sky and was lively with bent white accents from the reflected clouds. Tens of thousands.

"It is my vision," Teresita said.

"Yes."

"Every possible moment of my life, every choice, every minute."

"Yes. But what is different now?"

Teresita squinted. The eerie beauty of the scene made her eyes water. Tears ran down her cheeks.

"I see no pictures in the globes," she said.

"Look," Huila said.

Teresita saw her face in the nearest sphere. And then she saw her face in every sphere. Herself as a child. Herself as a bride. Herself as a mother. Herself.

"This is the culmination, child," Huila said. "There are no more paths. There are no more choices. In the end, you are left with this. Yourself."

She turned to Teresita and put her hands on her shoulders.

"You must ask yourself—do you like what you see?"

"I—" She faltered. "But I have been so wrong so many times."

"It happens."

"But I have failed so often."

"Indeed. That was part of your job."

"I tried, Huila, I tried very hard."

"Well, then," Huila said. "What's your problem? Listen, child—you tried far harder than I did. And look at me. I'm doing all right."

Teresita put her hand on Huila's arm.

"Huila! Am I...?"

"Hush, Teresita. See. Don't speak."

Huila pointed—Teresita followed with her eyes. A small sphere from the high left side of the sky trembled and rolled, like a raindrop on a windowpane, down the blue. It wiggled between the other spheres and hit the central sphere and was absorbed. And another. And another.

They fell gently at first, and then in a steady torrent. Out of the sky and into the globe of quicksilver that floated before her. It was a silent rainstorm. The central globe swelled, grew, wobbled heavily. When all the silver spheres had fallen into it, it burst silently. Its silver tide spread out before them in a vast, shining horizon.

"Oh!" Teresita cried.

It was a silver sea.

Huila took out her pipe and packed it with tobacco.

She lit it and blew an aromatic puff of smoke into the air.

"What do we do?" Teresita asked.

Huila said, "Well, it looks like a good day to go swimming."

"Huila! I cannot swim!"

"In this sea, you can," said the old one. "Besides, old Huila will be with you. Old Huila won't let you slip away."

They took each other's hands.

They stepped into the calm silver tide. It was warm. Teresita shivered once. She could see stars and moons reflected in the infinite water.

"When you get tired," Huila said, "float."

They waded in deeper, and when they were fully immersed, they swam toward the other shore.

NOTES AND ACKNOWLEDGMENTS

THE STORY is not the history.

Thomas Wolfe once said you could turn over an entire town's population of six hundred people to create one character. I think you can also turn over six hundred places to make one place in a novel. Six hundred incidents. Teresita made her way through the American fringe and heartland, setting down sometimes as lightly as a hummingbird, and falling to earth at others like a flaming meteorite. I have tried to make sense of this map and give a taste of the various landings as they happened. This, of course, is a novel as opposed to a textbook. It must be read as an imagining based on long research and a thousand interviews, letters, phone calls, and rituals offered by wise elders of many tribal peoples. Or, People.

It's my dream that follows the historical time line. But the duties of the novelist are different from the duties of the historian—six hundred peripheral characters might very well have been squeezed into one or two characters who carry the story without exhausting the reader's patience or sanity. Several assistants to Teresita, secretaries and book-keepers, for example, were magically processed into manageable form. There is some argument over the historical Mr. Rosencrans—was he actually called Rosecrans? Spellings vary. Since this is fiction, I went with the more fanciful spelling to give myself room to compose. His son was not named Jamie, though Teresita did heal him. Dr. Weisburd in New York comes not from textbooks or histories. He comes from Teresita's great-granddaughters. There are family rumors about his relationship with Teresita that were simply too much for me to pursue at this point. Some family members maintain that there was no doctor at all—that the man who supported them in New York was Rosencrans himself. "Weisburd" is a name from my own life and honored here. The Los Angeles episode did happen; I have moved it in time because novels have to make sense, unlike our messy hurtling lives.

All thanks and acknowledgments from the previous volume in this saga, *The Hummingbird's Daughter,* still hold. Family, spread all over the United States, Latin America, and Spain, took part in amassing the story: Urrea, Hubbard, Millán, Duty, Treviño, Kempf, Medlock, Nelson, Valencia, Herreras, Tully, Galicia, Zazueta, Van Order, Mann, Walker, Flores, Salazar—to name a few. Hello, Cousin Jeanne. Thank you for all the letters, talks, tacos, and family photo albums. Thank you for trusting me with your secrets and theories.

Great-granddaughters rule.

Geronimo appears in this novel in honor of my own Apache cousins, and of Manny (Manuelito), my Chiricahua medicine man/teacher. Although he was employed by Buffalo Bill, I am wishing for him that he could visit Venado Azul and eat ice cream undiscovered, and for a minute at peace. Also, Ambrose Bierce was working in San Francisco at the same time as Helen Dare; they certainly knew of each other. I hope he had the chance to join the cadres of reporters dogging Teresita. It's fun to think so.

※

Between the two books, I have spent twenty-six years in Teresita's world. Of all the experts and places, I am most haunted by my days in Clifton long, long before this saga took shape. Al V. Fernandez was the town historian. He told me then, "I am only eighty years old and wasn't old enough to meet her." He wore his railroad cap and wished that Clifton had a fine train station he could enjoy. I have offered his spirit both things in the novel.

Many real-life moments will stay with me forever: finding dear Lauro Aguirre's grave in El Paso, Texas, with David Romo; or the semi-legendary night when one of the scores of Teresita scholars revealed a carbine rifle at a public event and seemed to suggest he could easily kill me with it at fifty yards; or seeing beloved cousin Jeanne—Teresita's great-granddaughter, receive overwhelming love and applause from an eight-hundred-strong Pasadena crowd. There are still stories being revealed to me, even after all this time.

Since the first book came out, I have met more than a half dozen reincarnated Teresitas, and ten or twelve channelers who channel her from Heaven. I am led to believe that in the afterlife, one can go condo and inhabit all sorts of interesting new bodies at once. And, being spirit rather than flesh, one can also be in Heaven and Texas at the same time. I often wonder what Tomás Urrea would have made of all this.

As mentioned above, Jamie Rosencrans was a real child, though he had a different name. And he was actually healed in San Jose, not Clifton. He ended up later in life in Silver City, New Mexico, where he died. He, as far as I can tell, did not marry.

It would have been astounding to interview him or his kin. However, Don Luis Perez is alive and well in Silver City, and he was kind enough to show me the altar of the church in Tomóchic, which he has in his possession. Don Luis, for the record, will be presenting a factual history book about Teresita. John Van Order and Teresita did, indeed, live on East 28th Street in New York City. It houses a Kinko's today.

⁂

So—thanks. Again. Thanks to Little, Brown and everyone there. Geoff Shandler, the greatest editor anywhere—I will always remember arguing plot points in the woods near the Truckee River in California in a break from the Squaw Valley Conference. Thanks to everyone at the shop—among them Michael Pietsch, Nicole Dewey, Heather Fain, Liese Mayer, Allison J. Warner, and my goddess of publicity, Elizabeth Garriga. And deep gratitude to Peggy Freudenthal and Tracy Roe, my long-suffering copyeditors, who have done battle over these years with my idiot-savant obsessions, repetitions, and infelicities: unfurl it, Tracy! Thanks also to Pamela Marshall.

Thanks to my beloved agent, Julie Barer: we move forward with joy.

To my film agent and lifeline to sanity, Michael Cendejas at the Pleshette Agency in Hollywood. We have conspired and laughed and celebrated for a long time, but we are only beginning.

Thank you to Trinity Ray, wherever you are: you changed my game.

⁂

It was a thrill to meet the Ronstadts in Tucson. Tomás Urrea of Albuquerque gave me lessons in beekeeping.

Thanks to Ambassador Enrique Hubbard Urrea—mi primo. And a great translator.

And special gratitude and love to Mr. Valenzuela and the Yaqui people, who blessed me with their friendship, goodwill, and tribal tokens at the Tucson Festival of Books. And to the nameless holy man who came forward at the last minute and raised his hand over me in blessing. While I'm at it: thanks to Bill Viner and the Tucson Festival. Special love to Fitz.

The librarians of Texas Tech; especially the special collections wizards who gave me access to the archives of family letters, and the voluminous correspondence of William Curry Holden and Mr. Frank Puttman. Pure gold. Also their archive of family photos and such gems as the letters of Dr. Duty. (Note to researchers: there is an obscure listing stating that Texas Tech has, somewhere, a wire recording of Teresita's actual voice; we were never able to find it.) And to the library at my own UIC for arranging the transfers of information.

David Romo has argued with me and prodded me and challenged me and helped me for years now. He took me to Teresita's rooming house in El Chuco's Segundo Barrio, and he made good on his threat to take it over. At least part of it. He is creating a Teresita museum/library there now. His published account of Teresita's time in El Paso is of great value to any fan or scholar: *Ringside Seat to a Revolution*. We share an occasional publisher, Cinco Puntos Press, in El Paso. The great Byrd family that owns this venerable publishing venture has given me much love, care, and comfort over these years. Bobby, Lee, Susie, et al.—thanks for the bed and the vino!

Bruce Dinges and the Arizona Historical Society—perhaps Mr. Dinges will forgive me the fun I had with his wholly fictive ancestor in this novel; UTEP—particularly the late lamented Paso Al Norte Immigration Museum project, the library, and Ben Sáenz; to the National Hispanic Cultural Center in Albuquerque; to Tony Mares at UNM; to correspondents who sent me thrilling details I couldn't have known—the "chulo" material, for example, came from ranching families in the Tubac/Arivaca area. Thanks to Yuma sheriff Ralph Ogden, who gives me a good sense of the Arizona spirit when I need to write it. Also, Lisa Gezelter at the National Archives and Records Administration Pacific Region hunted down legal documents pertaining to various trials in the story. Thanks to Matthew Lara in Silver City. Thanks to the Masons and Freemasons who shared some data with me.

Felipe Molina's excellent Yaqui/Cahita dictionary was vital to both books, and this book relied on his fine *Yaqui Deer Songs: Maso Bwikam* (Tucson: University of Arizona Press/Sun Tracks, 1987).

In New York, the fabulous public library was heroic in its efforts to find me esoterica. The text of Teresita's letter from the Archangel Gabriel is actually to be found there. Sorry—no feather. And the staff and historian of the Marble Collegiate Church on the corner of Fifth Avenue and West 29th Street were very helpful. They provided me with research materials, a brief tour of the church, and the priceless story of the blue window and the big clock.

The University of Illinois at Chicago has given me a safe haven now for ten years and more. I am indebted to the institution for its patience and support of my wandering, distracted ways.

Thanks to my editor at *Playboy*, Lee Froelich, who sent me on assignment to El Paso/Juárez on a different investigation—a visit that, of course, opened new doors into the Teresita research.

As for the voluminous medicine/shamanic gratitudes—see the last book.

Lyn Niles did some late-inning genealogy and records mining.

Many writers have offered an open ear or a welcoming word over time. I can't thank you all, but I can tip my hat to you. Stewart O'Nan remains a great reader and guide through the manuscript mire.

César A. González has been a guiding light. And, of course, there would be no Teresita, there would be no me, without Rudolfo Anaya, nuestro tío.

The tidbit of the Americans being called "los Goddamns" by the Mexicans of southern Arizona comes from Elizabeth Brownell's priceless *They Lived in Tubac* (Tucson: Westernlore Press, 1986). The story of Teresita smiting the NYC attackers comes directly from her great-granddaughters.

My students and colleagues at Breadloaf, Fishtrap, and Squaw Valley have been wonderful inspirations and allies over the last six years. Thank you.

To that lovely man, Neil Gaiman—thank you, amigo, for suggesting the value of a haunted and lonely writing session in Las Vegas hotel rooms. It really worked. Though I thought the tossing palm fronds were devil monkeys coming in my late-night window as I typed.

Finally, the writers of the Cabin 20 community have monitored and upheld this entire operation—gracias, amigas y amigos. Fast-Horse Cathy Safiran was an early reader.

⁕

As always, my family supports me and suffers my eruptions. Cinderella, mi waifa, has battled through every desert and jungle with me. It has been a long season of work.

And now, we celebrate.

For further information about Teresita and the books, visit us at www.luisurrea.com.

Lios emak weye,

L.A.U
Chicago, 2011

ABOUT THE AUTHOR

LUIS ALBERTO URREA was born in Tijuana, Mexico, to an American mother and a Mexican father. His bestselling novel *The Hummingbird's Daughter,* the result of twenty years of research and writing, is a fictionalized retelling of the life of Teresa Urrea, the Saint of Cabora. The novel won the Pacific Rim Voices Kiriyama Prize.

He is the recipient of a Lannan Literary Award, an American Book Award, an Edgar, a Western States Book Award, and a Colorado Book Award, and he has been inducted into the Latino Literary Hall of Fame.

His nonfiction works include *The Devil's Highway,* which was a finalist for the 2005 Pulitzer Prize for general nonfiction; *Across the Wire,* winner of the Christopher Award; and *By the Lake of Sleeping Children.*

His poetry has been collected in *The Best American Poetry,* and a collection of his short fiction, *Six Kinds of Sky,* won the 2002 *ForeWord* magazine Book of the Year Award as Editor's Choice for Fiction.

He is a Distinguished Professor of creative writing at the University of Illinois in Chicago.